BLUE MOON

KAYLA LAFROTH

LITTLE FRIEND STORIES

First published on May 31, 2026.

ISBN 979-8-9958571-0-5 (hardcover) • ISBN 979-8-9958571-1-2 (paperback) • ISBN 979-8-9958571-2-9 (ebook)

Cover design by Destinee Nelson

Published by Little Friend Stories.

www.kaylalafroth.com

For those who feel too much.

CONTENTS

To humans, the Blue Moon is just another moon—little more than an interesting fact or a turn of phrase. For us, the Blue Moon is magic. It's the collision of fate, the makings of destiny, and the promise of the extraordinary. But then again, we are not like humans. For them, love is a game of confusion, turmoil, and heartbreak. For us, love is simply ours. Our soulmates are written in the stars, and like the tides of the ocean, fate cannot be controlled or changed.

At least, that's what I used to believe.

CHAPTER I

NOTHING IN BETWEEN

Tomorrow my entire life changes, but Aspen brings it up so casually you'd think it was just some human sweet sixteen.

"So, the big birthday's coming up."

The vibrant forest crunches beneath our sneakers as we make our way to my house. Moss and fern line the trail, a beaten down path of dirt and pebbles and roots.

"So it is," I say. We've just eaten breakfast, but my stomach is clenching and twisting. This is no ordinary birthday—I'm turning eighteen. And that means everything changes.

I close my eyes and draw in a deep breath. I smell damp moss, the whiff of squirrel hides, the needles of Douglas firs, and the scent of fresh dirt. The forest chitters with the life of late spring—a chorus of birds, the distant hammer of a woodpecker, the rustle of leaves.

I open my eyes. Patches of summer sunlight pierce through the foliage to dance on Aspen's face; he's watching me with that look in his eyes.

"How do you feel about that?" he asks.

I was prepared to respond to the usual gushing excitement —about how everything is going to change and there's no need to be nervous and how I'm so lucky that my birthday falls on a Blue Moon—but I don't know how to answer Aspen's simple question. Not with that look in his eyes, like he's peering through the cracks in the wall I built to hide my thoughts. I don't know how to tell him that tomorrow will be the day all my dreams come true—or the day my hopes are dashed like ocean waves upon the shore.

"I couldn't sleep the day before my birthday," Aspen says, saving me from answering. We're still walking along the path, and his tone is as light as the breeze. "I was terrified of turning eighteen."

"You were?" I ask.

"Yeah." He laughs. "I thought I'd have a heart attack, walking into school that evening. I was just waiting for her to show up at any moment, and then everything would be...I don't know. That would be the end of all that I guess."

I try to look stoic amidst the panic of flying thoughts. Is he saying this because he knows what I think? Has he figured out all that I feel?

"Yeah," I say. It's all I can manage.

When a werewolf turns eighteen, he or she can find their mate. If their mate is also at least eighteen, then they know it from the first moment they look into each other's eyes. It's been described as an instant, overwhelming attraction—an outpouring of love so full that your heart cannot contain it. They say that mates are written in the stars and gifted by the Moon.

"But hey," Aspen continues. "I haven't found my mate yet. It's been...what, six, seven months?" Seven and a half. "Maybe I'm a Lone Wolf."

"Oh please. You're not even nineteen yet. Don't jinx yourself."

"Maybe it wouldn't be so bad, being a Lone Wolf." He shrugs.

I roll my eyes. "Yeah right. Talk about a terrible fate."

"Who knows? Maybe I'd run off with some human girl and live the rest of my life with her." He wriggles his eyebrows with a cheeky grin.

I whack his arm. "Come on, don't even joke about that." I'm laughing, but something cold coils in my stomach. His ridiculous "what-if" would be inconceivable had anyone else said it, but Aspen has had a human girlfriend before.

His grin gives way to that faraway look in his eyes, and I know that brilliant mind of his is churning something. He's far from the forest path now, lost in some sort of dream.

"What are you thinking about?" I ask.

"Being eighteen."

"And what about it?"

He pauses, the way he always does before he shares an atypical thought. "It's just..." he starts. "It's just that being eighteen can be terribly unexciting."

"Unexciting?" I raise my eyebrows. "When anyone you meet could be your mate?"

His lip quirks upwards. "I know, right? That's what you'd think. I was so nervous to turn eighteen I thought I'd pass out— and then I finally got to my birthday, and time passed, and I realized it's all just...bland. I mean, think about it, Lu. From now on, if you meet any wolf who's over eighteen, you'll immediately know that they aren't your mate, and that's that. There's no excitement anymore. There's not much fun in liking someone who isn't younger than you because you already know the outcome. You either mate or you don't."

His words cut through flesh and bone and straight to my

heart. I should have more faith; I should trust in the Moon. I should be *over* the moon with excitement. They say it's magic when you meet your mate, that all others melt into background blur, but what if the Moon chooses wrong?

Aspen looks at me carefully—too carefully—and I wonder what he sees when he looks into my eyes. He breaks eye contact, donning some faux nonchalance with his next words. "I like the way humans do love."

"Humans?" The word jolts me out of my sappy thoughts. Sure, I'm anxious about my birthday, but I wouldn't trade my soulmate for that fickle, human love, plagued with confusion and break-ups and sorrow. We may look fairly human, but we are werewolves. We aren't burdened with such ridiculousness. We have our mates, we have our order; and thus we have our peace.

Aspen laughs, and his voice is sarcastic. "Don't look so enamored, Luna."

I scrunch up my lips. "I just—why? Why would you like anything about the way humans love?" Maybe he's never watched a rom-com. The ones I used to watch with Mom were nothing but stressful, fraught with misunderstandings and social blunders. Sure, the main couple got together in the end, but not before humiliating themselves.

"'Why' is a great question," he says, a smile tugging at the corner of his lips. He gazes at the canopy of trees overhead, his eyes sparkling with whatever he is going to say next. "When you're human, you never know." His easy smile grows. "You meet someone you like, and you don't know if they like you back. And so you test the waters and they test the waters, and it's exciting and fun and nothing quite beats that feeling of falling in love without knowing if it's going to work out."

My heart stops and quickens at the same time.

As he turns to look at me, a warm breeze blows through the

trees, tousling his blond locks. Soon it will be summer, his favorite season. "But I guess you wouldn't understand that feeling, would you?"

I could set him straight. I could tell him that despite believing in and preaching the werewolf way, I understand the feeling all too well. But instead I ask, "Why do you say that?" because it's easier to say than the truth.

"You've never dated anyone."

"So?" I snap. His tone wasn't patronizing, but his statement irks me all the same. "What would be the point?" My usual rhetoric starts spewing out. "I mean, I could have dated someone, but then what? Chances are he wouldn't be my mate. It's better not to waste time, not when we're all destined to find our mates." It's a true answer—the correct answer—and yet it feels like a lie. If hypocrisy were a smell, I would have reeked of it.

"Well, it makes sense you'd feel that way. You are the Alpha Daughter, after all. Our heir," he says. Normally, the words 'Alpha Daughter' are sung like a praise, but from Aspen it feels like a barb that pricks the back of my neck.

"What's that supposed to mean?" I kick a pebble with my Converse high-top. Though his tone wasn't cross, mine is.

"It just means you do things the wolf way," Aspen says. "Which is good, of course," he adds a bit too late. Annoyance stings my heart. His subtle digs against our way of life slice like papercuts. I haven't done everything perfectly, but that doesn't mean the wolf way isn't the right way. It's obviously superior to the human approach to love.

In some ways, we aren't so different from humans. We live in homes, we buy clothes, we use phones, we eat at restaurants. We're even forced to get some sort of education like human kids. Some humans don't understand why we wolves keep ourselves separate from them, thinking us nearly the same species. But we are not the same. We believe in our communities, in supporting the leaders of our hierarchy, in connecting with nature and our inner wolves. We believe in soulmates. My voice comes out in some pitiful half-whisper. "Why can't you be happy with the way we do things?"

Aspen's eyes widen. "I never said I wasn't." Maybe he's so used to reading me that he doesn't realize I can do the same, that I see the glimpses of quiet discontent simmering in his heart.

"Look, I understand that...I understand why meeting wolves and not mating would be frustrating. I do get that. But the problem with humans is that they never know if they've found the right person. That's why half of them get divorced. They pick wrong." Yes, this is why things are the way they are. Even if my heart shatters into a thousand shards tomorrow, *this* is why we have mates.

"Well, I think it's not simply that humans pick wrong," Aspen says. "It's that they stop loving each other. They choose to not love one another."

"I mean, yeah." I sigh. "But *we* never choose to stop loving our mates."

Aspen purses his lips. "I guess not." Bitterness creeps into his voice. "We just never get to choose at all."

While the gabbing woodland critters and the crunch beneath our shoes camouflage the tense silence between us, its pressure hangs heavy on my heart. The woods are thinning, we are close to home, and I don't want our time to end. This is the last moment I'll spend with Aspen before I turn eighteen. Tomorrow we'll look into each other's eyes and we'll know, one way or another.

"Aspen." We're approaching my backyard; it's a big hill leading up to the house with a pond at its base. "Do you think the Moon takes our choices into account? Does she care about who we would choose?"

As we emerge from the forest, Aspen slows his pace to a halt. "I don't know," he admits after several seconds. He turns to look at me, his eyes serious. Away from the shadow of trees, the setting sun washes him in gold, lighting up his blond curls and sun-tanned skin. "But I don't want to just wait for it to choose my life for me. I make my own choices."

My voice is just above a whisper. "You always have." We stand there, just looking at each other. The silence holds a different kind of tension than before. "Aspen?"

"Yeah?"

Heartfelt words dance on the tip of my tongue, begging for an audience, but I can't bring myself to release them. Seconds pass. I can't say it. I just laugh nervously. "Oh moon, I forgot what I was going to say."

"You forgot?" His little laugh lifts the weight of our conversation.

"Yeah." I shrug. "Probably some stupid question about humans."

"Ah, right. 'Cause I'm the human whisperer, is that it?" A crooked smile plays with his lips.

"You more so than anyone else I know." I strive for a light, casual smile as I drink in his appearance and scent for the last time. His beautiful mess of curls, his clean t-shirt and shorts with trendy sneakers, that easy smile on his face. The smell of freshly washed clothes and sun-kissed skin and ink-pressed pages. No matter what happens, tomorrow will be irrevocably different. Maybe to him, our friendship will be the same old thing, but for me, everything will change.

"Humans have such a different way of looking at things," Aspen says. "For us, it's so black and white. You're either it or you aren't. But for them, the possibilities are endless." He takes a step closer, his eyes dancing with his smile. "Isn't that something?"

My heart pounds in my ears. "Endless possibilities," I murmur. His face is so close that I can see the smattering of new summer freckles spilling across his nose and cheeks. "But... we're not human, Aspen." I look at his short, pointed ears. I glimpse his long, sharp canines just before his smile wanes. They mark us for what we are, mark us for what we are not. "We're werewolves. We're made differently."

I've never wanted to be human. I'm proud of my heritage, I love being a wolf—and yet, a sliver of my soul longs for the choice of which Aspen speaks. Because if I could, I would choose *him*. I'd choose him in a heartbeat.

As Aspen searches my eyes, I'm half-certain he's peering into the windows of my soul. His shoulders rise as he draws breath. "Now you're about to turn eighteen."

"Yeah."

"After tomorrow..." He doesn't finish the thought.

"Yeah," I say. After tomorrow, it won't be the same. Either there will be no potential future for us, all our little moments scattered throughout our lives for naught, or we'll be wrapped up in each other's arms from tomorrow forward with full assurance that we belong to each other.

It's either or, and nothing in between.

CHAPTER 2

STOLEN GLANCES

Aspen turns, and he and I start walking up towards the house, letting the moment pass like sand between fingers. Our conversation turns trivial. He asks what presents I hope to get for my birthday, and I rattle off some random wish list. Each step we take brings us too close to the house, and for once I wish this hill stretched longer. We're talking about nothing, but I don't want Nothing to end.

Then a scent hits my nose, faint but distinct pheromones marking another's presence. It's not long before Kodiak strolls towards us from the side of the house, his arms swinging back and forth with his brisk gait. He's wearing his classic grin, and while I'd normally smile and wave, some jolt of irritation sparks in my body. Why is he here an hour before the hunt starts, and why is he interrupting my last moment with Aspen?

"Well hello, Luna!" he calls. His voice is louder than necessary.

"Kodiak." I acknowledge him with a nod. Hopefully he gets the hint and scrams.

He doesn't seem to catch on, walking right up to us.

"Aspen, isn't it?" Kodiak asks. His smile reveals canines that are longer and sharper than just about any werewolf.

"Yes," Aspen says. His smile is polite and nothing more. "Good of you to remember me, Alpha Kodiak."

"But of course. You're a high beta, right? And your brothers are great hunters." Kodiak tilts his head and narrows his eyes, smiling like a hunter who's found his next mark. "I'm excited to see your skills tonight."

Aspen's smile remains, but I can see the strain in his eyes. "Yeah." He turns to me. "Well, I uh, I guess I'd better head back home before the hunt starts, get ready. I'll see you later, Luna, yeah?"

"Yeah," I say. My heart droops as I watch him scamper down the hill and back into the woods.

Tonight begins the Blue Moon Hunt, hosted by my father. While there are smaller inter-pack hunts, the Blue Moon Hunt is the only one that gathers wolves from all the Northwestern packs. Wolves from a dozen packs are gathering here in Dakota Ridge to launch the first of the two-night hunt. It's Aspen's first inter-pack hunt and I think he's looking forward to it about as much as I look forward to math tests. Meanwhile, I'm pretty sure Kodiak has been counting down the days to the Blue Moon Hunt like it's Christmas morning.

Kodiak is looking at me with a mischievous grin, like he's caught me stealing scraps of meat before dinner is ready. "So, is he your mate or something? You do know that your birthday is tomorrow, right?"

I clench my jaw against his mocking. I've known Kodiak my whole life, with him being from the pack closest to ours. He used to come over all the time. But still, that doesn't mean he gets to tease me about this. "Aspen is just a friend," I say.

Kodiak's eyes are as sharp as his smile. "You don't seem to think that."

"That's not true," I lie.

He takes a step forward. "I can hear your heartbeat quickening."

I purse my lips. I hate his stupid hearing. It's absolutely exceptional.

"Well, you wouldn't be the first wolf to have a boyfriend." His voice is a grating lilt. "I guess you'll know tomorrow if he's the one."

The gentle spring breeze now feels hot and bothersome. "I guess so." My voice snaps like a whip, which only makes his eyes and smile widen.

"Why are you so frustrated?" Kodiak has crazy eyes that are way too expressive for a normal face.

"I'm not frustrated, I'm annoyed."

"And that's different?"

"Yes. Because *you* are annoying, Kodiak."

"Wow. That hurts."

I roll my eyes. "Is Jael around? Why don't you harass him instead of me?"

"My sweet baby brother couldn't make it, unfortunately," he drawls.

"Probably *wouldn't* because you're so annoying." I turn and start walking towards the house.

He laughs. "Wow, I didn't expect a whole tantrum just because you like a boy, but what a treat!"

I whip around. "I'm not throwing a tantrum!" I say, in a tone that absolutely proves his point.

"I'm not throwing a tantrum!" He mimics in a high, infuriating voice. He stomps his foot in the grass for good measure.

I zero in on Kodiak's nose. It's a perfect target for my fist, but unfortunately he is Kodiak, and there's no way I could land a hit on him. "Wow, real mature," I say. He cackles and I let him know that he's "friggin' crazy" before walking off. I cross the patio and head up the stairs to the deck before entering the back door of the house. I'm greeted with the strong smell of sizzling bacon and the sight of Dad laboring over the frying pan. Pan-fried and grilled meats are about all Dad can make. He turns and smiles at me when I walk in—the kind of smile where his eyes crinkle and his sharp canines are on full display.

"Lulu! You're out and about early."

I glance at the digital clock on the microwave. It's 7:23 p.m.

"I visited Queenie," I say, settling onto a barstool. "She gave me a pair of earrings for my party tomorrow. I also got breakfast with Aspen, Anika, and Nova at Bruno's."

"I'm glad you still visit Queenie," Dad says. *"Even though Rory's not here"* is the part he doesn't say. "And how's Aspen feeling? Tonight's his first inter-pack hunt! And it's the Blue Moon Hunt, no less!"

I pause for a moment. "Well, he's really excited," I lie. Aspen's father, Alistair, is Dad's right-hand wolf. Aspen's family are high betas, ranked just below us at the top of the pack, and his brothers are beasts. Aspen's preference for books and philosophy over hunting and fighting wouldn't really enamor him to Dad.

"That's good," Dad says. "Sometimes I worry about him. The boy's got real good blood, but he just needs to come into his own. Accept the wolf within."

"Yeah. The wolf within." A cheesy smile rises on my face. Dad says that all the time.

"Speaking of good blood, it sounds like you ran into Kodiak?"

My stomach drops. I hope Dad didn't overhear too much of our conversation. "Yeah, I did."

"Now, Luna." He passes me a plate full of bacon before snagging a piece off the frying pan for himself. "We should really make one last concerted wish to the Moon so that she'll mate you with Kodiak. That would be a dream come true."

I chomp down on a piece of bacon. "For who? You?"

"Yes," Dad says, his mouth full of food. "He's an alpha, after all."

"Whoever my mate is will be the next Alpha," I say. Dad only had daughters, so I'm the new Alpha Heir of Dakota Ridge. My mate will take on the Alpha mantle beside me to lead our pack. "So it doesn't really matter anyways."

"Yes, but he's Midnight River's Alpha," Dad says. Because Kodiak is the neighboring Alpha, it would mean a merge—both of us ruling as Alphas over one large pack. "Can you imagine the two of you coming together?" Dad's got that twinkle in his eye, the slightest physical glow that appears when he teases. His irises are a vibrant purple, like mine. We have the same silky black hair, pale skin, and violet eyes. He's tall and I'm fairly tall, though I'm lean and toned where Dad is large and bulky. Of course, he also has a short, full beard, like any self-respecting male wolf who's found his mate.

"I'm just saying," Dad continues. "It would be nice if you could mate with him."

I take another bite of bacon—it's one of those bites where the meat crumbles perfectly and almost melts on your tongue. "Like you said," my voice grows quiet. "I can't very well choose."

"Good thing, too. You probably wouldn't choose Kodiak if you could, and then I'd have to disown you," Dad says, grinning.

A snort escapes my nose. "You're dumb." I throw another piece of bacon into my mouth while Dad laughs. Amidst the torrent of my emotions and the stress of an impending clock, Dad feels like the eye of the hurricane. Growing up, we had a standard daddy-daughter relationship. He'd come home in the mornings after a long night of running pack meetings, settling disputes, delegating work, or sometimes hunting or brawling. He would walk in the door, swing me around in an overly dramatic hug, and say, "Little Lulu," before kissing my head and telling me he was grateful for a pup like me. Our whole family would eat dinner together, and sometimes, when we were lucky, Dad would read us a bedtime story. I loved him, but we weren't particularly close.

But then Mom got sick.

After she died, Dad did not succumb to melancholy as we feared he might; instead he devoted more time and energy into his daughters. He would ask us about our nights, give us advice, take us on little road trips to other packs, drive us to human cities to go shopping or eat dinner—everything he could to provide the love of two parents. After Rory left, it was just me and him. Sometimes it feels like we are all alone in the world, here in this big empty house.

I finish off another piece of bacon. "Dad, do you think Kodiak's a Lone Wolf?"

The sigh Dad releases plucks a sad chord in my heart. "Probably." He shakes his head. "Poor thing." Dad might have lost his mate, never to find another one, but at least he had one.

My recently inflamed irritation with Kodiak cools as quickly as a dead animal in winter snow. "It must be awful."

"He could still find her," Dad says.

"Yeah," I say, though neither of us believe it.

Kodiak, the freshly minted Alpha of Midnight River, is bright, loud, and extroverted. He's the two-time victor of the Heir Trials and he possesses the most incredible physical prowess the wolf community has seen in decades. He's also twenty-three and still doesn't have a mate.

Most wolves find their mate within a year of turning eighteen, though it's not uncommon to find one at nineteen.

However, if you make it past twenty and still haven't found your mate, you likely don't have one. You're one of the very few lone wolves. While there are floating theories, we don't know the reason behind most lone wolves: only that they are tragic and pitiable. Being a Lone Wolf is my worst nightmare.

"So, how're you feeling, Lulu?" Dad asks. "Tomorrow's the big day."

"Oh yeah, tomorrow. It's uh, it's the full day of the hunt, right?"

Dad sighs in the way that only parents can sigh when they've heard a complaint a thousand times. "I know, I know. I wish I could be there right when you turn eighteen. But think about it: maybe your mate is from one of these other packs, and you'll get to meet him that much sooner. And it's going to be a huge party to celebrate both the hunt and your birthday—plus Rory's going to be here."

How good of Rory to show up.

"Yeah," I grumble. "I guess Grey had to come for the hunt, didn't he?"

Dad doesn't say anything for a moment, but I feel his heavy gaze. "Luna, Rory would have come regardless if there was a hunt or not. It's your birthday."

"Sure."

As if on cue, I hear someone calling out, "we're here!" from outside.

"Speak of the devil," I mutter. It's a human phrase Aspen taught me.

"Rory!" Dad's voice booms. He starts for the front hall and I hear the door hinge creak as Rory and Grey open it. I sigh, planting my feet on the ground and sashaying towards them. As sounds of joyous reunion echo throughout the house, I try to push down the thrumming excitement in my heart. I don't care that Rory is back. Why should I?

I enter the front hallway, overlooked by the large moose head hanging over the front door. Dad and Rory are standing atop the black bear hide as they hug one another, the waning sunlight from the window making Rory's blonde hair shine golden. Her mate, Grey, stands close to the door, watching with that placid smile of his. He's got cool blond hair, a trim beard, and the dullest look in his ruby eyes. Over Dad's shoulder, Rory locks eyes with me. She pulls herself from his arms and takes me in her own, trapping me in a warm hug. She smells nice, like earth and pine trees.

"Luna!" At least she sounds excited.

"Welcome home, Aurora," I say, hugging her back. She might have abandoned me, but the world still feels a little more right with her home.

"I've missed you so much," she says.

Doubtful.

"I missed you too," I murmur, because I can't think of anything else to say, and so the truth slips out.

Rory steps back, her hands on my shoulders as she scans me up and down like I'm a pup she's examining for scrapes. She smiles, her silver eyes crinkling and her sharp canines flashing. "You look so pretty, Lulu." Rory's always looked more like Mom, with her blonde hair and grey-toned eyes, but the resemblance is striking as she looks at me now. I see Mom's warm, proud smile like a wisp of smoke I can't quite grasp.

"Stars, it feels like it's been so long since we last saw each other," Rory says.

"Five months," I mumble.

"Has it really been that long?" she asks, though it isn't really a question. She swings her arm around me and pulls me closer. "I can't believe you're turning eighteen tomorrow! My baby sister is all grown up!"

My smile is limp. "I guess so."

"Congratulations, Luna," Grey says. I respond with the obligatory thank-you. I know the Moon put Grey and Rory together, but I still feel a spark of resentment whenever I see him. Of course, I wanted Rory to find her mate: I just didn't want him to live hours inland. I didn't want her to completely abandon us for him. Where are the weekend visits, the weekly phone calls, the daily texts? It was all swept away with Grey and the Northern Skies pack.

Once upon a time, before the Moon sent Rory off to the middle of the Rockies to live out her days with some hick alpha heir, Rory and I were the best of friends. Even though she was three and a half years older than me, she invited me to outings with friends, brought me to parties, snuck out with me in the middle of the day to go to Bruno's, and was always, *always* there for me. Yes, we did things with our own friend groups, but there was never a question in anyone's mind about our sisterly bond. An insult to me was an insult to Rory—proven by her sharp uppercut or mean kick.

During the school year, we'd stay up later than we should talking together well into the day, and in the summers, Rory would often shake me awake before the sun had set to go visit Queenie together. We'd talk with Queenie for an hour or two, always enjoying some sweet treat, before Rory whisked me across the border to the Midnight River beaches. Sometimes we'd spend our time either on the sand or cliff jumping with Kodiak and some of his friends; other times, it was just the two of us splashing in the water, watching the stars. We loved looking at the stars, even before Mom passed away. After Mom's death, Rory and I were even closer than before—the only two people in the world who could feel the loss of our mother the way we did. We'd put on some of her favorite movies (even though we had never liked them), we'd make her favorite foods (well, I made them...Rory can't cook), and we would tell each other every story about Mom we could think of that the other didn't already know. We did everything we could to bind our family of three together, to keep our father afloat in the wake of losing his one and only mate. Rory and I were more than sisters: we were best friends, and we were a team. I was going to do everything in my power to support her as our Alpha when her time came.

But then she met Grey, and I became chopped liver. What had once been our family of four now felt like a family of two—me and Dad.

Dad ushers Rory and Grey deeper into the house, saying he has a few extra pieces of bacon they can eat before everyone arrives. It's not long before people start trickling in, and by eight, the house is bursting full of wolves from Dakota Ridge, Midnight River, Crimson Star, Northern Skies and several other packs. I try to pick out their smells to distinguish their origins based on scent. Kodiak can identify which pack a wolf belongs to within two seconds.

The crowd is mostly comprised of male wolves priming themselves for the hunt in all manner of showy bravado. The she-wolves present are Dakota Ridge natives or the mates of the male wolves, the ones who don't have pups back home. They're draped on the arms of their mates as they watch them puff out their chests with lovesick eyes. Rory is talking and smiling with Dakota Ridge wolves, standing with perfect posture and confidence, while Grey talks with a couple of his pack members. I'll give it to Rory—at least she doesn't have to have her body pressed up against Grey's at all times.

The Dakota Ridge wolves look excited and almost awed to speak with Rory, and I wonder if they wish she were still the heir as much as I do. She was always supposed to lead our pack, but by mating with an alpha heir so far away, a pack merge was impossible. Instead, her new obligation became to help lead his pack, and her duty to lead ours fell to me.

"Luna!" Nova calls my name with all the excitement of a friend who hasn't seen me in months. We had breakfast this morning. Her light brown, chin length hair swishes as she makes her way towards me.

"Hey, Nova," I say, squished in the corner of the living room next to the fireplace.

"Found any prospects yet?" Another voice adds. Even weaving through a crowded room, Anika's gait is more like a confident saunter. She stands next to me against the wall and surveys the crowd with a smirk and sharp eyes. Her eyes are a nice green—she's not quite alpha-blooded, but there's some alpha a few generations back in her bloodline. She's from a high beta family and she carries that confidence with her.

"We should place bets on who your mate is," Anika says.

"It's got to be one of the alpha heirs! Or their brothers. It only makes sense," Nova says. "Mountain Falls has a really cute Alpha Son."

"Maybe my mate isn't here," I say.

"Yeah, sure, and maybe you're a Lone Wolf." Anika rolls her eyes.

I laugh. "You never know. Maybe me and Aspen—"

"You think he's your mate?" Anika asks, turning her head to face me. Nova watches us carefully.

My heart drops to the stomach. "No, I was saying maybe we're both lone wolves. It was a joke." The back of my neck feels hot under the press of the crowd, the cacophony of noise, and the stare Anika gives me, but my voice is calm. It betrays nothing. Anika and Nova may be my best friends, but they don't know about Aspen. He is a weakness—I know he is. A private, embarrassing, human-like weakness.

"Oh moon, is Aspen still going on about that?" Anika

shakes her head. "I swear, he *wants* to be a Lone Wolf. Probably thinks he's going to be some dramatic, tragic figure. He needs to stop reading that poetry nonsense."

I snigger with her, but I like his poems. I don't really get the ones that don't rhyme, but the ones that do and the ones that are lyrics to songs are my favorites.

Relief sweeps over me when the throbbing crowd starts heading out the backdoor, leaving me room to breathe. I step out onto the deck and peer over the railing to see Aspen in the yard with his brothers. He's bathed in the light of cotton candy skies as he gazes at the nearly full Moon, visible in the sun's last breaths. A creeping hint of dark blue rises from the east with the promise of night. Aspen turns his attention towards the ruckus of the crowd, standing still amidst the jostling and arm bumping and wrestling. A Lone Wolf in the chaos.

My breath hitches as I look at him and I'm struck with a stark dichotomy—either it was always going to be us, or it never was. Deep down, I feel certain that I know the answer, but my mind cannot divine the truth.

"You coming?" Anika asks. She and Nova want to enter the bottleneck of wolves making their way down the stairs.

I peel my eyes from Aspen and smile at them. "Of course. Just enjoying the view." I nod upwards. "The Moon is out."

"It's almost the Blue Moon!" Nova squeals as we make our way down. "It's so beautiful."

I look up at the Moon, a day before turning full, soon to be my Blue Moon. I wonder if she's staring down at me with pity for what's to come or with barely contained excitement. I was named after the Moon—I hope she cares for me now.

When I step off the stairs and onto the plush grass, I look at Aspen to find he's looking at me. His brother hooks an arm around Aspen's neck and pulls him down, digging a knuckle into Aspen's curls and yelling, "Let's go, Aspen! Let's go!" before letting out a howl. Aspen looks miserable.

I spot many friends amidst the chaos—alpha-blooded from other packs, wolves from my own. Raff is easy to find with his rust-colored hair and crazed howls. Logan turns from his dad to give me a glowing grin. Logan and Raff have been going on and on about this hunt for weeks. As high betas, this hunt is a chance to prove themselves not only to Dakota Ridge, but to all of the Northwestern packs.

"Luna!" Logan calls, running up to me. He stands in front of me and rakes a hand through his dark hair.

"Are you excited?" I ask. "The hunt is finally here."

"I'm over the moon," he says, his sharp canines almost glistening as he grins. "And then...when I see you next, you'll be eighteen."

"I know. It's an eventful Blue Moon."

"I'll say! I'll catch some good game," he promises.

"You'd better," Anika says. "Or I'll start a petition to make you the next Omega."

Logan laughs and whacks her arm. "Shut up, Ani." Then Logan's dad calls him over, and the second he's gone, Anika pokes my rib.

"Someone's got a crush on you." Anika's voice is sing-songy.

"Who can blame him?" Nova says.

"He looks like a lovesick puppy," Anika croons.

"He does not," I say, brushing off their teasing with a chuckle.

Our attention is diverted to a group of coordinated howls. Kodiak and his band of Midnight River betas walk from around the side of the house and down the hill. Kodiak is shirtless, revealing muscled arms and impeccable abs. He flexes—none of the she-wolves complain—and howls again before backflipping and walking on his hands to the frenzied chants of his betas.

None of his betas have their mates with them, and I wonder if Kodiak told them to leave them behind so they didn't draw attention to his lack of a partner.

Soon, many of the wolves start clapping and whooping for Kodiak as his physical antics ramp up. Nova's eyes are as big as the Moon, and Anika's looking at him the way she looks at prime rib. I glance over at Aspen, standing about ten feet away. He looks at me and rolls his eyes and shakes his head, as if to say "this guy." I laugh and shake my head in return.

Once all the male wolves are on the lawn, Dad walks forward, splitting the crowd until he's before everyone. He may be down the hill, but that doesn't diminish his tall, broad frame or powerful posture.

"Welcome, everyone, to the Dakota Ridge pack!" He calls out. If Rory were next to me, we'd mutter "alpha voice" to each other. While his voice is always deep, Dad's "alpha voice" develops an authoritative quality that demands attention and respect. "And welcome to the Blue Moon Hunt!" Dad throws a fist into the air and is met with cheers, and I feel the gravity and reverence of the Blue Moon descend upon my shoulders. "Tonight, we begin our hunt on the cusp of greatness, and tomorrow, we will hunt and celebrate under the Blue Moon herself!" Cheers ensue. "However, the hunt and the Blue Moon will not be the only cause for celebration." His purple eyes penetrate through the crowd to lock with mine. "We will also celebrate my daughter Luna's birthday. She will turn eighteen under the light of the Blue Moon!"

Now the roar of celebration is for me, and I try not to squirm under everyone's eyes. I'm alpha-blooded. I'm used to attention...just not this much. I plaster a canine-flashing smile and nod at the crowd.

"Without further ado," Dad says. "Let the hunt begin!"

There's a final chorus of howling celebration. Desperate

mates fling their bodies onto each other, trading sloppy, wet kisses. Too many she-wolves are misty eyed, promising that they'll die if their mate doesn't return. As if a moose could kill anyone in such a huge wolf pack. Nova's watching the final goodbyes with dreamy eyes.

"They say a kiss from your mate strengthens you!" she says. "That will be us soon, sending our mates off with a little extra strength."

I glance at Aspen, who's walking away from his brothers and their *affectionate* mates. He stands close to my father, who also stands without a mate to wish him farewell. My heart aches looking at Dad, standing alone, and it aches looking at Aspen. At the next hunt, I could be the one to bestow him a goodbye kiss, though I hope ours won't involve so much slurping and smacking. For once, I wish my hearing was as bad as a human's.

Mates finally tear themselves apart from one another and the male wolves start shifting into wolf form. The color of their fur ranges from butterscotch blond to jet black with varying coat textures. The lower betas have scrawnier wolf forms while the high betas and alphas are noticeably larger. Dad is a massive wolf with purple eyes that glow in the dusk and a thick black coat streaked with grey. I spot Aspen beside him, at least twenty pounds smaller, with a bright blond coat of curls. His brothers are crashing into him, trying to knock him off his hind legs. In wolf form, I doubt Aspen can hide his frustration from his brothers. Can't they feel it seeping from him? Does it only make them want to bother him more?

My father signals that it's time for everyone to leave. I don't pick up wolf cues quite as well in human form, but I can understand that, at least. Communication in wolf form is different from human form. The barrier of fumbling words is eliminated, replaced by sounds and body language and heartbeats. As a wolf, you emit those feelings that are too difficult to put into words. It's beautiful but terrifying, to be stripped naked like that.

Aspen shakes off his brothers and stands tall, for a moment belonging to a painting of baby pink skies under a nearly full Blue Moon—a portrait depicting promise and hope amidst uncertainty. To humans, the Blue Moon doesn't mean much; it's just something that happens every few years when there are two full moons within the same month. For us, the Blue Moon means so much more. The Moon herself is gracing us in her fullness twice in a month, and it's said that all sorts of beautiful, magical things can happen during the Blue Moon. It's the beginning of the "Blue Month", when its magic supposedly lingers in the air. As I look at Aspen, I wonder if the Blue Moon's magic will grant me my deepest wish.

When Aspen turns his furry head to look at me, I am thankful I'm in human form. I'm grateful for the fleshy barrier that withholds all that I feel. Then he turns his attention forward before running off with the rest of the wolves, leaving me behind. It's a warm evening, and I'm surrounded by weeping she-wolves and even friends, but I feel cold and entirely alone. That's the last time I'll see Aspen before I turn eighteen. I wish our last moment could have been our time in the forest, before Kodiak came. It feels like that meant a lot more than stolen glances in a crowd.

CHAPTER 3

SOULMATE

I'm anxious for the horde of leftover wolves and pack members to leave until they're gone. Without the noise, I can hear my own thoughts clawing against my skull.

"Thank the Moon they're gone," Rory says. She plops onto the black leather couch in the basement and leans her head against the cushions. I'm standing in the entryway to the hall, leaning against the wall.

"I was about to rip the throats out of those sniveling mates," Rory continues. "Do they really think there's any danger? On a Blue Moon Hunt of all things!"

I want to give no reaction, to withhold a moment of comraderie that will only make me sadder when she leaves again, but a snort escapes my nose. She smiles at my laugh.

"Maybe they're sad to part with their mates," I say, regaining cool composure.

"It's two nights," she scoffs, waving a dismissive hand.

You can't bear to leave Grey for two nights. You couldn't even bear to leave his pack in the last five months, I want to say. Instead, I say nothing. I should go upstairs, leave Rory to her couch. I'm not going to be her puppy dog, running to the door with a wagging tail just because she showed up.

"Man, in just a few hours it's your birthday," she says.

"Mmhmm," I say. Days and dates are strange for were-wolves. We operate twelve hours apart from our human counterparts, waking up in the evening and going to bed when the sun shines bright in the sky. The calendar date changes in the middle of our day, every day.

"When's your turn-time?" Rory asks.

"10:01 p.m." I want to be offended that she didn't know it, but your exact time of birth only matters when you're turning eighteen. Or if you're one of those human astrology girls.

"T-minus twenty-four hours." She grins at me. "Are you excited?"

"Yeah."

"Why are you standing around?" she slaps the cushion next to her. "Come sit."

I feel like that same stupid puppy when I obey her, settling next to her. I want to leave, and I don't. I can't decide between enjoying the moment and making a silent statement, instead existing in some uncomfortable middle. I mean, it's not like she completely forgot about me after she moved to Northern Skies. She still shows up for holidays and birthdays, she checks in every couple of weeks to see how I'm doing, she sends dumb mountain pictures here and there.

But it's nothing like it was before.

Her long nails feel good against my scalp as she scratches my head. "Our little Lulu," she hums. "All grown up."

I pray Rory doesn't mention Mom right now, because I'll cry if she does—and that's the last thing I want to do.

"You're nervous, aren't you." It's not a question. "It will work out, I promise. There's no way you're a Lone Wolf."

"Yeah, I know." As a child, becoming a Lone Wolf was my

greatest fear. I think I could bear it now, as long as Aspen is a Lone Wolf too. We could be two lonely wolves forging our own path together within the pack, "choosing our own destiny," as Aspen would say.

"What's going on?" Rory asks, looking at me with such tenderness that all I see is Mom. Rory doesn't even have to mention her to bring her into the room. I look away.

"I'm just nervous, you know? I mean, with this huge hunt, I'm probably going to meet my mate at the celebration party. It's a really big deal. And what if he—" I pause. "I don't know."

"What if he...what?"

What if he isn't Aspen? Of course, I can't say that to Rory of all people. Instead, I say, "What if I don't, I don't know—what if he's annoying or something?"

Rory's laugh is rich and hearty, just like Dad's. "He's your mate, Lulu. You're going to be obsessed with him. He won't annoy you. Well...most of the time."

I can feel her looking at me, so I turn to see her smile.

"I promise, you're going to love him so much you won't know what to do with yourself."

I try to picture loving some hazy wolf from another pack, of feeling everything I've ever felt and more for this mystery figure, but I can't imagine it.

Rory untangles her hand from my hair, leaving behind a lumpy ponytail, and leans against the pillows by the couch's arm. She drapes her legs over my lap like it's the most natural thing in the world.

"Alright, who's turned eighteen recently? Has anyone mated since I last came?"

I'm relieved she's pivoted the conversation away from my impending birthday. Here in the basement living room, with warm lamp lights and a worn-in couch, life almost feels normal. Rory loves the Dakota Ridge gossip. She sits straight up when I tell her that Juniper and Carlan mated, her jaw slack.

"You're kidding." Her voice holds the whisper of a scandal. "But Juniper's parents are the Omegas."

"Carlan's family was so upset."

"Yeah of course."

"But what can you do?"

"What can you do?" Rory shrugs. "It's the Moon." And the Moon did what she wanted—even pairing an upper beta like Carlan with an omega, of all wolves.

"Has Aspen found a mate yet?" Rory asks. It's an innocuous question, but my body freezes all the same.

"No."

"How long has he been eighteen for?"

"Seven months." My answer comes too quickly.

Her eyes sliver for a second, a flash of something that I don't like. "That's not too bad." Her voice is as casual as ever. "He's got plenty of time to find his mate."

Maybe I'm reading into things. "Yeah."

"Remember when you had that fat crush on him?"

I feel like some woodland animal that's landed itself in a trap. One wrong step and I'll be snapped up in its metal jaws. "Yeah," I say. I hope she'll drop the subject, that she'll ask me about another wolf and if he or she has found their mate.

"It was kind of cute. Kind of funny, really. You, the daughter of the Alpha. Worrying about him."

"He's a high beta," I say.

"Yeah, but you know. He's not like Ares, or Ace, or Alix," she says, rattling off his brothers.

I roll my eyes. They're strong, alright, but they're a bunch of brainless meatheads.

"Do you still like him?" Rory asks. It's a point-blank question, one that can only be avoided with a lie. Still, I try to work around it.

"He's a good friend."

Rory lets out a breathy laugh, leaning back into her couch pillows once more. Her legs are crisscrossed underneath her. "No way." Her voice is full of mirth. "You like wee little Aspen? Still?"

I refuse to look at her. I know there's no hiding the truth now. "Like you never liked anyone."

She laughs. "I mean, yeah. Obviously. You know I had a thing for Kodiak."

"You thought he was going to be your mate."

She swishes her hand like she's swatting away some insignificant fly of a thought. "Well I was wrong. Clearly. But I mean, Kodiak was an alpha heir, you know? Everybody knows he's crazy strong and his senses are off the charts. But Aspen...I mean, you know Aspen. The kid always had his nose in some stupid book. Ares used to complain about it all the time." She chuckles. "He's no fighter. I mean, if he didn't come from a good family, he'd have been bullied every day for all his nerdy sapcrap and human interactions." Rory laughs like we're in on some great joke together, ignorant to the sourness pumping through my veins.

What does *she* know about Aspen? She hasn't lived here for years. Despite Aspen's affinity towards academia, he is popular and well-liked because of his confidence, his way with people, and his authenticity. People like being around Aspen because he cares about them, because he's smart, and because he's a natural leader. He can get away reading books and hanging out with humans because of who he is, not just because he's in a good family.

"You know, I never harp on Grey." My voice is low. "I could talk about how he's basically a mute, and he barely makes an effort to get to know us, and he's always just standing around watching, and doing and saying nothing like some low beta servant. But I've never said those things before."

Gone is Rory's jollity and laughter; her face is as cold as her steely eyes. The warmth of the cozy basement has succumbed to chilling tension. "I tease you about your *crush,* and you decide to talk that way about my *mate?*"

I feel a prick of guilt and a stab of stupidity for dumping my frustrations about Grey like that. And yet, the way she emphasizes the words "crush" and "mate" dig at my skin.

Rory's eyes soften. "You shouldn't be so bent up over a boy, Lulu. I get it, I do, but Aspen? Really? I can't believe you still like him. What are you doing with such a big crush? You're going to meet your mate tomorrow and Aspen's not going to matter anymore."

Well, thank the Moon that Aurora is here to set me straight! Such a selfless hero—here to guide her foolish, wayward sister. Silly me with my silly crush. I'm so lucky she's deigned to come back for a day and act like she has all the say in the world about my life. And I'd better not say a thing about *her* life or *her* mate, or there'll be hell to pay!

I grip the edge of the couch cushion, wadding the cool leather in my palms and digging my nails into its surface. "Well, you're never afraid to speak your mind," I say, leveling her with a stare of violent purple. "Probably why the Moon dumped you with Grey. The Northern Skies pack needed at least one alpha."

Rory scoffs like she's in disbelief. She can't fathom that her little sister doesn't just buckle at the knees and tell her she's right about everything.

"And what do *you* know about being an alpha?" Rory cocks her head to the side. I grit my teeth against her next words. "You're throwing a hissy fit over a boy. Not a mate—a *boy*. I've never seen such pathetic human behavior in an alpha." She spits the word "human" like a curse.

It's moments like these when Rory looks so different from Mom. Mom's eyes were a soft grey; Rory's are a sharp, stainless steel that cut up my heart. I feel the first hint of tears. I want to say something back, to prove I'm just as alpha as she is, to hurt her as much as she hurts me. Instead, I rush out of the room so she doesn't see the hot tears rolling down my cheeks.

I go upstairs to hide out in my room until 11 p.m, when I start walking over to Anika's house. The fresh air feels good on my skin, especially in contrast to the tension in my house. I text Ani to let her know I'm on my way. She wanted to do a little preliminary birthday party, since the hunters won't be back until tomorrow at 3 or 4 a.m.

Late spring nights hum with the chitter of insects, a comforting sound that signifies the dark solitude of night. Under the baking sun, I feel as though my thoughts are on parade, but with the cloak of night, I retain an alpha composure worthy of respect. Tonight is not a dark night, not with the Moon a sliver away from full. I draw a deep breath, the lunar light dissipating the shadows of doubt cast by both Rory and me. I feel stronger under the Moon—more confident, more assured in my future. Tomorrow, I will see Aspen. Tomorrow, I will find out that he is my mate. He just has to be.

Anika's family are high betas, so their house is quite nice. As I approach the door, I hear chatter behind the walls until I deliver three crisp knocks and the house falls silent. Ah, a surprise party. I smile.

Anika opens the door, wearing a pink tank top and ripped shorts. Her light brown hair is pulled up into a messy bun. "Hi, Luna! Happy Birthday! Come on in!"

As I step into the house, I hear the breaths of a dozen people. We round the corner of the hallway into the kitchen, where a group of girls call out, "Surprise!" I pretend to look taken aback, but my smile is genuine. The girls gathered at the party are all upper Dakota Ridge betas except for Nova.

Despite the party revolving around my birthday, it takes my mind off my impending turn-time, adding a desperately needed levity to the whole affair. For a moment it's like any other birthday, with presents and a meat pie with candles. Anika is an impeccable host, with help from Nova ensuring that appetizers are refilled and drink pitchers are full.

I don't come home until after 4 a.m., laden with bags of birthday gifts. I head up to my room, plop my bags on the floor, and flop onto my bed. I don't bother turning on the lamp, instead pulling out my phone to look at my messages. Most of my female friends were at the party, most of my male friends are on the hunt, but I have messages from alpha-blooded friends from other packs and a message from Dad at 12:01 a.m., saying "Happy birthday, Lulu! I can't believe my little girl is already eighteen. I love you so much, and I'm so proud of the wolf you've become." I smile. Dad must have snuck his phone with him on the hunt and shifted into human form in some corner of the woods to text me with opposable thumbs.

Someone else did the same.

Aspen 12:04 a.m.

Happy Birthday, Lu

Aspen 12:04 a.m.

When's your turn-time?

My heart skips. With two little texts, all the levity I felt from the party is replaced with bone-eating anxiety. That's right, how could I forget? Even for a moment? This birthday is unlike any other birthday before or any birthday after. I have a turn-time, a second wherein I become a fully-fledged adult, a wolf looking for her mate whether she's ready or not. I draw in a deep breath.

Me: *Thanks, Aspen. It's* 10:01 *PM*

I tense up when I hear Rory walking down the hall. I click my phone off, plunging into the darkness of the night. The sun-blocking curtains over the floor-length window and balcony door impede the Moon's light from shining through. There are a couple of light knocks before Rory opens the door, silhouetted by the light of the hall. She leans against the door frame, her silver eyes glowing slightly in the dark.

"Hey, Luna." Her voice is soft. "How was your party?"

I sit up in my bed. "You knew about the party?"

"Anika's mom was talking with me at the hunt kick-off. She invited me over. Said it was a surprise party."

A pause. "Why didn't you come?"

"I thought you might not want me there."

"Oh."

I can feel the apologies dancing at the tips of our tongues, but Rory and I are alpha-blooded. We're too proud to say anything.

"Well." Rory pulls out her phone, glancing at the time. "It's already 4:15. We're probably going to want food soon enough—if you're not too full from your party, that is. What do you want for dinner, birthday girl?"

"Dinner?" I lean back into my pillows with an incredulous smile. Sometimes a couple of low beta women cook for us, but everyone is too busy preparing for the post-hunt feast tomorrow. "No way. Has Grey domesticated you? You know how to cook?"

She bursts into her rich, deep laugh. "Oh moon, no. I can't cook. I meant, what do you want for takeout from Bruno's?"

"I should have known." I'm grinning. "I guess having a mate can't change you that much."

"No, but it's really sweet you thought I could make something edible. I'm touched."

Rory's got a car, so she drives us to Bruno's to order steaks for takeout. Bruno is really happy to see the two of us and chats with us in between working the steaks on the grill. He invites me to pick a dessert from behind the glass, free of charge, for my birthday. Rory and I go home to eat our steaks, and we talk about everything—Dakota Ridge, Northern Skies, Bruno, Queenie, the new mates, the hunt, the Blue Moon, and everything in between. It seems like the only thing we don't talk about is our fight earlier. Or Aspen. We stay up late into the day, when the sun is hot and high in the sky. It's past 1:30 p.m when I crawl into a pair of cotton shorts and a white tank top and fall asleep.

I awake to a strange sensation, starting from the tips of my toes. The feeling reminds me of when my foot falls asleep, only more pleasant. It works its way through my legs, my torso, my arms, and finally the very top of my head before it's gone. I glance at my digital alarm clock. 10:01 p.m. I stare at the ceiling, clutching the covers close to my chin. So that's it then. I'm eighteen. I'm an adult. Less than a minute and my whole world is different. It's too late for me to fall back asleep, but I want to try. I don't want to think about my birthday party in six hours, I don't want to think about facing a hundred wolves, and I definitely don't want to think about seeing Aspen for the first time. I can't bear to face the potential reality that—

A knock rattles my thoughts—it's coming from my balcony door. I look over to it, its glass view obscured by the sun-blocking curtains. A muffled male voice introduces himself.

"Luna? It's Aspen."

My heart stops. In my half-asleep-half-turning-into-an-adult stupor, I hadn't heard Aspen climb up to the balcony. I lay as still and stiff as a dead critter. If I breathe, will he hear me?

Knock knock. "Luna? Are you in there?"

My heart starts again, beating far too fast to make up for lost time. My breaths return in shallow gulps of air. Why is he here? Why, of all people, is Aspen here? I had six hours! Six hours before I'd have to face him! Now he's here and he's outside my room. I dig my nails into my bed covers, holding it to my chin like a shield against this moment.

"Aspen?" My voice comes out in a just-woken croak. I sit up and clear my throat. "What are you doing here?" The covers are spooled at my waist, but my grip remains iron clad. There's a pause before he answers.

"I had to see you."

I draw in a long, deep breath. It's no coincidence he's here moments after my turn-time. Perhaps he needs to know just as much as I do. In the past seven and a half months, ever since he turned eighteen, I've imagined the moment our eyes would meet countless times, and I've waited for my turn-time with bated breath. Sometimes, the waiting felt almost impossible to bear, the anticipation so overwhelming it was suffocating. During every little moment I shared with him—be it a smile, a funny face, a conversation, a joke—I just wanted to know if he was the one. I had dreamed of 10:01 p.m. on May 31st. As I close my eyes, I renounce such longing and curse myself for pining after this day. Right now, I'd do anything for a hundred little moments more.

"Luna, are you still there?"

"Yes."

"Will you come out?"

I do not want to go out. I do not want to see him. Perhaps I will run away, away from this house, away from Dakota Ridge, away from him. I'll run away from a truth I cannot bear.

"Okay," I say. I plant my feet on the side of the bed, looking at the door handle beside those looming grey curtains like it's a ferocious wolf I'm up against in a spar. I take trepidatious steps towards the door, catching a glimpse of myself in the mirror. I'm still wearing my tank top and black cotton shorts, and my hair is a tangled dark mess. I pull out my hair tie and attempt to fix my hair, settling for a lumpy ponytail. I combat my breath with a mint, though it doesn't really matter. It only matters if he's the one so that our kiss isn't sullied with bad breath, but from how I hear the first moment is supposed to be, he probably wouldn't really care.

As I place my hand on the doorhandle, I feel as heavy as stone. I slowly open the door and step outside, my eyes glued to the dark wooden planks beneath my bare feet. I feel the fresh night air on my skin and hear the bugs in their nightly choir. I walk up to the balcony's railing and grasp onto it, the metal smooth and cool against my palms. I sense Aspen to my left, hovering in my peripheral.

"Luna." His voice is quiet. He leans forward against the railing, and I clench it more tightly, locking eyes with the Moon instead of him. It's gorgeous tonight, white and full and brimming with light. The Moon looms over the forest and pond below and it looms over me; I want to feel the strength of her lunar glow, to let it light up every dark crevice in my soul, but my insides are too coiled for even the Moon to penetrate me.

"It's the Blue Moon," I say.

He doesn't answer immediately, as though he's taking in the Moon. "It is."

"She's beautiful." The words come out almost choked. "They say miracles happen during a Blue Moon."

"So they say." His voice is quiet and smooth, like a soft summer breeze. "The Blue Moon can present unprecedented opportunities."

The aching in my chest pricks the back of my eyes with sparkling tears. I blink them away, turning my attention from the Moon to the ground.

"You left the hunt early," I say.

"I did."

"Are they going to be upset?"

"I went with the group bringing back yesterday's meat. They needed it in time for the party."

"I see. But aren't they expecting you back by now?"

"I had to see you, Luna." His voice cuts through the sounds of the night, lodging an arrow straight into my heart. It's one of the most romantic things he's ever said to me. It's one of the most heartbreaking things. All this time, has he felt it too?

A breeze flutters through the air, a gentle whistle in our silence. It wisps the loose strands of my hair and sends goosebumps down my arms.

"You won't look at me," he says.

I clench my jaw and release it. "I'm eighteen now."

"I know."

I don't answer. I don't know what to say.

"Why won't you look at me?"

My lip quivers. My grip on the railing is steadfast, my knuckles a chalky white. I close my eyes. "Why are you here?"

The following seconds are painful, as though Father Time himself has slowed the clock just to see me writhe. I wish I could see Aspen's face, but I dare not look.

"I have to know." His voice is quiet. "I have to know if it's you."

I open my eyes and stare at the Moon in a fervent prayer. If Aspen is my mate, I'll never ask for anything again.

"Okay," I say. I release the railing, my eyes trained on my bare feet atop wooden planks as I turn my body towards him. I take in one last breath, letting his scent wash over me. He smells like new books and wooden chessboards and ocean spray. I lift my head and look straight into his eyes.

Something is different.

I don't know if it happens in seconds, minutes, or hours. Father Time has removed himself. A warm flutter tickles my heart, exploding outward and filling every part of my body with warmth and euphoria, from the edges of my fingertips to the very hairs on my head. I feel my eyes light up as Aspen's begin to glow, and I'm falling into them like he's the ocean. My head is clear and fogged, crisp excitement and hazy joy. A clear echo sings in my soul: *he is my mate.* I loved him before and I love him now—more than I could have imagined. He is Everything and nothing else matters besides this moment, besides us.

There's no stopping my tears as a smile grows on my face. "Aspen!" I say his name like a prayer. I thank the Blue Moon with all my heart. Everyone was right after all—Blue Moons are lucky. And yet, it was always going to be us. Always. It's so obvious. I would feel stupid that I ever doubted Aspen was my mate if I had room for any emotion other than joy. I step forward, ready to take him into my arms and hold him forever. My body reaches for his in a powerful, primeval way it never has before, begging to be one with him. As I reach for him, Aspen steps back. Gleaming drops of sweat dot his brow. I do not understand.

"Luna." His voice is pregnant with emotion. His eyes waver with tears. Something pokes at my oversized heart, threatening to deflate it like a balloon. I don't feel any of that clear-headedness anymore. Confusion clouds my heart and mind. Something is wrong, but something can't be wrong because he is my mate. Nothing is wrong now nor ever will be again. So why is a warning clanging in my heart?

Aspen takes a forced step backwards, as though he's fighting his very body. His eyes are full of anguish, his lip is trembling. His voice comes out broken. "I was hoping it wasn't you."

All the warmth in my body dissipates as though I've been

shoved into icy water. I want to run to him, to pull him into my arms, to kiss him and love him, but I cannot move. I can't tell if I'm freezing to death or drowning.

"I—I am so sorry." Tears flow down his cheeks. "I'll—I will explain, I just—I have to do this. I don't want to, but—but I have to. I just—" He backs himself against the short side of the balcony's railing, clutching onto it as though he'll fall.

"What's wrong?" I ask. My voice sounds far away, like someone else is speaking for me. I cannot comprehend his reaction. Is the emotion too much for him? Is he scared of how much he feels for me? And why do I feel like I'm floating away from my body? I do not feel the wood beneath my toes anymore.

"Luna." Aspen squeezes his eyes shut like he's been looking into the sun. "I, Aspen, under the light of the Moon...formally..." His grip is white, his body is taut. I tilt my head and furrow my brow, the action feeling disconnected from myself. What is Aspen doing? His voice is a hoarse screech. "Apply to sever our connection!"

Then I'm thrown back into my body. Like a pin that has struck my heart, I feel a sharp, stabbing pain in my chest. My knees threaten to buckle and I have to grab the long side of the balcony railing to keep from falling over. "Aspen!" My voice is a ragged breath. I claw at my chest with my free hand to rip out the pain. Something is wrong. I cannot breathe. I look at him, desperate for an answer.

Aspen opens his eyes. They're full of sorrow and apologies, but they're those same ocean blue eyes I fell in love with years ago.

"Luna, I reject you as my mate."

CHAPTER 4

OCEAN BLUES

THREE YEARS, THREE MONTHS AGO

I am not sure when I first noticed that Aspen had blue eyes. When you've known someone your whole life, you don't remember when you met him or when you first noticed simple details. It was just a fact about Aspen—blond hair, blue eyes. His weren't a piercing turquoise nor a bright ice blue nor a shocking azure, but blue in a regular sort of way. Having brushed shoulders with alpha-blooded my whole life, I'd seen some of the most vibrant, stunning eye colors. Bright cyan, blood red, hot magenta, emerald green, sparkling gold. In the day, the sun's light revealed the eyes' full array of gorgeous color and in the dark, they glittered like stars on a clear night. Some were full of vivid color, and some, like Rory's silver eyes, were bold and piercing. Then there was Aspen, whose eyes were as ordinary as any other beta's—bland in comparison to the best. The only interest I took in his eyes regarded the direction they were pointed.

It was March 1st, a snappy day reminding us that spring was not yet here. I was almost fifteen years old. The cacophony of a hundred chatty teenage wolves bounced off the cold cafeteria walls and forced me to focus my hearing on the conversation at my table. We all had brown paper bags full of jerky and cold meats. We did not care for the government's idea of lunch, as their meals never provided enough protein. After many complaints with the school board, they maintained it would be unfair to provide the "night class students" with more quality meats than their human counterparts.

"We already have to pay your teachers more because you insist on holding school in the middle of the night!" I could imagine their nasally human voices. "We cannot allocate more funding to the night class student body's food than to any other school." The worst part was that none of us even wanted to go to school except for Aspen, but the government was heavy-handed about "all children receiving an education." Even the werewolf ones, apparently.

"We ought to revolt, you know." Logan was loud as always. I could see the flecks of cold ground venison he hadn't finished chewing. "If I gotta listen to Mr. Glade talk about cells and DNA till summer, I say we throw him in the woods for our next hunt. I can't take much more sapcrap." 'Sap' being slang for sapiens, as in Homo sapiens. Sometimes we called humans "the sapes." We got fangs and they got monkey brains.

Anika held out a hand, smirking. "Logan." She spoke in a gravelly tone, a stellar rendition of Mr. Glade's voice. "Tell me the cellular structure in my hand! Right now! Now! Have you been LISTENING to anything I've been saying?!"

Logan guffawed along with most of the table. Nova was giggling with a hand over her mouth, and even Aspen chuckled as he rolled his eyes. I did my best to laugh at Ani's imitation, smiling as I gnawed on deer jerky. I looked down at the plastic green table, chipped in some places and cracked in others.

"Don't worry, Mr. Glade. Next time I'm hunting," Raff

started, "I'll be sure to decipher the evolutionary history of my prey before going in for the kill."

More laughter from them. More faking from me.

I needed to stop feeling so sorry for myself. I tried to focus on the conversation, to care about biology and English and whatever else everyone was whining about. March held no special meaning for them. On the fifteenth, they'd all offer their condolences, talk about how great my mom was, but until then, it would hardly cross their minds. I thought Rory would come home this month and that we'd be together, but she was lovesick with her new mate. She did say she would stop by on the fifteenth, but I wondered if she could manage a tear over Mom's grave with all that happiness.

I gritted my teeth against swelling emotions. It didn't matter that Rory wasn't here. I didn't need her. I had my friends. I had my friends with their joking, teasing, happy—

There was one face that lacked the joviality of the rest. Aspen was staring at me, his eyes both soft and searching. I felt like he could see through me like glass and discern every emotion I tried to hide. He tilted his head and furrowed his eyebrows. *What's wrong?* His face asked.

"—Aspen. He's the sape-pet, after all," Anika said.

Aspen turned at the mention of his name, breaking our eye-contact. "What?"

"I said, all this raggin' on biology is gonna upset you. After all, you're some sort of genius, aren't you?" Anika's comment would come across as mean if I didn't see the glimmer in her eye, the smirk that veered closer to flirtation than cruelty. My eyes sharpened, but no one was paying me attention.

Aspen shrugged. "You call it genius. I call it trying. You should give effort a shot sometime, Ani. You might even escape a class with higher than a D." He smirked right back. That was the way to play it, to assert confidence and dominance, even if it was over something as trivial as grades.

"High school hot shot," Raff teased, elbowing Aspen's arm.

Logan waved a dismissive hand. "Yeah, yeah, but let's see how fast you are in a sprint, alright?"

"Someone has to keep you brutes happy and dumb." Aspen laughed. "If we all fail, the sapes are going to crack down on us."

The bell rang, and everyone started climbing out of the benches. The cafeteria echoed with shuffling feet and unbridled chatter.

"You all go ahead," Aspen said. "Luna and I can clear the trash."

Our friends stared at Aspen like he'd lost that smart-alec brain of his. "You'd make our Alpha Daughter, our Alpha *Heir*, pick up our trash?" Logan asked, his brown eyes huge and his lip curled in disgust. He turned to me and his eyes softened like butter in the summer. He smiled, as though apologizing for Aspen. *This guy.*

"It's all right," I said, crumpling up my bag. "An alpha ought to serve her people, right? You all can leave."

They looked confused and uncomfortable, but they weren't going to push back. They walked off and I started scooping up brown paper bags, once packed with lunches provided by groups of beta women. They were all empty—we didn't leave our lunches unfinished.

I could feel Aspen watching me, and I knew he wanted to say something. He may not have revered my alpha standing the way others did, but even he wouldn't suggest I stay behind to clean for no reason. The cafeteria was still noisy with the many stragglers who didn't pretend to care about the bell. I wanted to escape the noise, to find a quiet dark corner without blaring

LED lights overhead, to curl up and just *feel* without the world watching me.

Aspen and I crossed the rubbery cafeteria flooring, trash in arms. The floor had streaks of green and silver, school pride colors we couldn't care less about. We dumped the trash in the can by the door and walked out into a hallway full of delinquent wolves being snapped at by human teachers. I was a decent student, good enough to set an alright example for the wolves, but not too good to be considered a sape-pet like Aspen. The teachers didn't holler at Aspen and I for loitering in the hall, even sparing a smile for him.

"Let's go this way," Aspen said, nodding towards the right. Class was in the opposite direction, but I followed him, of course. We rounded a couple of corners before we entered an empty hallway. A light flickered overhead as Aspen touched my elbow. "Luna, is everything okay?" he asked, his voice quiet. He looked into my eyes. "You seem down."

That was when I really saw his eyes for the first time. No, they were not vivid blue like the clearest sky or the wings of a bluejay—they were blue like the ocean. His eyes were not a brilliant color that caught one's attention from across the room: they were eyes that were deep. The way he looked at me, the color and depth of them, I felt he could see my very soul.

My heart jumped to my throat as I tried to blink the tears away. "Everything is fine," I started, but his deep blue eyes looked so earnest and sincere. Sure, I was surrounded by friends and adoring pack members every day, but what did that really mean when I felt so alone? The only person who really understood me left for Northern Skies. "It's March," I said. My lip trembled and my voice wobbled. "It's March and Aurora isn't here."

His arms were warm and strong as he pulled me into a hug. My tears stained his shirt as his grip tightened. I felt stupid, the

Alpha Daughter crying about missing her sister. Crying over a mother who had been gone for two years.

"Oh, Lu." Aspen's voice was so soft it eased some of the shame I felt. I wrapped my arms around him. Since I'd already made a fool of myself, I might as well give in.

"I just, I feel alone," I confessed, my cheek against his chest. "She was...Rory understood. She knew. She knew what it all was like, and she was my best friend—and now I don't know who to talk to."

Aspen whispered, "I'm sorry," and held me for a minute more. When the bell rang to signify the start of class, I pulled away and wiped my face.

"Sorry. You'll be late to class."

He didn't move, nor was he quick to answer. I could see the cogs in his brain turning, working out something to say. "I'm... not Aurora." His voice was halting. "I know I can't replace her. But Lu, if you ever need to talk, I'm here for you. I mean it." He looked at me with those eyes, eyes that moments before were somehow mundane. It seemed impossible now that I ever could have thought that. "You know I love you, don't you?" he asked.

Tears sparkled in my eyes. My voice was quiet as a secret. "I know."

CHAPTER 5

LIGHT IN THE DARK

My legs give out and my knees crash against the hard wooden planks. I'm trying to catch my breath, but I cannot find it. *I reject you as my mate...I reject you as my mate... I reject you as my mate.* What did Aspen do? Something is wrong, something beyond my own thoughts. My body is processing something my mind cannot make out yet. What did he mean, "I reject you as my mate"? Why does my heart feel so heavy? Why do I feel so—

My breath hitches. It took a few seconds, but my mind understands what my soul already figured out. Aspen rejected me. My soulmate rejects me. He doesn't want me. He doesn't love me. He doesn't even care about me. Somehow, with a few words, he has petitioned the Moon herself to terminate our bond, to defile the most sacred part of who we are. He has destroyed us. He has destroyed me.

I look down at my trembling hands, ghostly pale in the moonlight. Aspen has already left. He's abandoned me in body and soul. I hold my hands against my mouth as my whole body shakes. I fall forward onto the balcony floor, tears pouring from my eyes as sobs rip through the night air. A pain I have never known racks my body, like the very stitches of my DNA are ripping apart. This is a primeval pain, something deep and intrinsic. Rejection from your mate. It is a desecration. An unthinkable cruelty. It's more than a birthright stripped away—it's a part of my being. I don't know how long I am there, drawing my breath in shuddering heaves, clawing my nails against the wood, until I hear a panicked voice calling my name. A flicker of hope in the black void of my heart. Aspen has returned. He'll stitch me together again.

I am pulled in with strong arms into a soft chest. My cheeks are wet and sticky, and my eyes are clouded with tears. I try to see through the haze of my vision and mind, and I first notice the bright full Moon above. The Blue Moon. They say it brings luck. I say it's a curse. I wonder if she mourns with me. I wonder if she's laughing. As I make sense of my surroundings, I realize it is not Aspen who holds me in his arms, but Rory.

"Luna!" Her voice is a throaty whisper, her palm is on my cheek. "What happened to you?" Her silver eyes are wild and desperate. I don't know if I've ever seen her so scared.

Cradled in my sister's arms, I wonder if I'll die. I hope I do. The black edges of overwhelming emptiness creep in from the corners. My mate has rejected me. My mate. My one and only mate. I try to speak, to tell Rory what has happened. "I—" The word is barely out before I'm overcome with a fresh stab of horrifying emotion. How can I say it? How can I speak the words aloud, say that I was rejected? It makes it too real and too tangible.

Rory carries me bridal-style into my room and sets me down on the bed before kneeling next to me. "Luna. Please talk to me. What can I—how can I help?" She takes my hand and squeezes it. "I'm going to call 911, okay?" She reaches for my cell phone on the nightstand.

"No," I manage to say. She's still holding my hand, and I try to squeeze it. "Doctors—they can't..."

"Okay, I won't call them." She scoots even closer. "But Luna, can't you tell me what happened?"

My lip is trembling as I nod. "Rory, I promise I'll tell you, but...I need some time. Please, can you give me that?"

She nods, solemn as the grave. "Of course. Of course."

I squeeze her hand once more. "Can you wait outside my room?"

I see the hesitation in her face, but she agrees, leaving me to my bed. I'm not sure how much time passes—maybe minutes, maybe hours. Just as I am born with the ability to change into a wolf, I'm certain these symptoms of a mate rejection—these uncontrollable, otherworldly feelings—were coded away inside me, set to trigger if I somehow found myself rejected by a mate. Set to prove that I've suffered some tragedy. As the perverse magic burns its last bolts of pain, I am left alone with my own thoughts. I realize it is not just my mate who has rejected me. It is Aspen. The magical attachment I felt to him is all but gone, the Moon's gift dissipated, and all I'm left with are my own feelings, just as they once were.

So I cry for myself.

I WOBBLE OUT OF MY ROOM AND DOWN THE STAIRS, WHERE I know Rory waits for me. I hear hushed whispers and I catch a whiff of dried flowers and antique furniture. Rory has brought Queenie. I step off the staircase and turn the corner to face the living room where they're looking at me, waiting for me.

I walk into the living room. "Hello, Queenie." My voice is as strong as a field mouse's.

"Hello Luna," she says. Her silver hair is pulled up in a bun, and her eyes are full of warm concern. I swallow the sob lodged in my throat.

Queenie is the oldest wolf in our pack. At least, I'm pretty sure she is. I used to ask her how old she was, but she always dodged the question, so I just assume she's immortal. Rory and I used to make up stories about Queenie late at night when we'd sleepover in each other's rooms. We'd speculate on where she'd been, how many human boys had fallen in love with her, and what her mate must have been like. We'd wonder if she was a spirit from the Moon sent to give guidance to wolves around the world, but the tight hugs from her plump body indicate she's no specter.

Those days of musing feel so long ago.

Rory and Queenie are on the couch, and I take an armchair across from them. Neither of them speak, waiting for me to do so. I draw a deep breath. "10:01 was my turn time," I say. It already feels so long ago, but how long has it really been? Hours? If that, even? Oh moon, the party is coming, isn't it? Oh no. Do I have to go? Is it really still coming? The world has ended but it hasn't stopped turning.

"And?" Rory asks when I take too long.

Right. My story. "And, shortly thereafter, Aspen showed up at my balcony."

Rory's eyes darken.

"He's my mate," I say. Rory's eyes widen, but she says nothing. Queenie purses her lips, looking graver than I've ever seen. "And he..." I choke on my words. I don't want to say them aloud. Tears flow down my cheeks. "He rejected me."

"He what?" Rory asks. She sounds confused. "What do you mean, he rejected you?"

"He said...it was funny the way he was talking. It was like

some sort of spell or chant, I don't know. But, he said he was formally rejecting me."

"What—" Rory whips her head between Queenie and I. "What is that supposed to mean? He rejects you? He can't do that. He's your mate." She looks at Queenie's solemn face. "This can't be right, can it? It's not..." She's looking between us. "It's not possible. It doesn't even make sense."

Queenie's sigh sends a ripple of silence through the room. I can hear the kitchen clock ticking, counting the seconds we wait for her wisdom. Queenie is the oldest, wisest person I know. Surely she'll know what to do. She'll know how to fix this.

"Strange things happen, once in a Blue Moon," she mutters.

"Strange things?" Rory cries. "Strange things! Her mate... rejected her? That's not just strange! That's—I've never heard of such a thing!"

Queenie rests her hand on Rory's leg, a quiet gesture that silences her. Queenie looks at me with brown eyes brimming with compassion. "A mate rejection is scarcely spoken of, but not unprecedented."

I suck in my breath.

"Those of us who know of these incidents do not speak of them. It is so incredibly rare that we don't want to worry youths looking forward to their mate. We don't want to plant false notions that it's common or acceptable. Rejecting a mate is considered a perversion of something sacred."

"What is this!" Rory leaps from the couch. Her eyes are wild with anger. "You can reject your mate?" Her voice is a deep, scathing hiss. "How dare he! Aspen rejected her? He rejected Luna? His mate?" She paces around the living room, huffing and puffing like some big bad wolf. "I've never even thought of something so...so vile." She kicks one of the armchairs, sending it skittering several feet across the wood flooring. "It's disgusting!" She slams her fist into the drywall above the mantel, leaving a gaping hole. Oh moon, what state will the house be in if she keeps this up?

I stand from my chair, walking towards her. "Rory..."

She turns to me, her silver eyes ravenous. "I will kill him."

"Rory, no."

"And Dad will kill him."

"No, Dad can't know."

"Of course he can. I'll tell him for you, if you'd like. That way we can all hunt for Aspen's head."

"I don't want you to tell Dad—and I don't want you to hurt Aspen."

"You don't want me to hurt Aspen?" Rory cries, offended by the very suggestion. She moves from the mantle, walking until she's right in front of me. She grips my shoulders. "How dare he! How dare Aspen reject you! And to reject your mate is just...just insane but to reject *you*? It's—" Her voice drops to a whisper. "It's unspeakable. Finding your mate, it's such a beautiful, sacred thing. He's made a mockery of that. He took that from you. You get one mate and he took that from you!" Her grip tightens. "He will suffer for it, Luna, I assure you."

My lips tremble. "Rory..."

Queenie's hand comes down on Rory's shoulder, gently pulling her back. "Aurora, Aspen is not your mate. He is Luna's. It is not your place to threaten him violence on your sister's behalf."

"He's not her mate anymore either!" Rory snaps, baring her sharp canines in a snarl. "He made sure of that!"

"It is not so simple," Queenie says, her voice and face stern. She nods to the couch, and Rory's shoulders sag before she sits back down. She crosses her arms under her chest and dons an expression that's colder than a winter storm. She's digging her long nails into her arm.

Queenie stands in front of me. "The Moon does not like it when her matches are put asunder. It is not easy to break a mate bond, and it requires specific, ritualistic wording to do so. The pair must apply to the Moon herself to dissolve such a bond."

"Aspen said something like that," I say. "He...applied to sever our connection or something. Then, he told me he rejected me." The realization hits me like a brick to the chest. He did what was necessary to break up a mate bond. He *knew* the right wording to say. "It's over. Oh moon, it's over, isn't it?"

"No, it's not." Queenie wipes away my fresh tears with her thumb. "For humans, it just takes one person to end a relationship. He or she decides that they no longer wish to be with the other person, and that's that. Not much can be done. It is quite different for werewolf mates. It takes two. From the moment you mated, the Moon determined you were to be one. A decision as hefty as deciding to sever that bond requires the two of you to come together in unison. You must both choose to break it off."

Hope alights in my heart like a twinkling star in the blackest of nights. Before I can reach out to touch its light, a cold fact strikes me in the chest.

"But Queenie," I start. "Something is wrong with my bond. It's not the same as it was. It's like those mate bond feelings have gone dark." All the love I still feel for Aspen is entirely my own.

Queenie nods slowly. Rory watches us in rapt attention.

"Imagine you and Aspen are tied by two strings," Queenie says, holding out two pointer fingers to mimic two strings between them. "He cut his string, thinking it would end the bond. However, this is not the case. By rejecting you, he has merely absolved you of your compulsion and strong feelings towards him. However, you have not cut your string, so he still feels that pull to you."

My eyes widen. "Wait, he still feels..." I remember the rush of euphoric feeling when we first mated, that desperate desire to take hold of him. "He feels all of that still?"

"Yes. Mate bonds fluctuate. It's stronger at times, weaker at other times, but he still is bound to you through all those feelings," Queenie says.

"Okay, but can Luna's feelings be fixed?" Rory butts in. "Does he get to feel all those wonderful mate feelings while Luna is cut off from that forever?"

"The bond can be repaired," Queenie says. She looks at me. "I believe if you two are intimate, your mate bond feelings will return. Or, you can reject him and your bond will be over for good."

The bond can be repaired! Everything can be fixed! I knew it! Of course. Hope blooms in my heart, like thin green tendrils curling around my veins. It's not over yet, not nearly. We are only blessed with one mate in life; Aspen was fated as mine, and it will still be us in the end. That has to be true. I know it is. We just have to move past this trial—I just have to show him how much he really wants me, and we'll have our happily ever after yet.

Soon Queenie leaves, promising to continue looking into the matter, and I charge upstairs to get ready for the party, fueled by my newfound hope. It's not long before I hear a knock at my door; I can practically feel Rory's concern emanating through it.

"I'm about to shower," I tell her, flipping on the water to let it warm up. I hear Rory enter the room.

"Luna," her voice is tentative. "About your party...maybe you shouldn't go."

I'm standing on the cool bathroom tiles; she's standing on the carpet of my bedroom floor. I turn to face her.

"I'll be fine."

"Luna, you were just rejected by your mate. I can't even imagine if Grey had done that. I'd be—"

"I'm fine." I need to go to this party. I need Aspen to see me. And I need Rory to stop looking at me like that. "You heard Queenie. Everything's going to work out. You'll see. I'll figure things out with Aspen."

Rory stands in the dark, scanning me as though I might fall apart at any moment. I avert my gaze. My hope is a thin glue holding together my shattered pieces, and if Rory keeps looking at me like that...

"I'm worried about you," she says.

I swallow the lump in my throat. "I'm fine, alright? I'm figuring it out. Just don't tell anyone about it, okay?"

"What about Dad?" Rory asks. "I really think we should tell him."

Dad often reminds me of a bear. He's big and cuddly, but when he needs to be, he turns fierce and deadly. If someone were to hurt his family, if someone were to reject his daughter as his soulmate, he'd unleash his teeth and claws and Aspen couldn't come out unscathed.

"No, you can't tell Dad," I say.

"Please," Rory argues. "I think Dad could help. He's the Alpha."

"No," I repeat. Even if Aspen's limbs could remain intact, I don't want Dad using his authority to force Aspen to be with me. Aspen must choose me, and I will be the one to make him want me.

"Come on, Luna. You've gotta tell Dad."

"No means no, Rory." I slam the door dividing the bathroom from my bedroom. I jump in the shower, trying to let the water lull me into a greater sense of peace and assurance than I feel.

I'm okay. I'm okay. I'm okay. I'm okay.

Just because my mate bond is a little broken doesn't mean I can't fix it. The party is in a few hours, and I'll look my absolute best. Aspen will see me and he will want me. I will smile and laugh and glow with every other wolf, and he will want that all for himself.

When I finish getting ready, I take a step back to admire my appearance in the mirror. My hair is pulled into a sleek, low ponytail that shows off a pair of dangling white-gold earrings with stars and crescent moons. I'm wearing a strappy, deep purple bodycon dress that hugs my figure and brings out my eyes. Though wolf girls don't often wear a lot of makeup, it's acceptable at an event such as this, so I've done my best with shimmering eyeshadow, eyeliner, mascara, and lip-gloss. I smile at my reflection, trying to look as happy and beautiful as I can. I look good. I picture Aspen's reaction when he sees me, how his pulse might race, how his eyes might widen, how his heart might feel.

I glance at the digital clock. The party starts in thirty minutes, which means the party *actually* starts in an hour. The male wolves must be back from the hunt by now, showering at the motel, reuniting with their mates, and bragging about their spoils. Dad must be home too, making himself presentable for the party. I need to find Rory and make sure the back of my hair looks alright, though she might be busy giving Grey some grandiose welcome back. I fling open my door to find neither my father nor my sister, but Kodiak, wearing nothing but a pair of black sweatpants. His black hair is wet and messy, freshly showered, and a towel is slung around his neck. He smells like forest and soap and a hint of iron. Kodiak's eyes are wide as they lock with mine before he sighs.

"Right," he mutters. He smiles and holds up a hand in a casual wave. "Happy birthday."

I find myself distracted by the drops of water trickling from his broad shoulders down his chest and defined abs. Sometimes I forget how fit he is under his t-shirts. "What are you doing here?" I ask.

"Your dad let me stay here instead of the motel. I uh, was headed back to my room." He jabs a thumb towards the guestroom door before interlocking his hands together and stretching his arms in the air, cracking his neck as he moves his head side to side. "We had a good hunt." He moves into another stretch with his arms, and it's impossible not to notice how muscular he is. "Though your little boyfriend's a lousy hunter. Nothing like his brothers."

It takes me a moment to register that he's referring to Aspen, and my heart drops to my stomach. Somehow he's both more and less than my 'little boyfriend'.

"Anyways, I'd better go make myself decent." Kodiak yawns. "This isn't my fancy party outfit." He laughs like he's made some ground-breaking joke. He turns toward his room, and I'm reminded that my last real moment with Aspen, before he rejected me, was interrupted by Kodiak. Then all I think about is Aspen rolling his eyes at Kodiak, how Aspen has always found a snide remark for him whenever they've had to cross paths. While Aspen's complaints have been amusing, I've always recognized that Kodiak is in some ways notably superior to Aspen. I watch as Kodiak stretches in a casual way that flexes his strong back muscles. Aspen, for all his brilliance, doesn't shine so brightly next to Kodiak, and I've caught glimpses of his quiet jealousy.

Jealousy...

Impulse takes hold of me as fast and powerfully as a wolf jaw on a doe. In a moment of reckless clarity, I'm grabbing

Kodiak's arm just as he's opening his door. He looks at me with those crazy, expressive eyes that spell out shock and confusion.

"You're a Lone Wolf, right?" My words spill out in a desperation before I can stop them.

The silence falls like a guillotine. My throat dries. Kodiak's eyes shift from bugged-out confusion to something painfully vulnerable. He pulls his arm away from my hand, and his chuckle is just a breath. "At least you asked me about it to my face." His eyes look so sad. "Most wolves just talk about it the moment my back is turned. Which is stupid, of course. I have the best hearing in the country."

I can't look at him. I'm staring at my strappy sandals against the hard wood floor, but I feel his eyes on me. How stupid of me to blurt that out like that.

"I don't know if I'm a Lone Wolf," he finally answers. "I probably am." His voice is just above a whisper, and I wonder if he's ever said it aloud.

My sudden onslaught of courage has sprung a leak, and I feel its reserves draining. Soon it'll be depleted and so I have to speak up now and solidify a plan to ensure my happiness. "Kodiak," I start. Maybe I should apologize first? Maybe I should get to the point. "Kodiak." How do I ask this? My heart is drumming in my ears so loudly it's chasing away rational thought, and before I can stop myself, I blurt out, "Will you be my mate?"

I dare a glance at him. Gone is that rare glimpse of raw vulnerability, replaced with flared nostrils and buggy, wild eyes. "Um, look, you do understand how the whole mate thing works, right?" He looks at me with horrified concern.

I clench my jaw, feeling my face turn pink. "Yes, I know how it works, but—"

"Look." Kodiak is clunky as he places his hand on my shoulder. His overly expressive eyes can't hide that he thinks

I'm insane, but he attempts a sympathetic smile. "Luna, you've been eighteen for what, not even a full day? I don't think you need to give up on finding your real, actual, Moon-given mate. Chances are you aren't a Lone Wolf."

I open my mouth to explain myself, to tell him I'm not a Lone Wolf but a rejected one, but my throat starts closing up over the words.

"Oh, please don't cry! Don't get me wrong, I'm really flattered!" Kodiak waves his hands in a panic. "I mean, I'd be thrilled to be your mate, honest! You're a lovely wolf, and uh, you know, I'd love to have a mate, but let's not have you give up hope just yet. There's going to be a million wolves at this party. Chances are you'll meet your real mate in thirty minutes."

This is going terribly. Now he thinks I'm either in love with him, or so psychotic that after a few hours I've convinced myself I'm dying alone.

"You're going to find your mate. I believe in you!" Kodiak sounds like he's talking to a five-year-old pup. His patronizing tone creeps up my neck like an itch.

"I already have a mate!" I hiss. "We had our bond moment a few hours ago."

Kodiak's jaw drops. He closes it. He blinks. He draws in a deep breath. "No offense, Luna…" His tone is lilting and light, but I see a lot of white above his irises as he looks down on me. "But what the actual—"

"My mate rejected me."

Kodiak stands very still, scanning my eyes for some trick. "What are you even saying? Your mate rejected you?" His eyebrows scrunch together. "He wasn't really your mate, then."

I don't want to go through this again, to explain and discuss what it means. I think about the hole Rory punched in the drywall. I'm not sure where Dad is, either. Is he outside directing party preparations, or is he inside listening in? If Dad found out, how would he react? What would he do to Aspen?

"Never mind," I mutter. My cheeks color once more as I turn from him. What was I thinking? This whole idea was ridiculous, and now Kodiak knows the humiliating truth. Hopefully he's just confused and he'll brush away the whole exchange as some weird but forgettable interaction.

"Wait." He catches my elbow with a calloused hand. "Explain it to me, won't you?"

He pities me. He pities me like some pathetic mutt at the bottom of the dogpile. I steel my bottom lip. I wonder if he can smell the salt of my tears in the corners of my eyes.

Kodiak removes his hand but looks at me gently and speaks quietly. "Look, let me get a shirt on. We don't need to stand around in this hallway, either."

So Kodiak puts on a shirt, and we end up in his guest bedroom, me on the desk chair and him on the edge of the bed. I explain what happened, leaving out Aspen's name, while looking down at the plush carpet beneath my feet. I do not cry. I tell the story as a distant, third-party figure—an omniscient narrator repeating events seen from above. I do not tell Kodiak about my conversation with Queenie, only that I no longer feel the mate bond. I'm met with cold silence as I finish my story, and I look up to see Kodiak staring past me. I'm used to his bright and zany expressions, making him fun at best and annoying at worst. Now, there's something dangerous in his countenance, a stark reminder that he is the Alpha of his pack. He's as quiet as death for several moments.

"So now he's turned you into a Lone Wolf," Kodiak says. The words "Lone Wolf" are a claw to the heart. What if Aspen and I can't reconnect? It would be like mourning a love that never was. Like being widowed before getting married. Like being a Lone Wolf. "Now you won't find a mate," Kodiak continues, "and if you choose to partner up with a Lone Wolf like me down the stretch, your pairing would be seen as lesser and illegitimate." He raises his eyes. "Which is why you want me to be your mate. If we pretend like we're seeing each other for the first time at your party and that we're mates, our marriage would be accepted and celebrated in society. If we wait until time has passed to form such an alliance, we would be looked down upon."

My stomach twists. It's true, I wanted to pretend that Kodiak was my mate, but this feels far more serious. I just want to make Aspen jealous enough to come back to me, but Kodiak is thinking about some long-term ruse. That's not what I want... but then again, what is my future should I fail to reconnect with Aspen? I'll be branded as a Lone Wolf, doomed to live alone for the rest of my life.

"This is our only chance," Kodiak says, his voice just above a whisper. "And of course, we're both alpha-blooded. We'd make an excellent pair, at least on paper."

"Yeah," I manage.

The atmosphere in the room is far more tense than I've ever experienced with Kodiak.

"Okay," he says. "I'm in. I'll be your mate."

I feel like I can't breathe. This is what I wanted, wasn't it? I wanted Kodiak to agree to pretend to be my mate, right? But no. This isn't really what I hoped for. I wanted *Aspen* to be my mate, for him to love me, to not have to resort to petty schemes to win him back. What will happen to Kodiak if Aspen chooses to be with me? Won't it be humiliating for him? No, no. It won't be. I won't let him be humiliated. I'll set it right. I'll explain the whole situation, even if it embarrasses me. People will be angry with Aspen for having rejected me, but they'll move on eventually. Besides, it serves Aspen right to squirm a bit after what he did. As for Kodiak, I'll explain that he was helping a fellow alpha, that he is the hero of our love story. He's the wingman from those human love stories who helps to bring two soulmates together.

"Okay," I agree. I feel very, very small.

As I'm leaving the room, Kodiak speaks up, his tone casual. "Oh, Luna?"

"Hm?" I turn.

"Who did you say your mate was again?" His eyes glow in the dark. Often they're full of warmth, like the sunshine. Now, they're a cold metal. Gold. His eyes have always been too expressive. His light tone and smile cannot hide the violence in them, and I'm certain that if I say Aspen's name, Kodiak will not ask for permission like Rory did. He will hunt Aspen down and he will kill him. I'll be left with Aspen's cold body and lifeless, shallow blue eyes.

I match the look in Kodiak's eyes with a threatening glower of my own. "I didn't say."

CHAPTER 6
IT'S YOU

I stand before the glass doors leading to the deck. I take a breath. In and out, in and out. All I have to do is step out onto that deck, stop at the top, smile like it's the greatest Blue Moon in the history of Blue Moons, and walk down the stairs. That's all I need to do next.

I try not to think about the "pretend Kodiak is my mate to make Aspen jealous" plan. I think about it anyway, and it sends my stomach into a somersault. It's a bad idea. I should call it off. But what if it's the only way to get Aspen back? And what if Aspen isn't coming back? I close my eyes. The latter is unthinkable.

I hear Dad's footsteps behind me, the floorboards singing their special creaks for his steps.

"Let me see you," he says. I turn around and smile at him. I won't think of anything else—just this exact moment, here with my father. Dad sighs and shakes his head. "Lulu, you look far too old and far too pretty. You're going to have to change. You've still got some footie pajamas, don't you?"

I laugh. "Oh, Dad."

He wraps me in a strong hug, and I inhale his warm, comforting scent. A wave of calm washes over my nerves like the tide upon the sand, and that glass door feels less daunting with Dad next to me. Through the glass, I hear the song of crickets, bursts of laughter, and howls of joy. I hold onto Dad for a few seconds longer before I face their music. When we step out onto the deck, the chatter dies down. I'm standing next to Dad so he can present me to the crowd. There are more wolves here tonight than at the hunt kick-off; everyone's been invited to the party. Under hundreds of eyes, I wonder if my shame will shine through—if, as a collective, they'll sniff out that I am so lowly as to be rejected by my mate. Dad seems oblivious to my anxiety with his proud, excited smile. I try to search the crowd for a pair of ocean blue eyes, ignoring all the ones that hope for a match with the Dakota Ridge heir. I can't find him. Oh moon, what if Aspen doesn't even show up? If he's hiding away at home, then what is all of this even for?

"Welcome all! We are grateful for our successful hunt!" Dad's merry voice booms across the backyard. Cheers follow. "Now, I know you are all hungry, so I'll keep it brief." Chuckles. "This night, we celebrate our hunt. We celebrate the wolves who have brought us this food. And of course, we celebrate the Blue Moon and the beginning of a Blue Month." Cheers. "And yet, there is yet something of utmost importance to celebrate." He puts his arm around me. "Today, my youngest daughter, Luna, has turned eighteen." He looks at me, his voice drawing quiet to hide its emotion, though we can all still hear him. "She is far more valuable to me than any hunting prize ever could be."

He turns back to the crowd. "And though we stand amongst warriors and victors of the hunt, I know that the greatest victor will be the lucky wolf who one day will discover my daughter is his mate." He looks at me with a smile that breaks my heart all over again. Dad wanted so badly to make this party special, to ensure I felt loved and important, and yet nothing he could do could take away the aching in my heart.

"Happy birthday, Luna," Dad says. The crowd of wolves echo his sentiment with a roaring "Happy birthday, Luna!" As I look out at the wolves below, Rory's eyes cut through the howls and cheers. They're pained with concern. I keep scanning the crowd, looking for Aspen, only to be met with a pang of panicked disappointment. If he's not here, I don't know what I'll do. There would be no point to my Kodiak plan, not really. There would be no point in me coming to this party at all.

Dad holds his elbow out for me to take as we walk down the stairs. I fake my most dazzling smile. All they will see is a brand new eighteen-year-old heir, excited and hopeful about her next stage of life. Heartbreak is just a concept she'll never know.

When we step onto the patio, I'm greeted with happy birthday wishes and congratulations. I'm the perfect picture of an alpha daughter—tall, strong, confident—when I glimpse a pair of eyes in the crowd. They aren't very bright in the moonlight, but they pierce me all the same.

He's here.

Relief and panic strike at once. Now that I know he's here, I try to push him into some dark corner of my mind, to focus on looking as happy and vivacious as I can without him, but he's an overbearing storm cloud that is impossible to ignore. I excuse myself from my current conversation, saying I'm getting food. I can't focus on what the she-wolf before me is saying, anyway. I let my nose guide me. Many of the lower beta women have been slaving away to prepare the hunt meat that was brought back early—the meat Aspen brought back early. The wafting smell of fresh, juicy meat makes my mouth water; it's been roasted and grilled and battered and fried and everything in between. After avoiding all food in my melancholy, hunger has hit me like a moose.

I feel the eyes of eager young male wolves trying to make eye contact with me, and when I glance at one, his shoulders droop. Little do they know I belong to someone who's never belonged to me. Indignation flares in my chest. Here are all these male wolves, trying to make eye contact and hoping for the privilege of mating with me—and yet, my one and only mate has rejected me. I will never have a soulmate again. The only person I've ever truly wanted wants nothing to do with me.

I'm almost at the buffet table when someone from behind puts his hands over my eyes.

"Logan!" I can pick out his scent, even if I can't see him. "What in the night are you—?"

"Happy birthday!" He cries. He takes his hands away and when I turn around, he's looking bashfully towards the ground. He holds out a small box with crinkled red paper. "I got you something."

"Oh, moon, thanks Logi." As I stare at the crude wrapping, my stomach starts to rumble. Geez, I'm hungry. "Should I... should I open it now?"

"Oh, you don't have to right now. It's up to you." He's still staring at the grass.

"Well that's really thoughtful of you," I say. Logan, like almost everyone else at this party, doesn't realize I'm already bound to my one mate, even if the bond is frayed. I tilt my head down to catch his gaze. His big brown eyes flick towards mine and widen before his face falls. "I'm looking forward to opening it," I say.

He swallows hard. "Yeah."

A shrill voice calls my name, but I turn to the buffet table instead of the sound of my name. I wonder if I can ignore her. One more detour between me and food might just turn into a bloody brawl.

"Luna!" Nova calls again. "I have food for you."

She's never said anything sweeter. I turn to the right, seeing her waving with a big smile and plate piled with meat. I dash towards her, my stomach leading the way, when I see Anika standing several feet behind her, right next to Aspen. My stomach turns, and not in hunger. He's wearing an unbuttoned grey suit coat over a white collared shirt, the top button undone. His curls are still damp and he smells like soap. Our eyes lock for far longer than the split second I caught them in the crowd, and his gaze sends a zing down my spine. My breath hitches.

Aspen breaks eye contact, snapping me out of our moment and bringing me back to the reality of this party and our situation. He rejected me. He doesn't want me. So why do I have to want him so much?

"Oh stars," Anika laughs. She's wearing a little black dress, her light brown curls pulled into an updo. "I thought you two were mates for a second." There's an undercurrent of nervous relief in her tone. I clench my jaw.

Nova's giggle is almost bashful. She's wearing the same blue maxi dress she always wears to special occasions. "I did too."

Suddenly I hate her and I hate Anika. I hate the way their innocuous words wound me. Aspen and I *are* mates. We shouldn't be a dirty secret. Everyone should be congratulating the two of us, not just offering me a birthday wish. In fact, he and I shouldn't even be here. We should be off in some private alcove enjoying nothing but each other.

Nova passes me the plate piled with my favorite foods, but as swiftly as it came, my hunger vanishes. "You're eighteen now!" Nova squeals. She glances at the gift in my free hand, and something almost sad flashes in her eyes. "From Logan?"

"Yeah, he gave me this."

"I can put it with the rest of your gifts, if you'd like," Nova offers her hand.

"Thanks." I pass it to her.

"Poor Logi. Probably heartbroken," Anika says with the weight of a feather.

"Probably not."

Anika saunters towards me. "Never mind him. You'll have to talk to every boy at this party. You know, one of them is likely your mate."

My eyes flicker to Aspen, and we both look away. Ani turns to Aspen, grinning. "Why are you sulking back there? Upset Luna isn't your mate, is that it?"

He takes reluctant steps forward. His smile is uncomfortable. "No, no. Nothing like that."

"That's right," I say. I try to sound jovial, but my voice comes out cold. "Aspen wouldn't want to be my mate anyways." I stop before my voice hitches.

"Oh please!" Nova laughs. "Who wouldn't want to be your mate?"

She blabs on about how great I am, how beautiful I am, how alpha-awesome I am, but I'm hardly listening. Aspen is looking straight at me with steely eyes and a clenched jaw. His shoulders rise and fall as he takes in slow, deep breaths.

"—looks great, doesn't she, Aspen?" Nova snaps us both back into her rambling.

Aspen blinks a few times. "Sorry, what did you say?"

"I *said*, Luna looks great tonight, doesn't she?"

I hold my breath for each second that follows, my body focusing every sense on this moment in agonizing anticipation of his response. Aspen's eyes trail my body, from my feet to my hands holding that giant plate of meat to my eyes. His fists are clenched. "She does." His Adam's Apple bobs. "I think...I think my dad needs me. So if you'll excuse me..."

"Rude," Anika teases, nudging his arm.

I can't stand to watch her touch him. I turn my head to look away, but my heart sinks into an even greater pool of dread when I see Kodiak looking straight at me. Oh moon, I forgot about him and our psychotic plan. It's the worst idea I've ever had.

"Kodiak..." my voice is shaky and breathy. I've got to signal it's off. I'll apologize later for burdening him with the plan.

Kodiak's expressive eyes dance in shades of gold as he looks at me, widening with awe. My own eyes widen with panic. Before I can cut him off, he says, "It's you." He speaks the words in a quiet reverence, like he's stumbled upon a lovely dream he isn't sure he can believe. I'm trying to think of how to respond. The plate of food in my hands feels cumbersome.

Kodiak's eyes begin to glow. "All this time," he says. "It was always you."

Tears sparkle in my eyes as an overwhelming longing fills my breast. This is everything I wanted to have happen with Aspen. I wanted him to look at me that way, with such tenderness as though any hard gaze might break me. I wanted him to tell me that it was me, that it always was, and that it always would be. Now my tears will only sell the ruse.

My eyes are glowing, a habitual response to Kodiak's glowing eyes. Whenever Rory used to glow up her eyes intentionally, I would glow them up back to prove I was just as alpha as she was. Now it further solidifies our faux mate bond moment. Our terrible, ridiculous scheme. "Kodiak..." I start. Can we still break it off? The crowd seems to interpret my emotion as the overwhelming rush of feeling that comes with finding your mate. Those around us have stilled, watching what they believe to be a beautiful scene unfolding. I'm distracted for a second when Nova silently takes my meat plate from my hands. When I glance back at Kodiak, he's right in front of me —and then his hands are on my face—and then he leans in and kisses me.

CHAPTER 7

HELL OF A LIE

My first kiss was with Logan, when we were eight years old. While playing a big game of tag in the woods, he was "it" and he'd caught up to me. Instead of calling out that I was "it," Logan pecked my lips and ran away. My second kiss—well, it's right now, and the way Kodiak is kissing me is very different from Logan's peck. Kodiak's hands are calloused and warm on my face, his kiss long and eager, and by the time he pulls away, I feel completely breathless. A real kiss was different than I thought it would be. I can't tell if it's weird or if I want to try it again.

I'm ripped away from such musings by the chorus of cheers at our public display of affection. Kodiak puts an arm around my shoulder and looks out at the crowd like that giant elk he brought back is nothing in comparison to me. While he's beaming brighter than the sun, my face is so red that the sun looks trapped beneath my skin. Upon closer inspection, I see a twinge of pink on Kodiak's cheeks. I survey the congratulatory crowd, spotting a huge grin on Anika's face and a slack-jawed Nova holding my food in one hand and Logan's gift in the other. Next to them stands Aspen. His face is contorted in a failed attempt to hide his anger. His shoulders heave with his breaths, his body trembles, and his eyes are a stormy sea. I stare at Aspen long enough to risk revealing my fraudulent bond-moment with Kodiak. Come on, Aspen. Come on. Call out our lies. Come on and claim me as yours!

"LUNA! KODIAK!" Dad's booming voice calls my attention. The crowd parts as he rushes towards us; he's like a bear with puppy-like enthusiasm. Oh right. How could I have forgotten? This is Dad's dream come true.

He's followed by Rory, whose silver eyes shoot me questions like bullets. She's not angry, not yet, but she's confused. When I think about explaining this scheme to her, my stomach feels queasy. Dad steals me from Kodiak's arm and swings me around like I'm as heavy as a stuffed animal. I'm glad I have an empty stomach. "Luna! I am so happy for you!" When he sets me down, he pulls Kodiak into a hug so strong that I hear Kodiak's back crack. "My boy!" he cries.

"Alpha Orion!" Kodiak is grinning, slapping Dad's back as he hugs him back.

Dad steps back. "I am so happy. You two have no idea."

Wow, I really did *not* think this through.

"This is one of the greatest things that has happened to me," Dad says. "To you both as well, of course!"

I hate myself. I really do. Rory's still looking at me, asking me what's going on with her eyes.

"Everyone!" Dad's voice booms once more. "My daughter, Luna, has mated with the Alpha of Midnight River, Kodiak!" If by some miracle someone had missed the news, they know it now, and with the way everyone cheers, I'm reminded more of crazed apes than wolves. A couple of Midnight River wolves even burst into tears. Kodiak takes my hand in his own, and it gives me an anchor to hold onto before I fall through the earth.

I wonder how we must look to everyone. This can't be believable, right?

A couple of wolves approach Dad—Aspen's parents, Alistair and Leah. "Alpha Orion," Leah speaks softly. "I'm sure they'll want to be alone now." She gives me this sly, knowing smile. "I think your bedroom might be more suitable than this party?"

Maybe I actually died when Aspen rejected me and now I'm in hell. A hell of my own making.

"Oh!" Dad's face flushes.

I want to shift into wolf form, dig a hole in the forest, and bury myself alive.

"Right, of course!" Dad's voice is marked with uncharacteristic stammering. "You two don't really need to stay for the party."

I look to Rory for help, hoping she can save me, but she's still confused. I look to Aspen, hoping he'll finally step up and put a stop to this madness, but he's gone. My heart drops to my stomach. He just left?

"Don't be embarrassed," Leah says. She must sense my discomfort. "It's only natural."

I manage a chuckle and clench Kodiak's hand more tightly —not because I'm looking forward to getting down and dirty with him, but because it's either crushing his hand or running away for one last cliff jump. "Right," I say. "I guess we'd better get going then." I glance up at Kodiak, who gives me a nod. We weave through the party amidst an onslaught of whoops and howls that turn my face scarlet. By the time we're in my room, my legs are shaking and my heart has twisted into a Gordian knot. This whole thing was a bad idea, and already the consequences are greater than I'd accounted for.

"Don't expect me to sleep on the floor," Kodiak says, his voice light as he tosses his black suit jacket on the carpet. While

I feel shaken to my core, he seems completely unbothered; then again, when he committed to this plan, he knew what he was getting into. For him, it was never just a temporary scheme to make someone jealous. For him, our plan is a total success—and for me, it's a failure. "I mean, obviously we don't have to—you know, *do* anything tonight, but we'd better get used to sharing a bed."

I feel sick.

He plops on the edge of the bed and pulls at the necktie by his collar. "So, what do you think? You think we fooled them all?"

I think of the tempest in Aspen's eyes, the way his body shuddered at the sight of us. Any pleasure I might have derived from that look is drowned out by the fact that he disappeared, not caring enough to step up and claim his mate.

"Probably," I say. Dad's jubilation makes my stomach curdle like sour milk. "They have no reason to believe we're lying." And that's what we're doing, really. Lying. I'm lying to my Dad, to my pack, to everyone. All in some desperate attempt to reclaim something that should already be mine. Love isn't supposed to be this hard.

"True," Kodiak says. "Though we've got to coordinate how we're really going to sell it, you know. Man, there's a lot we have to go over. We've got to think about it like if we actually mated, you know? What would be the next steps? How would we be acting? I mean, I know what we would be doing right this second, but what would we do and how would we act in front of everyone?"

I don't have the emotional bandwidth for this conversation. "One minute," I say. "I'm going to change."

"Oh, alright."

Walking towards the closet, I feel like something mechanical, a being outside her body pushing buttons and pulling levers to move forward. Kodiak mentions grabbing his comfy clothes as I shut the closet door behind me. It's a walk-in closet, leaving room for me to move around. I just need a moment away from Kodiak, away from all we have to do, away from everything. Shirts brush my face as I nestle against a wall and bring my knees to my chest. In the darkness, my tears fall in warm, salty drops and I try to quiet my shuddering breaths. When my nose starts to run, I have to use an old t-shirt for a tissue. Rory's words from the night before come to mind: *I've never seen such pathetic human behavior in an alpha.* I can't pretend my tears are induced by the mate bond; Aspen killed those feelings within me. My tears, this situation with Kodiak—this is all my fault. It has nothing to do with the Moon or cosmic circumstance. Another wave of sadness washes over me, and I have to hold back a dog-like whimper. I hate myself for getting into this mess with Kodiak, I hate myself for crying in a closet, and I hate myself for not being enough for Aspen.

CHAPTER 8
SO HUMAN
ONE YEAR, EIGHT MONTHS AGO

It was a crisp morning in early October, and my walk to Bruno's was one of scarlet, butterscotch, and gold. Nova had let me know that there were humans at the diner, so I told her I'd check out the situation. As soon as I stepped into Bruno's, I could smell them. Underneath the scents of Bruno's cooking and the humans' floral perfumes and deodorant sprays, there they were.

There was another scent I recognized as well: Aspen.

There was a semicircle booth in the back corner crowded with five people. I saw the back of Aspen's curly head. Why had he brought them here?

One of the human girls noticed my gaze, and her voice dropped to a hushed whisper. "Aspen, is that another, actual werewolf?" As if I couldn't hear her.

Aspen turned to me and smiled. "Hey, Luna." He didn't raise his volume, since he knew I could hear across the diner. "You want to come meet my friends?"

I didn't. I had no desire to fraternize with humans, but curiosity was burning me the way a hot stove sears bare skin. I'd heard that Aspen was spotted getting cozy with a human girl a few weeks back. Was she among them? Who were these humans Aspen thought were worth spending time with?

"Okay." I answered just loud enough so his wolf ears could hear me. "I'll order something and come over."

Bruno came out of the kitchen and smiled when he saw me behind the counter.

"Glad to see an actual wolf?" I teased.

His grin grew. "Glad to see you." Which was probably true. He was an older wolf with grey curls and a warm heart, and he liked me. I ordered food and walked across the black and white checked floor to their red vinyl booth. As I approached, the smell of their perfumes and body sprays was so strong I wondered how Aspen could stand to sit there. Then, I saw Aspen—a casual arm around a human girl with thin blonde hair and big eyes. Anger coursed through my veins and threatened to lash out in a gnash of teeth and claws. All the humans were gawking like I was some strange zoo animal. There was no room for me to sit.

"Pull up a chair," Aspen said, gesturing to the empty table behind me.

I'd never had to "pull up a chair" like that in my life. I always had room in the booth. My gaze was cold as I dragged a chair up to the table. It hissed out the slightest bit of air as I settled into the old, cushioned seat.

Aspen gestured to me like he was a tour guide. "This is my friend Luna." The word "friend" cut me in a way it never had before. Especially with his arm around Little Miss Mousy. "And she's actually the daughter of my pack's Alpha."

Everyone looked surprised. There were three human girls and one human boy, all with smooth, rounded ears and annoying smells.

"No way," the boy said. There was something wrong with

his upper lip—there was hair there, almost like a moustache, but there wasn't enough to really call it that. It came out faint and wispy. Werewolves had great hair—facial or otherwise—so I was always perturbed by the patchy fuzz on human teenaged boys or thinning hair and shiny domes atop older men's heads. "You're like, an 'alpha,'" he said. What were his air quotation marks supposed to mean?

"I didn't realize alphas were like, a real thing. I mean, I'd heard they were, but, that's like crazy," one girl said.

I didn't know what to say. I regretted sitting there, and I regretted seeing Aspen's arm around that mousy girl. I would have rather lived with the ghost of a rumor than the confirmation of its truth.

"Can you command Aspen to do stuff for you?" one of the girls asked.

"Yeah, Aspen," another girl butt in, grinning. "Are you like a slave or something?" She thought herself funny. Apparently her human friends thought so too because they laughed. Aspen, a slave? Were they serious?

A pack's hierarchy began with the Alpha and then the alpha-blooded, followed by high betas, mid betas, low betas, and finally the Omegas. All those above the midpoint were often referred to as upper betas, and all those below were called lower betas.

"Aspen is highly ranked within the pack." I glared at the humans. "His family is the top ranked beta family in Dakota Ridge. He is no slave."

"Bro..." the boy said, looking at Aspen with wide eyes. "You're a...beta male?" And he snorted and laughed like something about that was funny. Aspen at least had the shame to look a little embarrassed by his friends. Mousy had yet to speak. Aspen had yet to remove his arm from her. I was about to remove myself.

Mousy smiled at me when she spoke. "Luna, your eyes are like nothing I've ever seen! They're so purple!" Her own drab eyes were huge. "They're super pretty."

I blinked and then I looked at Aspen. "How do you know these humans?"

His smile was awkward, but he explained he met Mousy during the summer at the county fair, and she'd introduced him to her friends. I didn't ask how they decided to start dating. I realized I didn't want to know. Bruno brought me my food, and I wanted to eat as fast as I could so I could leave.

"Can you turn into a wolf?" one of the girls asked, as I chowed on my burger.

"Yes."

"No way! Can you show us?"

"We're in a diner."

"Well outside when we're done eating?"

I ignored her.

One of the girls started talking about this boy she just broke up with and how she hoped they could get back together. Her friends were emphatic in telling her it was a bad idea, that her ex was a jerk, and that she deserved better. Another girl talked about how she'd asked a guy out on a date and had gotten a flat rejection. Her friends consoled her, telling her that guy sucked. Their experiences were so different from mine and my friends' that I forgot I was trying to eat as fast as I could to leave. Maybe I had it all wrong. I wasn't the caged animal Aspen was showing off to his human friends. Instead, he was bringing the zoo to me.

"Speaking of dating," the boy with the weird lip said, "Luna, are you dating anybody?" He smiled wide and slow.

I was polishing off my fries. "What?"

"You know, do you have a boyfriend?" He leaned back into the booth and folded his arms. "'Cause I mean, if you're looking for one, I might know a human guy willing to give a werewolf a shot." He winked at me.

The girls at the table laughed and started teasing the boy, calling him a flirt.

"Stop, stop," he said. "She might get a bad impression of me."

Aspen bit his lip and scrunched his eyes shut for a second, like some migraine had just swept over him. "Travis, Luna doesn't want to go out with you."

"Now that's for Luna to decide," the human boy said. "I mean, *you* like humans. Obviously. Maybe she would too."

Everything he said was offensive. The suggestion that I'd be interested in him—and even worse, his mentioning Aspen's affinity for human girls. I took a napkin and started wiping my hands with unconcealed disgust. "Has Aspen told you humans anything about being a werewolf?" I curled my lip and the humans stiffened. It seemed like it was only then that they realized I didn't like them. Aspen looked at me in such a guarded way that I was sure he regretted inviting me over as much as I regretted agreeing to it. "We have mates," I said, annunciating every word and speaking so slow a pup could understand. "Do you even know what that means?"

There was a moment of silence before they realized it wasn't a rhetorical question. "I mean, I've heard of it," one girl mumbled. "I didn't know if it was—"

"It's real," I said. "And it's the backbone of our society. It's deeply a part of who we are. When we turn eighteen, we can find our soulmates. And once we do, that's it. Nobody else matters." I looked at Mousy. I wasn't like Rory, who was always bold and strong. I was softer, I was quieter, I was content away from the center of attention. She was supposed to be the heir, not me. But in that moment, I remembered who I was: an alpha, with precious blood in my veins. I was no weepy, wimpy human. And I didn't like Mousy. She shouldn't have been there. She shouldn't have been with Aspen. She had billions of humans to choose from. Why did she have to take the one werewolf who meant more to me than anyone?

"Aspen isn't exempt from this." I was looking right into her eyes. "In a year he'll turn eighteen, he'll meet his mate, and anything that happened in the past won't matter." I turned back to the boy with the weird hair above his lip. "So no. I don't have a boyfriend because I have a mate."

And as annoying as they were, I actually felt bad for those humans at the table, for their sad conversations about unassured love and failed relationships and confusion and rejection. Yet as I looked at Aspen, his arm pressed against Mousy's, I mostly felt bad about myself, for being so human in how I loved.

CHAPTER 9

PERSONAL

I end up wearing the crumpled white tank top and black cotton shorts I wore earlier, since they're the only pajamas in the closet and the rest are in my dresser. It's the outfit Aspen rejected me in. Wonderful. Kodiak's already back in the room by the time I leave my closet, sitting on my bed dressed in shorts and a t-shirt that shows off his muscled arms. I'd be jealous of him if I were Aspen, but it seems that Aspen does not care.

Kodiak glances at me, his face twisted in some awkward pity. "You doing alright?"

I'm standing in the middle of the carpet, feeling like a guest in my own room. "I'm fine." I walk to the dresser and grab a makeup wipe, rubbing at my smudged mascara and red-rimmed eyes. It doesn't take a super-heightened-senses alpha to figure out I was crying, but I want to pretend I wasn't all the same. I feel his eyes on me, and I want to retreat back to my closet where I can't be seen. At least he doesn't have X-ray vision.

As I finish wiping off the last smear of makeup, Kodiak approaches me.

"What is it?" I ask.

He says nothing for a few seconds, shifting his weight from foot to foot. His pointed ears redden. "Um, I'm going to give you a hug now."

I feel the tears welling up for round two, so I lean into his embrace just so he can't see me cry. Kodiak wraps his arms around me, pulling me into a warm, strong hug. I press my cheek against his chest and soon I'm holding onto him like he's a lifesaver in the middle of the ocean. His voice is soft. "I'm sorry."

We stay like that for a while until I pull away from his arms. Kodiak watches me carefully, his golden eyes glinting in the night.

"I'll kill him, you know," he says. "It'll be easy."

There's a very real part of me that's angry, that wants Aspen to feel just as miserable as I do, but I'd never want him dead. "Sorry," I say. A ghost of a smile wriggles on my lips. "But Aurora already called dibs on him."

When Kodiak laughs, it's like a pin has poked through the black cloud of pressure in the room, and I feel a tiny ray of light peeking through.

"She would," Kodiak says, his voice warm. I remember when Rory and Kodiak were younger. I remember the way they looked at each other. I remember the look on Kodiak's face when he found out she'd mated with Grey. Dad had had such high hopes for them. "So," Kodiak says. "How many people know that you were rejected?" He sits down on the bed, and I sit next to him.

"Just you, Aurora, and an older she-wolf in the pack. Queenie."

"And him," Kodiak says. "He knows."

"Yeah." My voice grows quiet. "I guess there's also me and him."

"So five," Kodiak says. "Five people who know we're a sham, present company included." He flops backwards, scrunching up his face. "Your pathetic excuse for an…ex-mate will probably never tell anyone unless he wants to get killed."

"Queenie wouldn't say anything either," I add. "She's like the village sage or something. I don't know. But she can keep a secret, I know she can. I trust her."

Kodiak narrows his eyes. "Then there's Aurora."

I grimace. "Yeah."

"You think she's going to go along with all this?"

"Honestly, I don't know."

"We could tell her that we're actually mates." Kodiak sits up in some flawless crunch. "You know, Blue Moon magic and all that. You got rejected and the Blue Moon granted you another, obviously superior mate."

I snort. "Yeah, maybe. I don't know if she'll buy it though."

"We could, I don't know, act super lovey dovey tomorrow. Feed each other breakfast and all that nonsense!"

"That's so cringy."

"Most mates are pretty cringy, Luna."

I laugh as Kodiak and I discuss how we'll fool everyone, some suggestions legitimate, some ridiculous. There's bad and good to planning this all out. There's a part of me that feels like I've dived too deep into the water and I'm not sure I'll make it to the surface in time to breathe. The other part of me feels relieved, distracted from my sorrow and distracted from *him*. It makes me feel like my life is just some silly plan hatched from a movie rather than a colossal mess that I can never clean up. Before long, the drama of the night catches up to my body, and I feel a tiredness that sinks all the way down to the bone. I walk over to the curtain and peek outside, the party still swinging, the moon still in the sky.

"Maybe you should get some rest," Kodiak says, watching me from the bed.

As I look out at the sky, the Blue Moon carves melancholy in my heart. I can already see the hints of first light, and soon the Moon will fade to nothing under the power of the sun. This so-called magical night will end...and while it's only brought me sorrow, it's a night where I still had hope, where for a fleeting moment, Aspen truly was mine. I want to sleep away the rest of this wretched night almost as much as I want it to remain as a frozen time capsule to my briefest bliss.

"Maybe I should," I say, peeling my eyes away from the Moon. "I'm tired now."

I crawl into bed and curl the covers around me, staring at the lavender paint on the wall. In the night, color is obscured, and it's hard to see such subtle shades. It's too early to retire for the day, but I'm tired and I don't want further conversation about how we're going to fool everyone or about what the future will look like for Kodiak and me. Soon, I hear Kodiak shuffling around before the room lights with the dim glow of a laptop screen. As I fall asleep to the sound of Kodiak's slow, rhythmic typing, thoughts of Aspen and Kodiak and soulmates swirl in my head and bleed into fitful dreams.

The night succumbs to morning. I wake up several times throughout the day while Kodiak sleeps in a soft purr. A slice of sunlight sneaks in from the gap between the curtains and cuts across the bed. I check my phone. Aspen has texted me! Excitement courses through my veins.

Aspen 5:28 p.m.

Hey, can we talk?

Aspen 5:28 p.m.

I think we need to rethink what happened

Aspen 5:29 p.m.

I made a mistake. I miss you.

I wake up. There's a faint light from the waning sun creeping in at the edges of the curtains and casting a soft glow in the room. I blink through the bleariness of a restless day of sleep before memories of Aspen's text messages flash through my mind. I snatch my phone from the floor and click it open, desperate to read Aspen's texts, desperate to respond to his request to talk—only to discover that there are no texts. They were just a dream. I feel a bitter wave of disappointment well up in my heart as I set the phone down.

The sound of short, heavy breaths draws my attention to the right. Kodiak's side of the bed is rumpled and empty, but the wolf in question is on the floor, going up and down in one-armed shirtless pushups. I'm distracted from my distress over imagined text messages as I ogle Kodiak's impeccable form, his gorgeous muscles made glossy by a light sheen of sweat as he performs perfect one-armed push-ups. He switches seamlessly from his right arm to his left and turns his head toward me with a cocky smile.

"Good morning, princess." His tone is as strained as if he were on a light morning walk, not in the midst of one-armed push-ups.

"You make it look so effortless." I'm gawking. The one-armed push-ups I've attempted haven't gone so well.

"Well, it took lots of effort for a long time," he says, dipping down and pushing up. "I don't look like this for nothing. Though I won't lie, my genetics certainly help."

Werewolves are usually toned and muscular due to active lifestyles and high-protein diets, but they don't often look as good as Kodiak. "I suppose you do workouts like these every evening," I say.

He grins, his eyes flashing with mischief. "Especially when pretty girls are watching." He laughs as my face flushes before pushing himself off the floor. "I don't know about you, but I'm ready for breakfast. I'm absolutely starving."

Neither of us got to eat the mouth-watering spread at the celebration last night.

"I'm going to pass away from hunger at any moment," I say.

He laughs. "Then let's get some food, love bug!"

We get dressed, and soon we're seated around the dining table full of leftovers for breakfast. A small chandelier hangs over us, lighting the room in lieu of the setting sun. Kodiak is beaming from ear to ear, Dad's looking like a pup on Christmas, and Grey lives up to his namesake by looking as placid and drab as always. Kodiak and I are eating like our lives depend on it as I try to avoid Rory's hawkish gaze.

"You two have quite the appetite!" Dad laughs. Then he blushes, as if he's said something dirty. I want to die.

"I'm starved, Alpha Orion!" Kodiak's mouth is full of elk. "Luna and I hardly ate anything from the feast, after all."

"No doubt still enjoying yourselves," Rory says, her silver eyes glinting.

Kodiak matches her gaze with gold, his sharp grin sliding up his mouth. "We weren't miserable."

I slam my hands down on the table. "Can we just...not, please?"

"Let's look towards the future!" Dad cuts in. He seems as uncomfortable as I am. "With Midnight River bordering Dakota Ridge, I think we have some great opportunities ahead of us for our two packs now that you both have mated. I predict a pack merge will be in our future."

"Dad, we haven't even talked about the wedding," Rory says, withholding a laugh. She's fiddling with a piece of fried rabbit leg. "You're already talking about our packs merging?"

"Well..." Dad falters. "Of course, that's part of the wedding plans. We have to figure out how we're going to host the wedding."

A long time ago, werewolves didn't do weddings. They're unnecessary, of course, since you're already committed to your mate for life. However, as the years went on, it became commonplace to celebrate the match, and we eventually adopted the term "wedding" to describe that celebration and the traditions that accompany it. Since she mated with someone from another pack (and their Alpha Heir, no less), Rory had two weddings. One to say goodbye and one to say hello.

"We probably only need one, since our packs are so close," Kodiak says.

"Two would look excessive, ten miles apart," Rory says.

"As the Alpha, we should probably host the wedding in my pack," Kodiak says.

Dad frowns. "Luna is still alpha-blooded, and the current heiress to Dakota Ridge."

"Yes, but she'll be moving to Midnight River. You're still the reigning Alpha here. She'll be celebrated as Midnight River's new Alpha Female."

"She'll eventually be the Alpha Female of Dakota Ridge as well; likely you two will reign over both packs, which is why—" Dad makes a pointed look at Rory. "We need to discuss our two packs coming together and what that looks like."

Pack merges only happen in the rare instance that two neighboring alpha heirs mate. Dakota Ridge and Northern Skies were too far apart for a merge, so Rory had to give up Dakota Ridge for Grey's pack. But because we border Midnight River, I can remain Dakota Ridge's heir *and* become Midnight River's Alpha Female. At least, I could if I were *actually* going to marry Kodiak, which I'm not.

"Merges are uncommon." Kodiak rubs his eyes. "I don't

know how well Midnight River is going to like expanding the community like that."

"I know. But fortunately, they all go to school together, so it's not like we're total strangers," Dad says.

"Yeah," Rory says. "But the two packs are likely to maintain their identity. They'll see themselves as Midnight River *or* Dakota Ridge, not as one pack. It's going to be..."

I don't feel a part of this conversation. Instead, I'm nothing more than a pricey asset bringing two companies together. This should be the time I'm planning my wedding, gushing over dresses and flowers in order to share my newfound love with Dakota Ridge. The current conversation feels like we're conducting a business deal. And yet, that is exactly what Kodiak and I are—a desperate deal made between two people incapable of receiving love. The conversation is as cold and hollow as I feel inside. How would it be if Aspen were sitting next to me? I imagine the two of us as smiling, blushing mates with our chairs scooted close enough that our arms are touching. Aspen's parents would be there, of course, thrilled their son is joining our family. We'd have a beautiful wedding here in the yard, with music and flowers and dancing and the wonderful food Aspen had hunted. I would be drunk off happiness instead of stiff in a wooden dining room chair.

"We can bring the rest of her things over time, but for now we'll pack a suitcase," Kodiak says. I reenter the conversation. What's happening?

"Huh?" I ask.

Kodiak turns to me, and I wonder if this is the first time he's noticing I'm here. The way he places his hand on my shoulder looks terribly awkward. "We're going to pack your suitcase so you can come with me to Midnight River tonight. I've got to head back, and I'm obviously not leaving you behind."

"Tonight? We're going to Midnight River tonight?" My throat feels dry.

I can see a flare of panic in his eyes at my hesitation, but he smiles through it. "Of course. We're mates now. I can't leave you here." His eyes are so wide he might as well be screaming to the whole room that this is a sham.

But I can't go. He doesn't understand. If I leave, I won't even see Aspen and any chance at our reunion will slip away like we were nothing more than a hazy dream. Instead, I'll be ripped away from everyone I know to share a bed with someone I do not love. And yet, refusing to go with him is as good as admitting that this is all a lie—even Dad will see right through it, and where does that put all of us?

"Let's slow down a little bit," Rory says, moving her hands downward. "Kodiak, I know you're really excited to bring Luna home. And Luna—" She gives me a piercing stare. "*Obviously,* you're head-over-heels for Kodiak, but Luna can't move out just yet." I see Rory fighting a grimace. "Luna needs to finish school."

"School?" Kodiak says the word like it's the most inane thing he's ever heard.

"Yeah. She has less than a week left before she graduates," Rory says. Rory dropped out of school her senior year when she mated with Grey. She doesn't give a rat's tail about school.

And Kodiak knows that, with the glare he levels at her. "Since when did you care about getting some sape degree, Ror—Aurora?"

"I don't, but Luna does." Rory glances at me. "She's always cared more than me. And she's less than a week away from it." Rory leans back in her chair, the first two legs coming off the ground. "But I don't really care, so I guess it's whatever Luna wants."

I feel four pairs of eyes focus on me, and I'm beyond

grateful for the opening I've been given. "You know, in the midst of everything, I think I forgot about school." My voice comes out in a nervous laugh. "But Aurora's right. I can't leave yet. I've got to finish out my last year." If Aspen is going to be anywhere, it'll be school.

Kodiak, however, isn't going to let me go that easily. I can see determination in his eyes and bewilderment in Dad's—new mates are supposed to be inseparable, sickeningly in love. We go back and forth, Kodiak saying how he can't bear to part from me with angry eyes, me telling him it breaks my heart too, but that I've got to finish up school and he needs to get back to his pack. I'm only able to get away with this ruse by promising to spend the weekend in Midnight River. When we return to my room, Kodiak's face is twisted in frustration.

"What are you doing?" he hisses.

I click on the lamp light. "I'm finishing school." I turn to him from my bedside table, crossing my arms. "I've said it a million times."

"Don't you understand?" He walks right up to me, and I smell the soap from his recent shower. "I *can't* show up in Midnight River without you."

"So you've said. Look, no one else is around. You can drop the act."

He rolls his eyes. "It's not that I can't emotionally bear to part from you, Luna. Do you understand how humiliating it will be? To return home without you? Everyone will think it's some sort of joke."

"It'll be fine." My swishing ponytail grazes his chest as I head towards the balcony window. I pull back the curtain, peering at the night sky and the Moon. It's the beginning of the Blue Month. "We've got forever to be 'mates', don't we? What's a few more days? They'll get over it."

"Luna." He says my name through clenched teeth.

"It'll be fine. Do you need help packing?"

He argues with me, but I remain firm on my "dedication to education." Besides, I actually do care more about school than the average wolf. Sure, the bar is pretty low, but still. When Kodiak finally acquiesces to my will, we're in his guest room and he's shoving the few things he brought into his backpack, crouched on the floor.

"Are you going to see me off, or is that too much?" I can taste the bitterness in his words.

"Of course." My voice is soft. Despite my adamance about staying in Dakota Ridge, I do feel bad. I know he's upset and I hate doing this to him, but it's for a greater purpose.

Kodiak's eyes do not glow; they're dark and stormy. "You'll have to pretend like you're sad, you know. Since I'm your mate."

"I know."

The carpet feels hard beneath my feet in this cold atmosphere. I take a few steps forward and place a gentle hand on Kodiak's shoulder. His hands slacken on the backpack, and as he looks up at me with surprised eyes, the Alpha before me seems like he's no more than a pup. I've known Kodiak my whole life, but in this moment he feels like a stranger, and I realize I've only seen a fragment of who he truly is.

"When you go, I'll kiss you like the love of my life is leaving," I murmur. If either of us are going to keep up this charade, Kodiak is right in that I have to try and act like I'm in love with him.

He lowers his gaze, long dark lashes looking at the ground. He reminds me of myself in that moment, weak when he's expected to be strong.

"I'm sorry," he says. He zips his backpack and stands up without looking at me. "You deserved to be with him. You had a real soulmate."

As Kodiak leaves the room, I wonder how I would feel if this charade was all I'd ever had.

At his departure, I try to drum up the sadness echoing in my chest, but it still feels foolish and performative. We're all out on the front lawn of the house, and with a romantic canopy of stars overhead, I wonder how the North Star is judging my performance. Dad's given his handshake and back pat, Rory and Grey have offered cordial goodbyes, and now it's my turn for the showstopping finale. I've already tried to cry and failed, instead opting for a pouting face. Now, I put my arms around Kodiak's neck and my heart pounds within my shaky body against his chest. They think we've done everything by now, so they wouldn't understand the fluttering nerves in my stomach.

"I'll miss you." My voice is quiet. Then I kiss Kodiak for the second time, pressing my lips against his in my best attempt at a kiss. Kodiak's lips move against mine like he's got all the time in the world, and his arms wrap around my waist and pull me against this chest. I like the way his body feels against mine, and I'm surprised by a pang of disappointment when he lets me go.

He puts a calloused hand on my cheek, his golden eyes soft as honey. "I'll miss you more."

I didn't expect the emptiness I feel when he's out of sight. With Kodiak, I wasn't so alone. He distracted me from my thoughts, provided companionship when I had none, and now I've sent him away.

Dad gives me a hug, telling me it will be okay. I wonder if he saw that glimmer of genuine sadness, or if he's just seeing what he expects to see—a recently mated she-wolf already missing her mate. Dad must think it's some grand trial for me to watch my soulmate walk away for a couple of days, but I've seen mine try to leave for good. Without Kodiak, it's just me and Aspen, forced to deal with all that's passed between us.

Rory walks up to me. "Luna, can I talk to you?" Her voice is neither hard nor soft.

"Maybe later." I don't want to explain myself to her. "I...I need some fresh air."

"I can walk with you."

"I want to be alone."

Dad puts a hand on Rory's shoulder. "Let's give her some space."

I smile a thank you at Dad before jogging off to the backyard. I shift from human form to wolf until I'm all black and glossy and I'm running on four paws. I love the feel of the summer night against my fur and the way my senses sharpen and my mind quiets. I run towards the forest, smelling the moss and the trees, listening to critters singing, and feeling the wind on my face. I run without a destination, the Moon my guiding light through the trees, when a scent stops me in my tracks. My ears stick straight up, my body tenses, and I can't decide if I want to run towards the scent or away from it.

He's coming closer now. At the crest of a hill, I see a large wolf with butterscotch curls looking down at me with deep blue eyes. Emotions I hide in human form begin to spill out in wolf form. I can feel Aspen now, too. He's confused, he's unsure of himself. He's hurt. I want to pry deeper into his feelings, but I'd risk exposing how I feel, and I feel everything. I shift into human form, severing the outpour of feelings, and lean against a tree trunk, my eyes cold as I look at him.

"What are you doing here?" I ask.

Aspen shifts back into human form, from fur and snout to tanned skin and golden curls. He's wearing a t-shirt and shorts over Vans; his hands are in his pockets as he surveys me.

"I'm allowed to go for a run," he says.

"Okay." Since when does Aspen go running in wolf form?

Is he upset, trying to burn off energy? Anger and hope fight for a place in my heart, and I don't know what to say to him.

"So," he says. Then nothing. He's usually more prolific than this.

I wait a few moments. "So what?" I ask.

Nothing.

I wait.

"What are you doing with Alpha Kodiak?" He finally asks.

"What kind of question is that?"

"You know what kind of question that is." He sounds agitated. I want to pick at that tone like a scab, to make it bleed into full-blown jealousy.

"We're in love." My voice is haughty. "We're mates."

Aspen says nothing.

"I was surprised too," I continue. "I mean, after all, you and I—" I freeze. "Well, it must have been the Blue Moon. They say it's a magical time. Must have given me another mate, another shot." My words fire off like an accusation rather than giddy gratitude for the Moon's miracle.

Aspen's eyes narrow, and I know he's trying to read me. Sometimes, I too can read him like a book, but tonight he's nothing more than blotted out words in the distance.

"Well good," he says. "That's what I was hoping for. It's better this way."

His words cut me like canine teeth ripping into me. *It's what he was hoping for. It's better this way.* To an outsider, maybe it would seem better. Me, an alpha's daughter, mating with the neighboring Alpha. It means the uniting of packs, it means offspring with great genetics, it means everything is bigger, stronger, *better.* But as for me, I did not want better. I wanted *him.* Now I'm left with a sham and a broken heart.

"Con-grat-u-lations." I drag out the word in long, scathing syllables. "Thank the Moon your dreams came true."

He sucks in a long breath. "It wasn't personal, Lu." *Lu.* The nickname, once the sweetest syllable I'd ever heard, is a jab that mocks me. Aspen clenches his fists. "I swear it wasn't personal."

He came to my room the second I turned eighteen, just to see if it was me, just to reject me. I swallow the lump in my throat. "It felt personal." My voice is a hiss against tears. I should stay, of course I should. He's jealous, he's fighting his feelings for me, he's conflicted. Now is the perfect time to dig into him, like stabbing a fishhook into his heart and pulling it out. And yet, I can't bear to show him my tears and prove that I love him more than he's ever loved me. So I shift into wolf form and run off before he can see them fall.

CHAPTER 10

SHOOTING STAR
NINE MONTHS AGO

"Look," Aspen said, pointing at the sky. "Do you see that star right there?"

We were lying in the sand, the night breeze brushing our skin.

"Yes?"

He laughed. "It's right there." He leaned in an inch closer, the smell of saltwater and ocean on his skin. "You see it?"

The waves crashed against the shore as I scanned the skies for that elusive star. I loved looking at the stars. I loved it even more with Aspen next to me. "I think...I think I see it!"

I could hear the smile in his tone. "That's the start of Leo, the beginning of his head. And then, just a little bit to the left, left and up—" He stopped when a streak of light whizzed across the sky. "A shooting star! Quick! Make a wish."

Aspen was the first wish that came to mind. With his 18th birthday in just over a month, I'd been thinking about him more than ever, so I closed my eyes against the sky, wishing on that shooting star that Aspen and I could be soulmates.

I opened my eyes and turned my face towards him, my

cheek against the sand, my hands resting on my stomach. He rolled to face me, his sandy curls blending with the beach we lay on.

That easy smile of his rose on his face. "What did you wish for, Lu?"

I smile and shake my head. "I can't tell you. It's a secret."

"Ah, you're no fun." His voice is quiet underneath the roar of waves.

"What about you then?" I asked. I moved my face just an inch or two closer. "What did you wish for, Aspen?"

His smile turned mischievous. "I can't tell you that."

"Oh, come on, you asked me." I poked his arm.

He laughed. "Well it's like you said, Lu." His blue eyes sparkled with some mystery I could not see. He moved his face another inch closer. "It's a secret."

And for a moment, as my every heartbeat became striking and important, I was certain that his wish was the same as mine.

CHAPTER II
SHE COULD HAVE

I feel Rory's stare when I come out of the woods and into the backyard, even from a couple of acres away. She's sitting on one of those plush chairs on the deck, her silver eyes glowing, and while I can't make out her facial expression from this distance, I already know I don't want to face her. I consider running back into the woods, but she might chase me down and she's faster than I am. I shift back into human form and make my way up the hill. I'm slower that way. As I approach the patio, Rory stands up and leans over the deck's railing, gesturing for me to come with a curling finger. It feels like a silent threat. I trudge up the stairs and stop in front of her with folded arms.

"Yes?"

Rory rolls her eyes. "What do you mean, 'yes?' You can quit it with that act. Dad had to go to Loki and Sheena's to deal with some squabble, so he isn't going to overhear us." She falls back into her chair, somehow looking down at me from below. "What in the *night* is going on?"

I dig my nails into my arms.

"By all means, take a seat, Lulu. I've got all night. All day, if we need it." She swivels in her chair and gestures to a matching seat next to her.

I breathe in. I breathe out. "We don't need to be here all night. It's not that complicated, alright?" I do my best to look sincere as I try a smile on for size. "Kodiak and I really are mates."

Rory blinks real slow. "Luna, just sit down."

"It's true!" My voice nearly cracks. I take the seat across from her and lean forward with what I hope comes across as emphatic sincerity. "It must be the Blue Moon or something, I don't know!"

"I'm offended you think I'm that stupid."

"It's the Blue Moon!"

"Luna, I'm trying to have a real conversation with you." Rory rubs her face. "The only reason Daddy even bought your crap act at all was because he has no reason to suspect you're lying. So why are you and Kodiak pretending to be mates?"

I shrink into my seat. "We're not—" Rory fixes me with such a glare that I fear she'll rip out my hair if I lie again. "Okay, fine. We're pretending." My voice is just above a whisper.

"I got that."

"So there you have it."

"Why are you doing this? You already have a mate, Luna. And don't pretend like you're over Aspen, either. You heard what Queenie said. You could still fix the bond if you wanted to. So what's with this fake-relationship sapcrap?"

I don't want to have this conversation. I don't want Rory staring me down with an evil eye judging decisions that I already judge myself for. I look down at my feet. "I—I don't know. It just kind of happened. I just thought—I mean, if Aspen still feels any of the mate bond, it's gotta be driving him crazy, right? To see me with Kodiak? And so, I don't know, it just seemed..." I'm not sure how to finish.

"So this is all some scheme to make Aspen jealous?" There's anger in her tone. "Does Kodiak realize that?"

I purse my lips.

"Oh stars, Luna," she says in an exhale. "Look I get—no, actually I—" She freezes. "Do you realize how unfair this is to Kodiak? How much you're screwing him over? I mean, it puts him in a terrible situation. Did you think about that?"

I stare at my fists balled against my knees, her words amplifying the guilt coursing through my veins. She and Kodiak used to be close. I don't know if she's more sickened by my behavior or if I am. I dare a glance at her—her forehead is in her hand, elbow resting on her knee.

"What a mess," she says.

I personally think this is closer to a catastrophe than a mere mess, but I still don't like Rory telling me so. "Well good thing you don't have to deal with it," I say. "Aren't you and Grey leaving soon anyways?"

"Grey already left for home."

I raise my eyebrows. Grey...left? Without Rory? She's actually staying here with me? I thought she'd be getting out of here as soon as possible. "And...you're not going with him?"

"Of course I'll go back eventually," she says. "But, well, you've got a lot going on. I need to be here now."

My silly little heart softens like chocolate on a warm day. "Oh, I see." My voice is quiet. "I'm surprised he was okay with you staying here for a bit."

"Of course he was," Rory says. "Grey cares about you too, you know? He's really worried about you."

I furrow my brow. "Worried about me? Why would he be worried about me?"

"Because of everything that's happened," Rory says, as if

it's the most obvious thing in the world. "Obviously, you've been through a lot the past day or two, and—"

"And how would he know about that?" I ask, horrifying realization creeping over me. "'Cause I certainly didn't tell him."

Rory doesn't even bother to look remorseful about her betrayal—just confused by my reaction. "Luna, Grey would never go around telling people what happened."

"But apparently you would." I'm angry at her and I'm angry at myself for being on the verge of tears for the past two days.

"Grey is my mate!" Rory cries, as if that's supposed to make everything better. "And you know him. Do you really think he'd go around telling people what happened? He's just worried about you, like I am, and like I'm sure Dad would be too if I told him—but oh, wait—I didn't tell Dad anything, did I? Because I *do* respect your privacy, even though I think Dad should know what happened. I mean, maybe you wouldn't even be in this whole fake-mates mess you've landed yourself in if you'd just let me talk to Dad!"

"Wow. You're right!" I cry, jumping up from my seat. "As always! I'm sure Dad could have perfectly fixed this unprecedented incident and everything would have been perfectly fine. Too bad I'm just a stupid mutt who ruins everything."

Her sigh is short and annoyed. "I didn't say that and you know it."

"Well, would you look at the time," I say, staring and tapping at an invisible watch on my wrist like some sape. "I should be headed inside. I've got school tomorrow, and I'll want a good day's rest!"

I walk inside and slam the door behind me. I storm up to my room and wrap myself in my indigo bedspread until an hour later, I hear a gentle knock on the door. I sigh. Dad must have settled the argument that had taken him from the house.

"Come in, Dad," I call, untangling myself from the covers to sit upright.

The mouth-watering smell of venison brisket intensifies as he opens the door. Leftovers from the post-hunt feast. Dad's holding a plate of it in large, scarred hands, looking unsure as he watches me.

I still remember when he tried to braid my hair. It was the first day of my junior year, and I'd broken my wrist in an official inter-pack spar a few days prior (a spar that I won). Mom had always braided my hair the first day of school, and then Rory, so Dad took the task upon himself. I remember the feel of his thick scarred fingers against my scalp as they stumbled over the glossy black waves. The braid was clumsy and lopsided, but I wore it to school anyways. And really, who would critique the Alpha Daughter on her father's braid?

"I brought you something," Dad says, holding out the plate like a peace offering, even though he's the only person in this house who I'm not angry with.

"Thanks, Dad." My smile is tired and grateful. "That smells great."

He walks over to the side of my bed and passes the plate and a fork before taking a cautious seat at the edge of my bed. Maybe he knows that my tears can be set off by anything and everything in my current emotional state. The plate rests on my lap atop the pool of fabric swirling around my waist. I stab a slice of brisket with my fork and tear into it with my canines.

"You must miss him," Dad says, but there's uncertainty to his tone.

I swallow my bite. "Yeah, I do." I could be an award-winning actress if I was talking about Kodiak.

Dad's deep voice is quiet, like the distant roll of thunder. "I miss her," he says.

Maybe Dad isn't worried about making me cry.

"I wish she were here," Dad says. "She always knew what to say."

My bottom lip quivers. "Yeah." It's not the first time I've imagined what it would have been like if Mom were here. She would have known all along about Aspen, about how much I had wanted him to be my mate, and she would have been the first person I told when he rejected me. She would have understood, more than anyone else in this whole wide world possibly could, just what that meant to me. She would have mourned with me. And then...well, I'm not sure what she would have done, what she would have said, but it would have been just what I needed. Unlike Rory, I don't think Dad could have fixed everything if I'd told him what happened, yet with all my heart, I believe that Mom could have.

CHAPTER 12

RAINDROPS (PART ONE)
ONE YEAR, THREE MONTHS AGO

"Is it wrong for me to say that I miss her?" Aspen asked. He and I were sitting on the patio in plastic chairs under the deck as thick drops of rain splattered on the ground and pounded against the wooden planks overhead. A bunch of kids were in the yard, playing and running and roughhousing in the rain. Logan and Raff were wrestling in the mud while Anika cheered them on, and Nova was staring up at the sky as the rain hit her face.

I glanced over at Aspen. Rainwater dripped off his curls, his chin, his eyelashes, and his shirt clung to his body. I gathered my hair from behind my back and combed through the wet strands.

"Miss who?" I asked, twisting my hair to wring out the water. "Your girlfriend?" They'd been dating for five months now. I tried not to sound bitter, but maybe he'd sat by me to gloat.

He chuckled softly. "No. I was talking about your mother."

I let my hair fall against my shoulders.

"You were thinking about her, weren't you?" he said.

It was March 13th. Two days before the anniversary of her death. "Yeah," I said. It would mark four years since her passing. The rain *pat pat pat* overhead and I shivered from the chill of wet skin and cool air.

"She was your mom," Aspen said. "And you have every right to mourn her more than I do, but..." he paused, and his eyes were hazy with a memory I couldn't see. "Well, I miss her too."

Logan turned his attention from Raff and wrapped muddy arms around Anika's waist, swinging her around while she shrieked. A couple of the younger high-school-aged wolves were racing across the yard—one slipped in the mud and howled—but they all were all drowned out by the rain.

"She was the best Alpha Female we could've had," Aspen said. "Maybe one of the best ever."

Raindrops rolled down my cheeks.

CHAPTER 13
OUT OF CONTROL

The next evening, I wake up to three unread texts. They're not from Aspen.

Kodiak 1:23 p.m.

hey luna my butterfly princess moonlight starshine sparkle of my eye

Kodiak 1:24 p.m.

i'm coming for dinner tomorrow so let your cooks know. i eat a lot!! can't bare to be away from my puppy pumpkin sugarbear bride baby much longer

Kodiak 1:27 p.m.

also good luck at school today

The sickening combination of human and werewolf pet names makes me laugh through my bleariness at 6:00 p.m. I respond "see you this morning" before walking into the closet to pick out my outfit. More than any other school day, I need to look my best today. At least, I need to look my best without looking like I tried too hard. I settle on a black tee tucked into blue denim shorts with a plaid, red flannel shirt tied around my waist. I put on my favorite necklace—a crescent moon dangling from a thin chain—and sport my classic moon-shaped stud earrings and three tiny hoops climbing up my left ear. I like the color of silver, but it really irritates my skin, so all my jewelry is white gold. I glance at the small pile of makeup on my dresser and decide to splurge on a little mascara and lip gloss. I pull my hair up in a ponytail, throw on a pair of Converse, and examine my appearance in the floor length mirror. It's pretty good.

I shrug on my backpack and head out the door, opting to cut through the woods instead of using the beaten roads. School is just past the edge of Dakota Ridge's territory; we border a human town, so we use their crappy school at night when the humans aren't there. We share the school with Midnight River and Crimson Star, but their attendance is somehow even worse than ours. Our classes are now separated by pack, since they found it led to less fights. Outside the school, three beta women stand behind a table covered in brown paper bags that they pass out to students. Years ago, even as her own health was declining, Mom implemented our own school lunch program, since the human school board refused to provide more meat for our lunches. She convinced the Alphas and Alpha Females from Midnight River and Crimson Star to join in on the program, so now all three packs set aside animals from hunts for teams of skilled beta females to prepare for our lunches.

I approach the entrance to Adam Douglas High, renamed after the so-called illustrious man who decided to force werewolves into going to school. Along with everyone else, I flip my middle finger at his name above the front doors out of habit. Most of the teachers loathe the "night class" students.

This time of year, it's still light outside at 7:25 p.m., but as the sun sets, the LED lights overhead will shine with the softness of blaring headlights in the night. The school always reeks of humans whenever we first get there: BO and body spray and sweat and probably misery. In fairness, their smells aren't all bad, but we like to complain about the worst of it. My friends and I always play a guessing game of what they served for lunch when we get into the cafeteria. Raff once told us that we should be grateful we don't have to enter the boys' locker room.

Today, everyone looks extra ticked off about returning to school. We had three days off for the hunt, even though we were so close to the end of the semester, and nobody wants to be back here. A lot of people aren't.

Nova is the first person to spot me when I walk in, and she runs up to me and gives me a huge hug. "Luna! Oh my stars! I thought you'd be in Midnight River!"

"If only!" I say in my most convincing tone. "But I'm so close to graduating, so—"

"Hey!" a voice shouts.

Nova steps away from me, and I turn to face a boy, probably a freshman or sophomore, with scraggly hair, brown eyes, and a scrappy build that'll fill out when he's older. He's from Midnight River.

I raise an eyebrow, the sort of way Rory would when she didn't like the way she was addressed. "Hey what?" My voice is cool.

"Is it true that you're Alpha Kodiak's mate?" he asks, his eyes ablaze. A couple of his friends are standing next to him, watching for my reaction.

"Yes," I say. "Which means I'll be your Alpha, too."

The boy's lip curls. "Then what are you doing here? Why aren't you with him right now?"

"I'm trying to finish up school. I'm a graduating senior, so these last few days are important." I fold my arms. "Kodiak and I have the rest of our lives together."

"That's the most stupid thing I ever heard!" the boy growls.

I grit my teeth. Next to me, Nova is fidgeting and looking down at the ground. I step forward and take in a couple whiffs of the boy's scent. His cronies are still eyeing me, waiting to see what I do next. I can tell the boy is a lower beta, so I ought to put him in his place. Ask him what he thinks he's doing, questioning an alpha. And really, what *is* he doing? Why does he care if I'm glued to Kodiak's side or not? Why is he concerning himself with this issue? Who does he think he is? My attention is pulled as two people walk in through the front door: Logan and Anika.

"Kodiak finally gets a mate," the scrappy boy says. "And it's some selfish mutt like you." The words strike me like a slap.

"YO!" Logan shouts. "How dare you talk to her like that, litter runt!" He approaches and shoves the boy to the ground.

"Who do you think you are?" Anika pipes in, her teeth bared.

One of the boy's friend steps forward and strikes Logan's chest with his forearm. "Hey, he spoke out of turn. You can back off."

"Back off?!" Logan cries. He laughs incredulously. "He called our Alpha Daughter, our Alpha Heir, a MUTT!"

The first boy must have some scrap in him, because he's back on his feet and bold as ever. "What kind of alpha is she if she can't even do her basic duty to her mate?"

It feels good to watch Logan's fist crash against the boy's cheek. The boy wobbles back, and Logan jabs him with his left, sending a stream of blood flying out the boy's mouth. The friend steps up and lands a solid blow on Logan. Out of nowhere, Raff comes running down the hall. "I smell blood!" He shrieks. His eyes light up when he sees the fight and he jumps the friend. Soon, Anika is tangled up with a Midnight River girl, punching and scratching, and Raff and Logan are fighting the two Midnight River boys. A crowd circles around them, pumping their fists and howling and cheering. Human teachers stand back looking scared or tired, but either way, they don't want to catch a stray fist to the face by stopping the fight.

I'm unsure of what I should do; the role of an alpha-blooded female differs from that of my male counterpart. More important than a demonstration of dominating violence is maintaining a visage of cool control. I should have crushed the boy when he questioned me—reminded him of his place. If Rory were here, she would have shut down this fight before it began, and if Rory were here, she'd know how to stop it. What if I try to break up the fight and I fail? I grit my teeth. I have to do something.

I approach the girls first, pulling the Midnight River girl by the back of her shirt and throwing her away from Anika.

"Ani, stand down," I order. Anika's huffing and puffing and she looks ticked, but she obeys. I grimace as I turn to the boys. I've got to break them up and—

Midnight River girl starts running at me. She scratches my cheek before I elbow her in the face, followed by a kick to her stomach. The crowd oohs and cheers. She goes down hard, and I put my foot down on her chest, a Converse shoe against a bloodied t-shirt.

"The fight is over. Stand down or else," I snarl. I may not be Rory, but I don't lose fights—especially not to mid beta brats.

As I turn my attention to the boys, another person pushes his way into the pseudo ring. Aspen's eyes are wide as they survey the fight before he rips Logan off the bloodied rude kid. Aspen is naturally quite strong, like most of my friends. Except for Nova, they're all high betas. He's trying to get Logan to stop and keep Scrappy Rude Boy away while I break up the fight between Raff and his opponent. I'm grateful for Aspen's help, yet I'm embarrassed that I needed it.

Once everyone is separated, huffing and puffing, I realize I need to make some sort of speech. Everyone is looking at me, including Aspen. His eyes are wider than the Moon.

"Alright," I say. "That's enough." Oh moon, what am I supposed to say? How do I end this altercation? I look to my friends and give them a nod, a token of my appreciation. "We're all just standing up for our own," I say. I walk up to Rude Boy. "And as for you, I am alpha-blooded. And while I understand your concern, you'd do best to remember your place." I leave him with a cold glare and turn back to my friends. The hall explodes into chatter while teachers yell that it's time to go to class.

"You okay, Luna?" Logan asks, reaching towards the cut on my cheek.

"Don't touch her!" A voice rips through his action. Aspen's eyes are wild, and my friends and I stare at him like he's been possessed by some beast. Aspen himself seems surprised at his reaction, his lips parted and his eyes wide. "You—you don't want to hurt her."

"I'm fine," I tell Logan, offering an apologetic smile. "But you all look a bit roughed up."

Logan shrugs, rolling his shoulders. "Eh, nothing gets you up in the morning like a good scrap."

Anika grins. She's got a shiner that'll turn purple. "You're the Alpha Daughter. We're not gonna let some mutt talk to you like that."

"Wait, what did he say to her?" Raff asks. We all start laughing. Of course Raff would jump into a fight he knew nothing about.

"So," Logan starts. "Kodiak, huh?" He scratches the back of his neck. Logan's always had a little thing for me—chances are he's more upset about Kodiak than Aspen is.

"Logan! Rafael! Anika!" Mr. Miller plows towards us like a tornado intent on destroying everything in its path. He gives me the stink eye but says nothing. He knows it's not worth it to pick on the Alpha Daughter and incur everyone's wrath. Another teacher is already chastising the Midnight River kids to no avail. "That's detention for you!" Mr. Miller barks.

"No thanks," Logan says.

Mr. Miller's red, balding head looks like it's going to erupt any second. He's stuck with the night class for another year, and he's not happy about it. I shake my head and start walking towards class. The bell rang five minutes ago, and I have to show I'm making an effort to graduate, since I'm forsaking my "mate" for school. Most of the kids are yapping at the teachers, telling them to lay off, but Aspen is sprinting up to me. My heart skips a beat. I don't know what to say.

"Luna." He reaches out to grab my arm, but stops himself just before making contact. "You're bleeding."

"Oh." I bring my fingers to my cheek and feel cool, sticky blood.

"Come here," he says, stepping into an empty hall. Many halls and classrooms go unused by the night class, since there are far more human students than werewolf. Aspen fishes around his pocket and pulls out a dark handkerchief. I almost laugh. I made fun of him when he bought it, but he said it would come in handy with all the fights we have. Aspen raises the handkerchief and dabs my cheek, the fabric and pressure as soft as a peck. His skin never touches mine. His jaw is clenched and his eyes flit between the cut and my eyes until they land on my lips. His breath shakes and mine stops.

"I..." He looks into my eyes. "I don't know if I can do this any—"

The sound of approaching voices makes him step away. Feelings of relief and anger flood my system—relief we weren't caught, anger that the moment is ruined. And then more anger that I should even have to worry about being caught with my mate.

"Here." Aspen hands me the handkerchief without his skin touching mine. "I'll—I'll see you in class."

He rushes into the main hall and I'm left with nothing but a bloodied handkerchief.

The sky is inky black by the time school lets out. I'm grateful to escape the harsh fluorescent lights and slip into the shadows of the night. Of course, wolves still see very well in the dark, but the darkness is a relief—a break from LED lights shining in my face while I'm pestered with questions about Kodiak and what this means for the pack now that I've mated with the neighboring Alpha.

Almost as soon as I'm off school grounds, I'm back in Dakota Ridge boundaries. We've got dirt roads we hardly use and worn-down footpaths for sidewalks and countless trees. If I keep following the road, I'll get to Bruno's diner, the town square, the general store, and the motel that's always booked up full when we host inter-pack events. A few houses line the road near the center of town, but most are tucked away in clusters of cleared-out plots in the forest, often grouped by caste.

Midnight River and Crimson Star wolves are carted home in buses, but Dakota Ridge kids prefer to walk. It's only a few miles—nothing for a werewolf. I cut away from the dirt sidewalk into the forest's embrace, weaving through trees I'd know with even feeble human eyes. Branches snap underneath and leaves rustle overhead as I run my hand along the trunks, trying to let the comforting smell of dirt and birds and vegetation overpower my vexations, to transport me into a floated ether unattached to my life and its problems. I bolted out of school without lingering to chat with my friends, claiming Kodiak as my reason. They didn't know I was running away from them, from their questions, from myself.

Rory is right. She always is. I *am* a mess, and everything that's happening is because of my own stupidity. They want to know when the wedding is, if it's going to be here or in Midnight River, if the packs are merging, and if so, when and how, and "I don't want to merge with them," or "I think it would be cool," and "How are you going to navigate the merge" —but never "How are you?" I feel sick from questions I cannot answer; they slosh around in my stomach and swirl like a whirlpool that threatens to pull me in, never to breathe again. My life is a shattered vase on the concrete, one I threw in a desperate attempt to fix things. I can't even take the reins of my own life, let alone the pack. Let alone *two* packs. I never wanted to be heir—I was content as an alpha daughter, content as the heir's sister, more than content to mate with a beta who loves poetry and sunlight. Now I'm expected to rule over two packs with a wolf I pretend to love and a power I do not possess.

I fall to my knees, sticks and stones grinding against my bare shins and dirtying my skin. It's a cloudy night, blocking the Moon's light from piercing through the trees, but it's just as well the Moon cannot see me: an alpha-blooded so weak that I'm surprised I do not reek of the stench of an omega. I bury my face in my hands, both my nose and tears running, hiding my face from a world that does not see me. How could I blame Aspen for rejecting me? How could I be angered by his so-called audacity? I am weak and I am pathetic. I feel so disgustingly human when I should be a pillar of strength for wolves to rely on.

I stay there for a while before pushing myself off the ground, swiping at my smudgy eyes and attempting to still my trembling lip. I trek through the forest, trying to scrape a balm for my soul from the trees and finding there is none.

For the rest of the day after he gave me his handkerchief,

Aspen had been the picture of all that I should be: cool, collected, even indifferent. I did not matter to him any more than Anika or Nova or Raff; I was just another wolf attending the same school and the same classes. His eyes did not pierce me with a longing gaze during the few times he bothered to glance in my direction. Perhaps he's moved on from it all, and that lingering mate bond in his veins has evaporated like the morning dew. For him, the rejection was a single moment, one painful flash of time to power through. For me, the rejection exists in a thousand moments. It's in the path we used to walk, the food we used to eat, the music we used to listen to, and the plans I used to dream.

CHAPTER 14
WHITE FLAG
ONE YEAR, FIVE MONTHS AGO

It was a snappy day in late January, and we were bundled up in coats and scarves outside the school bus. I was late, but when my classmates saw me, they ushered me to the front of the line. The bus was old and smelled of human sweat and heavy body spray, but we were forced to endure it for our field trip. I walked down the aisle, scanning the rows and empty seats, when I saw Aspen by one of the windows wearing a corded earbud. He smiled at me, and hesitation knotted in my stomach. Most of my friends were in the back of the bus, and I knew I should go to them. Aspen had made his choice with a human girlfriend.

Then again, *he smiled at me.*

"This seat taken?" I asked. I'm so stupid.

"By you," he said.

The seat was ripped, exposing yellow foam beneath the grey vinyl, and I was foolish and spineless for sitting in it, but I already knew that if I'd sat anywhere else on the bus, I'd have longed for this seat. Aspen pulled out his earbud and coiled the cord in his lap.

"You're late, Lu." His eyes were full of mirth.

"It's 3 p.m.," I yawned. There were still humans milling about the school grounds. "No museum is worth getting up this early." We all only agreed to come because it seemed better than being stuck in Adam Douglas High again.

He grinned. "We might be quiet for once. Everyone's going to be too tired to cause trouble."

"Or too sleep-deprived for self-control."

"One of the two. But look." He pointed across the aisle, where a pair of Crimson Star wolves were nodding off against the backs of the seats in front of them. "It might be lights out."

"True," I said. I glanced out of their window, hoping I didn't see Aspen's mousy girlfriend among the lingering humans outside. After the last wolves in our grade entered the bus, Mr. Appleby stood at the front. He was a balding man with glasses who was looking forward to transferring out of the night class. He droned on and on about the importance of the art gallery, why it was meaningful, blah blah blah. I think everyone except for Aspen and I were either chatting or sleeping during his announcements. Mr. Appleby sat down, and from the back of the bus, Raff and Logan clapped and hollered in exaggerated excitement about the art gallery, prompting others to join their fun, and Mr. Appleby started muttering about his new school like he was going to the promised land. The bus began to roll, and I leaned back against the seat with drooping eyes.

"You look tired," Aspen said.

"Mmm hmm."

"I'll wake you when we get there."

Though sleep beckoned me, I doubted I could get away with sitting next to Aspen on the way home. Sleeping through the ride would be a waste.

I nodded at the earphones in his lap. "What were you listening to?"

"Music."

"Human?"

"Even *you* have to admit, humans make the best music."

I smiled lazily. "Well, there aren't many werewolf artists."

"No, there aren't," he said. "Which is a shame. I think we've got stories to tell."

I sat up straighter, pushing past the tiredness from behind my eyes. "I think we do, too."

"Plus, the werewolf artists we do have aren't very good," Aspen said.

"Well, I wouldn't say—"

"They suck."

I pursed my lips, thinking about the songs I'd heard. "Okay, they're not the greatest," I admitted.

Aspen laughed. "Human songs tend to have more emotion, more meaning. Here, I have an idea." He took one of his earbuds and held it out to me. "I'll show you a song, and you can tell me what you think it's talking about."

My fingers brushed his as I took the earbud. I put it in my left ear while he put the other in his right, connecting us together by a chord. I was glad Aspen's hearing was not good enough to pick out the quickening of my heartbeat without paying close attention.

And so it began, our bus ride to the art gallery, cheeks close together and songs playing in one ear. He would play a song and pause it, asking me for my thoughts as we went along.

"Okay, last one," Aspen said. We would be arriving soon. "This is *White Flag* by Dido." The beginning notes swelled in my left ear, and I closed my eyes to focus and pick out the words. The song was sung in first person, a woman expressing that she was still in love with someone. She knew she shouldn't confess her feelings, but hiding how she felt wouldn't change her emotions. She claimed that she wasn't trying to start things up again, but as the chorus started, she sang that she wouldn't surrender, that she wouldn't put up a white flag.

Aspen paused the song after the chorus. "What do you think so far?" he asked.

I swallowed the emotion rising in my chest. "Well, I guess the verse is pretty straightforward. She used to love this guy, they probably dated, and she's still in love with him. But she thinks he doesn't want that. Her to love him, I mean."

"Yeah, I think so too. I also like how the verse talks about how if she didn't say it, she'd still have felt it. Just because she doesn't say anything, doesn't mean those feelings aren't there."

"Yeah." And I wondered if he knew all along, if this was all a ploy to talk about me.

"What did you think about the chorus?"

"I thought it was beautiful."

He raised his eyebrows. "Yeah?"

"It sort of reminds me of mates," I said, scrolling through the lyrics on his phone. "When your mate dies, you still always love them. You don't surrender that love."

In the depth of his eyes, I could see that he was really listening to me, considering my words as carefully as he would the songwriter's. "I never thought about it that way."

I felt a tingly surge of pride for making him think about a song he liked in a new light. "But of course, it is different." My voice grew quiet. "The person she loves doesn't love her." *Maybe he has a girlfriend now,* I didn't say. "Mates are true to each other, but she's the only one who remains true." I stared at the seat in front of me instead of Aspen, as though looking into his eyes would reveal all that I felt. "Her relationship with him, it's like a sinking ship, you know? He doesn't love her, but she's not abandoning the ship. She still loves him, and she's not going to pretend otherwise. And it's kind of a…I don't know. Almost a contradiction?" I managed to peek at him, to look into deep eyes that clung to every word I said. I felt an echoing pang in my heart. "She loves him, but she's accepting their fate."

CHAPTER 15

ACROSS THE DIVIDE

The sunrise is dull and colorless behind the thick canopy of clouds. I have dirty skin and ruined makeup and ignored texts from Rory asking where I am. Instead of using the front door, I opt to climb into my room through the balcony. It hovers over the corner of the deck and can be climbed through the supports. My muscles flex as I take hold of the wooden balustrade and hoist myself over the railing. I wonder if Aspen climbed it the same way, his heart pounding from more than physical exertion. Now standing on the balcony, I look down at the wooden planks where I crumbled before him, broken and weak. I don't linger there.

I head into my room and turn on the shower. The hot water doesn't heal all that I feel inside, but it's warm and soothing on my skin and washes me clean of the day's grime and tears. I change into an oversized t-shirt and black cotton shorts before I attempt to braid my wet hair. I can't braid as well as Mom or Rory, but it turns out alright. As I come down the stairs, I hear and smell Kodiak amidst the clamor of pans and sizzle of bacon, talking with Dad and Rory in the living room. They're discussing what the pack-merge will entail and how to break the news to everyone and when. Before I come into view, Kodiak stops mid-sentence and bounds into the front hallway as I'm descending the stairs.

He comes right up to me; his grin is big, but his voice is quiet. "Hi, darling."

I try not to laugh at the pet name. "Hey, Kodiak." Dad and Rory are likely peering into the front hallway from the living room, so with the added height of a couple stair steps, I wrap my arms around his neck and lean in to plant a kiss on his forehead. His smile turns bashful, and his ears turn red. Kodiak is an unusual alpha—sometimes he seems too boyish for the role.

Dad enters the hall from the living room, smiling at our embrace. "Luna's been missing you," he says.

Kodiak raises an eyebrow, his eyes wide and surprised. "Were you?" He sounds pleased.

Dad thinks my moping was all for Kodiak. "Of course," I say, placing a hand against his sharp jawline, his five o'clock shadow brushing my palm. That's right. He has a mate now, so he can grow out his facial hair. "You're my mate."

His smile flickers.

Dad starts shuffling out of the room. "I'm going to check on dinner." Bea and Kya—lower betas who sometimes act as our chefs—are in the kitchen whipping up some aromatic concoction of venison and bacon and herbs. I take my arms off Kodiak and step down onto the main floor to head towards the living room, but he tugs on my t-shirt and pulls me back to him. My heart jumps at the unexpected movement. When he places a calloused palm on my left cheek, I wonder how much of this is a facade to him. Then again, everyone can hear us. Maybe Rory's watching us, but I don't feel the prick of her cold, silver stare. Kodiak rubs a thumb just underneath the cut on my cheek. It should heal, but there's a thin red line marking where the Midnight River girl scratched me, marking my failure to control the situation.

"What's this?" he asks, eyebrows raised, tone light.

"Fight at school." I don't want to explain that the fight started because our mating was questioned, and that it was one of his wolves who nicked me.

Kodiak's smile is sharp, his golden eyes half-lidded. He lifts my chin with his thumb. "Did you win?" he asks.

I think of the elbow to her face and the foot I planted on her chest. "Of course."

Kodiak's grin widens. "Good." He pulls his hand from my face to take mine, leading me from the hall to the kitchen. I'm grateful he doesn't ask more questions, though I feel a little silly that a single word and proud look from him are enough to make me wonder if I'm not the worst alpha-blooded after all.

Rory walks up to me with a big stack of white porcelain plates. "Take these."

I let go of Kodiak's hand in time to balance the plates in my arms.

"Bea and Kya are busy finishing up dinner," Rory says, marching back into the kitchen and tearing open the silverware drawer. Bea and Kya smile apologetically as Rory takes out fist-fuls of forks and knives. "Dad's outside on a call. We gotta set the table."

Rory and I walk into the dining room while Kodiak asks Bea and Kya if they need help with anything. Of course, they insist they don't, and Kodiak should feel free to relax. That's how Bea and Kya are. I'm sure Rory forced them to let us set the table.

"Why did you give me so many plates?" I ask, setting the stack at the edge of the dining room table. "We only need four."

Rory surveys me like I'm a landmine that could explode any second. "Didn't Dad tell you?"

"Tell me what?"

She turns her eyes to the forks and knives she's placing on white linen napkins. "Oh, well, Alistair's family is coming." Her tone is light, her gaze is grim. Kodiak's yapping with Bea and Kya in the kitchen, so I doubt he's listening, but I try to sound casual just in case.

"Oh, gotcha."

At least Kodiak isn't in the dining room, listening to my heartbeat quicken. Alistair's family is coming, which means Aspen is coming. It's good, isn't it? Aspen will see me and Kodiak, he'll be jealous, he'll realize his mistake, and everything will be made right. A mess made clean. So why is my stomach in knots? And why am I wearing this huge ugly shirt and shorts? My hair is in a wet braid. I don't look my best. Would it be too strange if I changed now? Probably. I guess I'm stuck looking like this.

When Alistair and his mate Leah arrive, they bring two of their four sons—Ares and Aspen—since the others are tied up with pups. Ares has brought his mate, Misty: a classless lower-mid beta who was thrilled to get a high beta catch like Ares. The two mated their senior year, when Aspen and I were freshmen, and they were about as insufferable as mates could get. They couldn't keep their hands off each other in the halls nor at lunch, and they'd constantly sneak off to closets where everyone could hear their UNNECESSARILY LOUD rendezvous through thin wooden doors. We were all relieved when they were kicked out of school.

We take our seats at the dining room table. Dad sits at the head, with Rory on his left and Alistair on his right. Rory's row is her, Misty, Ares, and Aspen. Alistair's row is him, Leah, Kodiak, then me. Somehow Aspen has ended up right across from me.

Dad is telling Alistair about how some wolf from the hunt

left a hole in the wall by the mantle while Misty talks to Rory. "It's so great to see you again, Aurora!" Misty places a hand on her shoulder like they're old pals. Rory had been friends with Ares, but she certainly wouldn't have spent time with the likes of Misty. "But where's your mate?" Misty asks with huge eyes. "I guess he's an alpha, right? Why are you here without him?"

Rory's silver eyes slide to Misty's hand on her shoulder and then to me across the expanse of a table. I wonder how Misty cannot see that she's seconds away from getting her hand crushed.

Dad at least notices, and breaks from his conversation to save Rory from further conversation with Misty. "Aurora, why don't you tell Alistair how things are in Northern Skies?"

I turn to my plate of juicy venison steak with mashed potatoes and green beans cooked with bacon. As I'm about to pierce the steak with my fork, my chair jostles and is dragged a few inches to the left—Kodiak pulling me closer to him. He isn't looking at me as he does so, he's listening to Alistair's conversation, but a mischievous smile touches his lips. I glance at Aspen. His eyes are burning. Meanwhile, Ares' eyes flash like he's just discovered the cure for Lycanthroma and pulls Misty's chair closer to him. I'm sure Rory's relieved about the extra nine inches of space from her. Misty giggles, and Aspen watches her and Ares rubbing noses together in poorly concealed disgust. Maybe he rejected me for fear of becoming like them. If so, I almost can't blame him.

"You were too far away from me, puppy," Ares says, his voice a growl. Oh, I definitely can't blame Aspen now.

"I can never be close enough," she says, her eyes ravenous.

If they start going at it on this table, I hope Dad or Rory or somebody kills them. Rory looks like she might not wait until it gets to that point. Dad is wearing that same uncomfortable look from the Blue Moon party when Leah suggested Kodiak and I should be alone. Alistair and Leah look a bit embarrassed, and Aspen looks like he'll die of shame. Meanwhile, Kodiak wears a goofy grin, and he turns to me with the softest of whispers. "We should use those lines next, 'puppy'."

I turn his cheek to whisper back into his ear. "I'd rather die."

Kodiak's laugh puts a smile on my face until I feel a pair of eyes pricking my skin. Aspen is clenching the fork and knife in his hands like he's going to use them on one of us instead of his food.

"Oh moon, this is so *embarrassing*," Kodiak says, drawing out the last word. He leans forward with his arms crossed on the table, looking straight at Aspen. "But I seem to have forgotten your name. I know, we were just on the hunt, but..."

I try to remain calm, to keep a steady heartbeat. I know that Kodiak knows Aspen's name. He talked to him before the hunt, when Aspen was walking me home.

The look in Aspen's eyes is one I have scarcely seen, like an angry, storming ocean. "I am Aspen." He keeps his voice calm.

"Aspen," Kodiak repeats. His smile shows his long canine teeth and is anything but comforting. Then, he glances at Ares. "You were a beast during the hunt, Ares."

It's of little surprise that he did so well, but Ares' smile still spreads from ear to ear.

"That's my wolf!" Misty says, clinging to his arm. Rory rolls her eyes.

"That's high praise coming from you, Alpha Kodiak," Ares says. "And it means a lot. I live for hunts."

"Me too!" Kodiak grins. He turns back to Aspen. "What about you, Aspen? What do you live for?" He laughs. "Because I don't think it's hunting."

Aspen flushes and shifts in his seat. Dad, Alistair, and Leah are deep into their own conversation, oblivious to the rest of us, but Rory is smirking and Ares and Misty are chuckling. As if Misty has any room to judge Aspen. I wish I could enjoy watching Aspen squirm as much as the rest, but all I want to do is step in and put an end to this, the same way I tried to stop the fight at school. My fists ball up against my thighs, good for nothing but digging my nails into my palms.

"What do I live for?" he asks. "That's quite the question."

"I live for *you*," Misty says, resting her head on Ares' shoulder. Rory rolls her eyes.

Sometimes I feel like I'm the only one who understands Aspen in a world to which he does not belong, and yet, other times I cannot predict what he'll do or say next. What *does* he live for? Books, chess, human girlfriends?

Aspen loses the rigidness in his shoulders, his eyes trailing to the window full of grey morning light. His eyes become lost in a vision only he can see. "I live for a better future," he says, turning back to Kodiak.

"A better future?" Kodiak asks, leaning back in his chair. He makes a show of grabbing my hand and interlacing our fingers. "What's wrong with the life you have now? Are you that miserable?"

Aspen narrows his eyes for a second. "That's quite the logical leap, Alpha Kodiak. You assume that working towards a better future means that I am miserable. And yet, isn't that the point of life? To learn and grow? To progress? As an alpha, I'm sure your goal is to make your pack even more prosperous and happy." He tilts his head, staring at Kodiak with that hunter's gaze that's so intrinsic to werewolves. "Then again, maybe that's not your goal. Perhaps you're content with everything the way it is. That makes sense, when you're at the top of the food chain."

My eyes widen. It's the strange paradox of Aspen—he's not one for physical brawls, but he fights with his words. They've earned him the occasional black eye or bruise, but those scraps haven't stilled his tongue. Aspen has never worshiped the ground I walk on for being alpha-blooded. Unlike many of my peers, his affection felt more personal: he liked Luna, not the Alpha Daughter. I assumed it was because he saw through my alpha-bravado facade, but perhaps it was an intentional rebellion, a sign of deep-rooted resentment towards the alpha pedestal. I purse my lips. Perhaps that resentment extends to me.

I look at Kodiak, fearing his reaction to such provocation. Thankfully, he doesn't look too angry. His eyes are narrowed, but he seems more thoughtful than anything. Meanwhile, I can see that Rory's eyes are full of fury, and she's only holding her tongue to let Kodiak respond.

"You're right," Kodiak finally says. I didn't expect that. "You're right in that we should be trying to improve and make better lives for our community and our posterity. That's what I try to do, as an alpha. And there's always room for growth. But I still think you should be careful about living for the future, better or not. There's always going to be some distant, better future just out of reach." Kodiak squeezes my hand and lifts it up. "You may not appreciate what you have in the present, but one day you might look back and long for the past."

Aspen looks at me and then down at his plate. His ears fall back just a bit, like a chastised dog. "Wise words, Alpha Kodiak," he concedes. "You and Ares live for the present thrill of the hunt. I live for an unknown future."

"I live for more than hunting." Kodiak sounds peeved.

Aspen's eyes, unbright as they may be, are piercing. "And I live for more than dreams."

"Moon, Aspen. You're so dramatic," Ares says, slapping his brother's arm and laughing up a storm with Misty.

"Yeah, yeah," Aspen says. His smile is faker than my relationship with Kodiak. Aspen turns to his plate, cutting the venison and shoving it in his mouth. I can see he's pulling away now, like a turtle creeping back into its shell, shutting out the outside world. I want to hear more about what he's thinking, to learn what this better future he envisions entails, to ask if he resents me for the blood in my veins.

But I can't.

Not here, not with Kodiak, and not across this table that feels as deep and wide as an ocean between us.

CHAPTER 16

CHECKMATE

ELEVEN MONTHS AGO

Last summer, I wandered into Bruno's in the mid-afternoon—a time when I should have been asleep, but I was wide awake. The diner was different at that time of day. The usual clanging of dishes and chatter and laughter was gone, replaced with something quiet, clean, and peaceful. The warm electric lights were replaced by the sun's rays shining in through the windows, and Bruno was replaced behind the counter by a boy resting his head in his arms.

Aspen looked up when the bell at the door sounded, his curls frizzy and his eyes bleary. The panic in his features gave way to a tired smile as he nestled his cheek against his arm on the counter. "Oh, it's just you."

"Just me?" I asked, my tone as light as his. The sound of my shoes against the black and white checked floor accentuated how quiet it was that day. I settled on a red barstool across the counter.

"Mmhmm," he murmured, nodding his head against his arm. "Just you, Lu." His eyes shut and his smile deepened.

I reached across the counter to wrap one of his curls around my finger. "You know, just about anyone else would have jumped up the moment I walked in."

His laugh was soft. "Our Alpha Queen. That's what Logan would say, right?"

"Something like that."

Aspen brought his head up and I pulled my hand from his hair. He stood up from his barstool and presented himself to me, arms outstretched. "How do I look, Alpha?" He was wearing the Bruno's Diner uniform, inspired by the 50s like the rest of the diner, with a white collared shirt underneath a pinstriped red and white apron. His white hat, which looked sort of like a paper boat with a red stripe, was tossed on the counter along with his red bowtie, revealing his messy hair and matching eyebags.

"You look like crap," I answered, my smile sweeter than Bruno's ice cream sundaes.

Aspen laughed. "Moon, I need a coffee. You want one?"

"Sure."

He took the coffee pot and poured steaming streams into cherry red mugs. He dumped sugar and cream in his and offered me my typical plain coffee. The aroma was warm and soothing as I took a sip. "Drinking black coffee," Aspen said in between a swallow of his sugary concoction. "Like an alpha."

I rolled my eyes as I chuckled. "You're a flea."

"Compared to you, my queen."

"You're on one today."

"I'm tired."

"I can tell."

Aspen threw his mug back, taking a big swig of his coffee. Every summer, he worked the dreaded day shift at Bruno's Diner, and it seemed he hadn't adjusted to working all day just yet. "Luna, have you ever played chess?"

"Chess?" That was out of nowhere.

"Yeah, you know, the game with pawns, knights, the queen and all that?"

"I know what chess is," I retorted. "But...no, I haven't played it."

Aspen's grin grew. "Okay, Lu. I've got an idea. I'm going to teach you to play."

"Chess? Why?" I asked. Few things sounded duller than sitting around some checkered board and moving pieces turn after turn.

"It's good for your brain," Aspen said, tapping his head. "It's a game of logic, prediction, strategy. Let me show you."

My eyes widened when Aspen pulled out a tattered old chess box from under the counter. The cardboard corners were worn and fuzzy and one side of the box was completely torn, but Aspen looked at it like it was a treasure.

"Why do you have that here?" I was incredulous.

"I like to play when it gets slow."

"With who?"

His smile turned funny, his ears turned pink. "With myself."

I burst out laughing. I couldn't help it. It was such a funny scene to imagine. "That makes no sense!"

"It's not as weird as you think it is!"

"Do you, like, sit at a booth and run around the table when it's the next turn?"

"No, I just twist the board."

"Moon, Aspen. You playing chess by yourself has to be the saddest thing I've ever heard."

"Well that's why you should play with me. So I can be less sad." He shook the box, chess pieces rattling against the cardboard. "Nobody in this pack plays."

I finally stopped laughing and leaned forward against the counter. "And what's in it for me?" I asked. Of course, I knew I would say yes, but it was worth it to make him sweat. He and that human girl had only just broken up, and after months of being forced to watch their torturous courtship, he didn't deserve to have my cooperation quite so easily.

Aspen narrowed his eyes, examining me while he tapped his chin like some sort of cartoon character. "Hmm." After a few more seconds of mulling, he said, "If you win, I'll worship you like the alpha-blooded heir/queen you are for, I don't know, at least a week."

"A whole week?" I dropped my jaw in faux shock.

"Maybe even more. Who knows?" Aspen shrugged with a grin.

"And what does this worshiping entail? Are you going to kiss the ground I walk on?"

"Lu, if you beat me at chess, consider the ground kissed."

My laugh echoed joy in that empty diner. "Well, with an offer that tempting, I guess I'll have to."

He was still grinning. "I knew you couldn't refuse."

My smile was slight. He was right, of course. I couldn't refuse. I couldn't refuse him even when I wanted to.

I teased him often as we played that summer, telling him to pucker up every time I took one of his pieces. In our close matches, he'd ask me what my favorite form of groveling was. Of course, I couldn't have cared less about him pretending to worship me, but it made him laugh when I joked about it. When I finally won, I was planning to tell him to forget about the week of worship, to tell him that I never did and never would want that from him.

But I never won. I never beat him. Not even once.

CHAPTER 17

AFTER ALL THESE YEARS

The rest of dinner is about as enjoyable as the start of it. Ares and Misty continue to be the absolute worst, Rory looks ready to rip one or both of their heads off, and Aspen is quiet and sulky. Kodiak does not provoke him further, instead talking with Alistair and Dad. As the foremost beta in the pack, Alistair is privy to the upcoming pack merge and wants to determine logistics. I don't say much, and I steal too many glances at Aspen. Once, our eyes meet, and I feel a thud in my chest before looking away.

When dinner finally ends, Rory excuses herself for the restroom, and I know we won't be seeing her again. Alistair and his family head to the front door to leave, walking over the black bear rug under the eyes of the moose head above the door. Misty lingers so she can say goodbye to Rory, but has to give up on her fond farewell when Rory doesn't reappear. Aspen is outside while his family stands in the front hall, his hands shoved in his pockets and his foot tapping against the porch. The gray sky casts a somber hue on his skin.

"Aspen, come say goodbye," his mother says, fixing him

with a look that tells him to *be polite*. Aspen walks in, mumbles an apology, and shakes Dad's hand. "Thank you for dinner, Alpha Orion."

"Of course. We're always happy to have you," Dad says. "You've always been such a good friend to Luna."

Aspen's smile doesn't reach his eyes.

"Nice to meet you again," Kodiak says, stepping up to Aspen with a handshake so firm that the veins in Kodiak's forearms flex. Aspen's smile turns pained.

"Always a pleasure, Alpha Kodiak." There's a drawl to his tone. He glances over at me, but doesn't say anything, instead turning to his family. I guess his mother thinks that's good enough, and their family starts heading out the door. Aspen looks back at me, something vulnerable and sad in those eyes of his, and shuts the door. Staring at that big wooden door, something empty and blue settles in my stomach. Why do I crave Aspen's presence so much when he always leaves me sadder than before?

I feel Kodiak's eyes on me. I fear he suspects the truth about who Aspen is to me.

"Are you headed back to Midnight River tonight?" Dad asks me.

Oh right, *that*. It's now Saturday morning, which means I have two days I'm not in school before we finish up on Wednesday morning. Yesterday was the last day of school for the humans, but our last day was pushed back for the hunt. I'm sure the human teachers hate us as much as we hate them.

"Of course," I answer Dad. I don't want to go to Midnight River, to dig myself deeper into this hole, but maybe I should accept that this hole is my life now. Order a La-Z-boy and a rug to cover up the dirt floor. "I've been looking forward to it all night. I just need to pack."

Kodiak offers to help me, but I leave him with Dad, telling

them that I'm sure they have a lot to discuss. In my room, I throw unnecessary schoolbooks out of my backpack and stuff it with clothes. I have homework due on Monday and finals to study for, but I don't think Kodiak will accept that excuse to push off Midnight River even longer. What Kodiak doesn't realize is that everyone is going to be furious when they find out we're frauds, and spending time in one another's packs will only make it worse. But then again, maybe they'll never find out. Maybe this *is* life now, La-Z-boy and all. And for the rest of my life, I'll see Aspen around Dakota Ridge, and I'll know he is my one and only soulmate, and he'll know I'm his—and I'll be married to someone else.

I grip my backpack straps, the meshy fabric rubbing against my palms. I can't live that way, like living in a desert with an oasis dancing in my peripheral. How could I be content with heat and sand when I have to face a constant reminder of all I should have had? I can't just give Aspen up, not when the future without a real soulmate looks so dreary. I refuse to accept this fate. I am alpha-blooded; I will wrangle my destiny from the stars themselves if I have to.

There's a knock on my door. "Luna?" It's Rory.

"Yeah?"

She opens the door and makes herself at home on my bed. "We need to talk."

Nope. "I'm almost done packing," I say, walking into my bathroom and grabbing what I need for the next couple of days. Should I bring makeup to look my best amongst the Midnight River wolves? Maybe, I don't know.

"Luna," Rory says.

If I was in wolf form, I'd flatten my ears against my head. I look at my small bag of cosmetics. I might as well bring my makeup. Though, maybe it will be better if I'm unimpressive to

Midnight River—they'll be less disappointed when it all turns out to be a great con and I'm not their new Alpha Female.

Rory's leaning against the bathroom doorframe now, arms folded and hard to ignore.

I sigh, my hands full of toiletries. "Yes?" I ask.

She takes the toiletries from me and walks off. I peek my head out of the bathroom, watching her drop the toiletries on the bed and dumping out my backpack before folding my crumpled clothes into a crisp pile. Rory, like Mom, is very neat and organized when it comes to these sorts of things. I'm not a slob, but my room was often messier than hers. My life too, apparently.

I step out and watch her fold a pair of jeans, and a funny smile rises on her face. She looks up at me, a twinkle in her silver eyes. "You know, I was this close to ripping Misty's throat out." She holds her thumb and index finger out with only a centimeter between them. "*This close.* She's lucky Ares was such a good friend of mine."

I laugh. "Oh moon, I could tell you were about to lose it. I don't know how she couldn't see that."

"She's denser than a sape."

"Well, at least you were already gone when Misty and Ares first became mates. We all had to go to school with them."

Rory makes a gagging noise.

"It was awful," I say.

"I can only imagine." She had dropped out to live with Grey only a couple months prior. "I'm proud of you for not killing them. They're one of the worst mate pairs I've ever met, and I've met a lot of annoying pairs." Then she laughs. "Grey would have been so uncomfortable, oh stars! I wish I could've seen his face." Just the thought of him lights Rory up with a huge smile.

"You must miss him," I say, my voice soft.

Rory shrugs as she folds my tank top. "Of course I do." There's no pining in her tone, just spoken as a matter-of-fact.

"When are you going back?" I ask.

"I don't know," Rory says. "When it's time to go back."

"But you miss him," I say. It's why she hardly ever comes back without him, why she never drops by on a whim, why she abandoned me.

"Yeah, but you're more important than that," Rory says. She pauses her folding for a moment, looking at me with caution. "And...I know you didn't want me to tell him about everything going on, but Grey agrees. He wants me to be here with you."

I think of Grey, so quiet and sullen. It's hard to imagine he wants Rory to stay here with her little sister instead of going home with him. Rory just keeps packing my backpack, squeezing in my schoolbooks, content in the silence. Even though she can be mean and frustrating, I feel my caked-up resentment giving way to relief that she's here, like a river pushing up against a mud wall.

"I don't know what to do." My voice is just above a whisper.

Rory zips up my backpack and pats the spot beside her on the bed. I comply—as I always do—and as soon as I'm seated next to her, Rory puts her arm around me. I rest my head against her, her piney scent filling the air, and tears slip out of my eyes. It's so unlike Rory to say nothing, but I revel in her silent support while I can.

"It's going to tear you apart," Rory whispers after a few minutes. We're trying to keep our voices down. "Being halfway in and halfway out. You can't do both, Luna. You can't be Kodiak's fake mate while you're Aspen's real mate. You need to see it through with Aspen, make him mate with you and end this whole charade, or you need to kill Aspen and commit to a life with Kodiak."

I pull away from her and grimace. "I'm not going to kill Aspen."

She sighs. "I know. Wishful thinking."

I shake my head and roll my eyes, but I know her words are true. I need to put an end to this mess, and soon. It can't go on like this.

"I'm going to talk to Aspen as soon as I'm back," I whisper. "We'll figure it out." Somehow, I know we will.

Rory clasps her hands in her lap, and she's watching me in a careful way that tells me she has something unpleasant to say. "What about Kodiak?" she asks. "What you're putting him through...it's unfair, Luna."

A knot coils in my stomach.

"I know he's not your mate. I wouldn't have expected you to give up your real mate for him, but this whole thing he's a part of now..." She squeezes her eyes shut as though she's wincing in pain. "Moon, I just feel so—oh, that poor wolf!" She looks at me. "You realize, don't you? The victim of this whole plan of yours? You have to figure out what you're doing, and fast. Not just for yourself, but for Kodiak."

I know what I've done. I try to avoid thinking about how Kodiak will feel when I reconnect with Aspen, about what everyone will say about us, but the thoughts plague me still. I feel rotten inside, but instead of telling Rory that she's right and that Kodiak is my victim, something defensive slips out instead. "I know, okay!" My whisper turns into a hiss. "You think I don't know that? Geez!" I stand up and walk away from her. I don't know why I'm acting like this, why I feel so hurt. I guess I wanted her to unconditionally take my side, since I can't do that for myself. I wanted her to tell me that it was okay, that I did what I had to do, that it will all work out. But of course I shouldn't have expected that. Rory has never been the lying type.

"Luna." She says my name like a soft chide, the way Mom used to when I was about to do something naughty. "Don't act like that." Rory stands up, taking my zipped backpack and gently placing it in my arms.

It strikes me how much she's changed over the past few years. The Rory I know would have smacked me in the head with the backpack and told me to stop acting like a baby. We would've started scratching and wrestling until Dad made us break it up.

I don't know what to say. I should probably apologize, but the words are frozen in my mouth. Instead, I mutter, "Thanks for staying."

Rory lets out whatever frustration was simmering in her face with a long breath. "Good luck in Midnight River this weekend. When you get back, let's talk to Queenie, alright? She probably knows more about this rejected mate business than any of us."

When I walk down the stairs, Kodiak is waiting for me, and a fresh pang of guilt strikes my heart. *What you're putting him through...it's unfair.* We exchange quick goodbyes with Dad and Rory before hopping into Kodiak's truck with its smell of old carpet and gasoline. The fabric seats are worn, the windshield is grimy, and the air conditioning barely works, but Kodiak's got the windows rolled down, and the wind that whips my braid cools us both. I try to remember the last time I was in a car...it must have been two months ago when Dad took me out for steak dinner in the city. Kodiak has one arm resting out the window and the other on the steering wheel, his fingers tapping along to the song on the radio. His golden eyes are on the road, but there's a faraway look to them, like he's entered some quiet, peaceful world.

My heart swells when we hit Midnight River's famous coastline: a road atop the cliffs that drop into beaches and ocean. I've always loved the ocean—the smell of fresh air and salt water, the push and pull of the tides. Secretly, I've envied Midnight River for their coast, but I'd never tell any of them that. It's a strange realization that I'm headed to Midnight River to be introduced as their new Alpha Female, that an ocean that belonged to Midnight River will belong to me and Dakota Ridge too. Except...none of that will last. When I fix my broken bond with Aspen, I'll lose the ocean.

I close my eyes. I can hear the waves crashing over the rumbling sound of Kodiak's truck. I breathe in the scent of salty fresh air. I feel the way the wind brushes my face. After a few moments, I glance over to see Kodiak watching me with eyes that remind me of honey.

"What is it?" I ask.

He turns back to the road. "Do you like the ocean?"

"I do." My voice is quiet.

A smile rises on his lips. "I'm glad."

Oh moon, what am I going to do with Kodiak when Aspen and I fix our bond?

We take a left onto a road that leads away from the ocean, deeper into the forest where the heart of Midnight River is carved out amidst the trees. Soon, we're parked outside the Alpha House, one that I've visited several times in my life. It's large and made of dark wooden planks mixed with black metals, and unlike my house, the yard has not been cleared out, leaving a forest instead of grass. Kodiak takes my backpack from the back seat and jumps out of the truck.

"Well, this is it," he says as I join him outside. "Home sweet home."

It's ten o'clock in the morning—late enough that I can start getting ready for bed, I think. Kodiak steps towards the porch before freezing, taking in a long whiff of air.

"What is it?" I ask.

His jaw flexes. "My brother is here. It seems he's brought some high betas with him."

My muscles tense. "Why are they here? At 10:00 a.m.?"

Kodiak shakes his head. "I told them we didn't want to be disturbed this morning."

"And they didn't listen?" My eyes are wide. When my dad tells someone to do something, they listen. "Do you think it's a surprise party?"

Kodiak swings my backpack over his shoulder and takes my hand. His voice is low and dangerous. "I doubt it." Then he drops to a whisper. "Luna, I know this is all very difficult for you, but please." He squeezes my hand. "Pretend that you love me, alright?" He's staring at the front door like it's a ferocious monster that will attack him if he moves.

I squeeze his hand back. "Okay."

Kodiak's brother, Jael, is Rory's age, twenty-one. While he's closer to my age than Kodiak is, I didn't see much of him growing up. Neither of us were the heirs, so Kodiak came to Dakota Ridge more often than Jael, and Rory went to Midnight River more often than me. However, in the interactions I did have with Jael, whether at school or one of our homes, I never really liked him. I always sensed a bitterness in him bubbling beneath the surface of his glowing eyes. I wondered if it was because he liked Rory too, and next to Kodiak, Jael was smaller, weaker, and overlooked. I tried to connect with him once—both of us alpha-blooded, neither of us destined to rule—but there was something in the way he looked at me that made me feel small. Where Kodiak had crazy eyes and a loud laugh, Jael had a cold glare and permanent sneer.

I don't want to see Jael again.

Kodiak opens the front door, and that's when I smell not just Jael, but three other people. Kodiak brings me through the front hall and into the living room, where Jael sits on the large love seat. He's wearing a sharp smile that reminds me so much of Kodiak, though his canines aren't quite as long as his brother's. "Surprise," he drawls.

The other wolves in the room are high betas, and a couple are scanning me over from head to toe with cold eyes. I make a conscious effort not to fidget under their gaze.

"What are you doing here?" Kodiak asks.

"I wanted to welcome home our new Alpha Female!" Jael's magnanimous voice is as sincere as a human car salesman. He's sitting on the love seat like it's his throne, and I remember that's where Kodiak's dad used to sit before he passed the Alpha mantle to his son. Ah, I see. Jael must have wanted to be the Alpha. But he must have known his whole life that he wouldn't be, so why is he pulling this stunt?

"Hello, Jael," I say. "It's been a while."

"It has been. Look at you—all grown up now," he says. Jael looks grown up, too, with a full auburn beard that matches his hair. He found his mate right after he turned eighteen, though I've been to so many weddings that it's hard to remember how his went.

"Yes, I turned eighteen during the Blue Moon," I tell him. "I don't remember seeing you at the hunt."

"Well, someone had to watch over Midnight River while Kodiak was away," Jael says, nestling deeper into his seat. Two of the betas have sharp eyes, but one is smiling at me. He stands up and walks over to me, shaking my hand that isn't in Kodiak's.

"Luna," he says. "We are so excited that Alpha Kodiak has found his mate, and that it's you, no less! We were worried... well, this is a wonderful turn of events. We're excited to see how the pack's future evolves, what with you as the reigning heir of Dakota Ridge."

"We can thank the Moon. She must want our two packs to unite," I lie.

"I must say," Jael interrupts. "We were surprised when you didn't come back with Kodiak yesterday."

"Luna had other duties to attend to." Kodiak glares at Jael.

"Right. Of course," Jael says, his eyes fixed on me. His are not a true gold like Kodiak's; they're more yellow, but even still they remind me of him. My heart pounds in my chest. Does he suspect the truth of what Kodiak and I are, or is he just trying to cast a cloud of doubt in a desperate power ploy? His eyes and words spin a spider's web that I must avoid. What would Rory do? She wouldn't like that Jael is here, undermining Kodiak's authority. She'd put him in his place. She always knew just how to do that.

"It's uncommon, though," Jael says after a moment's reflection. "I'm...*impressed* you could be away from Kodiak like that, considering you just mated."

He is questioning us, that's for sure. If it were just me and Kodiak here, I could let it slide as brotherly concern, but the fact that he's brought an audience into Kodiak's home—without Kodiak's permission—makes this a disrespectful attack. Kodiak is the Alpha. I don't understand why Jael thinks this sort of behavior is acceptable. I never would have done something like this to Rory had she become the Alpha Female of Dakota Ridge.

I think back on my time with Jael as a youth, when we were always seated together at dinner tables. Jael and I had the same standing—siblings to the heir—and putting him down, putting him in his "place," never crossed my mind. Now here he sits, as wide-legged and comfortable as if he owned the home, staring at us with cutting yellow eyes. What would Rory do?

I straighten my posture. "I had other obligations I was bound to. While it was difficult being away from Kodiak, we did what we had to," I say. I try to invoke the commanding tone Rory has when speaking to inferiors. "But of course we understand why it might seem so strange and confusing. None of you have ever been the Alpha or the heir, so you really couldn't understand what it means to put duty over desire."

Jael's eyes burn like an unnatural flame—too yellow to be a true fire.

"But Luna and I still have limits to our self-control," Kodiak adds. "And we were looking forward to being together this morning. *Alone.*"

The betas look to each other and to Jael, their conflicting loyalties obvious on their pathetic faces. Was Kodiak not clear? What is wrong with them? Why are they so insolent? Maybe it's because Kodiak has only been their Alpha for nine months? But no. That is no excuse. He's been their heir since birth. Jael's jaw is set, and I look at Kodiak to see an angry vein popping out of his neck.

"Let me be more clear," Kodiak says. "Get out of my house before I have to physically throw out your broken bodies myself."

Only then do the betas stand, offering apologies and well wishes. Jael gets up from his claimed throne with the speed of a chess king. Such insolence. "Sleep well, Kodiak," he says, offering no apology for his intrusion. He looks at me. "And Luna, welcome to Midnight River."

The tension in my muscles does not relax until they've all gone. I look to Kodiak, who has yet to let go of my hand. I pull mine from his and stand in front of him, searching his eyes. Their golden color has turned dull, as though the anger that burned him has left him barren.

"What's wrong with them?" I ask, my voice low and cold,

my nostrils flared. "You are the Alpha. How can they treat you like that?"

His eyes meet mine and he holds my gaze for several seconds before answering. "It will be nice to have...a partner. After all these years." The softest of smiles grazes his lips before he turns away and heads upstairs.

CHAPTER 18

YOU WOULDN'T
UNDERSTAND

That day Kodiak and I slept in the same bed. I thought about taking one of the several spare bedrooms, but I was afraid some unwanted visitor might show up and blow our story to bits. Kodiak's room befits an alpha, with dark furs draped about, scarlet red sheets, and a dark grey bedspread. After a full day's sleep, I'm still wrapped up in cozy covers while he takes a shower, planning how to avoid meeting as many people as possible. If Aspen and I—no, *when* Aspen and I get back together, it will be better that I avoided the Midnight River wolves.

Kodiak walks out of the bathroom, droplets of water dripping from his inky black hair. He wears only a towel around his waist, leaving little to the imagination.

"Moon, where are your clothes?" I ask, pulling the covers up to my chin as though his nakedness could expose my own.

Kodiak grins. "Better get used to the view, Luna." He holds his arms out to present himself like a trophy, and I thank the Moon above that his towel does not fall to the ground. "It's all yours, now."

"At least put some pants on," I grumble, turning my body away from him with a flop.

"Why, are you shy?" Kodiak lilts. I hear the soft thud of his towel dropping to the floor, followed by the sound of a creaky drawer opening. Whatever somber mood he was in last night has given way to unabashed brazenness.

"Shy?" I repeat, covering my head with the bedspread. "No. I just don't want to look at you waltzing around buck naked!"

He laughs and I hear the ruffle of fabric and a zip. "I'm decent now, Luna. You don't have to hide anymore."

But I'm comfortable in my cocoon of billowing sheets and blankets, if not a little hot. The mattress creaks and shifts as the weight of another person joins the bed, and I feel a tap on my shoulder through the covers surrounding me. "Luuunaaa," he says in that sing-song voice I know so well. "You can come out now."

I sigh and pull the blankets off my head. Kodiak's on his stomach and his face is hovering over mine. I see the extra bright flecks of gold in his eyes, the growing facial hair on his jaw, the pink in his smiling lips. I smell the soap on his skin and the mint from his toothpaste on his breath.

"Good morning, darling." His mouth pulls into a mischievous smile.

I smile back at him. "You don't have to call me that, you know, when no one is around."

He takes the strands of hair that have fallen out of my braid and wraps them around his finger. He doesn't say anything for a moment. "Then what should I call you?" he asks. "Puppykins?"

"Ew."

"My 'good girl'?"

"Awful."

"My goddess?"

"Well, I was named after the Moon, so that's not too bad," I tease.

The way Kodiak smiles at me stirs my heart, and for a moment I wish that we were real, that he had been the one on my balcony that night and that he would have accepted me. Maybe then I could have forgotten about Aspen. He'd be a silly memory instead of a powerful presence clouding my mind. But that rush of feeling on the balcony, that joy so full I thought I would burst—I've never felt that before, and if Aspen and I can't figure it out, I'll never feel that way again.

Kodiak's face stills. "You doing okay, Luna?"

His question catches me like fabric on a briar bush. "I...I guess so."

Kodiak twists to his side and rests his head on his arm, looking at me for several seconds.

"Why are you staring at me?" My voice and laugh are nervous.

"You were thinking about him, weren't you?" His voice comes out soft, almost sad.

I just look at him in return, my chest heaving with my breath.

"He's not worthy of you, you know," Kodiak says, his face inching closer. "He's an embarrassment, the lowliest of trash. Despicable."

I try to picture Aspen in a garish light instead of lovely rose. I think of him dating that human girl, Mousy, who I hated with all my heart. I think of how he rejected me, how he ignored me at school, how he didn't say goodbye when he left dinner—and yet, outside of his indifference to me, there is nothing so terrible about him. In fact, he hasn't even been indifferent. I think back on all his warm hugs, his bright smiles, his funny texts, his wise insights, his assurances that—at least in his own way—he loved me and was there for me. I wish he were some cruel monster that I could hate, but when I try to twist him into the villain that Rory and Kodiak are so sure he is, I can't quite snuff out all the light he's brought into my life.

My voice is quiet. "It would be easier if he really were so awful."

Kodiak's brows furrow, and his voice takes on an agitated tone. "What do you mean, 'if he were'?" His lip curls, revealing a long canine. "He rejected you! His mate. I mean that's like, I don't know, he's got to be evil or something."

"He is not evil."

"Are you sure about that?"

"Yes."

"Well, point him out to me, and I'll decide that for myself."

"No."

"Why are you protecting him?"

I turn away from Kodiak and untangle myself from the covers. Loose strands of my slept-in braid are slick against the back of my neck in this warm room. I stand up out of bed.

"Seriously, answer the question," Kodiak says. I don't like how he's demanding answers like this, that he can't let it be, and that he can't understand. "Why are you protecting that little mutt? Why do you care at all about his well-being?"

"You wouldn't understand, Kodiak," I say.

"Why you're hung up on a loser? You're right, I don't understand."

I whip around to face him. "He's not a loser!"

"Clearly he is, Luna!" Kodiak gets off the bed. "And he doesn't want to be with you, got it? So he's not worth any more tears."

His words sting me like a lash of a whip. *He doesn't want to be with you.* "You don't know what it's like."

"What it's like to love a loser? I sure don't."

I clench my jaw. Those vulnerable glimpses of Kodiak the past few days led me to believe he might understand, that there was some romanticism underneath his flashy exterior, but I was wrong. He's a fighter, an athlete, a leader—not a lover. He's never had a mate. Maybe the Moon gave him so many physical gifts without someone to call his own because that is who Kodiak is destined to be: a strong, Lone Wolf who doesn't need to rely on anyone. I envy him, that strength of body and mind that leaves him unaffected by the pathetic wiles of love. The only reason he's pretending to be my mate is to strengthen his position and to merge with Dakota Ridge.

"You don't understand what it's like to actually love someone like that," I say.

He scoffs. "I don't know what it's like?" He shakes his head, as though my words belong to a petulant child. "You know, I forget you're just a teenager. You think you're so special and unique."

"Well you don't know, Kodiak! You *actually* don't know! You've never had a mate. You don't know what that feels like, to find the one and have that taken from you."

"'Taken from you.'" Kodiak uses air quotation marks. "As in, he rejected you. This wasn't some slip of the rug or trick of the Moon. He. Chose. This. He chose to put you through this hell."

My eyes shine hot with angry tears—still embarrassing, but at least my face is fierce instead of pitiful. It's true, isn't it? Aspen did reject me. Aspen chose this fate for himself and for me, but with Kodiak yelling about it to me, I realize that I believe there is more to the story. Sure, I've felt plenty sorry for myself, I've felt humiliated and rejected, but Aspen isn't some merciless cartoon villain inflicting suffering for fun. I saw the guilt in his eyes and the sadness in his countenance. I know—

even if no one else does—that Aspen cares about me. He always has.

"It's not that simple," I hiss, angry tears streaking my cheeks.

Kodiak draws in a deep breath and releases it like a kettle letting out steam. His shoulders relax and his eyes soften as he looks at me. "It seems like it never is."

We don't say much else. I start getting ready for the night while Kodiak heads downstairs to start on breakfast. I can smell the sausage sizzling on the frying pan as I let out my braid and comb through my hair with my fingers, letting it fall into braid-made waves. There's still a red mark on my cheek from yesterday's cut. I'm wearing jean shorts and a white tank top with my usual white-gold jewelry when I come into the kitchen, my stomach gurgling at the smell of cooking meat.

"Someone's hungry," Kodiak says, flipping a fried egg with his spatula before serving sausage on a plate. He slides the plate across the granite countertop, and I'm grateful he's decided to feed me despite our argument.

I snatch a sausage link with the tips of my nails and take a bite. "Thanks."

"You're welcome, *my goddess*."

Despite our recent argument, I can't help but smile at the dramatic pet-name. His eyes light mischievously. When he's finished with the fried eggs, Kodiak joins me at the kitchen table and we eat kitty-corner from each other. I compliment his cooking, telling him I'm impressed he can make a fried egg on his own. He explains he lived on his own for a bit before becoming Alpha, and didn't have lower betas at his disposal to cook for him. As I'm shoveling another bite of food in, Kodiak stops mid-sentence. His ear twitches and he raises an eyebrow.

"What is it?" I ask. I haven't heard anything yet, but I hope whatever's caught Kodiak's attention is not Jael.

"My assistant is coming to the door," he answers. "He's young, but he's been my...secretary? I guess you could call him that. I made him my secretary right after I was appointed Alpha."

A knock clashes against the front door.

"Come in, Raulin!" Kodiak calls before taking a huge bite of his sausage. I hear the clicking turn of the handle and the padding of feet across the wooden floors, but it's his scent that catches my attention, one that is as shocking and noticeable as a scarlet dress at a funeral. My nose curls. There's something wrong with him.

Raulin enters the kitchen. He looks about my age, with floppy, fine brown hair and hazel eyes. He has a crooked nose and a few scars on his face and arms, probably from various scraps. He smiles at us, revealing the typical long canines. "Good evening, Alpha Kodiak." He bows his head at him and does the same to me. "Luna. It's a pleasure to meet you. I'm Raulin."

"Hello," I say, my voice taut. I can't figure out what's wrong with him. He smells unlike any werewolf I've ever encountered. Of course, everyone has a different scent, but his is one that feels so alien—and yet familiar.

Kodiak glances at me like he's trying to say something with his eyes, but for once I can't read them. Then he offers Raulin a seat at the table. Raulin's clutching one of those smart tablets in his hands and is explaining the pack's earnings and spendings last month, and I'd probably be more impressed that a wolf my age was placed in charge of the pack's budget if I wasn't so distracted by his smell. It almost reminds me of how Adam Douglas High smells, that conglomeration of leftover human smell and human teachers mixed with our scent. My heart freezes at the revelation. Oh moon. Raulin...he couldn't be, could he? If he is, why is he sitting across from the Alpha at his own kitchen table?

Raulin rakes a hand through his hair as he explains the increase of honey sales, brushing his hair back just enough to reveal ears with smooth, rounded curves. Stars, it is true! Raulin is a half-breed! What is a half-human, half-werewolf doing here at the Alpha House? And as Kodiak's secretary? He's got to be below even the Midnight River omegas! I have so many questions. How did he come to exist, what is his role in the pack, how come I've never heard of him, and why is Kodiak associating with him? But I don't demand an explanation right here, right now, because it could undermine Kodiak's authority in front of an inferior.

And unlike his brother, I don't want to do that.

Raulin's eyes flicker towards me, catching my unabashed stare, before he refocuses on his tablet. "We could afford to decrease…" His voice trails off and he fidgets in his seat. "We could afford to decrease spending in gasoline, since ATVs aren't strictly necessary. We could use our savings to allot more towards Blue Month festivities. And…" Raulin looks right at me. "I know you must have questions."

He's taken me by surprise. "About the gasoline?"

"No. About me. You can tell, can't you?" He tucks some loose hair behind his soft, human ears. "You can tell I'm half human."

I won't lie to him. "It's the way you smell."

"So I've been told. You're alpha-blooded too, so your nose is better than most."

If I were Rory, I'd probably ask Kodiak why he is working so closely with a mutt, but it feels wrong to demand such answers with the half-breed staring straight at me.

"How old are you?" I ask.

"I turned eighteen in April."

He's my age. I should have met him in school. I know a lot of the night class by name and the rest by their face or smell, and I couldn't have missed the stench of a half-breed. "I am also eighteen," I say. "How have we never met?"

To my surprise, a wry smile rises on Raulin's face. "I'm not exactly Midnight River's pride and joy."

I furrow my brow. That still doesn't explain—

"And I went to school with humans," he continues. "I didn't go to the night class."

A pack member of Midnight River, attending high school with humans? Aspen may have spent time with humans—even dated them—but at least he was never so shameful as to forsake werewolves for human school. Then again, Aspen isn't a half-breed.

"I see. How was that?" I ask.

"Good." Raulin shrugged. "Pretty different from the night class, from what I've heard. This past year, all the human seniors have been stressing about getting into college and whatnot."

"Yeah, that's definitely not on any of our minds."

He laughs. "Yeah...secondary education isn't exactly a werewolf priority."

It's hardly a thought, much less a priority.

"I'm going to college, though," Raulin says.

"You are?" My nose wrinkles. "Why?"

He laughs like I've said something funny. "Kodiak made the same face when I told him."

"Yeah, I don't get it." Kodiak shrugs. "Sounds like a crap time, but I suppose his half-human side makes it possible, I don't know."

"Don't you have to pay for it?" I ask. The money werewolves make from selling goods and taking odd jobs only goes so far, so I can't imagine a bigger waste of money than paying to go to school. You might as well use cash for bonfire kindling.

"Sort of," Raulin says. "But I have a scholarship. There are tons of grants and scholarships available for students with werewolf heritage since almost no one uses them."

I'm not sure if I should congratulate him or offer him my condolences. "Well that's...I don't know. That's nice I guess."

Raulin chuckles and Kodiak guffaws. "See, my bride understands!" Kodiak says, slapping a hand against my back.

As the sun sets behind the large glass windows, Raulin finishes his financial report before going over our schedule. Today, Kodiak's supposed to hold his weekly petition hours in the Town Hall, and afterwards, we'll have dinner with Kodiak's family at his parents' current residence.

I'm anxious for Raulin to leave so I can ask Kodiak all about him and how his existence came to be. As soon as he's out the door, Kodiak says, "I know. You're curious about him."

"Am I that obvious?"

"Naw, not really. Way less obvious than most." Kodiak grabs our dirty plates and brings them to the kitchen sink. "I just figured you must be wondering."

"Well you're right on that one." I lean forward against the granite kitchen island as he starts running the hot water. "This whole time you all had some secret half-breed running around?"

"Yeah, I know. Pretty scandalous." He grins, scrubbing the grime off a plate. "Obviously, this all happened like eighteen years ago."

"Is his dad a human, or his mom?"

"Dad. His mom was born and raised here in Midnight River. She was one of our Omega Daughters."

"Figures," I scoff. It would be an omega that would fool around with a human.

"You know what it's like, being an omega." He glances over at me. "Well, maybe you don't."

"Stars, you act like I don't come from a functioning pack."

"Oh, I know you do. That's why you don't really know what it's like," Kodiak says. "Honestly, I probably don't know that much either, us being at the top and all, but you know...we can imagine it really freaking sucks. Everyone crappin' on you all the time, taking out their problems on you. So Raulin's mom, Mina, was born to the Omegas. Her best hope was mating with some mid beta, but chances were she'd be the next Omega. Anyway—and keep in mind, I'm like four when all this was happening so I've gathered most of this after-the-fact—Mina apparently met some human kid at school. She had gone super early to school that day for some reason and he had extracurricular activities and they ran into each other."

Kodiak places the washed plates in the dish rack and starts on cleaning the frying pan. "I guess they fell in love. Or something. At least, she fell in love with him. She'd sneak out to see him, blah blah. Her parents didn't really stop it." Then Kodiak's scrubbing slows and his voice softens. "The human boy was kind to her. More kind than any of us were." He resumes his normal pace and cadence. "Anyways, most of the pack had no idea that Mina had a human lover, but when she got pregnant at seventeen, it was a huge uproar of course. She didn't have a mate, and now she was pregnant."

It is the ultimate taboo, giving your body to someone before you find your mate. Sex before that point is an enormous betrayal, but conceiving or siring a child forfeits your opportunity altogether to find a mate.

"So obviously everyone knew she was locked in to be the next Omega Female," Kodiak says. "And everyone was trying to figure out who the father was. Who in our pack had done this to poor Mina? Taken advantage of a naïve Omega Daughter?

Or was it someone from another pack?" Kodiak sighs. "When they found out it was a human...I mean, I'm glad I'm too young to remember what that was like. Probably was horrible." He shakes his head. Kodiak turns off the sink and starts drying the plates with a hand towel. He looks at me as he leans back against the sink. "Raulin's dad was also seventeen, and you know how human teenagers are. They're like little children in their culture. Not even thinking about marriage or family until way down the road, so he was freaking out, and Midnight River was freaking out. But once everyone calmed down a bit, it was decided Mina would be the one to raise the baby and we would all be there for her. In our own way. You know how it is."

Every pack may have a strict hierarchy and clear roles, but we're all there for each other. We rally around our own. Omegas might have to deal with more grunt work than most, but no one is ever abandoned. No one ever goes without. We take care of each other.

"So yeah. Raulin, our little half-breed, was born, and it was a huge deal for the pack." A mischievous smile grows on his face. "But hey, if you and I get caught in our lie, at least it won't be Midnight River's first scandal."

My stomach curdles. I don't want to be associated with a scandal like Mina's in any way, shape, or form.

"I can't believe she'd do that, get that close to a human," I say. Aspen and his stupid human girlfriend pop in my brain. I know he still felt iced out, but I wonder if Aspen knows just how much I shielded him from everyone's spite while he dated her. Glares and snarky comments were nothing compared to the claws and teeth I spared him from. "I mean, she got pregnant by one," I amend. Going out with a human was bad enough, but carrying a human's child?

"Oh, make no mistake, Midnight River is to blame," Kodiak says, placing the dried plates in the cupboard.

"Yeah, yeah. 'The strongest is ours, the weakest is ours,'" I recite. We had to say that all the time growing up. It's the idea that we all bear the responsibility for the shortcomings of our weakest pack members, and that we all share in the glory of our strongest.

Kodiak laughs. "It's more than that, Luna." He shuts the cupboard door and faces me. "At least, in this case it is." His eyes, so expressive, look a bit sad. "We drove her to him, to that human boy. We didn't take care of Mina like we should have. If we'd treated her better, things would have been different for her." He sighs. "But we didn't, so we all have to live with that."

Nova comes to mind for some reason. Of course, she's nowhere near Raulin's social pariah status, but there were some comments when I first started spending time with a low beta like her. Stuff about her status, stuff about her brother.

"But Raulin himself is a great kid," Kodiak says. "He's real smart, good with numbers. Probably that human brain." He taps his head. "I'll miss him when he leaves, but he's probably going to be happier with the humans."

"Yeah," I say. I'm not sure what I think of it all. It's a lot to take in. "Probably."

Kodiak steps up to me and plants a kiss on the top of my head.

My eyes widen. "What was that for?"

He laughs. "You can't look so blushy over something like that." But he looks quite pleased as he takes my hand and pulls me towards the front door. "We're supposed to have done a lot more than that, remember?" He winks.

I roll my eyes. "You just caught me off guard, that's all."

"Well, it's time to get on your guard, my darling goddess." Kodiak opens the door. "Because we're about to face the wolves."

CHAPTER 19
UNKNOWN SIDES

Midnight River's paths are lined with solar lights staked into the ground, providing a warm glow as we make our way to the heart of the pack.

"You can join me today during my petition hours," Kodiak says, squeezing my hand with a grin. "I don't usually get too many people, but more might come now that you'll be with me. Plus, with the Blue Month, people are bound to be upset over some petty decoration or something."

Dad also holds petition hours in Dakota Ridge's Town Hall, when pack members come forward with grievances for Dad to address. Mom often accompanied him before she got Lycan-throma. Sitting next to Kodiak to help guide his pack is about the last thing I want to do. It will only make things worse when our ruse is dismantled.

"About that," I start. "I know we're...*mates* and all, but I'm not the Alpha Female of Midnight River yet."

He furrows his brow. "I mean, I guess not technically. But you basically are."

There's not a lot of precedent for this situation, since most heirs already have a mate by the time they become the official Alpha. During that ceremony, his mate is crowned Alpha Female alongside him.

"I won't be the Alpha Female until the wedding," I say. In situations where very young heirs become Alpha due to an unexpected death, their mate is crowned at the wedding. "So maybe we should hold off on me doing Alpha Female things until then."

His eyes turn suspicious as a hint of glow lights them up.

"Otherwise, what's the point of the whole passing-the-mantle, crowning ceremony?" I argue. "Some might think it's pretentious."

"I highly doubt anyone is going to pitch a fit if my mate accompanies me to petition."

"I'm still an outsider," I push back.

Kodiak snorts. "You're literally from Dakota Ridge. You're basically from our backyard, not outer space."

"You know how packs are. We like to keep to our own." I think about the fight at school yesterday. The way that scrappy wolf jumped to Kodiak's defense by coming for my proverbial throat. I don't know how Kodiak would feel about Midnight River and Dakota Ridge wolves getting into a fight over us.

"Well then they're going to have to get over that," Kodiak says. "You're my mate now, which means you're their Alpha." I'm not sure how I'll convince him to let this go, but he continues, "That being said, I get if you're hesitant to start that up today. You still need to get to know Midnight River better. We can wait on petition until after the wedding."

Relief washes over me. "Okay, I think that's a good idea. Thank you."

Soon we hear the echoes of a bustling pack enjoying their Saturday night. The sounds of little feet pounding against the dirt road, a pup crying over a game of claw tag gone wrong, the chatter of wolves swapping the latest news. There's the wafting smell of breakfast skewers cooking over smokey campfire wood amidst the muted scents of earth and trees. When we walk into the clearing, several of the pups nearby abandon their game of claw tag to run up to us.

"Alpha Kodiak!" they cry, slapping the hands Kodiak holds out for high-fives. They look at him with a mix of excitement and awe.

"Cal, Nara, Clover, Zev..." Kodiak rattles off the kids' names one by one as he high fives them. Their love and admiration for Kodiak radiates from them, clear as a scent. Maybe last night's intrusion with Jael and the other high betas only represents a fluke faction.

"This is Luna." Kodiak presents me to the pups with one hand on my back. "She's the current heir of Dakota Ridge, and now she's my mate."

"I heard you had a mate now!" One of the little boys cries. His hair is sticking out all over the place. "That's awesome!" Most of the pups are offering their congratulations, save for a couple of broken-hearted looking ten-year-old girls. Soon we're attracting the teens and adults of Midnight River, and as we make our way to the Town Hall, I'm shaking hands and receiving congratulations over and over again. So much for my low profile. I recognize a lot of the wolves who look around my age, but the rest are mostly strangers. We walk on the main road past a little bakery, a small motel, and a stand selling breakfast skewers. The building roofs are lined with bulbs of warm yellow light that remind me of huge fireflies. Crisscrossing strings hang over the road, tied between buildings and holding up blue crescent moons and other hand-painted banners to celebrate the Blue Month.

My eyebrows shoot up when I spot Scrappy Rude Boy, the instigator of yesterday's fight. He's watching us from behind the corner of the general store, an embarrassed look painting his features. Kodiak glances over and smiles widely. "Finn!" he calls, waving him over. Scrappy Rude Boy looks surprised, but he comes up to us. Kodiak places a hand on his shoulder. "Finn, this is my mate, Luna. Luna, this is Finn. He's got a lot of heart. He'll make a great hunter when he gets older."

Scrappy Rude Boy—or rather Finn—seems like an entirely different wolf from the one I met yesterday. Gone is his spitfire spunk, replaced with a slight blush and guilty gaze as his eyes flick to the cut on my cheek. But when he looks at Kodiak...oh, there it is. There's this sparkle of pride in his eyes and that same clear sense of admiration that I recognized in the children. I wonder why Kodiak called this boy over, why he shows a lower beta like Finn such warmth and favor—but it explains why Finn was so insolent yesterday, why he took it upon himself to call me out and defend his Alpha. Kodiak is, without a doubt, Finn's hero. He looks at Kodiak like he could save the world.

"It's nice to meet you, Finn," I say. He called me a mutt yesterday. He started a fight that I needed Aspen's help to end. And yet, I feel a strange hint of affection for him that I did not have moments ago. The way Kodiak treats him, the way he treats Kodiak...what would it be like to inspire such admiration and warm loyalty, rather than shallow, distant fealty? A small smile rises on my face. "I think I've seen you around Adam Douglas."

His smile is sheepish. "Yeah, I've seen you around too. Especially since you're the Dakota Ridge heir and all." He pauses a moment. "It's good to see you here with Alpha Kodiak."

"You're going to love Finn," Kodiak tells me. "He's got a lot of fight in him." He tousles Finn's hair before we move forward. We don't make it far until some wolf comes up to us and claps a hand on Kodiak's back. It takes me a second to recognize him with his beard, but I used to see him around school. He's a year older than me and is a mid beta, if I'm remembering right. I'm surprised at his familiarity with Kodiak—I don't remember him being very remarkable—but maybe that's how Kodiak is. Super friendly with inferiors, like Finn.

"Kodiak!" the mid beta says. "Finally graduating from werewolf *boy,* after all this time!"

My eyes widen so much that I feel a strain before I try to look normal. What is this sort of behavior? Calling him 'Kodiak' instead of 'Alpha Kodiak'? Insinuating that he is only *now* fully grown, when Kodiak is four years his senior and his Alpha? I try to picture anyone in my pack speaking to Dad that way, and find that my imagination is drawing a blank. I wonder if this wolf is some friend of Kodiak's, a charitable cause like Raulin or Finn, but the look in Kodiak's eye leads me to believe otherwise. He looks frustrated, maybe even embarrassed.

That wolf is not the only one who makes a strange comment. One of the male wolves says, "Alright, alright. We'll let you grow a beard, now," to Kodiak. His tone is in jest, but the suggestion that they can tell him what he can and cannot do with his own hair is highly offensive. Inappropriate comments continue—one joking that the pack is saved, another laughing that Kodiak must not have a secret love child after all, and more comments on Kodiak's hint of facial hair. We're almost to the Town Hall when a mid beta says, "We finally have a real Alpha!"

That's when I snap.

"Excuse you?" I whip my whole body to face him, some bearded twerp who couldn't be more than twenty. I think I've seen him at school. "Who do you think you are?"

His face blanches as I step right up to him, my eyes blazing like purple stars in the night. I know the ears of a hundred wolves are tuned into this moment, but I'm so upset I don't care.

"You are talking about the victor of the Heir Trials here, your *Alpha*. And Alpha Kodiak is more than a real Alpha, with or without me. So why don't you show some respect before he makes you show it?" I didn't even have to ask myself *what would Rory do?* This wolf's disrespect was so nauseating that I threw it all up without having to think about it.

"I'm...I'm sorry." He looks like a frightened doe as his eyes flick between me and Kodiak. "I didn't mean it like that. I meant no disrespect, Alpha Kodiak."

"Try harder next time," Kodiak says, putting a hand on my shoulder and leading me away from the twerp. As soon as we walk into the Town Hall, I want to explode and rage against the nonsense from outside. I want to ask Kodiak what's wrong with him, why he didn't shut down every one of those comments. I want to tell him that the golden boy Kodiak I grew up with would never have allowed such insolence. But we're not alone.

We're in the Town Hall's reception room, facing a half-circle mahogany desk. Raulin is there, smiling at us from behind the desk, but it's the she-wolf sitting in a waiting chair that puts me on edge. She has slicked-back blonde hair and cat-like eyes that are green enough to indicate she's got some alpha heritage in her. The sweet baby pup in her arms doesn't hide the sharpness to her smile.

"Long time no see," Kodiak says to Raulin, chuckling at his own joke. Then he turns to the she-wolf with the baby and offers her a brisk nod. "Alena."

"Jael's in the office," Alena says.

"I know."

"Fang was getting fussy." She's bouncing that chubby little pup on her leg. I'd forgotten that Jael had a baby. He's probably around one year old.

Kodiak's smile widens as he looks at little Fang, and even though I'm no fan of Jael's, I have to admit that Fang's a pretty dang cute baby. "It's because he's been missing his uncle," Kodiak says, walking up to the baby and giving him his finger to hold. "Isn't that right, Fang?"

"You make a great babysitter," Alena says. The lack of warmth in her tone makes it seem like a dig, one that snarls in my heart. The Moon really outdid herself with Jael and Alena. She really found two of the most spiteful wolves and brought them together. Alena's probably upset that Fang isn't going to be the next Alpha of Midnight River.

Kodiak doesn't seem to notice Alena's sourpuss attitude and takes Fang from her. "Hi buddy!" His voice goes high and babyish. "How's it going, snugglebear?"

"Don't call him that," Alena snaps, standing up and snatching her baby back. "Fang is a warrior."

"Fang is an infant," I say.

Kodiak laughs. "Well, it's always a pleasure to see you, Alena, but people are going to be coming in soon, and I don't need you or Jael's help with petition hours." He puts an arm around me. "Also, you haven't even said hi to my lovely mate, Luna."

Alena adjusts how she's holding Fang, her face pinching at the sting of chastisement. "Hello. I'm Alena. I'm Jael's mate."

"I gathered that." A slow smile crawls up my face. "I'm Luna, daughter of Alpha Orion and heir to Dakota Ridge. I'm looking forward to being your Alpha Female." I know I shouldn't say that, because I'm not really going to be Midnight River's Alpha Female, but—*moon* is she obnoxious. She, Jael, and half the pack could stand to lose their attitude.

Jael saunters out of one of the closed doors, presumably leading to some office or conference room. "Kodiak, Luna. It's great to see you two," he says. I wish I could say the same—but then again, I guess I could if I wanted to lie like he just did. "You two are coming to dinner tonight, right?" Jael asks.

More than anything, I'm dreading this family dinner with Kodiak's parents and Jael's annoying family. It's a huge shovelful of this trench of a lie we're digging.

"Probably," Kodiak says. Who knew that a semi-noncommittal word could sound better than a choir of songbirds? "Probably" is not "definitely."

"Probably?" Jael repeats.

"Yeah," Kodiak says. "Anyways, I'm going to show Luna around the Town Hall, but you all take care of yourselves." Kodiak snags my hand and leads me through the big French doors into the large part of the Town Hall, allowing the doors to swing shut behind him.

"So annoying." His whisper is so quiet I doubt they'll be able to hear it. "Welcome to the Town Hall!" He speaks normally. "This is probably where we'll get married."

Married. We're supposed to have the wedding in a couple of weeks. I never imagined I'd feel so queasy about my own wedding. I feel the loss of what should have been sparkling anticipation.

We strut around the ballroom-type area, mostly waiting for Jael and Alena to leave, before entering the office-type space again.

"Thank the Moon they're gone," Kodiak says when we walk back in. Raulin wears a funny smile. "I know, Raulin," Kodiak says. "They suck."

He shows me the various offices and the fancy meeting room where he'll be holding petition. "The doors are 'sound-proof.'" He uses air quotation marks. "For privacy."

It's not long before pack members start showing up to meet with Kodiak. Because I'm sitting in a chair in the lobby, I have to make small talk with some of them, but the homework on my lap deters most of them from starting a conversation. As much as the schoolwork irritates me, I'm grateful for it. It somewhat keeps my mind off my life and Aspen.

I snap my chemistry book closed and sigh, squeezing my eyes shut against the mental imprint of the periodic table. I hate chemistry. I hate solving the stupid little equations. I hate all the numbers looming at me—a final homework sheet to prepare for our final.

"I hate this sapcrap," I mutter, dragging my face down with my hands. The door Kodiak sits behind is mostly soundproof, but I can make out the muffled voices if I really pay attention. An older she-wolf is complaining about some pup who's been stealing her eggs. Apparently, she's been raising these chickens for a long time and—

"Whatcha working on?" Raulin says, drawing my attention.

"Chemistry," I say.

"Looks like you're having a blast."

I grimace.

Raulin laughs and hops out of his swivel chair. "Let me help you," he says, coming from behind the desk and plopping down next to me. I'm not sure how I feel about a half-breed like Raulin treating me with such familiarity, telling me that *he* will help *me*, and yet, something akin to déjà vu aches in my chest. Raulin reminds me of Aspen; there's no way around it. Aspen had a confidence in himself that outweighed any apprehension he might have felt about my being the Alpha Daughter, a confidence that allowed him to see right through me. As Raulin sits next to me, helping me through my worksheet, I feel the strange comfort of a friend. Maybe I shouldn't feel this way. Perhaps I am so weak that he sees me not as an alpha, but merely a sheep in wolf's clothing.

I need to stop such musings. I should just focus on my homework.

We work through the problems, and when I get stuck, Raulin gently guides me through the steps I need to take. I feel awkward when the egg lady comes out of her petition with Kodiak and gives us a side eye, but Kodiak's smile makes me feel better. He asks us how the homework is coming along and assures me that Raulin is a whiz with all that nonsense. Soon Kodiak is back in his room for another round of petition with another she-wolf, and Raulin and I are back to chemistry. When we finish the last problem, I breathe a sigh of relief and say, "Thank the Moon it's over," before I realize that my brain now has space for all my thoughts—being here in Midnight River, my inadequacies as an alpha-blooded, my broken dreams with Aspen.

"You know, I'm glad you're here." Raulin interrupts my mental spiral. "Here with Kodiak."

I'm surprised by his sudden statement. "Oh, yeah. I'm glad I'm here too," I lie. The longer I'm here, the more impossible my predicament becomes—and the worse I make things for Kodiak.

"Are things very different here from Dakota Ridge?" he asks.

I'm not sure where Raulin is going with this conversation, but I'll run with it. I could use more information about Midnight River, about what's wrong with the wolves here. Sure, Kodiak is a Lone Wolf, but that alone can't justify everyone's behavior towards him. I start packing up my homework. "In many ways, it's similar," I tell him, shutting my textbook. "But..." How do I say this without embarrassing Kodiak to an inferior? "The way Kodiak's brother talks to him...the way the betas...it's just, it's different. The wolves here are more, uh..." Disrespectful? Completely and utterly insolent? "Casual, I guess." I shove my books into my backpack.

Raulin looks me over in a way that tells me he knows what

I'm really insinuating. He sighs. "They treat him that way because he's a Lone Wolf." He gestures at me. "At least, they thought he was."

"But he's still the Alpha," I say. Being a Lone Wolf is a pitiable fate for any wolf, but that doesn't change the fact that Kodiak is the Alpha. There has to be more to their insolence.

"He almost wasn't," Raulin says.

My eyebrows lift. "What do you mean?"

Raulin scans me over as though he's assessing how much he should tell me. "I suppose since you're his mate..." he says. Raulin leans his head against the wall, looking up at some past I do not know. "Everyone loved Kodiak growing up. He was like the sun or something, I don't know. Everyone revolved around him. He was stronger and faster and had sharper senses than any of the other packs' heirs. The first two years after Kodiak turned eighteen, everyone was excited about who he was going to mate with, since she'd be our future Alpha Female. A lot of people thought it would be..." He casts a swift glance at me, then looks away again. "Well, that doesn't matter, because then people started to wonder if there'd be a future alpha female at all. Some felt it wasn't right to have a Lone Wolf for an Alpha, assuming he was one." He pauses. "Then, Jael turned eighteen and found his mate that very same day." Raulin's lip curls. It seems he's about as fond of Jael as I am. "Some thought it was a sign from the Moon, that Jael was supposed to be the next Alpha. So when Kodiak's father passed down the mantle of Alpha to Kodiak anyway, there were many who disagreed with the decision. They felt that they were being led by someone... incomplete. Someone who, by tradition, shouldn't even grow his facial hair. They considered him defunct and insufficient." Raulin is staring at the ground with a glare that could burn.

"People have speculated, of course, why he might be a Lone Wolf. Some thought that it was the price for his gifts. The

Moon blessed him with so much strength, she had to take some-thing away. Or the other way around. Because he was not blessed with a mate, she gave him the strength of two. Those people argued that Kodiak was more than enough to lead Midnight River. Those people still love him—are *still* fiercely protective of him." I think of scrappy Finn, the way his eyes burned at me during school when he thought I was doing Kodiak wrong. He was right, unfortunately. I am doing Kodiak wrong. The more Raulin explains, the sicker I feel.

Raulin's eyes glaze over. "Others didn't see it that way. Some speculated he had a secret child, which was why Moon had taken away his mate. Many blamed..." he pauses. "Well, whatever their reasoning, many still think Jael should be Alpha." Then, a smile. A look my way. "At least, that's what they thought before you showed up."

I'm sure my smile is as weak as my stomach feels. "Yeah. I guess we can put all those rumors to rest."

We sit there in silence, with only muffled snippets of Kodi-ak's conversation to pull my mind away. I feel completely awful. This whole time, Kodiak has been under such scrutiny for being a Lone Wolf—and now when it seems his problems are solved, I'm supposed to sweep the rug out from under him? Make everything a hundred times worse? Moon, how did I get myself into this mess?

"I know someone from Dakota Ridge," Raulin says. He must feel the need to make conversation.

"Do you?" I refrain from rolling my eyes. Of course he knows someone from Dakota Ridge, he lives just—but wait, no. He's an actual mutt. A student of the human side of Adam Douglas. Who would hang around him?

Oh. The answer hits me half a second before Raulin says it.

"Yeah. Do you know Aspen?"

Somehow, I manage to feel even worse. I'm so glad Kodiak

isn't in the room, listening to my heartbeat increase, smelling the sweat threatening to form on my temples.

"Aspen?" I ask. "Yeah, I know him." Would Kodiak hear that my casual tone is forced, or does he lack the ability to detect lies?

"Makes sense." Raulin laughs to himself in a way that does not seem at all forced. "Stupid question. Obviously you know him." His laughter feels like a taunt. *Obviously you know him. He rejected you.* "Do you talk with him much?"

I resist the urge to grit my teeth against his questions. "Well, yes. His father is my dad's right-hand wolf. He and his family are high betas."

"No way, really?" Raulin looks surprised. "I didn't even know he was upper beta, let alone high." His wide eyes return to normal and his brow crinkles a moment before he smiles. "Then again, I guess it makes sense he didn't tell me. That's how he is."

There's something frustrating in the way Raulin talks about Aspen, like he knows him so well and I'm just the casual acquaintance. I never knew Aspen was friends with a half-breed; but then again, Raulin was likely part of Aspen's human experiences that I had wanted no part of.

"How do you know him?" I ask, because the only thing I want more than to stop talking about Aspen is to talk about Aspen.

"Mutual friends," Raulin says. "Not werewolf ones though, ironically. He was dating a human friend of mine."

Ugh. Her.

"A bunch of us went out for food one day and my friend was bringing her new boyfriend along. When Aspen walked up to the table, he looked straight at me. He must have smelled something was off immediately and asked me if I was part werewolf." There's a smile on Raulin's face. "And you know, that was the only time I'd been asked that by a werewolf who didn't look at all...you know, off-put. He smiled at me. Like a real smile. He told me that was cool." He chuckles to himself. "Can you imagine that? 'Cool.' A werewolf telling me it was cool to be half-human? And apparently a high beta at that."

I say nothing, only picturing the scene in my mind. Aspen's easy smile, his kind, simple answer to a boy who was a stain on his pack's pride, a tucked-away shame.

"He's probably my best friend," Raulin says. "At the very least, he's my best werewolf friend."

It's strange to me that this is Aspen—*my Aspen*—that we're talking about. This boy who claims Aspen as a best friend is someone who, before today, I did not know existed. I thought Aspen and I were close—that if nothing else, he and I were true, best friends—and yet he never mentioned Raulin. I think of my first reaction to seeing Raulin, the way my stomach curdled and how I didn't understand why Kodiak would even associate with him. Ah. I suppose that's why Aspen never mentioned him to me. He must have known me well enough to know I wouldn't look fondly on someone like Raulin. For some reason, I feel ashamed.

"Do you guys talk much?" I ask Raulin.

"Yeah," he says. "Lately we haven't seen too much of each other, but we keep up over text."

"Really?" My voice borders on dull, but my eyes must be alight as I look at Raulin. He's not just Kodiak's half-breed secretary, but a messenger, a bridge to Aspen I can cross now that we've destroyed ours. It's not as if I have no way to contact Aspen—I have his number, I know where he lives—but it feels like I can't, that I must wait for him to initiate contact. But now, here is Raulin. "How has Aspen been?" I'm casual as can be, sitting back without a care in the world, making small talk about some mutual acquaintance.

"Good," Raulin shrugs. "Busy."

"End of the school year," I mutter.

"Yeah."

I crave more information than the three words on how Aspen's doing. *Is Aspen upset about me? Is he struggling with all this half as much as I am? Has he told you about me at all?* But I don't know how I can ask anything more.

The she-wolf comes out of Kodiak's office. "And you'll talk to the boy about it?" She's looking for confirmation.

"I will, Ana. Promise," Kodiak says, giving her a comforting pat on the shoulder. Ana almost deflates in a sigh of relief. Then, she glances at me and back to Kodiak. I wonder if she's going to say something about why I'm sitting next to a half-breed.

Instead, she whispers, "she's very pretty."

Kodiak grins. "She is."

As soon as Ana leaves, Kodiak stretches his arms up towards the ceiling, lacing his fingers together and yawning. "Petition is done for the day."

"Good job," I say.

Raulin claps.

"Thank you, thank you very much." Kodiak bows three times in different directions to us and his invisible audience. "Well, that's a wrap for all of us. You're free to go home too, Raulin." Kodiak walks up to me and offers a hand. "And you get to come home with me, darling."

As Kodiak and I walk back towards the Alpha House, I notice the sky is a lighter shade of blue. The sun will be up in a couple of hours. Kodiak is smiling at everyone as he passes and calling them by name, one hand waving and the other holding mine. I think back on my conversation with Raulin. There are sides to both Aspen and Kodiak that I haven't known, revealed to me by a half-breed I would have overlooked.

As I watch the smile on Kodiak's face, my heart aches. He's such a good alpha. His love for his pack—even for the outcasts like Raulin—radiates from him. He's strong, confident, and capable, yet under constant scrutiny for some trick of fate he could not control. So now he's taken fate into his own hands. Now he has me. Now they're going to respect him. And now I'm going to let him down.

CHAPTER 20

LONE WOLF
SEVERAL YEARS AGO

It's a fragment of a memory, perhaps one made up from a hundred similar moments. I was tucked snugly in bed, my mother sitting beside me with her halo of blonde hair and soft grey eyes. As she caressed my hair, I asked for just one more song before I went to sleep.

She smiled, and I knew she'd cave in. She always did. "Alright, Lulu. Just one more." Her voice was gentle and soothing. "Which song do you want?"

"Lone Wolf," I said. It was one of my favorites. I liked its haunting tune, and Mom could sing so beautifully.

"The Blue Moon was bright," she sang.

"We heard his howl that night.

A solo amidst duets,

A mate he never met.

His song upon a hill,

We feel its eerie chill."

She squeezed my little arm as she stood to leave.

"And though night turned to day,

His world remained forever gray."

CHAPTER 21

CURSED DESTINY

Kodiak doesn't let go of my hand, not even when we're out of sight from the rest of the pack. For him, our upcoming marriage isn't just a cardboard house built to last a few days. He is planning to start a real life and marriage with me, so to him, holding hands is probably the least he can do to show that commitment. I remember learning about human history in social studies, about how their royalty participated in arranged marriages based on politics instead of love. Those marriages were considered as real and valid as any other in the sight of their God. Some of them even grew to love each other. Would the outcome be the same with me and Kodiak, should we go through with this? But no, we can't go through with it, can we? If I give up Aspen, I'll never feel the love of a true mate bond again. How could I forsake that feeling?

"I have a crazy idea," Kodiak says, swinging my hand as we walk.

"What's that?" I ask.

"We skip dinner with my parents and Jael, and instead, I show you someplace kind of cool. What do you think?"

"I think that the best crazy idea I've ever heard."

Kodiak laughs. "Guess I don't have to convince you. Well, I get it. Jael's a huge pain in the tail."

"You can say that again."

"Alena's not much better either."

"The two were made for each other."

Kodiak guffaws. "You know, I think the exact same thing!"

When we get back to the main house, Kodiak drops my backpack off inside and grabs his car keys.

"We're going in the truck?" I ask as he holds open the passenger door.

"Makes it more of an adventure." He winks.

The truck sputters as Kodiak turns on the ignition. Kodiak peels out of the driveway and we make our way down the wooded dirt road until we reach the paved road, with towering pine trees on one side and a dark ocean on the other. A dark blue sky promises the light that will soon come with sunrise. Kodiak parks in a dirt overlook and jumps out of the car. I follow his lead and peer over the edge to see a rocky beach and a quaint little house built against the cliff.

"Come with me," Kodiak says, his smile wide enough to show off his canines. He offers me his hand and he leads me down a thin, rocky trail full of switchbacks until we reach the house. It's small—a one-story house of glass and wooden planks, perched on a shorter cliff jutting from the main rock wall. There's no sidewalk leading to the entrance, just trampled-down vegetation, and Kodiak lets go of my hand to pull keys from his pocket and open the front door. "Come on in," he says, smiling like a wolf boy who's brought home his first deer.

The home is small. It's draped in a dozen fur pelts for carpet. It boasts hodgepodge furniture: a rickety table, a plaid couch, a metal framed twin bed. The kitchen is little more than a corner with a refrigerator, microwave, sink, and hotplate.

Overall, the decor is pretty awful, but floor-to-ceiling windows make up the western wall of the house, showcasing the beach and the ocean. I pad across the hides of a moose, a bear, and several deer until I'm a foot away from those windows.

The view is breathtaking, even in the night. Ocean waves crash against a beach made of black rocks and sand. A canopy of stars twinkles in the sky. Sunsets from this view must be something to behold.

"Wow," I whisper.

Kodiak walks up to the windows, stopping a few feet to my left. I feel his eyes on me for a moment before he looks out towards the ocean.

"What is this place?" I ask.

"It's my house," Kodiak says. "Or at least, it was. I started building it a few years ago, when I was twenty and still just the heir. I wanted my own place not under my parents' roof."

Different packs have different expectations about moving out. Some packs have a culture of never moving out, of staying within the ancestral home until it's so crowded someone is forced to leave. In other packs, like Dakota Ridge and Midnight River, wolves stay with their parents until they find their mate. I wonder if this was yet another controversy surrounding Kodiak, that he'd chosen to leave before he found a mate.

"Your house is far away from the heart of your pack," I note, glancing over at him. His eyes are transfixed by the ocean.

"I know," he says. There's a pause. "I wanted to be close to the water."

"I can see why." The sound of the ocean waves crashing against the shore, the melodic, rhythmic pulse of the water, the steady assurance that the waves will always come and go—things I've always loved about the ocean. And for all the allure of the sea, perhaps its distance from the pack had its own appeal.

"Of course, once I became Alpha, I had to move back into the main house, but sometimes I like coming back here. Helps me think." He turns to me. "Well, what do you say? Should we go down to the beach?"

I keep my white tank top on, but Kodiak has brought me a spare pair of swimming trunks to replace my jean shorts. I have to cinch the trunks with a tight knot, and I hate how loose everything feels without my underwear, but it's better than diving in with jeans and sneakers. Kodiak does not look the least bit uncomfortable in his trunks and shirtless torso, once again showing off his impressive physique. I remember the way Anika gawked at him during the Blue Moon hunt, and I try not to stare at him that way. Apparently, I'm not as immune as I'd like to be to the allure of an attractive body.

My steps are trepidatious as I navigate through slick black rocks and patches of brown sand towards the water. Kodiak offers his hand a couple of times, but as a point of alpha-blooded pride I decline his offer and make my way on my own. Besides, I shouldn't get too comfortable taking his hand. I finally arrive at the decent-sized patch of rock-free sand, and I run into the water, howling at my first splash of icy ocean spray. Kodiak laughs and runs in after me. The sunrise is gradual as we swim. I bob with the waves, my toes touching the sandy bottom, until a wave lifts me up, over and over again. Kodiak is swimming with more purpose, doing laps back and forth that probably contribute to his muscular arms and broad shoulders.

When I've had my fill of bobbing, I move to the beach and plop down onto the sand, digging my feet in. Kodiak comes in from his swim and sits beside me. As the cool water laps my ankles, a memory itches at the back of my mind. Once, it was Aspen who sat next to me in the sand. Aching longing fills my heart as I pull my knees to my chest and rest my head atop them. I imagine this house, this place, with Aspen at my side, his smile as easy as the ocean breeze and his eyes as blue as the water. The wind would push against his curls and his arm would push against mine as we buried our feet in the sand, creating our own little anchor in this world.

But I'm not here with Aspen.

Kodiak is scanning the water with those golden eyes, his black hair wind-tossed, his mouth a surly line. I sense there are thoughts churning in his head, but he gives them no voice. I understand the feeling well. As alphas, we must withhold so much of what we feel. We must be pillars of unquestioned strength for our communities. What must it have been like for Kodiak, with all his gifts, to have his strength always in question?

"I didn't know how bad it was," I finally say. "The way they treat you." The waves crash against the shore. Sandpipers run from the icy blast. They chase the waves two or three more times before he speaks.

"I was sixteen years old when I entered the Heir Trials." Kodiak's eyes remain fixed on the horizon.

I was nearly eleven at the time, but I remember the story he's about to tell. The Heir Trials take place every four years, when the heirs from the region come together and fight one another in a one-on-one tournament. Usually, the heirs are at least eighteen when they join the Trials, but Kodiak was the exception.

"I fought against peers only a couple of years older than me; I fought against full-grown wolves well into their twenties. Whatever their demographic, it didn't matter. I beat them all."

It had been an upset. It had been decades since any heir had won every single fight—and it was a sixteen-year-old, no less. I'd never seen Rory look so smitten. Even I developed a trivial crush on Kodiak.

"And four years later," Kodiak says, "when I was twenty, up

against all my peers—all my peers with their precious mates—I beat them all again. Maxum, Kingsly..." he hesitates a moment, "...Grey. And the crazy part, Luna?" He looks up to the sky and laughs to himself. "It wasn't even that hard. Sure, it was a good workout, but there was never a moment where I feared I would lose. I am just that much stronger, do you understand? I always have been." His eyes soften as he watches a scene from a past he can never return to. His voice is just above a whisper. "They said I was blessed by the Moon."

I dig my feet deeper into the sand and look at my knees instead of Kodiak. It feels like an intrusion to stare at him while he relives an era gone by. The waves do not still for us nor for this moment, but continue their never-ending push and pull with the shore.

"The morning after the trials, I heard my parents talking in their room." His jaw flexes. "I hear everything."

My heart drops to my stomach. I think about the private conversations I've had with Rory while Kodiak's been in the house. Did he hear us, or was he preoccupied enough that our words fell upon deaf ears?

"My father was so proud of me. Of course he was. Two heir trials in a row—undisputable champion. Some dream come true." In his eyes I should see unbridled pride, but instead there's a look I know all too well. It's the same one I face when I look into the mirror—shame. "My mother told him that it wasn't enough. Jael, two years younger than me, already had a mate. I couldn't be the leader of Midnight River. Even if I was the strongest, the fastest, it wasn't enough if I was a Lone Wolf." He slowly claws the sand, balling his fingers into a fist. "I was angry." He holds up a fistful of sand and lets the grains fall. His voice turns into a whisper. "I was hurt." He scoffs. "Imagine that? Her words wounded me more than any alpha heir could during the trials. I left the house...went running in the woods just so full of anger." A pause. "I came across Raulin."

Kodiak closes his eyes; his nostrils flare. "He smiled at me when he saw me. He congratulated me on my performance in the Heir Trials." Kodiak's eyebrows furrow. When he opens his eyes, they're racked with guilt. "You know, people used to blame him. Raulin, I mean. There were rumors and whispers they thought I couldn't hear. They said that Raulin was a curse, that the Moon must be punishing our pack because of him. The Moon turned me, their heir, into a Lone Wolf because Midnight River had produced a half-breed. We could hide Raulin, our pack's dirty secret, but we couldn't hide the fact that I had no mate."

It makes sense that people would think that. In truth, we know very little about the Moon and her whims, but it's very plausible that she'd be angered by a half-breed. The Moon, who puts wolves together in sacred bonds, watching a she-wolf waste her precious powers of procreation on some lowly human? A she-wolf throwing away her chance to have a true mate? Perhaps the Moon was angry, and what better way to teach Midnight River a lesson about fooling around in love than to strip their prize heir of his mate?

"I didn't pay those rumors much mind." Kodiak continues. "I mean, I had no compassion nor love for Raulin. I never would have associated with the likes of him, but that didn't mean I believed the nonsense spouted by old biddies." He looks down at the sand. "But then I saw him that night. I saw Raulin, and when all he did was give me a genuine compliment, I decided that he must be mocking me. I decided that he was to blame for everything." He draws in a deep breath. "I beat him." Kodiak says the words so slowly and clearly that they cannot be missed. "Punch after kick after punch until my hands and clothes were drenched with his blood. I told myself it was his fault that I hadn't found my mate, that the Moon was cursing me for it, that he deserved it. And then I stepped back and saw —really saw—what I had done to him. He was so beaten and bloodied he was hardly recognizable. Me, an alpha-blooded, the heir of my pack, the champion of the Heir Trials…and I chose to beat him up. A half-breed. A poor, defenseless bastard. I almost killed him for a rumor. For something he had no control over. For nothing."

I see the regret and guilt wracking his soul like a ravaging disease.

"I had to take Raulin to the hospital, and when people in the pack found out what had happened, no one even questioned it. No one, except his mother, seemed to care what I had done to him. He was a half-breed, lowlier than an omega. Whatever it was, he probably deserved it." Kodiak lies back, his bare back against the sand and his face looking up at the heavens. "Because in their eyes, it doesn't matter what Raulin does. It doesn't matter how smart he is, or how hard he works, or how capable or competent he is. Raulin is half-human. He is unlike the rest of us, so he will never be enough."

I look back at Kodiak, and in those golden eyes I see a sorrow I didn't know he could possess. Kodiak has always been so full of life, of confidence, of bravado. He isn't the type of person to be weighed down with regret or inadequacy—yet here he lies. It's like I never knew him. Or maybe I did, once upon a time, when he used to run around with Rory and he had the whole world before him. I knew him as he was—the golden boy—but didn't notice that his shine had tarnished, didn't realize he was only projecting an image of someone he once was. I wonder if he keeps Raulin close out of guilt, an atonement for his brutal beating by protecting him with the alpha cowl, or if he keeps Raulin close because he sees himself in the boy.

"Rory and I..." Kodiak starts, but he pauses. Anyone else using her name, her *nickname* reserved for family, would be quite strange. But Kodiak used to say it often. "Aurora and I," he corrects. "We always used to say that there were only two types of people: the strong, and the weak. And I believed that. I really did."

The rhythmic sound of the waves fills the silence between us. The strong and the weak. It seems so black and white, and yet that is our existence, our nature. We have a clear hierarchy, we have clear roles, we have clear mates, and that spectrum of gray belongs to humans too fond of over-philosophizing.

But Aspen sees gray. He sees a whole array of color that most of us are blind to. He sees half-breeds like Raulin and struggling alpha daughters like me and he sees a world of possibilities. He sees some distant, better future that I have not imagined. Aspen is not like Kodiak. He's not an exceptional hunter, nor an incredible fighter. He can't hear a heartbeat from across the room or sniff out a wolf half a mile away, and while he's got more strength than the average wolf, he hardly engages in fights. But Aspen has a steely gaze, a fearlessness in the face of alphas, a deep-rooted confidence that we all can feel.

And then there's me, cosplaying strength when there is none. In Rory's world of weak and strong, which category does she put me in?

"What do you believe now?" I ask.

"I don't know," he says. "I guess, like you said earlier today, it's not that simple."

I draw in a deep breath. "Yeah. I wish it was, though." I long for the simple world of my youth, before the days of confusing feelings and difficult situations. I miss when I believed that everything would always work out for the best because the Moon was watching over us. My mom was never supposed to get cancer, Rory was never supposed to leave,

Aspen was never supposed to reject me, and someone like Kodiak was never supposed to be a Lone Wolf.

"Do you think the Moon is laughing at us?" I ask. I pull my legs closer.

"What do you mean?"

My voice is so quiet it could be a whistle of the breeze. "Maybe she's just disappointed in me."

I feel Kodiak's eyes on me. "Why would the Moon be disappointed in you, Luna?"

I shouldn't have said anything. It was stupid to say it aloud, but now the words are out in the open air. "I don't know."

Kodiak lets out a noise of exasperation. "Come on, Luna. What are you thinking?"

It takes me a few seconds to respond. "Maybe I'm being punished."

"Punished?" he asks. "Punished for what?"

"I don't know." My voice threatens to break. Oh please, no more tears! I can't display the very weakness the Moon must be disappointed in. "For being pathetic." For falling in love before I should have, for moping about my long-dead mom, for whining about my sister leaving, for feeling too much.

"What makes you think you're pathetic?"

"I just am, Kodiak. I'm supposed to be strong, I'm supposed to be an example, and I'm just not. I'm weak. And that's probably why the Moon gave me a mate who would reject me. She gave me everything, and all I did was act weak and pathetic." I turn my head. I don't want him to look at me. His shame is, what, beating up a mutt? Being better than everyone at everything? It's not his fault he's a Lone Wolf, but it's my fault that I've become one.

Kodiak takes his time before he responds. "People say the Moon didn't give me a mate because I was too strong. That I was given enough gifts as it was. I wondered if she was punishing me for my arrogance—and yet, as an alpha, that's basically my prerogative. Now, you think you've lost your mate because of weakness. So which is it, huh? Does the Moon punish us for strength or weakness?"

I don't know what to say, but I do look at him. His attention is back on the ocean.

"Sometimes, I—" Kodiak pauses. "Sometimes I wonder if the Moon actually cares, or if it's just a big rock in the sky." He sighs. "If the Moon really is controlling our fate, why is fate so cruel?"

I hug my knees tighter to my chest, trying to find an answer to his question. Wanting to fall back on my childhood upbringing to assure Kodiak that everything will turn out as it should. Instead, all I say is, "I don't know."

Fate. It always seemed so magical and exciting. Now, it feels like a curse.

CHAPTER 22
SECOND CHANCES

The following night through early morning passes similarly to the previous one—I meet more people, sit outside of more meetings, and feel even worse about myself and this situation I've gotten myself into. Kodiak takes me home at 9:00 a.m. Rory is in the living room when I walk into the house. She sets her cellphone aside.

"So?" she asks. "How was it?"

I shrug.

"You in love with Kodiak yet?"

I give her the stink eye. "No."

"Why not?"

"Because he's not my mate." And because he's not Aspen. There's a world where, had Kodiak and I been closer in age, and had I grown up with him the way Rory had, I would have been head-over-heels for him. But in the world we live in, Kodiak and I weren't that close and it's hard to forget everything I have with Aspen because of a nice couple of days with Kodiak.

"Fair enough," Rory says. "Did you meet the whole pack?"

I groan. "Pretty much. We avoided dinner with his family, thank the Moon, but I'm pretty much solidified as their future Alpha Female." I back flop onto one of the couches. "It's a huge mess, Ror."

"Yeah, it is," she says. "Which is why we're going to see Queenie."

"Queenie? And she's going to fix everything?"

"She's not. That's up to you. But hopefully she's going to give us some useful information. Get up," Rory stands up and offers me her hands. I take them and she peels my limp body off the couch.

"It's late," I argue. "I have school in the evening." A part of me is scared to see Queenie, scared she'll tell me that too much time has passed, that it's over with Aspen. Every day that goes by, it feels less and less likely that we'll come together in the end.

But Rory wins out, per usual, and she and I walk to Queenie's house, nestled alone on the edge of Dakota Ridge's territory. It's a quaint log cottage with a porch full of plants and a singular rocking chair. I'm brought back to summers gone by when Rory and I would visit in the early evenings while most wolves were still asleep.

Rory knocks on the door, and after several seconds, Queenie answers. Her long silvery hair is pulled back in a braid, and she wears dangling golden earrings that sparkle. Queenie's smile is warm and genuine. "Aurora, Luna. Please, come in."

As we step inside, we aren't met with the usual animal hides or heads that adorn most wolf homes. Instead, it's a cozy place with brocaded furniture, thick embroidered rugs, and shelves stuffed with books and trinkets from places I can only imagine. There's a lingering smell of cookies and a scented candle in the air, something with pumpkin and apple spice even though it's not the season. Queenie offers us a seat, and Rory and I fall back onto a purple couch. Its velvet furnishing is rubbed nearly raw in certain spots, but it's broken in and so comfy. Queenie goes to the kitchen and comes back with a plate of gooey chocolate chip cookies that melt right in your mouth.

"Please, have as many as you'd like," she says, setting the plate down on the wooden coffee table. I wonder where the table's nicks and scratches come from—did she used to have little pups running around? Did she buy this used from some human family?

"You don't have to tell me twice," Rory says with a grin, grabbing a cookie and eating half in one bite. Rory loves meat as much as any other wolf, but she's got an incurable sweet tooth. "Oh!" she moans. "I missed these, Queenie. So good."

When Queenie smiles, there's a twinkle in her deep brown eyes. "And we've missed you, Aurora." Her dangling earrings make the smallest tinkling noise as she walks over to her book-case. I nibble on a cookie. It's warm and sweet and soft, but my tangle of nerves is choking my appetite. Queenie runs her hand across book spines with long, knotted fingers that must have been willowy and elegant when she was young. She pulls a book with a faded green cover and yellowed pages and takes a seat in the embroidered, cream-colored loveseat. Rory polishes off her second cookie. Queenie flips through the book with her thumb.

"When someone's mate dies, do they get another?" Queenie asks.

Rory furrows her brows, her mouth stuffed full of sweet, chocolatey goodness. I lean forward. Why is she asking such an obvious question?

"No," I answer. "You only get one."

Queenie looks at me, her eyes rich and intense. "Months

ago, Aspen came by. He asked me the same question," she says. "I gave him the same answer. Then, he asked me, 'What if you're rejected?'"

My heart drops to my stomach.

"He asked me if rejected mates got a second chance." She places the green book on the coffee table. There's gold embossing on a cover so faded that I can't read the words. "Aspen has always visited me, as you two girls have. But he would come and read. He's always asking questions, searching for answers, trying to discover more about who we are."

Rory's mouth finally isn't full of cookies. "Discover who we are? What kind of sapcrap is that? We already know who we are."

"There's always more to discover about ourselves, Aurora," Queenie says.

"Still!" she sneers.

"Amidst his readings, he must have found a reference to rejected mates." Queenie looks at her crowded bookcase and sighs. "These books, they hold a great many secrets."

"What did you tell him?" I ask. My body is taut with tension, holding so still so that I cannot miss the answer. "When he asked about rejected mates?"

"I told him what I knew," she says. "And I told him that we do not speak of rejected mates, that it's a mockery of the Moon, of who we are. We never spoke of it again. I didn't think much of it until the night of your party, when I realized his question held far more weight to it than I'd realized. I never thought he was planning to reject his own mate."

I don't know what to make of this revelation, that he'd been contemplating this for a long time. Was he always planning to reject his mate, or just one he didn't like?

"Since your birthday, I've been looking through my books," Queenie says. "I wanted to be sure." She leans forward and taps the green book with her long nail. "It's in this book, a book that Aspen took home with him one weekend." As she flips through the pages, I see that the book is a conglomeration of typewritten words and scrawled-in pen notes. Queenie lands on a page and begins to read from it. "'While a wolf whose mate has passed away can never find another mate, one who has been rejected has a chance to find another one, as long as the bond between the original mates is completely severed.'" She looks at me carefully. "This means, Luna, that if you accept Aspen's rejection, there's a possibility you could find another mate."

Rory's eyes widen, and I find I cannot move. I am frozen to that purple velvet couch cushion, frozen to that point in time, frozen in front of my next move.

"That's impossible," I finally whisper. "We only get one mate."

"You used to think it impossible to be rejected," Queenie says.

"So if Luna dumps Aspen," Rory says. "Officially and all that, then she'll get another mate?" She smiles even wider than when she was offered cookies.

"Not necessarily," Queenie says. "There's a *possibility* she'll find another mate. There is no guarantee. It's far, far less certain than a regular wolf's chances of finding a mate."

"How certain are we talking?" Rory asks. "Eighty percent? Ninety?"

"There are not many recorded instances of rejected mates," Queenie says. "But of the few we know of, some found new mates and some never did. It's quite uncertain."

Rory's smile gives way to anger. "Well that's stupid. What's Luna supposed to do with that?"

"That is entirely up to her," Queenie says, calm in the face of Rory's storm. She reaches for her bookshelf and plucks out another book, a thin one with a black leather cover, the word "rituals" embossed on the front. She thumbs through crinkled pages, and when she reaches the last one, she places the book in my lap. Even in the warmth of a summer morning, the words before me chill my bones. My hands tremble as I pick up the book.

Rejecting a Mate

Should you feel compelled to reject your mate, you must recite the following under the light of the Moon.

I, [state your name], under the light of the Moon, formally apply to sever our connection. [State his or her name], I reject you as my mate."

The memory washes over me, as cold and harsh as a wave of icy ocean spray on a February day. I see Aspen before me, white knuckled and paled, the agony in his eyes. The words in my memory sounded far more labored than they appear on the page, but they were all the same.

I, Aspen, under the light of the Moon, formally apply to sever our connection. Luna, I reject you as my mate.

I flip that cursed page over, but there's only the black leather back and a ripped paper seam. I shut the book and place it on the coffee table. Why does Queenie even keep such a malicious text in her library? Why didn't she burn this information years ago? If she had, Aspen never would have known how to reject me. Right now, I'd be drowning in bliss instead of misery.

"That's what he said to me." My voice is quiet and low. "The night of the Blue Moon, that's what he said."

Queenie takes a folded piece of paper from her pocket and puts it in my hands. "This is the last page from that book, Luna. I took it out years ago. If you want to reject Aspen, to chance finding someone else, you have the power to do so." She looks at me with those wizened brown eyes. "You have the information now. What you want to do with it is entirely up to you."

My eyes widen as I hold the piece of paper in my hands. When Queenie first told me that I could sever my connection with Aspen—cut him off with an unfixable finality—I hadn't even considered doing so. Now, if I end things with him, there's a chance I'll find a soulmate again, that there could be someone else out there for me.

This information should rock my world, should make me rethink everything—and yet I find myself wanting to tear the page into a million pieces. I wanted Aspen as my mate long before I knew he was my mate. I never wanted to find someone else. It was always him, and the hazy half-promise of another wolf is as inconsequential as a wisp of smoke against the reality of Aspen.

The only real upside would be if I could mate with Kodiak. He's far more tangible than some future unknown mate, and honestly, mating with him would be far more convenient. Our lie could become truth. I wouldn't have to disappoint anyone, Kodiak wouldn't have to be humiliated, and we could live our lives as Alphas over two packs.

He's handsome and strong and kind. I could fall in love with him...couldn't I?

But what if I don't mate with Kodiak? Do I live with the threat that some other soulmate besides Aspen is floating around? Do I still marry Kodiak? Do I still hope we'll fall in love with each other?

And what if I *do* mate with him?

I know you're supposed to feel everything for your mate, that no one else is supposed to matter, but perhaps I only felt all those feelings when I mated with Aspen *because* it was Aspen. Even before the Blue Moon, I felt that way about him. If Kodiak and I were to suddenly be soulmates, would I lie next to Kodiak every day, still wondering what might have been with Aspen?

I look up at Queenie. I try to smile, but it's weak against my paled skin. "Thank you. You've given me a lot to think about."

CHAPTER 23

IT MIGHT HAVE BEEN

EIGHT MONTHS AGO

Aspen passed me a creased piece of paper. The typed-out poem had lines slashed out with pencil. I was seated in a plush chair in the school's moonlit library; Aspen was standing in front of me with his hands clasped behind his back. It was 3 a.m., and the school did not bother producing a librarian for the night class. Most wolves avoided this place like it might have some contractible human disease, but of course Aspen was quite fond of it.

"You ready, Luna?" he asked.

I rose an eyebrow. "You're the one that has to recite it, Aspen. All I have to do is read."

He smiled. "I'll take that to mean you're ready." Tomorrow would be our English test for the poetry unit. Ms. Turner had asked us to choose a poem to recite, and since Aspen chose one that was so dang long, he was allowed to strike out a few lines.

"Yes, I'm ready when you are," I said.

Aspen dramatically cleared his throat before starting his recitation. "Maud Muller by John Greenleaf Whittiker."

"Whittier," I corrected.

"Whittier." He smiled sheepishly.

"Maud Muller, on a summer's day,

Raked the meadow sweet with hay.

Beneath her torn hat glowed the wealth

Of simple beauty and rustic health.

But when she glanced to the far-off town,

White from its hill-slope looking down,

The sweet song died, and a vague unrest

And a nameless longing filled her breast,—"

His eyes turned just a bit glossy, and his voice grew quieter.

"A wish that she hardly dared to own,

For something better than she had known."

He resumed his normal cadence and continued his recitation, infusing it with inflections and rhythm and character. He was going to blow us all out of the water for our test, but that was of little surprise. The poem went on to tell Maud Muller's story, where she met a rich judge who came down the lane. The two shared a moment and dreamed of what it would be like to be with each other, but they chose to go their separate ways. The judge married another wealthy person, and Maud Muller married a poor man, but often their minds drifted to each other, wishing things could have been different.

Aspen whispered to me, "This is the best part."

Then he drew in a deep breath and put a dramatic hand on his heart, holding out the other one towards the sky. I chuckled and rolled my eyes.

"Alas for maiden, alas for Judge,

For rich repiner and household drudge!

God pity them both! and pity us all,

Who vainly the dreams of youth recall."

Then he looked right at me with those deep blue eyes, and

his voice drew quiet, like the patter of rain or the soft rumble of
a distant storm.

> *"For of all sad words of tongue or pen,*
> *The saddest are these: it might have been."*

CHAPTER 24

GREEN

Aspen and I will meet in the library, after the final bell rings. No one will interrupt us there. We'll talk about everything; we'll solve everything. I know there's still hope for us—I can feel it in my bones. I'm entangled in the web I've spun with Kodiak, but I'm sure Aspen and I can figure out how to unravel me from this wayward plan's sticky grasp. We have to.

It's Monday evening, the second-to-last day of school, and I've arrived at Adam Douglas with plenty of time before the first bell rings. Most wolves arrive late to class, but chances are Aspen will be waiting in first period English alone, where I'll ask him to meet me at the library after school. The halls are basically empty except for the human staff and some nerdy lower betas, so I'm surprised to see Anika leaning against a locker. When she sees me, she straightens up. Her eyes widen with something akin to fear before she plasters on a big smile.

"Luna, you're back from Midnight River!" Her loose brown curls bounce as she walks towards me. She's got a blue bruise around her eye from the fight a few days ago. "It's so good to see you!"

I narrow my eyes. What's wrong with her? "What's up with you, Ani? You're acting like Nova."

Anika's laugh is pitchy. "Yeah, I can see why you'd think that. Ha. Honestly, it's just good to see you, you know?"

"Um, good to see you too," I say. I glance up the hallway. Normally I'd like to chat with Anika, but I wanted to catch Aspen alone and I don't know how to go to class without her walking with me.

"We can start heading to class," Anika says.

Since when has Ani cared at all about class?

"Sure."

Anika's pace is as slow as a toddling pup's gait. "How was your weekend?" Her smile is bright. "With *Kodiak?*" She wiggles her tone along with her eyebrows.

"It was great," I lie. Sure, there were good moments, but 'great' is certainly an exaggeration. "I got to meet a lot more of the Midnight River pack, spend alone time with him. And we even went to the beach."

"That sounds romantic."

"It was." I realize I need to smile, to look like I'm lost in some dream, and so I find one. "He took my hand and we ran across the sand till we were in a little alcove hidden from the world. I didn't want to get wet, but this big wave rushed in and caught us both." A real smile. "We laughed so hard."

Anika's smile seems genuine. "Aw, that's so fun. I'm so happy for you and Kodiak. You two are great together."

"Yeah," I say. I don't want to give more false details, so I ask her how her weekend was.

"My weekend?" She sounds almost breathless, and I quiet my own breathing to listen to her heartbeat. Faint and soft, but there it is, an erratic ticking in her chest. Just the sound of it makes me nervous. "Funny you should ask," she says, her smile pained. "It's been kind of crazy!"

Why do I feel so apprehensive? "Was it?" I ask, my tone a couple shades too cool.

"Yeah. First of all, I just want to say, I really am so so happy for you and Kodiak."

"Right." A sense of dread slithers in my stomach. "You said that."

"Of course, sorry," Anika says, her smile nervous. Her uncharacteristic lack of confidence is shaking mine. I want to end this conversation now, to tell her we'll talk next month about her crazy weekend, to run to English class and lock the door behind me. "So, Aspen and I hung out a bunch this weekend," she says. That dread is coiling around my organs, squeezing them until I feel nauseous. "And, well, truth is, I've always kind of had a thing for him. I mean, I don't know if you could tell. He's really different from me, of course. Totally a nerd." A nervous laugh. "But I don't know, there's something about him. He's really smart and he's funny. And, you know, he's pretty cute too. But I, you know, I didn't ever want to do anything with it 'cause, well, and you're going to laugh now, but I always thought you maybe liked him too."

I do not laugh.

"But, like I said, we were hanging out a lot this weekend, and we were staying up super late one night and I told him I always kind of liked him, and..." She pauses for a second, and I wonder if I can make a break for it, if I can dash down the hall and never hear what she has to say next.

"Aspen kissed me," she says.

Once, I was arguing with an alpha-blooded girl from Pine Peak, and she sucker punched me in the stomach. Just like that, I couldn't breathe, she'd knocked the wind out of me. If Rory hadn't stepped in to pummel the girl, I'd have been totally defenseless. I feel that same way now. Sucker-punched. Unable to breathe. And no Rory to rescue me. He kissed her? *He* kissed *her?* Aspen kissed Anika?

"And um, well, I guess we're kind of together now? I don't really know. It's all kind of a whirlwind! But I'm really excited of course." I can feel Anika's green eyes on me, too green for your average beta, waiting for a response. "Stars, this must be kind of a shock. I mean, I'm sure it seems totally unexpected, Aspen and I."

I have to say something. She's waiting for me to respond. Her eyes are on me. I have to speak, but I don't want to say a thing. I can't say anything that might validate their 'relationship'. It's not even a relationship. It's not real. It can't be. It is just a nightmare I have to wake up from, not something that exists in reality.

"It is unexpected," I say, fighting to withhold venom from my tone. "I mean, he's not your mate."

"Well...technically we don't know that. I mean, I turn eighteen in August."

But I *do* know that, because Aspen is my mate and he'll never ever be hers.

"Yeah, but what are the odds of him actually being your mate?" I say. "You know it's a waste of time to date."

"Okay, fair. So let's just say he isn't my mate. Let's say it doesn't last. I mean, at least we're going to have a good time for the next couple of months!" The way she smiles, I know regular, confident Anika is returning. "So I'll enjoy it while it lasts."

I don't know what to say in response. How can she be so casual about him when he means everything to me?

"Besides, you're going to be all tangled up with Kodiak every day from here on out. I need someone to keep me company this summer."

"Gotcha," I say, because I can't think of anything else.

Anika and I walk into our English classroom, and Aspen is waiting there at his desk. I'm not sure how to read his expression, but Anika's is excited and satisfied. She walks up to him and plants a kiss on his lips, marking him as her own. I think something breaks inside me. Maybe it's my heart. I'm malfunctioning. What if I just dropped dead, right here right now? Would he rush to my side, or just worry about how Anika might handle my death? Aspen's eyes flit to mine, and I wonder if he can see how hurt I am or if he even cares.

"I told Luna on the way in," Anika says. She's standing and he's sitting, so she rests her arm around his neck. "Of course, she doesn't approve of dating." She winks at me. If I wasn't malfunctioning, I'd know she's being her usual teasing self, but my system is falling apart and loud green alerts are flashing and all I can see through that sickly shade is malice. Anika is taunting me with that wink. She's trying to hurt me. She's rubbing Aspen in my face before she stomps on it.

"Well," Aspen starts, but it seems he has no idea what to say. His words just stop.

"Well, what?" Anika prods.

"Well, uh, I don't know." Then Aspen contracts the nervous laugh that Anika has shed. "Luna's always believed in not dating, in waiting for your mate."

"Well now she's got Kodiak, so I guess that worked out for her."

She doesn't fool me. I see what she's trying to do. She's reminding me of my mating with Kodiak, binding my tongue so that I can't object to their horrible pairing.

"It's just general advice I give out." My tone is prickly. "So don't come crying to me when it doesn't work out in the end."

"I know, I know, I'm just teasing you," Anika says.

"Oh hello," a voice interjects. Our English teacher, Ms.

Turner, has walked into the classroom. "Nice to see all of you here."

"You're probably not used to this," Anika says, taking her desk. It's next to mine.

"Can't say I expected some popular seniors to show up early the last week of school, no," Ms. Turner says, smiling. Ms. Turner is my favorite teacher. Most wolves are a little easier on her than other teachers, since she's only in her twenties. Normally I'd be friendly with her, but I'm too sick to speak. I don't say anything to her and neither does Aspen. I sit at my desk in perfect silence.

Anika has to fill the space with the words we lack. She's telling Ms. Turner about what's next after school ends, events she's looking forward to.

"I can't wait for Luna's wedding," Anika gabs.

Of course she can't. I'll officially be cut off from Aspen forever. She can have him all to herself.

"That's right!" Ms. Turner turns to me. "I heard about that. You found your mate last week, right?"

My throat is dry. "Yeah." My eyes flick to Aspen. His eyes flick away.

"That's so exciting! He's the Alpha of Midnight River, right?" she asks.

"Uh huh."

"What's his name, again?"

"Kodiak."

"Kodiak. I like that name. Do you have a picture of him?" She asks.

I know Ms. Turner is trying to be friendly, but I just want her to leave me alone.

"Um, maybe," I mumble. I haven't taken a single photo with him this last week. I'd have to dig through my camera roll to find him.

"Alpha Kodiak is really handsome," Anika pipes in. "And he's got dark hair like Luna. They look great together. Aspen was telling me how good a pair they make, too."

It takes everything in me to wear a blank face, to not look at him in some hurt accusation. I imagine Anika tangled in his arms, Aspen telling her how happy he is for me, how Kodiak and I are so great together. I shake my head. I can't think of that. The image of the two of them, their bodies pressed together, their *lips* pressed together—it's so gut wrenching that even Ms. Turner should be able to hear my heartbeat pound. Pound and pound and pound until it explodes.

"Oh yeah?" Ms. Turner says.

"Mm hmm." Anika glances at Aspen, waiting for him to join in. She flicks his shoulder, the way she always does. It seems so much worse now.

"Oh, yeah," he says. "I mean, he and Luna are both alphas. Cut from the same cloth. It's...it's great. All we could have hoped for."

All we could have hoped for.

"And Luna's going to make the most beautiful bride." Anika turns to me and smiles in a way that is so genuine that I know she really means it and I can't even pretend that she's trying to hurt me in any way. She takes my hand and squeezes it, as if to remind me that she's one of my best friends and always has been. "I'm going to miss her, but she's got her soulmate now."

A lump jumps up in my throat, but I swallow it down.

Then Anika turns to Aspen. "Luckily for me Aspen is still a Lone Wolf, so I'll have someone to keep me company."

"Well, the pleasure's all mine," he says, though his voice is missing some of the usual charisma it has when he banters with Anika.

"Yeah?" She leans forward and smiles at him in her flirty

way. Maybe that's the face she made right before he kissed her, when he cupped her cheeks in his hands and brought his lips to hers and they kissed and kissed and—

I look away.

Anika pivots the conversation, trying to coax Ms. Turner into dropping our final. It becomes a blur of background noise as my mind stages a mutinous play. The way he might have looked at her, the way he might have touched her, the way he might have whispered to her. The playwrights of my brain even provide a dialogue of words he said to her that he'll never say to me.

I feel Aspen's eyes on me, burning through my flimsy facade of nonchalance. I can't bring myself to look at him. Not only has he rejected me, but he has chosen Anika over me. In the past, I could comfort myself that he was just attracted to silly human girls and silly human ideals, but now the truth stares at me with mocking scorn. He has chosen Anika, a werewolf, over me. He knows me better than almost anyone, and I still am not enough. I am still not his choice.

Anika is complaining to Ms. Turner, but there's still a glow about her. Something happy. Something beautiful. She looks back at me and loudly whispers, "Do you think I'm wearing her down?"

Ms. Turner chuckles, and despite it all, so do I. And so does Aspen.

I hate him.

I really do. I hate him with all my heart, and I hate Anika too. I hate Anika for being better than me and for winning Aspen over, and I hate Aspen for choosing to date someone I can't really hate.

CHAPTER 25
BIG BAD WOLF
ONE YEAR, EIGHT MONTHS AGO

Two Octobers ago, Principal Jones and Vice Principal McLaren of Adam Douglas High had the brilliant idea of hosting a joint dance for the human and werewolf students— or as they called it, "the day and night class." They slotted the dance for Halloween and encouraged costumes. We weren't sure if they'd chosen that day because some part of them still saw us as the monsters of their myths, or if they wanted us to mingle with humans as one under the guise of costumes. We all hoped it was the former, but figured they were stupid enough to believe in the latter, as if we couldn't sniff out humans from wolves. While they needed to see our ears and canines to know we were different, it was clear to us from the moment they stepped into the room.

All of us wolves thought it was an absolutely stupid idea to hold some interspecies dance. I mean, we were going to go of course, but that didn't mean it wasn't stupid. We were just curious to see how those sapes would act at some Halloween dance and wanted to know what might happen when they threw us all together. Anika and I had decided to get up early on the weekend to go into town. It was about 7:30 p.m. when we got to the costume store. As always, it was odd seeing and smelling so many humans, but we soon acclimated to their scent and were enjoying ourselves.

Anika ran her hands along plastic weapons splattered in red paint. "You know, I sort of like horror movies," she said.

"Do you?" I asked, flipping a fake knife and catching it.

"Yes." She grinned, showing off canines that would have alerted those around us to our true nature, were they paying any attention. "I like to imagine how I would act in such circumstances. If Michael Myers came knocking at my door, I'd be all claws and fur and teeth. I'd probably rip off his leg."

I laughed. "I wouldn't have thought you, of all people, would fantasize becoming the humans' savior in a horror film."

Anika wrinkled her nose. "Moon, Luna, are you trying to annoy me? Obviously it's not about saving the humans."

"Just showing off that you wouldn't die when they would?" I wore a wry smile.

"Exactly," Anika said. We were moving away from the fake weapons to a section full of costumes packaged in clear plastic bags. "I like horror movies because I know I would survive."

"Who knows, Anika? Maybe an axe murderer will hit the Halloween dance."

"Moon, I hope so. That would make my night."

I laughed even as I rolled my eyes. Anika had always been bold and vivacious, viciously confident in her abilities, and I admired her for it. She was a fiery blaze compared to my frosty, controlled demeanor, but she often said or did what I wished I could, and for that I was grateful.

I tapped the bag of a Little Red Riding Hood costume. "You know, maybe I'll go as Little Red Riding Hood. The humans will be surprised when they find out I'm also the Big Bad Wolf."

"Oh Luna, you should!" Anika said, pulling the bag towards her. "It's not an ugly costume either. It might even be cute."

"I do kind of like it," I admitted.

"Maybe I'll go as the Big Bad Wolf from the Three Little Pigs," Anika said.

"All you need is to find some sapes to dress up as pigs."

"Run, run, run, as fast as you can."

The hairs on the back of my neck stood, some instinct kicking in before I consciously recognized the scent. I managed to choke back the growl in my throat.

"What's wrong?" Anika asked, her voice serious.

"Unpleasant company," I answered, turning my face away from the smell. It was too late. She was approaching.

"Is that you, Luna?" Her voice was so sweet that it was nauseating. I had to look at her, didn't I? Talk to her? Play pretend?

"Well," Anika said, her voice quiet and drawled. "I guess we found some humans to compliment my costume."

Aspen's little sape girlfriend stepped up to me, all five feet of her with her wispy blonde hair and a smile so bright it could blind me. Mousy. She was with a couple of friends that I didn't recognize.

"It *is* you!" Mousy said. I wondered if she really was oblivious to my distaste or if she just didn't care. "Do you remember me? We met at the diner?"

Anika's eyes flashed in recognition. I'd told her about my wretched dining experience with Aspen and his human gaggle. I hadn't had to divulge my interest in Aspen for Anika to get annoyed with the humans and with Aspen for bringing them.

"Why would she remember you?" Anika asked, her lip curling. "Luna is an alpha."

Mousy blanched. Apparently, it took an overtly rude

comment for her to realize that this conversation wasn't welcomed.

"Oh, well, we met a couple of weeks ago," she said. I wished she had just said sorry and skirted off. "I'm Aspen's girl-friend. He's in your tribe, right?"

Using the wrong word for *pack* was annoying. Introducing herself as Aspen's girlfriend was infuriating.

"Yes, I remember you," I said. "I don't forget a scent so easi-ly." I wished I didn't remember her, as Anika had suggested. I wished she had been as inconsequential as some pesky gnat, nothing more than an annoying human interaction. I wished her scent wasn't burned in my nose, that her visage and her stupid humanness didn't enrage me. I wished I didn't hate her so much because I wished she didn't even exist.

Mousy smiled at my acknowledgement like I'd introduced her as my best freaking friend. Moon, so annoying. "Are you guys buying costumes for the dance?"

"Yes," I said. Would she not just go away? Why was she even talking to me, trying to act like we were friends? Now I had to be polite just so she didn't go crying to Aspen about the big, bad wolf Luna.

"We are too!" Mousy said. She gestured to her forgettable friends and introduced them to us. "This is Luna. She's Aspen's good friend."

I hated her.

"And...you must be Luna's friend?" she looked at Anika.

"Yeah." Ani did not elaborate any further.

Mousy gave me a sheepish smile, as if she and I were friends sharing secret glances about some strange rude person we'd just met. But Anika was my friend, not Mousy, and Ani's visible display of hostility was only a fraction of what I felt inside. My stone face did not crack at her smile.

"What are you all thinking of dressing up as?" she asked.

Why would she not GO AWAY? I never wanted to see her ever again. I had already considered foregoing the dance entirely just so I wouldn't run into her and Aspen canoodling on the dance floor, and now here she was trying to make some grand show of friendship.

"Little Red Riding Hood," I said.

"Oh yeah?" Then she laughed. "Oh wait! That's actually so clever."

I refused to be flattered by her words, to let her cool down the furnace I'd stoked against her. "Thanks," I said, offering a fake smile. "We thought it would be a bit ironic."

"Hey, you gotta lean into being a werewolf, right?" Mousy said.

Ani let out an exasperated sigh.

"Right," I said, attempting a smile.

"What do you think I should go as?" Mousy asked me. Then she laughed to herself. "Aspen tried to give me some ideas, but I want to surprise him."

"Maybe Little Bo Peep," I said.

"Hm, that could be fun!"

And despite my fervent wishes to the contrary, Mousy did not seem to take the hint. It was like she was desperate to establish some connection, to prove to herself and the world that we were friends. She kept coming up to Anika and I as we were shopping, asking my opinion on some costume or other when all I wanted was to give her a good knee to the stomach.

Finally, Ani and I got in the long checkout line to leave this nightmare.

"Who does she think she is?" Ani hissed. "I don't know how you had the patience for her."

"I'm just glad we're leaving," I said. "We made it through without incident, and now we won't have to deal with her again."

I felt eyes watching me, and I glanced at the group of teenage boys in front of us, staring at Ani and I with either fascination or hunger. Moon, human boys were almost as bad as Mousy.

"No way," one of the boys said. "Are you two actual werewolf girls?"

"Ughhh." Anika let out a guttural sound and rolled her eyes.

"Hey we're not here to give you guys a hard time," another one said. "Honest! We're, like, into werewolf acceptance and all that. You guys are just really pretty."

Anika and I looked at each other. These sapes were hitting on us? Like we would actually want to speak with them?

"Hey!" a high voice butt in. Oh moon. Not her. Mousy was wearing some heroic face. "They're not interested in you."

Well thank the Moon that Mousy was here to save the day! Whatever would we have done without her. I looked up at the cash register, where some customer was giving the cashier a hard time. Couldn't they kick that customer out so that the line could move forward faster?!

"You're one to talk, Sarah," one of the human boys said. "Aren't you dating a werewolf?"

"I am," Mousy said. "And these girls are his friends. Trust me, they're not interested."

"I'm going to kill Aspen," Anika whispered. "When I get my hands on him—"

"You're actually so annoying, you know that?" the human boy said. Finally, something we agreed on.

"If *you* think I'm annoying, that's a compliment," Mousy said.

"Moon, what is holding up this line?" Anika asked through gritted teeth.

Mousy joined us in line. "Don't worry about them," she said. "They're obnoxious but they're spineless."

"We weren't worried," I said. "Anika and I aren't scared of a few sapes."

"A few...what?" she asked.

"It seems like you know them."

"Yeah, unfortunately. We're all seniors, all in the same small town."

"You're a senior?" I asked, showing interest in her for the first time. The line moved a few people forward. The traffic block human must have left. "That's exciting." Many human seniors in high school left home after they graduated, off to some university that would hopefully be very very far away.

"It is!" She smiled. "I can't wait. I'm planning to do my undergrad in biochemistry before going to med school."

"That sounds fun," I lied. Anika yawned.

Mousy's eyes flitted to mine, then to the floor. She held the plastic bag of her costume against her chest, wrapping her arms around it like a hug. "I want to do cancer research."

I paused a moment. "I see."

"I want to research underdeveloped areas, you know? There are, uh, there are certain diseases that only target certain people, like uh, like werewolves. And, well, I want to look into diseases like Lycanthroma. See if there's a cure, or at least better treatments."

The noise of laughing teens, the shouts of surprise and jolts of fear, the clanging quarters buried in pockets and the cash register opening and closing—it all faded into muted background sounds, and I turned to look at Mousy fully. I was far taller than she was, and she seemed especially small as she looked down at the floor, hugging that costume.

"I...I heard about your Mom," she said. "I'm so sorry. That shouldn't have had to happen. My parents, they're both doctors. I'm not one myself yet, but I really believe that there are cures and solutions to be found for your community. I've wanted to do this for a long time."

Several seconds passed before I responded, before I could choke back the emotion that had risen to my throat. "I see." My voice was quiet.

There Mousy stood with her mousy blonde hair and soft little ears and smartsy school-minded human brain. Aspen chose to date a human, of all things, and it had made me angry that he'd chosen a basic sape like her. I hated that she was human, and yet, in that moment, I realized I wouldn't have had it any other way. She could be my enemy and I didn't have to feel an ounce of guilt. She could be ignorant, obnoxious, foolish, OTHER. She wasn't supposed to use her stupid human ambitions to cure Lycanthroma, to try and save my people from the same fate my mother had suffered. Mousy was supposed to be the monster. In the story of my life, she was supposed to be the big, bad, irredeemable wolf—and more than anything, I hated that she wasn't.

CHAPTER 26

HATE

The rest of the night is as miserable as the start. In between finals I catch Aspen and Anika brushing hands, smiling at each other. Whatever tortured gaze he had for me at twilight disappears as the night deepens. Logan and Raff tease them about it, parroting the usual talking points about how dating is useless, but there's no real chastisement in their tone. The more they talk about Aspen and Ani's budding relationship, the more I realize that no one else cares that much about not dating before finding your mate. Logan even brings up some young couples in our school that I was not aware of. Perhaps the only reason my friend group never dated was not because of their conviction to hold out for their mate, but because of their conviction to please me, the Alpha Daughter. Maybe Aspen has wanted to date Anika for a long time, and he had to wait until I was too busy with a mate to care.

But I do care. Every nudge, every glance, every smile they share creeps across my skin like poison ivy and I just want to burn it all away. Usually, it is Aspen who would look right at me with those deep blue eyes, who could pierce the calm and collected front I'm trying to put up with just a glance. But his eyes barely graze over me, so Nova has to take up the mantle. She is quiet throughout all our conversations. She is watching us all, and she is watching me. While Aspen's knowing looks made me feel vulnerable, there was also something euphoric about him seeing me for who I was. With Nova, I feel even more stressed out than I already am. It's one thing for Aspen to really know me, but Nova is a different matter altogether. While she is my friend, she's also a low beta, and I certainly can't let my true emotions slip in front of her.

By the time seventh period rolls around, I'm at the end of my leash. I'm exhausted trying to hide everything I feel, and I can't bear to look at Aspen or Anika anymore. Of course, because *of course*, Aspen and I share a table in seventh period. I want to ask the teacher if I can move to a different spot, but I know that would incite questions that I cannot answer.

About five seconds after the teacher plops the science final in front of me, I know I'm going to bomb the test. I can't focus on chemistry with Aspen right next to me, with his scent, with his betrayal, with his—

"Excuse me." Aspen raises his hand, looking right at our teacher. Mr. John looks surprised, but he scurries over to our table.

"What's up, Aspen?"

Aspen's ears droop a little. "Um, well, would it be possible to move to another seat? Like that empty table in the back? I'm just super nervous and I can't concentrate."

Mr. John gives me the stink eye, like I'm the one who's done something wrong when it's the other way around. If Aspen was looking at me, he'd see my widened eyes, my surprised lips. Mr. John turns to Aspen with a magnanimous smile. "Of course, Aspen. Move where you feel most comfortable."

Whispered musings and jokes begin to fly, and I stare down

at my paper with the intensity of the sun to keep the heat out of my cheeks. I hear Aspen's chair scrape against the floor as he heads to the back. Mr. John yells at everyone to be silent while taking our test and that he's not afraid to fail us.

It was hard to concentrate with Aspen sitting next to me, but it's harder now that he's made his public escape from me. So many thoughts are racing through my mind, and none of them are related to the chemistry on the page in front of me. I do my best to soldier through, to pass a class that I pretended to care about to avoid everyone in Midnight River, and I weakly hand in my finished test to Mr. John when he collects them. With the test over, Mr. John tells Aspen he can return to his original seat. Aspen sits beside me, but I do not look at him. Mr. John is giving his farewell speech, his hopes that we'll remember something we learned in the future, how even though school is over, that doesn't mean learning is over. Blah blah blah. I'm sure Aspen finds it riveting, that he's soaking up every little word about the value of education with some dumb smile on his face, but that's only a guess since I'm not looking at him.

Oh Aspen! What have you done to me? You've ruined my life! You've turned me into the wretched, weeping creature I've become. Now I'm in a pretend relationship with Kodiak and you're in a real one with Anika. With Anika! My best friend Anika.

I hate him. I really hate him.

But no, that's not quite right, is it? It's not that I hate him.

It's that Aspen hates me.

There it is! Clear as a summer sky! The ugly, awful truth I never realized. *Aspen hates me.* It's so obvious, isn't it? He hates me. Maybe he always has. He hates that I'm an alpha, he hates that I'm not smart like him, he hates that I wouldn't have been friends with someone like Raulin, he hates that I parade as something strong and competent when I'm weak and pathetic. All this time, any show of nicety was for his own survival, to stay on the good side of the pack's precious Alpha Daughter turned heir. He wants to punish me. He wants to pound me so deeply into the earth that I can never crawl back to my alpha pedestal. And what better way to do that than to reject me? To turn me into a Lone Wolf like Kodiak, who has to prove himself every day despite the golden blood in his veins. Why else would Aspen have gone against everything that is good and right, against everything his body desired the moment we mated, if not to punish me? His hatred of me must have been strong to overcome something as potent as a mate bond. I was so stupid to hope we could repair anything when he so fundamentally dislikes me.

I'll never hope again.

The bell rings, and cheers and hollers erupt as people jump out of scraping chairs. My whisper is almost inaudible amidst the chaos. "I never knew."

"Never knew what?" Aspen asks. I guess he heard me. I guess he's speaking to me.

A good alpha wouldn't say anything. She'd be strong and confident, cool as winter mornings, but Aspen already knows the truth about what I am. He hates me for it. So my hurt spills out in a broken voice. "I never knew how much you hated me."

I race for the door without even glancing at him, tears blurring my vision. I have to get away from Aspen, away from everyone. They can't see me like this. As I run down the hall, I ignore the teachers telling me to slow down, and I listen to peers speculating that I must be off to see Alpha Kodiak, that I've been aching to see him all day. Why else would I be in such a hurry? Despite the drama it's caused, in that moment I'm grateful for Kodiak and our ruse so that the world can assume I'm better than I am.

Once outside, I shift into wolf form and run on four legs. At 2:30 in the morning, the night sky is almost as dark as my fur. My emotions are spilling from me like water from a cracked vase I cannot plug. As I approach the woods near my house, I realize someone is following me, someone who's been running with more urgency than myself.

Aspen's wolf form is all golden waves and glinting blue eyes, and I sense his desperation to catch up to me, his frustration, his confusion, and even sadness. He barks at me. He wants to talk, in human form. He wants to know why I'm feeling this way. I flip into human form, cutting off the leaking tap of my emotions.

"Why did you follow me?" I demand as Aspen is shifting into human form. "Huh? Why aren't you chasing after your latest girlfriend?" I feel like some incompatible mixture of oil and water. I'm excited that he's followed me, and I'm angry that he's somehow made me hope just after I swore I never would again. "Am I some sort of sick joke to you?

"You said that you think I hate you!" Aspen cries. "I don't hate you, Luna. How can you even say that?" He slaps a hand against his chest. "I have always loved and cared about you. You know that, right?"

"How am I supposed to know that?! You don't care about me at all, I know you don't." I feel my throat closing, my eyes watering. Even in human form, my emotions are far too obvious. "I mean, really? Dating Anika out of nowhere like that? Did you even think about how much that would hurt me?"

"Hurt you?" His eyebrows furrow, his nostrils flare. "Hurt *you*, when you're the one parading around with KODIAK?" His voice breaks into a growl I've never heard him use before. "KISSING him in front of me, in front of everyone. Whispering to him at dinner, holding his hand, going to Midnight River for the weekend, all while I'm listening to EVERYONE talk about it ALL THE TIME." His blue eyes are wide and wild, and they hold a glow usually reserved for alpha-blooded. His muscles are taut and his mouth is turned into a dangerous snarl. "I had to watch ALL OF THAT." His voice keeps breaking into a growl, almost how a teenage boy's voice breaks into a high pitch. "Did you think of how it made me feel?" He's taking long, heavy steps towards me, and my breath catches in my throat. "Do you even understand how much I loathe to see you with him, the way it tears at my body and heart?"

He's so close now I can't breathe. The sounds of the forest, the scents all around us, all of it fades as I lock onto this moment, lock onto his eyes. "I had to do it," I whisper. "You rejected me. You left me with no other option." I clench my jaw and draw in the deep breath he's stolen. "I had to do whatever it took to get you to wake up and see me."

His eyes widen with realization, and I see my Aspen shining through as his eyes dim, taking back control of his own body, but he still looks pained. "Lu." His voice is so quiet. "There's so much to say." The emotion in his voice is close to tears. "And I've been trying so hard not to touch you, because I just know that if I do, I'll never let you go."

This is it. This is what it's all been for. The tears, the scheme, the lies, the heartache. It's all been for this moment. I can hear my heartbeat pounding in my ears. "Then *touch me.*"

Oh no.

Oh no oh no.

He's here. I sense him.

My heart drops to my stomach and my face falls. "Aspen, you need to shift NOW!"

"Shift? Why—" And then Aspen realizes it too and shifts into wolf form just as a huge, black wolf with golden, glowing eyes bounds into view. No no no no no no.

"Kodiak!" I cry, but it falls on deaf ears as Kodiak leaps in a ferocious pounce straight onto Aspen. Aspen lets out a whine of pain followed by panicked barking. I have no doubt that Kodiak can rip Aspen to shreds, and I'm desperate to stop it. "KODIAK!" I scream before shifting into my own wolf form and charging at Kodiak, knocking him off Aspen. In wolf form, I feel Kodiak's rage radiating from him like sonar. I can almost taste his bloodlust, metallic and sticky on my tongue.

I position myself between him and Aspen, making it clear he is not to touch him. Kodiak crouches and growls, the fur on his hide sticking up like a thousand tiny needles. He bares his huge teeth as hot saliva drips onto the forest floor. He's telling me he wants me to move. He's threatening me, even, but I stand my ground. It's not that I think he couldn't kill me if he wanted to, but deep down I believe he won't. He lashes out in an angry growling fit, and I match him with a low growl of my own. He starts charging towards me, and I clench my jaw and brace for impact when Kodiak flawlessly flips into human form just inches away from me and starts screaming at Aspen.

"I KNEW IT WAS YOU! I KNEW IT WAS YOU ALL ALONG, YOU PATHETIC MUTT!" Spit is flying out of his mouth. "Do you realize how selfish you've been? What you've done to Luna? So stop hiding behind her and fight me so I can kill you! You understand? I'm going to kill you. I'll kill you right here and now."

Aspen is backing away, his blond ears flat against his head and his hind legs buckling. He could run, but he'll never outrun Kodiak. We all know this. Kodiak starts shifting back into wolf form, and I flip into human form and throw my arms around Kodiak's wolf neck.

"Please, Kodiak!" I beg, and tears streak down my cheeks as I bury my face in his fur shoulder. "Just let him go! I know you want to kill him, I know you have all the power to kill him, but you can't!" I scramble back and place my hands on both sides of

Kodiak's long wolf face. His fur is so dark against my pale hands. His eyes burn a shockingly bright gold, like a fire in the pitch-black night. "You can't kill him, Kodiak. Please. You just can't." Tears are running down my face, and his snarl retreats. His heartbeat starts to slow, but his eyes remain angry as ever. I turn to Aspen and throw out my arm, gesturing for him to leave. "Get out of here! Leave, Aspen!" Please, please leave.

Aspen runs off as fast as his four legs will take him. Looking into Kodiak's furious golden eyes, I can imagine the anger that must be rippling from him in wolf form.

"Thank you, Kodiak," I whisper. "Thank you, I—"

He flips into human form. "What was that, Luna?!" And now all that anger is focused on me.

I swallow the lump in my throat.

"He followed me home," I say. "I—I got angry with him at the end of school, and, and he wanted to talk to me. And so, and so we—"

"And what did you say to him? Because maybe, just maybe, my hearing was off for once, but it sounded like you said that you did what you had to do so that he would see you. That he should *touch you*. Did I get that right?"

My mouth has gone dry. I don't know what to say. Kodiak is so close to me, he is so angry, and I am both ashamed and frightened.

"Did I, or did I not, Luna?" He demands. Kodiak's voice, musical and lilting in nature, has transformed into something terrifying. Even after the Heir Trials, when he beat down heir after heir with ease, I never saw him as an intimidating, hard Alpha. I thought he was just light and breezy and golden. Turns out, like with everything in my life, I was wrong.

Kodiak's eyes are hotter than burning coals as they bore into me. "Because with that kind of talk, it seems like to me that everything you and I have done to show the world we are mates, to make a life for ourselves—everything was just so you could make him jealous. So you could win back that scrap of hide and then go off with him. That was your plan all along. Or am I wrong?"

My heart has dropped to a stomach of painful, tight knots. I want to tell him that this is all a big misunderstanding and that he's gotten it all wrong, but neither statement is true. Kodiak is right. Everything I've done with him was in pursuit of a selfish plan to win Aspen back. I went forward with such a public charade on a naive optimism that everything would work out all right. Seconds tick by as I scour my mind for the right words to say, and the wild look in his eyes morphs into something hard.

"So it is true." His lip curls. His disgust is palpable.

Tears start to run down my face, or maybe they never stopped. "Kodiak, I'm sorry. I never meant for all this. I just—it became so much more complicated than I thought, and, and I thought—"

"You thought? No, Luna. You didn't think at all. Because you were selfish and thoughtless." He isn't yelling, but his voice is cold and deep, and that might be worse than if he were screaming at me. "You didn't think it would be complicated? For me to publicly announce you as my mate, and then a week later you tell everyone that I was lying? That it was all some stunt and that you're actually mates with Aspen? That you and I took the sacred mate bond and pretended it was ours? You didn't THINK about it?!" His voice has risen again, and I pray no one is anywhere near us to hear everything. Then I'm ashamed of the thought. I deserve public humiliation for everything I've done, don't I? I was willing to put Kodiak through it for my own gain, after all.

"You're supposed to be the heir of Dakota Ridge and *this* is how you behave? What kind of alpha are you, Luna? It's embarrassing that you would stoop so low." His words are claws ripping up my heart, and by now I'm crying so much that my nose is clogged and I can hardly smell. Without my sense of smell, I feel blind and vulnerable in the dark woods.

"Stop sniveling like some pathetic omega," Kodiak growls. Then he shifts back into that large, beautiful wolf, and he runs back the way he came, leaving me alone with the person I hate most.

CHAPTER 27

IT SHOULD HAVE BEEN US

A barrage of thoughts batter my soul. It's too much; it's too overwhelming. I switch into wolf form. When I'm all wolf, my mind doesn't work the same way as it does in human form. My thoughts become simple and blunt, and the humanesque complications and nuance turn into an out-of-focus backdrop. If I'd been in wolf form this whole time, then this entire situation would have been avoided. I'd never have involved myself in such a disastrous scheme because I wouldn't have thought it up in the first place. I shift and curl up on the forest floor, closing my eyes and feeling my mind slow. In exchange for dulled thoughts, sharp, primal emotions and simple, piercing thoughts fill my head and chest. I feel terrible. I feel guilty. I feel sad. I messed up. I am a bad person.

It's not long before Rory finds me, and she places a hand on my furry shoulder. "I overheard Kodiak yelling at you," she says. Her voice is gentle. She sounds like Mom. "Do you want to stay here or go home?"

I do not move. It does not matter. I feel so sad.

Rory sighs and sits cross-legged next to me. She starts scratching my head with those long nails of hers. It feels good, but I still feel so sad and guilty. She starts singing "Hey Little Wolf Cub" quietly. Rory has a nice voice. She really sounds like Mom when she sings. Time passes. The sun is rising. Rory nudges my shoulders.

"Come on Luna," she says. "We have to go to dinner. Dad invited Kodiak over."

I shake my head. No. I can't go. I feel too bad.

"Yes, you need to come," Rory said, pulling my body from the ground so that I'll stand on four legs. I let out a grumpy growl, and Rory flicks my ears. "It will be alright, Luna."

No. I don't want to see Kodiak. I am a bad person.

I yelp as Rory takes me by the scruff of my neck and starts dragging me forward. I wriggle out of her grip and snap my jaws at her before walking forward on my own. Mean Rory. I don't want to go.

"Things have a way of working out," she says. "We'll figure it out, okay? I'm here to help you."

No one can help me.

We make our way up our hill of a backyard and enter the basement's sliding door. "Come on, Luna. You can't sit at the table like that. You'll shed all over the food." I let out a growl, and Rory flicks my ear again. "You growl at me once more and I'll tear your teeth out." She looks annoyed, but her voice is calm. I don't want to go to the dinner table. I don't feel like switching to human form. I want to go back to the woods. I feel so bad, but I shift into human form.

It takes a moment for wolf-brain fog to clear, but once it does my thoughts crash against my mind like ice-cold water. I replay my conversation with Kodiak in my mind. The blooming anger in his tone. The way he looked at me, like I was patient zero of a flea infestation. I am selfish and thoughtless, far crueler in my actions than he was in his gaze. Just on the brink of a breakthrough with Aspen, I had to face the consequences of my actions that got me to that point. I want to dissect everything that happened with Aspen, to pull that memory apart and extract the shining gold nuggets of hope—yet it feels wrong of me to think about my own happiness when I've caused so much stress and chaos.

"Rory, I—" Tears fill my eyes. "I can't go. He hates me. I've really messed it all up. I've caused such a mess, and—"

"Don't cry again. Your face will get puffy." She snags a tissue from the coffee table and passes it to me.

I dab at the tears blotting my face before blowing into the tissue. "I can't go," I whisper.

Rory draws in a deep breath. "Maybe you should take a quick shower, wash all those tears off. Dinner's not going to be ready this hot second. I'll dazzle them with my small talk in the meantime."

I almost laugh. Rory hates small talk.

She puts her hand on my shoulder, and I see sympathy in her eyes. "I know it's hard. I know there's a lot on your mind, but you have to face Kodiak. This is part of what it means to be an alpha. You don't run away from your problems—you address them head on."

I purse my lips. *What it means to be an alpha.* But she must know that I'm weak—she's seen it on full display this past week. The only thing alpha about me is my genetics, and that's nothing I had control over. "But I'm not like you, Rory," I say. Maybe that's why she left for Northern Skies with hardly a thought to spare for me. I am nothing more than a lower beta in her eyes, some pitiful creature beneath her radar.

Rory rolls her eyes. "Of course you're not like me, Luna.

Moon, we've always known that." My stomach drops. *We've always known.* This is, of course, no new development for her. But Rory continues. "I am me and you are you. What's your point?"

"What I mean is—" I find myself stumbling over the words. "What I mean is I'm not strong and brave like you are."

Rory surveys me with soft silver eyes. So much like Mom's in gentle moments. "Luna, you and I are different. Like I said. You feel so much more than I do."

So she does know. She knows all about my sappy, sape-y feelings.

Her smile is kind. "And that makes you much braver."

On the main level, Bea and Kya are cooking and Dad is wearing headphones as he finishes up some call. Good, he wouldn't have heard us talking. He pulls off his headphones to tell us that dinner is almost ready, and he looks at me when he says that Kodiak is waiting out on the deck.

"Luna's gonna take a quick shower," Rory says. "Make herself pretty and all that for 'im." She motions for me to go upstairs. "I remember when I was always making sure I looked my best for Grey."

"It was the same for me with your mom." There's a special warmth in Dad's voice that only comes out when he talks about Mom. As I head up the stairs, I listen to the tail end of their conversation. "Made sure I smelled nice, that my hair wasn't too much of a mess."

"Mom loved your hair."

"She did."

I make it to my bathroom and turn on the shower. While I wait for the water to warm up, I look at myself in the mirror, at my red-rimmed eyes and puffy skin. The healing scratch on my cheek. I wonder how things might have turned out today if Kodiak hadn't arrived when he did. Would I be such a teary mess? Would my conversation with Aspen finally heal what he had broken, and would everything be fine? No, everything couldn't have been fine, even if it had worked out that way. I still would have had to figure out how to handle this Kodiak situation. On the night of the Blue Moon, Aspen and I made irrevocable choices. Our moment on the balcony was a gift as golden as Kodiak's eyes, and we as good as threw it into the ocean. I still hope we can forge a new treasure, reclaim some lost gold, but we'll never get that piece back. At the fork of destiny, Aspen and I made decisions we cannot unmake with consequences we cannot run from.

The rising steam lets me know that the shower is more than hot enough now. I'll get in soon, but first I pull back the curtain on the bathroom window to steal a glance at Kodiak, and I see that Rory is sitting with him on the deck, her hair golden in the sunlight. Over the sound of water hitting the bathtub floor, I can't make out what they're saying, but curiosity compels me to inch the window open.

"—sure the wedding will be beautiful," Rory says.

I put my back against the wall—I don't want either of them to glance up and see me eavesdropping. I'm praying Kodiak won't somehow know that I'm listening, that he'll assume my shower has overtaken my senses.

Kodiak's laugh is derisive. "Assuming there is a wedding."

Rory does not answer. I wonder if she's looking at him, eyes full of sympathy, or if they're trained on the forest ahead, unsure of how to answer.

"You knew, didn't you?" he says. "That this was all some scheme to win over that pathetic mate of hers—that they still had a bond?"

I purse my lips. The bitterness in his tone makes my stomach curdle all over again.

"Yes, I knew," she says.

He lets out a huffy breath. "I see."

She sighs. "I know."

"How could she do something like that? Was she trying to humiliate me? To tear me down even more? I don't know how anyone will respect me after this. She just as good as gave away my birthright."

My guilt only intensifies at his words, a stabbing reminder of how thoughtless and cruel I've been. I gave no consideration to anyone other than myself, and now Kodiak's been dragged into a mess that never was his.

"Luna acted rashly," Rory says. This is where she tells him what a disgrace I am, how she lectured me to figure it out, how she told me it was going to hurt him, how she knew I was thoughtless and selfish. "And so did you."

"*Tch.*"

"You should have known better than to jump into such a precarious situation last second." Despite the accusatory nature of her words, Rory's voice is calm and even. "And with an eighteen-year-old who was just rejected by her soulmate. Did you think she'd be over him just like that?"

Kodiak doesn't say anything.

"You had your own selfish motivations, and had either of you thought to consult me, I would have advised against it."

"We didn't have time for a consultation session," Kodiak says. "We only had a little time before the party."

"You two could have chosen to get married later on," she says. "You didn't have to put on a whole performance and lie about being mates. There are cases of widowed wolves getting remarried, and neither of you really even had a mate to begin with."

"It wouldn't have been the same and you know that," Kodiak chides. "We never would have been respected in the same way."

Rory doesn't refute his point. As the seconds pass, I wonder if that's the end of their conversation and if I should actually get in the shower when Rory speaks again. "Is it bad? The way they treat you?"

The sound of my shower water fills the long pause.

"Half of Midnight River wanted Jael to be Alpha," he says.

"Jael?" she sounds shocked.

"Yep."

"They wanted *him* to be Alpha? What's wrong with your pack?"

"Well, he has a mate."

"Still!" Rory breezes past his somber tone, incredulous at this development. "Having a mate doesn't magically change someone into some mature being. I've met so many pairs of mates who are the absolute worst."

"Like Ares and his mate from the other night. What was her name?"

"Misty! Moon, they are awful," Rory groans.

Kodiak laughs. "You were so close to losing it."

"I mean, why was she acting like she and I were best friends?"

"I guess you're both in the new-mate, pre-children stage of life."

"Yeah, not a good reason to get cozy with me. She's lucky I didn't rip her hair out."

He clicks his tongue. "So violent, Rory."

"Right, you're one to talk. Remember when that Crimson Star beta told you that their Alek was a better heir than you?"

"Oh, moon."

"Do you remember what you did?"

"Maybe."

"You kicked him in the face."

"First of all, that beta was super annoying and condescending for no reason. And second of all, it was a beautiful kick," Kodiak says. Rory laughs. "I had to skip detention for a week after that but it was totally worth it."

"It was a gorgeous kick," Rory concedes. "Violent, but gorgeous."

"Do you remember Reika?"

"Not her," Rory groans.

"Her nose is still crooked."

"What, are you trying to make me feel bad about it?" Rory asks. "She was so annoying."

"Was she?"

"Well I'm sure she wasn't that way to you, but to me?" She groans. "The way she would glom onto you? It was infuriating. I don't even regret it."

"How heartless."

Rory snorts. "Whatever. You know—and maybe you feel this way too with being Alpha and all, I don't know—but now I have to be level-headed all the time and diplomatic and mature, and sometimes I miss those days when I just did whatever I wanted to, when I would just go around goofing off with friends and bugging the sapes, and when you and I would—" she pauses, catching herself on whatever she was going to say. Her tone shifts. "Well, I suppose it doesn't matter now. We all have to grow up. I can't be as impulsive as I once was."

A silence falls between them that I do not understand. I dare a glance out the glass, praying they don't see me. I feel a warm breeze against my skin from the crack in the window. In the light of the early morning sun, Rory and Kodiak are looking out at the forest, not each other. It seems they're lost in some daze of a past gone by, and I feel there is something being said in their silence. When Kodiak speaks, his voice is so quiet that it's little more than a whisper in the wind.

"It should have been us."

Rory does not flinch, does not widen her eyes in surprise. In fact, she seems so stoic in her continued gaze forward that I wonder if she'd been thinking the same thing. Then, she draws in and releases a deep breath.

"No. If it was supposed to be us, it would have been."

The steaming shower behind me mimics the sound of falling rain as I wait with Rory and Kodiak in their silence. Kodiak doesn't respond, doesn't even look at her. It's Rory who speaks again.

"I love Grey. He's...not like me. He's far more quiet, thoughtful, observant. He's my other half. He softens my edges and I sharpen his. We round each other out, we make each other whole. I am a better person because of him, and I love him so, so much."

"I know," Kodiak says. "He's your mate."

Seconds tick by, and her voice is so quiet that I hold my breath to hear her words. "But there's a part of me that will always love you, Kodi, in the part of my heart where that girl who was wild and free still lives on."

Kodiak turns his head to look at her. I cannot see his eyes from my window, so I'm left to imagine what his face must look like. Rory looks at him, something rueful in her lips and in her gaze. "But I'm not that girl anymore, and I suspect...you're not that boy either." She looks at him for a few seconds more before she stands. I wonder what she's thinking and feeling in this moment, how her emotions are twisting and curling around her heart. As she heads for the back door, she pauses and turns back to Kodiak.

"I never thanked you."

"For what?" Kodiak asks, twisting in his seat to face her. A ghost of a sheepish smile dances on his lips. "Dragging your sister into a huge mess?"

I can imagine the amused quirk of her lip. "No, not that." A pause. "For not killing Grey at the Heir Trials. I know you could have. I know you wanted to. But you didn't."

There's something so sad in Kodiak's expression, even from my spying out a window, that I wonder how Rory can stand to look right at him. "I didn't do it for him," he says.

She waits for a beat. "I know."

CHAPTER 28

A COUPLE OF SENTENCES

At dinner, I can hardly pay attention to anything Dad is saying. He's going on about wedding plans, and Kodiak and I are giving half-hearted answers. Rory's back probably hurts from carrying this entire conversation, interjecting to give her opinion and stating simple facts to elicit nods from me and Kodiak. My eyes keep going from Kodiak to Rory, trying to catch some sizzling spark in their gaze. Kodiak's eyes have lost their usual bright expressiveness, and he's donned the placid smile I usually see on Grey. Rory is fighting to make it seem like all is well, and is giving us both a look that begs us to try harder. I don't sense the anger and hostility that rippled off Kodiak earlier, and I wonder if he's depressed about me or Rory. Maybe it's both. Maybe he's just depressed about everything. I always knew that he and Rory sort of liked each other, and they used to hang out enough that he almost felt like an older brother to me, but I never realized how deep it ran. I guess most wolves don't like to advertise pre-mate relationships, but still. She told him she had loved him. That's a big deal, isn't it?

As I look between them, envy flickers in my heart, even

though I shouldn't feel that way. I wonder if Rory felt at all the same when Kodiak kissed me at the banquet and announced to the world that I was his mate.

Kodiak's phone buzzes and he checks the screen. "I have to head out," he says, standing up from his chair. "They need me back in Midnight River." I wonder if that's true or not, but at this point I don't care. I just want this day to end. But I feel Rory's expectant silver eyes on me, and I know I have to be a little brave.

"I'll walk you out," I say, holding his hand for show.

After Dad says goodbye, I walk Kodiak outside and he lets go of my hand as soon as the front door closes.

"See you." His voice is gruff, but it lacks the fury from earlier. His eyes hold that hint of expression once more, and I realize that his big bad blow-up was just the explosive reaction to how hurt he felt.

I want to hold my tongue, to let him run off, but I muster up my courage and blurt out, "Can we talk?"

His stare is that of a wounded animal—angered but hurt. He isn't saying anything, and as much as I don't want to talk, I'm more scared he'll just say no and I'll be awake all day worrying about it on top of everything else.

He finally speaks. "Yes. We need to talk. But can we do it tomorrow?" My heart sinks. So much for getting sleep today. "I have a lot on my mind, and I think I'll be in a better place to talk then."

It's not the answer I was hoping for, but it will have to do. "Okay."

He nods and turns to leave.

"Kodiak?"

He looks back at me.

"I'm sorry. I know that doesn't fix anything, but I'm sorry. I really am."

He draws in a deep breath and sighs before taking a step towards me. My eyes widen when he plants a kiss on the top of my head. He looks so sad, like the weight of life has hit him all at once. His puts his hand on my forearm and gives it a light squeeze. "I'm sorry, too."

A DAY OF POOR SLEEP IS FOLLOWED BY A NIGHT OF SCHOOL. The summer sun is still up by the time I'm in front of Adam Douglas High, collecting my meaty lunch from the lower beta women outside the school. When I see Aspen in class, I take my usual desk near him, and everything from yesterday rushes towards me—the way his voice would break into a snarl as he spoke of me and Kodiak, the way he looked at me with longing eyes, the way he was so desperate to touch and not touch me. Aspen winces as he fidgets in his plastic seat. Though his face is unmarred, I'm sitting close enough that I can smell the healing wounds underneath his clothing.

"Are you okay?" I ask just under my breath. More students are filing into class, laughing and joking with each other.

Aspen's jaw flexes against some pain, and his eyes are cold and steely. "It's just part of being a werewolf." He does not try to hide the bitterness in his tone. Kodiak pounced on Aspen the second he showed up, dug his claws into him. My stomach churns to think of the consequences had I not stopped him.

"Do you need help?" I whisper.

His lip curls. He doesn't even look at me. "There's nothing you can do. This is just life here."

Moon, he's really upset. "Aspen, what do you mean?"

"Hey Aspen!" Anika takes her desk in front of Aspen and grins at me. "And Luna. Always good to see our gorgeous heir."

I smile back at her, as it's what I should do. Besides, now that I know that Aspen is still struggling with his feelings for me, I'm feeling far more magnanimous towards Anika than I was yesterday. "Evening, Ani."

Anika looks Aspen over. "You don't look too good."

"I'm alright."

"Class, we need to get started," Mr. Miller says. No one stops talking.

"You sure you're alright?" Anika's legs are kicked out to the side of the chair as she leans in to sniff Aspen. "Moon, are you wounded?"

"It's not a big deal."

"What happened?" She doesn't sound overly concerned, more curious than anything. Aspen isn't one for fights like Logan or Raff.

"My brother and I got into it, that's all," Aspen says. "Wolf form."

Anika laughs. "Stars, Aspen! You date me for a couple of days and already you're acting more like a wolf. Good for you!"

I wonder how she cannot see the insincerity in his smile.

When Logan walks in, Anika waves him over. "Loges! Guess what! Aspen actually got into a scrap!"

"No way!" Logan is all smiles as he claps Aspen on the back. Aspen winces. "Now that's what I'm talking about! Wait until Raff gets a load of this."

"AHEM!" Mr. Miller says in the form of a loud cough.

"Where is that stupid little mutt?" Logan mutters. "YO RAFF!" He cups his hands around his mouth.

"Logan!" Mr. Miller yells.

"LOO-gan!" Some of the wolves mimic the teacher.

"What's up!" Raff runs into the classroom. Must have heard Logan from the hall.

"It's Aspen!"

"What about 'im?'"

Moon, this is so chaotic. Aspen's irritation is obvious now as he tells them class is starting. Mr. Miller tries to start class as his bald head turns redder and redder. Nova walks in announcing she got us all snacks, and gives everyone in our friend group a jerky stick. Raff pokes Nova and tells her Aspen got wounded in a fight with his brother.

"Uh, is he okay?"

"'Course he's fine." Raff snorts.

"IF YOU ALL DO NOT GET IN YOUR SEATS, NONE OF YOU WILL GRADUATE. *I MEAN IT!*" Mr. Miller shrieks.

"Oh no. What a nightmare." Logan deadpans. Half the class laughs.

"Logan, you should find your seat," I finally say. "Class is starting. We might as well graduate if we've suffered this long."

"Oh, alright. Only 'cause *you* said so."

The day goes on as usual, or about as usual as it can be. It still upsets my stomach when I see Aspen and Anika brush hands or smile at each other or tell private jokes, but through the glossy sheen of a new relationship, I can see that Aspen's mind is troubled. Perhaps he's thinking about last night as much as I am and how close we were to one another before Kodiak pounced. He told me that he has so much to say, and I'm desperate to hear him out. I have to talk to Kodiak tonight—I have to figure out so many things—but I need to know why Aspen rejected me. I need to know if I'm really the problem or if there's something else. Everything that's happened between us couldn't have meant nothing to him.

Today is the last day of school. I hear that it's some sort of emotional day for human seniors, that people cry saying goodbye to their friends and teachers, but there isn't a tear to be found among the werewolf student body. The closest we get is when Logan says he's so happy it's over that he could cry. Not only do we have little interest in school, but no one is leaving their respective packs. All this means is that we'll meet up in the woods, the town square, and the Alpha House rather than dingy, LED-lit hallways.

At lunch, I'm sitting across from Logan, Anika, and Aspen on the same plastic green bench as Nova and Raff. The whole conversation has mostly consisted of Logan, Anika, and Raff complaining about everything we've endured while Nova and Aspen and I eat our food. Logan's mouth is full of venison-burger as he reminisces. "And let's not forget about Mr. Apple-body's cologne." He swallows and breaks out into a fake cough. "I could smell it from down the hall."

"Apple-body! Ha!" Anika laughs. "My nose always stung when he wore that sapcrap."

"And those big textbooks they made us read? I'd burn them all in a huge bonfire if the next kids weren't forced to use them."

"Well I kept every essay I ever wrote," Anika says. "Just so I can burn them to celebrate."

"NO WAY! You're a genius, Ani!" Logan cries.

"Ughhhhh," Raff whines. "Why didn't I think of that?"

"'Cause you're no brains and all brawn," Anika says, taking a bite out of her burger.

"Better than the reverse," he says.

"I can't wait to get out of here." Logan throws his head back in a blissful sigh. "Twelve years of torture are over. And when I find my mate, everything will be perfect."

"Amen to that!" Anika smiles at Aspen and puts her shoulder against his. I almost scoff. Like she'll be his mate.

"You know, it really wasn't all that bad," Aspen says, eyeing Raff, Logan and Anika. "And there were some good teachers too."

"Like who? Mrs. Pugface?" Raff's laugh is akin to a hyena.

Aspen grits his teeth, his eyes glower. His voice snaps like a whip. "Mrs. Smith was a perfectly nice teacher, especially considering how poorly you all treated her!"

A thick silence sweeps across the table like a strong gust of wind. They don't know how to react to Aspen's anger. Nova's shoulders hunch, even though she hadn't even participated in bashing the teachers.

"None of you ever respected them. None of you ever tried. You got mad about the littlest things, and whenever a teacher tried to help you, you all ignored them. It's like you all want to be as dumb as possible!"

Their eyes are wide. Mine scan him carefully, watching the pain in his eyes.

"We've had some really good teachers. Think about Mr. Bass or Ms. Turner. Ms. Turner even added a whole section dedicated to werewolf literature! Think, these teachers willingly applied for the worst of all the teaching jobs—the night class. They have to go against their natural clocks to deal with a bunch of disrespectful mutts, and most of them do it because they want to try and give us a good education. If any of you had reached out, if any of you had actually tried, they would have helped you. And yet, all you can do is spit on them and make fun of them." Aspen stands up, snatching his brown paper bag. "We assume we're just so much better than humans without ever bothering to take a look in the mirror." He stalks off across the cheap plastic flooring towards the entrance, leaving us with his condemning words. My stomach churns. I wonder how much of his speech applied to me. I've always been nicer to teachers than most, but I haven't been without my share of complaints. Is this part of why he rejected me? I didn't love the human teachers enough?

Anika looks stunned, but her wide eyes quickly give way to

teary ones. "Excuse me," she mumbles. She bolts towards the cafeteria door and leaves the four of us alone in a painful silence. I'm not sure what I should say, or if I should have chased after Aspen myself. Raff is the first to break the ice.

"You know...I will kind of miss the human teachers," he says. For the second time in this conversation, we're all stunned.

"Really?" Nova asks.

"Yeah." A maniacal grin grows on his face. "I remember when Ms. Turner first got here and saw one of the first fights of the year. She looked like she was going to faint 'cause of all the blood. I'll miss seeing that look on new teachers' faces."

"You're so stupid," Nova mutters, and Raff and Logan burst out laughing.

"Moon, what was with Aspen's whole speech?" Logan is shaking his head and chuckling. "Like any of this school stuff even matters."

I look down at the burger patty in my hands, my stomach wound so tightly that it hardly looks appealing anymore. I feel my phone buzz. Aspen—he's texting me. I shove the last bite of food in my mouth and click open my phone. No, it's not Aspen, but Kodiak.

Kodiak 12:14 a.m.

I will pick you up from school

Kodiak 12:14 a.m.

Then we can talk

"Is that Kodiak?" Raff asks, chomping loudly.

I almost jump. "Oh, yeah. He's going to pick me up after school."

"Must be nice to have your mate," Raff says. "It's been two months already. I'm going to die a Lone Wolf like Logan."

"Shut up," Logan snaps. Raff laughs. He turned eighteen in April, Logan in January.

When school lets out, I'm almost relieved to see Kodiak's dented truck in the distance. It was the perfect excuse to avoid Logan's plans to celebrate the end of school at Bruno's. The rest of the school night had been awkward, with everyone avoiding Aspen, and Anika wearing these dejected puppy eyes. We don't have yearbooks to sign—no one but Aspen volunteered for a yearbook team, and he didn't want to do it by himself—so most wolves are headed home like it's any other day.

"That's Alpha Kodiak over there, isn't it?" Logan says. We're standing just outside the front doors, and Kodiak's truck is the only running vehicle that isn't a school bus.

"Yeah, that's him," I say. There are a lot of students rushing past us, shouting in unbridled excitement that the school year is done. "A bunch of you guys are celebrating at Bruno's, right?"

"Yeah." Logan pauses. "I wish you could come."

"Oh, me too," I lie. "But you know."

"Yeah. You have a mate now. That comes first."

I smile and shrug.

"Do you remember that time we went to Bruno's after school? Just you and me could go. Last spring."

"Oh yeah, I remember," I say, though really it's little more than a vague memory.

This smile stretches on his face, but there's something almost sad in it. "Yeah. You got that big ice cream sundae, and it was too sweet for you, so you made me eat it with you. You didn't want to let it go to waste, make Bruno feel bad." His laugh is slight. "That was real nice of you. You know, to think of him."

I'd forgotten about that. "Oh yeah! It was a big, oh, what kind of a sundae? A big—"

"Peanut butter fudge," he says. "Super rich."

"Right, right." I look over at where Kodiak is parked. I

should probably start walking towards the truck instead of down memory lane.

"Are you happy with him?" Logan asks. I turn my face to him, and he shakes his head. "Ugh, stupid question. Sorry. Of course you are. He's your mate. And he's, you know, he's all that. Alpha. Heir Trial victor. Of course, of course you're happy."

I take a moment to look at Logan carefully. He's agitated, acting unlike himself. I think about Raff's joke from lunch. "Hey, Logan, you know what Raff said earlier, about you being a Lone Wolf. You know that's not true, right?"

"No, no, I know."

"Six months is nothing to be worried about, especially as a male."

"Yes, that's not...it's not that. I'm sure I have someone. It's just, well, I thought maybe—" his cheeks color. "I had an idea of who it might be, and it's not her. So. Whatever. But like, I'm happy for you, you know?"

Logan's had a little crush on me since forever, as far as I can tell. Oh, he gave me a birthday gift, didn't he? I forgot to open it. Oh well. Logan is feeling bad now, but I know he'll find his mate, and when he does, none of those inkling feelings for me will matter.

"Hey," I say, touching his arm. "You'll find someone, okay? You'll find your mate. And when you do...I mean, the past will just be that. Past. None of it will matter. You're going to be so happy you won't know what to do with yourself. And I'm excited for that for you. Really. You deserve it. So keep your head up, alright? Be patient and the Moon will bring your soul-mate to you."

Logan's smile is large, but it lacks any sign of life. "Yeah, for sure. Thanks, Luna. Appreciate it." He gestures to the truck. "I'll let you go see your mate now. I'll see you around."

As Logan walks off, I wonder if his feelings for me ran deeper than I ever realized. What I brushed off as a trivial crush, could it have meant the whole night sky to him? Could his feelings for me be even half as much as my feelings for Aspen? It seems impossible that my friendship with Logan could produce such emotion in him, but I don't really know, do I? Maybe Aspen sees me the way I see Logan, and every moment we shared was under his generic friendship umbrella. The story of his life starred Mousy and Anika as leading ladies, and Luna as a side character. Without the Moon's interference, perhaps I would have been little more than a couple of sentences in his diary of life.

And then I wonder how I would have felt, were I in Logan's shoes and Aspen in mine. If after finding a mate, all Aspen could muster for me was some trite, clichéd, "be patient. You'll get your soulmate one day."

I grimace as I approach Kodiak's vehicle, where he looks ahead with some simmering glower. I've probably hurt Logan with my thoughtlessness, and now I have to face the person I've hurt most of all. I pause outside the truck and rest my hand on the handle for a few seconds, taking a deep breath to muster my courage. Then, I open the passenger door.

CHAPTER 29

NORTH STAR

Kodiak does not look at me when I climb into the truck. The "thanks for picking me up" I was going to say dies on my lips. He drives away from the school and onto Dakota Ridge's dirt road, the vehicle jostling with every imperfection of the path beneath.

"How was your last day?" he asks without much warmth.

"It was fine. It's over now, at least. I graduated."

"Well, school is apparently very important to you." There's a hint of a sneer on his lips.

I tighten my jaw. "Well it's over now, so you don't have to worry about me going to school anymore."

"Your schooling is the least of my worries now," he says.

Another jab to bruise my spirit, to remind me of the colossal mess I've made. We drive through the center of town, with its few buildings and businesses. Wolves turn to look at the unusual sight of a car on the road with curious eyes that light up when they realize it's me and Kodiak. I wear a fake smile through the glass until we're out of their sight. Kodiak navigates through dirt roads until we reach human-made pavement, leading us outside of pack territories. The Moon and the truck's headlights illuminate the road as we cruise past pine trees. I lean back against the headrest and a deep sigh escapes my chest.

"I screwed up, Kodiak," I say. "I know I did." The truck rumbles and hums in our silence. "When I asked you to pretend to be my mate, I wasn't thinking clearly at all. I didn't think of the long-term implications. I was just thinking of myself, and I was desperate. By the time I realized what I had done, that this whole thing was a terrible idea, it was too late. We were in the middle of it all. And I wish, I wish so badly I could go back in time. I wish I could fix everything. I wish I'd never done this to you, and I don't know what—" My voice breaks. I don't know what I can even say. I don't know what I can do. I look out the passenger window because I can't bear to look at Kodiak's face.

Each ticking second of silence is a painful prick on my heart, but when he speaks, his voice is softer than I expected. "I've been thinking about us a lot, about our situation." A pause. "About you and Aspen."

I brave a glance at him. Kodiak's gaze is fixed on the road ahead as he draws in a breath. "Tell me about him."

The invitation feels like a trap. I think about Aspen all the time, and over the past few years, I've often wished for someone to confide in about my feelings for him, but I don't want to do so now. Not after everything that's happened, and not with Kodiak.

"Well, you know most everything already," I say, looking down at my lap. I quickly rehash the rejection and explain what Queenie told me that night. "I found out that we're still connected by a thread. He still has those mate bond feelings for me, even though he's trying to fight against them. And when I saw you, I thought..."

"You thought you could use me to make him jealous." Kodiak sounds impatient. "Yes, I know all this. I asked you to tell me about *him*, not about this situation."

"About...him? What...what do you want to know?"

"Obviously you care a lot about him. There's more to it than just this past week, isn't there? Remember, I saw you two just before the hunt, and you were already defensive about him." Kodiak's golden eyes fall on me. "So, what is it about him?"

And with how much there is to say, I find myself lost for words. It takes me several moments to say anything. "He's...my best friend." I look down at my fidgeting hands. "He's smart and kind and thoughtful and funny. And when we're together, we can laugh and joke about trivial stuff, or we can talk about things that are deep and meaningful. And honestly, after Rory left, he was the one person left who really saw me. He always knew who I really was." I pause. The truck's soft rumble beneath us creates a lulling noise. "Rory mated with Grey about a year and a half after my mom died. I was still having a really hard time with my mom's death, but Rory was gone." Tears fill my eyes. "She was off in Northern Skies, living a new, perfect life, and I was left behind in Dakota Ridge. And during that time, Aspen was there for me. He's always been there for me, even when no one else has been."

I feel the weight of Kodiak's careful eyes. "And you love him."

It takes a moment for me to say it. "Yes. I love him." Then, my voice lowers to a whisper. "Much more than he loves me." The admission makes my heart drop to my stomach. The thought has been rattling in my head for this past week—if I'm being honest, I've been wondering about it for years now, but saying it out loud makes it feel as real and hard as the asphalt we drive on. "All this time, I thought...I thought there was something special between me and Aspen." I shake my head, so disappointed in my own optimistic naiveté. My volume starts to increase. "This whole time, I've been telling myself that everything is going to work out in the end, that somehow we'll get some fairytale ending, that we'll overcome the challenges. That with every stupid decision I've made, it's all going to be made right when he and I work out. But that's ridiculous, isn't it? Absolutely, completely, stupidly insane!" My laugh is a cold, short barking sound. I imagine standing before a version of myself, one wearing that purple dress for her eighteenth birthday, her eyes full of tears and her heart full of delusions. How stupid was she. "I mean, think about it." I lean forward and wipe away the tears of my past mirage, shaking my head in pity. "Even the very best of cosmic circumstances couldn't make him love me." Then gone is the image, and I'm back in the truck next to Kodiak. The smell of gasoline, the stains on the carpets, his rich, woodsy scent. "And still I dragged you into a mess that never was yours. We shouldn't even be here, having this conversation. You should be home in Midnight River, blissfully unaware of all this. Instead, I made it your problem in some desperate attempt to get Aspen to care about me." I think of the anger in Kodiak's aura the night before, the hot and fuming saliva dripping from his wolf fangs. "And it's all my fault."

I've upended Kodiak's life for nothing, for a person who has never and will never love me the way I love him. So Kodiak's next words are the last thing I expected him to say.

"I forgive you, Luna."

My eyes widen, and I look at him to see he's looking at me with eyes like warm honey. His words and eyes flood my heart with a wave of warmth and relief that I didn't know how much I needed. For a brief moment, there is a lightness in my body I haven't felt in days.

Kodiak returns his eyes to the dark road ahead. "That is, if you'll forgive me."

I tilt my head. "Forgive you?"

He strengthens his grip on the wheel. "Yes. For getting so angry with you. For blaming you for everything as though I had nothing to do with it. I should have known better, I should have thought it through more. You had just been rejected by your mate. Of course you wouldn't be thinking very rationally. And..." He furrows his brows. "I think a part of me knew that. I knew this was a small window where it could work, knew that if we thought it through and considered the risks and the backlash, that we wouldn't go through with it. One or both of us would back out. So I decided we had to rush forward without thinking—and in that way, I was selfish. I did what I wanted for myself, without really thinking through what was best for you. I thought..." His shoulders slump, and those expressive eyes seem to droop. "I thought it was the only way."

I think of their faces—Midnight River wolves full of relief when they met me, the way they were so emphatic about their excitement that Kodiak finally had a mate. I think of Jael sitting in Kodiak's chair, the snide remarks about Kodiak's facial hair, the blatant impudence some showed their Alpha. As desperate as I was to get Aspen back, Kodiak must have been just as desperate for their respect. Kodiak is an incredible specimen, and for his own pack to pity and disrespect him is nothing short of a tragedy.

"You just wanted your pack to respect you." My voice is quiet.

"Yes," he says. He leans his head against the headrest and his lips curve downward. "And I didn't want to be alone anymore."

I raise my eyebrows, turning to face him more fully.

"It's..." His sigh is frustrated. "How do I put this? You told me that I don't know what it's like to lose a mate."

I bite the inside of my cheek and look down. I feel ashamed at that outburst.

"And, I mean, technically you're right. I *don't* know. But...but you don't know what it's like to be alone. And I hope you never know it, Luna, I really do. Because when we were all young and freshly eighteen, we were all in the same boat, all of us hopeful and excited together. And then, all your peers start finding their mates, and then the kids you thought were so much younger than you start finding theirs—and you have to watch as year after year everyone around you finds the love of their lives and you are still alone. And everyone's asking you if you've found the one, or asking what you're doing to meet new wolves, or saying your time will come—and it's so exhausting. And then one day...the questions stop." He pauses, his eyes trained on the night sky ahead of us. "And you realize that you aren't sure what's worse...everyone asking you if you've found your soulmate, or when they've given up on asking all together."

In the last week, I've thought about lone wolves more than I ever have in my whole life combined, and yet I was still so caught up in my own heartache that I didn't think about Kodiak's. I assumed the only thing that would really affect him was his pack's judgement or mistreatment of him, but it's clear that it goes much deeper than that. I think about his conversation with Rory on the deck, that terrible look on his face, and the ache he hasn't been able to heal with a love of his own.

"It's lonely, Luna," Kodiak continues. "To want to find that so badly, and feeling like there's nothing you can do." His eyes move over to me. "But then you came to me, asked me to be your mate." He looks back at the road. "And I knew you didn't love me and that I didn't love you, but there you were. You were so vulnerable and beautiful, and it seemed like maybe, just maybe, the Moon hadn't completely forgotten me. I told myself that this was a gift to me after all these years. It was my opportunity to *do* something. One of those Blue Moon miracles." He sighs. "I was coming to see you when I heard you and Aspen talking in the woods yesterday, and in that moment it was so clear to me, the mistake I'd made. How foolish I'd been. And more than that, I was jealous. I was so jealous, and it all felt so unfair. You are alpha-blooded, and really nice to talk to, and kind, and very, very beautiful. If you had been my mate, you would have been a dream come true." His grip on the wheel is so tight I can see the veins in his arms. "But you were his, and in that moment I was angry—with you, with him, with the Moon, with life, and with myself—and I took it all out on you."

I hadn't imagined that Kodiak would offer any sort of apology in this conversation. I thought I'd be more than lucky if he even deigned to forgive me. But here he was, admitting his shortcomings, telling me I would have been a dream.

"Will you forgive me?" Kodiak asks, looking at me with those syrupy puppy eyes.

Would *I* forgive *him?* After everything I've put him through, after all that's happened this week? What a ridiculous question. "Of course."

We drive in silence for a spell until Kodiak pulls off on an overlook over a dark forest. "Sunrise isn't too far off." He's opening his car door. "Let's enjoy the Moon while we can."

Kodiak hops out, and I follow suit. Kodiak sits on the edge of the truck bed with his legs dangling over the side, and I climb up to join him. With the waning Moon, more stars are visible in the sky, creating a gorgeous canvas above us. It's said that when a werewolf dies, he or she joins the Moon as a star in the night sky.

The chorus of nature at night fills the air—the sounds of

owls, the chitter of bugs, the rustling of the leaves in the breeze. I wonder how much more Kodiak can hear than I can, if he hears a whole symphony in the music of the night. I wonder how much more he can see, if he can trace more patterns amongst the tapestry of stars.

Sitting outside without tears and snot running down my face—as has been the norm for the past week—is a soothing balm for my weary heart. Kodiak's heartbeat drums a quiet, steady rhythm that calms my own as his eyes search the heavens. I'm the first to speak after several minutes.

"When my mom first died, I used to sit outside every night and watch the stars for hours." I feel Kodiak's eyes on me. "I would search the sky, trying to see if one of the stars would wink at me. I was trying to figure out which one was hers." I release a breath of a laugh. "I was mad she died in the spring and not the fall. It meant the nights got shorter and shorter."

"Did you ever figure it out?" he asks. "Which star she is?" His arm is so close to touching mine that his body heat tickles my skin.

"No," I admitted, scanning the skies. "I could never make up my mind. So eventually, I decided she was the North Star. I mean, of course, the North Star has been there for forever, but now I always think of her when I see it. I wanted her to be my guiding force, showing me the way to go." There's something surreal in telling Kodiak all this, telling him the sort of thing I would only tell Aspen. But here Kodiak is, warm and present beside me, while Aspen is probably off trying to make up with Anika. Sometimes I wonder if he lives more in my mind and memory than in my reality.

"What do you think she would tell you to do?' Kodiak asks me, his voice as gentle as a caress.

What would Mom tell me to do? I wish I knew. I wish she

could beam down a ray of wisdom, guiding my next steps in this billowing mess. "I don't know," I admit. "I wish I did."

Kodiak tilts his head, his eyes locked onto the North Star. "I didn't know your mom as well as you did," he says. "But from all my encounters with Alpha Lyra, she had a really good heart."

I find myself waiting for his next words with bated breath, as though he is divining my mother's will for me.

"And I think she'd want you to follow yours," Kodiak says. "I think she would trust you to make the right decision."

I smile ruefully. "That's not very helpful or specific."

"Well I can tell you what I would do, if I were you," Kodiak says.

"Oh, what's that?" I ask.

He doesn't answer for a few seconds. "If it had been me, Luna, if the love of my life had been my mate, I would have done whatever it takes to see it through. I would have done anything to be with her. And if it still didn't work out, at least I would have known that I tried and that I did all I could. If I were you, I would pin Aspen down and get some real answers from him." He turns to me and smiles sheepishly. "Without some handsome, strong, awesome Alpha interrupting by threatening Aspen's life."

I laugh, I can't help it. "You think I should?" I ask.

"I know you should," Kodiak says. "Don't live your life with regret. And if it works out with him, we'll figure out how to handle this situation with you and me. Yeah, everyone's going to be all upset about it for a bit, but people move on. They'll find new drama to worry about." He looks forward. "It will all work out."

My heart melts faster than ice cream on the hottest summer day. I am so undeserving of such kindness from Kodiak, but here he is all the same, telling me to pursue Aspen even to his own detriment. What would it have been like, had Kodiak been my real mate from the beginning? If my heart feels this full now, how happy could I have been?

I lean my head against his shoulder. "You are too good."

"No, I'm still thinking of myself." He takes my hand in his. "I'm still thinking of a boy who would have done anything for the chance you have. And I can't take that away from you."

A breeze blows by, bringing an echo of eavesdropped words. *It should have been us.* Kodiak pulls his hand from mine, instead wrapping his arm around me running his hand up and down my arm against the chill.

"Sometimes I wonder...do you think we have more than one soulmate?" he asks.

"What do you mean?" I furrow my brow. "More than one soulmate? Like some human rom-com love triangle?"

"No, no, nothing like that," he says. "I mean, yeah, you only get one—but what if there were multiple wolves who *could* be your soulmate, multiple potentials. Like, there could be a pheromone or something that even we can't consciously recognize, and everyone who emits that smell could be your mate, and it just works out with the first potential mate you see and that's the only one from then on out."

His words hit me with force, and I recall Queenie's words about rejected mates, that they have the chance to find another one. Maybe Kodiak is right...maybe this is how it all works; that if I were to reject Aspen, I'd just have to run into another person in my pool of potentials. It is far less romantic, far less fated to think that there are several wolves we could mate with instead of the one-and-only the Moon hand-selects, but there's something hopeful in that when said one-and-only has rejected you. There's something hopeful in that when you're sitting next to a wonderful person who's still looking for his soulmate.

Kodiak has the same look in his eye that Aspen gets when

he's far away in some distant scene. He's no longer next to me on a truck-bed beneath a canopy of stars. "Sometimes I wonder, what if I'd gotten there first?

And then I see his scene too: that blistering, December day. His legs buried in snow, my dad's hand on his shoulder, that look on his face.

Kodiak's eyes are lost in the stars. "What if I was there before him?"

CHAPTER 30

IT'S HIM
THREE AND A HALF YEARS AGO

Dad had been anxious all day, and I didn't know why. Snow fell in puffy white tufts outside the living room window as Dad's foot tapped against the rug, his face furrowed the same way it always furrowed when he was running the lines of an upcoming speech through his head. I couldn't think of any upcoming speeches, however. Rory and Grey would have their wedding soon, so maybe Dad was worried about that, but his anxiety felt more urgent.

"Is everything alright?" I asked. I sat beside Dad on the couch. "You seem on edge."

"I'm fine." Dad gave me a reassuring smile. "I'm...just thinking of the upcoming trade. Kodiak and his father just finished their long hunt several hundred miles inland, so they're going to have different game than we're used to eating. Kodiak offered to do some initial negotiation, so he's coming over."

"Dad, it's just Kodiak." I rolled my eyes. "You have nothing to be so worried about. This trade isn't that important, is it?"

Dad smiled again, but there was still something off. He

patted my leg. "You're right, Lulu. I'm sure it will be fine." Then Dad's ears moved back and his body stilled. "He's here." He wore such a grave expression; I couldn't understand him.

"Cool," I said. "When you're done with him, tell him I want to show him some of my Christmas presents. I think he's going to like the punching bag."

"We'll see," Dad said, standing up and walking towards the back door.

"You're going outside to greet him?" I asked, watching Dad shove on a pair of snow boots.

"Thought it might be polite," he said. Geez, Dad was on one today. Kodiak wasn't even the Midnight River Alpha—just the heir.

"I can greet him for you if you want. Since Rory isn't gonna do that anymore," I snorted.

"That's alright," Dad said. "I think it will be better if I go." He took heavy steps out on the snowy deck, and I watched him from the window, burning with curiosity about his strange behavior. I lifted the window a crack, and a gust of chilly air blew in through the window screen. Dad walked down the deck stairs and greeted a beaming Kodiak, who made his way up the hill with snow up to his knees.

"Alpha Orion! Hello!" He waved. His voice was as jolly as the holiday we'd just celebrated, and his cheeks were a merry, cherry red. "It's good to see you."

I expected Dad's usual warmth and cheer, but he trudged through the snow like it was a great, heavy burden he had to plow through. "Hello, Kodiak." Dad did not speak in his usual booming tone, and I had to strain to hear him through the sound-dampening snow.

Kodiak lifted up a brown burlap sack like he was Kris Kringle. "Before we get into the trading, I've brought you all gifts. Something for you, little Lulu, Rory."

I sniffed at '*Little Lulu.*' I had totally outgrown that stupid nickname. I was already fourteen years old.

Kodiak slung the bag over his back, but his smile faltered looking at Dad. I couldn't see Dad's face from my angle, but it must have been something solemn.

"She's not here, Kodiak," Dad said.

Kodiak's smile turned wonky. "What do you mean?"

Yeah, what the heck, Dad? I was still here and I wanted my present from Kodiak.

"Do you know Grey, the Alpha Heir from Northern Skies?" Dad asked.

Kodiak stood very still. He took a couple of seconds to respond. "Yeah, I know him." There was an odd edge to his tone.

"He came with his father a few days ago," Dad said.

"It's cold, Alpha Orion. Let's go inside."

But Dad did not budge, like a huge, unmovable boulder.

Kodiak was fidgeting again. "Come on, Alpha Ori—"

"I'm sorry," Dad said, and whatever he was sorry about, he sounded really, truly sorry. Kodiak's eyes widened, his head shaking back and forth.

"No," Kodiak said, his nostrils flaring. "No."

Dad took a step forward and placed a big, gloved hand on Kodiak's shoulder, freezing him in a wide-eyed look of terror. Dad's words were quiet. "It's him, son. It's him."

That was the first time I realized that Kodiak, that invincible, golden boy, could be hurt. The look that dawned on his face was so piercingly, hauntingly sad that it took my breath away.

I never knew someone like him could look so broken.

CHAPTER 31

HUMANITY

The stars fade as the sky turns purple and then pink. The light from the yawning sunrise fills the sky. My vibrating phone informs me that Nova is calling.

"Do you need to get that?" Kodiak asks.

"I'm sure it's fine."

But when she calls again, I pick up the phone with a prick of irritation. If she's calling over some stupid conflict...

"Nova," I say. "What's up?"

"Oh, hi Luna! Thanks for picking up."

"Uh huh."

"It's just, well, um, I know you're probably out with Kodiak, but I think you should come back to Anika's house. Anika's pretty upset right now."

Moon, she was calling for a stupid reason. It's not my job to console Anika because Aspen is upset with her. In fact, that's about last place in my list of priorities. "Look, I told her not to come crying to me when it didn't work out with Aspen, didn't I?"

Silence fills the other end for a few seconds. "Yeah, it's just, well, I really think you should come, Luna. I really do." Her quiet voice drops to a whisper. "Please come over. I think...I think you'll want to know what's happening."

My curiosity is more than piqued, now. Nova makes silly calls all the time to tell me what's happening, but she's never asked me to come over like this, not with that pleading tone in her voice.

"Nova, what's going on?" I ask. There it is again, that coiling sense of dread, that wave of apprehension washing over me, like whatever she's about to say could rock my world.

"It's about Aspen," Nova says.

"What about him?" My heart starts to hammer against my chest. Did something happen to him? Did he get hurt? Did someone attack him? Or maybe he just dumped Anika, maybe that's the big news.

"Um, maybe I should let Anika tell you."

"Moon, Nova! Is he okay? What's going on? What's the big deal over there? Tell me!"

"He's okay, he's not hurt or anything. Just...just please come, okay?"

And then Nova hangs up the phone, leaving me to the dark abyss of the unknown. I'm just staring at my phone. Why is this the one time Nova decides to be blasted cryptic?!

Kodiak hops off the truck bed and offers me a hand. "Let's get you to Anika's."

Soon we're on the road, and I'm catching him up on the events of that day.

"Apparently they're dating or something? It's stupid, obviously. I'll bet he dumped her and that's what the big news is. I mean, they were only a thing for a couple of days. I don't get why I have to be called in for this," I rant. "They shouldn't have even dated in the first place. Oh, turn here."

Kodiak drives down a wide path covered in rocks and sticks —the road to Anika's house.

"And Nova should have just told me what was going on. It's so annoying."

There's nothing to worry about. This is all about placating Anika's silly feelings over a two-day relationship. Nova yanked me from who she thinks is my mate for something that Anika could have informed me about in a text. This is all just a dumb detour.

I feel Kodiak looking at me. "You're nervous," he says.

I look at him with wide eyes.

"I can hear how fast your heart is beating," he says. "I can smell your fear."

My cheeks color. I feel like I've been caught naked. Truth is, I hope Anika's just being dramatic and silly. I hope I can leave with a simple chastisement and a blanket statement on why you shouldn't date before you have a real mate.

"I'm sure everything's fine," I answer, speaking more to myself than to Kodiak. "It's just...well, it's going to be fine. Nova and Anika are overreacting about whatever's going on." I reach to grab my backpack from the backseat. "We're almost there. This road is rough for a vehicle. I'll run from here."

"Okay," Kodiak says, slowing the car down. He watches me carefully. "Good luck, Luna."

I offer him my bravest smile and hop out of the truck, running towards Anika's house. I feel an anxious rush to get there, to scoff at their petty concerns before heading home. When I walk in the front door, I hear sniffles and Nova's soft, comforting words from upstairs. I make my way up the wooden staircase and enter Anika's room. She's sitting on the floor against her bed crying, red-nosed and puffy-eyed, while Nova offers a tissue and a concerned look.

"Luna." Anika's mouth wobbles. "Thank the Moon you came."

My eyes widen. "Moon, Ani, what's wrong?" I ask, crouching down beside her. I put a hand on her arm. "What's going on?"

"It's Aspen!" she wails, taking the tissue Nova's offering and blowing into it. "Stars, I can't smell a thing. But yeah, it's Aspen."

"What did he do?" I ask. I hope he dumped her.

"Okay, so you know how he was acting all weird and pouty at lunch?"

"Yeah."

Her bottom lip quivers. "So, I went to talk to him and he was being all cold and dismissive and whatever, and it really pissed me off, but after school I figured he was just feeling weird because it was the last day and everything. So I went over to his house. His mom told me I could go to his room. When I got up there he was shoving all these papers and stuff in drawers and trying to shut down his laptop. I asked him what was going on, and he was avoiding me and it was a whole thing—and then I found out what was going on, and oh Luna—it's just terrible!"

I'm scanning her eyes, trying to make sense of what's happening in this story.

"And...what happened?"

"Aspen is leaving!" she wails.

"Leaving?" I ask. "What do you mean?"

"Aspen is leaving the pack!"

My heart drops to my stomach. My body turns cold. The sound of Anika's weeping sniffles gives way to a ringing silence in my ears. "What?" I whisper. Leaving the pack? What does that even mean? Where is he going? *Why* is he going? What is she talking about?

"He's going to California," Anika says. "He's going to college there. Some university that starts with an S. He's leaving the pack to go to college."

"That can't be right," I say, even though I know it's absolutely right. It makes too much sense for it not to be. He's leaving. He's not even planning to stay in Dakota Ridge. He's going off to college like those humans he loves so much. He always was the smartest of us. And yet, that can't be right. This can't be real. He wouldn't really just leave, would he? *Could* he?

"That's what I thought!" Anika cries. "I thought it must be some sort of sick joke. How could he think of leaving the pack?"

It is wrong to leave your pack. You only leave the pack for a mate. You don't leave just to go to some college.

"Are you...are you sure?" I ask.

"Look at this sapcrap!" Anika jumps up off the floor and snags a folder sitting on her dresser. She shoves it in my arms. "I took it. He's got this folder full of this application stuff. You gotta stop him. Here's all the proof you need. Talk to your dad. Talk to whoever you need to. You've got to stop him, Luna. Stop him from leaving the pack, from leaving everything that's good and right. This is wrong."

I look down at the folder, white with a big red S logo with a green tree inside. The words "Stanford University" are printed underneath it.

"He can't just leave the pack!" Anika says again. "It's wrong and you know it, and you need to stop him. You're the Alpha Daughter. You're the heir. You can stop him."

"Anika, I—" I don't even know what to say. I am overwhelmed with so much emotion that I can't even discern what I'm feeling. I don't know what to say to her, or to myself. She's looking at me with expectation, with some desperate hope that I'm going to fix everything. Nova's looking at me too, but there's a different note in her gaze.

Something sad, something that seems to recognize more than it should.

"I'm going to look into this, okay?" I say, shaking the folder for emphasis. "I'm—I'm going to figure this all out. Just, um, just don't tell anyone else about this yet, okay? If word gets out that Aspen's planning to go to college..."

"I know, I know." Her nods are frantic. Aspen's lucky that the pack has put up with his scholastic tendencies as much as they have.

I stand up on wobbly legs. "I'm going to figure this out, so just don't do anything yet, alright?"

"We won't, we promise," she says.

As I leave her house, I'm struck with the strange irony that it's a good thing Anika likes Aspen so much. If he had been anyone else, she would have led the persecution against him for abandoning the pack for human wiles. I'm only a few yards away when I hear the front door open and close. Nova is standing there, looking at me tentatively.

"Are you alright?" she asks quietly.

For some reason, Raulin comes to mind. Maybe it's the talk of college and humanity. Maybe it's just the fact that Nova is so far beneath me in the eyes of the hierarchy.

I hold the incriminating folder closer to my chest. "Yeah," I lie.

She's watching me with those eyes, the same ones she had at lunch a couple of days ago. Eyes that are seeing too much. She steps up to me and puts a hand on my arm, something earnest in her gaze.

"It's a lot to take in," she says. "I know how much you care about him."

And with the way she looks at me, the way her hand is both gentle and firm on my arm, I know that she knows. I don't know how she's figured it all out, but she knows my feelings for

Aspen. Maybe she even knows everything, from the fact that we are really mates to the truth that Kodiak and I are not. For a split second, I consider ripping my arm away, telling her that I care about Aspen as much as any other pack member. I want to tell her that I'm fine and that she just needs to shut up and go back to Anika. A low beta should not be able to spot my weakness with such clarity.

But Raulin comes to mind once more.

I wonder, have I ever really seen Nova as a friend, the way I see Anika or Logan or Raff? Or have I considered her more like a low beta pet, best used for playing fetch? The answer, I fear, is somewhere in between. When was the last time I bothered to watch Nova the way she watches me? The way she always anticipates my needs, like how she'd already gotten me food at the Blue Moon Hunt party by the time I made it to the buffet table. When was the last time I bothered to actually care about her?

Nova takes her hand from my arm and gives me a meaningful nod before turning back to the house.

"Hey, Nova."

She turns back to me.

"How's your family been?" I ask. "Your little brother. He's, what, like eleven now?"

The surprise on her face is almost painful to watch, like she can't believe I care enough to ask her such a basic, polite question.

"Koen's thirteen now," she says. She wears a bewildered smile.

"Wow, already? I guess he'll be going into high school next year."

Nova nods.

"How's he been?" I ask.

Her smile isn't exactly cheery—there's something

emotional in it. "He's doing a lot better now. Thanks for asking."

"Really?" I ask. That's great news. Koen was born with a lame leg. It was pretty much a given that he'd be designated an omega when he came of age. "I'm so glad his leg healed up."

"Oh, no, his leg will never get better," Nova says. She dons her usual sweet tone. "But they don't beat him anymore."

My heart sinks like a rock to the bottom of the ocean. I think of little Koen, same brown hair and hazel eyes as his sister. Small and smiley and weak. *They don't beat him anymore.*

"Thank you," she says, looking at me like I'm her salvation.

"What...what are you thanking me for?" I ask. I feel like acid is sloshing in my stomach.

"Well, you know." She shrugs a little. "I'm not...I'm not like you. Or Anika. Or Aspen, or Raff, or any of them. I know I'm not a high beta. But because you let me spend time with you... you know."

"They don't beat him anymore," I say, my voice hollow. "Because you're my friend." Because I pretended to be a friend, when I never saw her as an equal. I don't know the last time I truly sought to know how she was doing past the expected pleasantries of "how are you?"

"Yes," she says. I hate how grateful her smile is, and it strikes me that she never really saw me as a friend either. The hierarchy has always been too present in our relationship. I kept her around for convenience, and she stayed for her family's survival. She accepted my paltry friendship like a cherished gift because it was the only thing saving her brother.

"I'm glad to hear it." The voice feels so unlike my own, like some disconnected puppet speaking on my behalf.

Nova wishes me good luck and heads back in the house, leaving me alone with Aspen's folder and with my thoughts.

My heart thrums from the anxiety of the folder, and my stomach twists from the revelation about her little brother Koen. The worst part is not that I didn't know about Koen. It's that maybe I did. It's that I'm aware that low betas aren't treated well. I may not go out of my way to kick 'em down—it would be beneath me as an alpha—but I've never put much effort into stopping such behavior. Never campaigned against it when I so easily could have. If Aspen were the heir, what would he have done?

When I'm far enough away from Anika's property, I plop on the ground and sit against a tree, staring at the proof of Aspen's social transgression. In the eyes of the pack, he's the one that's in the wrong. He wants to abandon his pack. And yet, am I much better if I stay and continue in my self-absorption? I shake my head. I'll have time to think about Nova and the low betas and the role I should play later. Right now, I need to focus on what's in front of me, on Aspen potentially leaving. Nova called me in to solve this problem, didn't she? I may not have been the best of friends to her these past years, but if I did anything right, it was that I always addressed the crises that she brought to me. For all my shortcomings, Nova has always trusted me to take care of various situations, and the least I can do is fulfill this latest request.

So back to the folder. I'm burning to open it, to pour over the contents of the papers within, but I feel like it's some sort of Pandora's box. Once I open it, it will mean this is all real. It will mean that Aspen really is planning to leave everything he knows and loves for some human-styled life. Before me is the key, I'm sure of it, the answer to the question that's been plaguing me...but do I really want to see what's inside?

I open the folder. Of course I do. I have to.

The first thing I see is a page printed on Stanford University letterhead, an acceptance letter welcoming Aspen to the university. Oh no. He's in. He's not just applying. He's been accepted. I find various letters of recommendation from our teachers at school. In Ms. Pugmire's letter, she says: *"He is the bright spot of his school. He does not settle for the celebrated mediocrity of his peers. His determination mixed with his pleasant nature, along with his unique background and perspectives, will be great additions to the Stanford University campus.*

Mr. Bass also wrote a letter of recommendation:

"Aspen is committed to making a difference in the world and in his communities. He's even made a difference in his school. Whenever Aspen was in my class, his peers behaved just a little bit better. His example meant something to them. I believe he could help change even the prestigious Stanford University students for the better."

And then there's Ms. Turner, a teacher I used to sort of like until this moment. Her concluding paragraph reads,

"Aspen has maintained a passion for academic excellence amidst a student body who does not value, and at times even scorns, such efforts. It was clear early on that Aspen would be the uncontested valedictorian of Adam Douglas's Night Class, but he was not satisfied with a mere title. In all his work, Aspen committed to going above and beyond what was expected of him, showing a true dedication to learning and education. He is sociable, respectful, smart, persevering, and ambitious. In my years of teaching, there is not another student who I could recommend more highly than Aspen."

A strange feeling comes over me, an understanding that this all has been in the works for a long time, that many of our teachers at Adam Douglas knew what was happening, and all us wolves were oblivious to it. I wonder if Aspen's family knows about it, but I can't imagine they do. His father would never let him leave for college. His brothers would never let him hear the end of it.

There's another page, an essay written by Aspen himself. When we had to learn about applying for colleges in school, Ms. Turner told us we would have to write essays in our applications. We all scoffed at that notion. At least, I thought we all did. I hold the essay with both hands, as though it's some precious artifact that might fly away in the wind and take its secrets with it.

Some students have a background, identity, interest, or talent that is so meaningful they believe their application would be incomplete without it. If this sounds like you, then please share your story.

My Story

I am a werewolf.

Like most in my species, I grew up in a pack—a small, loyal, tight-knit community that keeps to their own. There are certain expectations when you're a werewolf and unspoken rules that you must follow. I must defer to the Alpha. I must understand my place in the hierarchy. My worth is based on the blood in my veins and how much blood I can shed. I should never leave my pack and I must live there until the day I die. There are many elements to my own culture that have frustrated me. We place no importance on education, and little to no importance on interacting with the world outside ourselves. There are problems to be solved, government representation to ask for, werewolf diseases to be cured, but we're too concerned with "sticking with our own" and following tradition to make such improvements.

While I am often frustrated with my community, there are also beautiful things about werewolf culture. We all have a deep-rooted connection with each other, and we make sure everyone is cared for, and fed. We have the joy of shifting into wolf form together, a feeling and sense that is hard to explain but that is special. We even have soulmates, something many humans would give anything for. We werewolves also connect over the fact that we are different and separate from most of the world. We are not human, and werewolves like to emphasize this fact and focus on our differences.

As werewolves, we pride ourselves on our animalistic instinct, on our rigid hierarchies and defined lives that differ so vastly from our human counterparts. We call ourselves wolves above all else, and yet the irony is, I find I have much less in common with an average beast than I do with mankind. We may be called "wolves", but the truth is, we wolves are far more human than we care to admit. We cast aside ambiguity and critical thinking, branding such terms as overcomplicated human matters, but we DO have complex emotions! We do face conflicts and moral dilemmas that aren't as black and white as we'd like them to be. We focus on the beast within, but we are so much more than animals. And I want to help both wolfkind and humankind come to understand this.

I want to attend the prestigious Stanford University because I want to make a difference in my community. I want to bridge some of the misunderstandings between humans and werewolves, and above all, I want to show werewolves that it is okay to embrace their humanity. We are more alike than we are different. I may be a full-blooded werewolf, but my heart is very human.

I shove the page back into the folder and slam it shut along with my eyes. *"My heart is very human."* What is wrong with him? We aren't human! We just aren't! Perhaps there is room for improvement, I'll grant him that. I know I still have a lot to learn, a lot to atone for—but to sell it all for a human experience? Our lives weren't supposed to be this way! We were supposed to live a simple life! He was supposed to be my mate and the future Alpha of Dakota Ridge! He could have fixed all these problems, problems he finds so damning that he's abandoning his heritage. We should have been happy, and I never should have experienced such heartbreak. But no. I had to fall in love with the one werewolf who's decided he wants to be a human, no matter who he hurts in the process.

And yet, was it not Aspen's humanity that made me love him?

I pound his number on my cellphone. The phone rings and rings and just when I think it will go to voicemail, he answers.

"Luna?"

"We need to talk, Aspen."

There's a moment of silence. "I know."

I grit my teeth. Why do I feel like crying again? Why is this awful feeling sweeping over me?

"Where are you?" he asks.

"In the woods. I'm not too far from Anika's house."

I hear his sigh through the phone. "Okay. I'll come find you."

My heart pangs. "Okay."

He hangs up the phone, and I'm left with staring at his Stanford folder in silence. As I wait for him, a sense of déjà vu comes over me, the same feeling I had when Raulin told me he was Aspen's best friend. Every piece of paper in this folder reveals something I didn't know about Aspen. I always thought we were special to each other, that he saw all of me and I saw all of him, but now there sits a stack of tangible evidence that proves I didn't know him as well as I thought—that while I fully trusted him, he never felt quite the same.

CHAPTER 32

RAINDROPS (PART TWO)
ONE YEAR AND THREE MONTHS AGO

"I have this memory of your mom," Aspen told me. "Something I don't think I'll ever forget." It was that rainy day in March, and we were still under the deck on the patio. The pitter patter of the rain pounded over our heads, and our wet clothes clung to our bodies. The errant drops of water camouflaged the stray tears that rolled down my cheeks.

"What is it?" I asked, my voice quiet. All my attention was on Aspen now, away from the ruckus of our friends and classmates. A story about Mom that I did not know! I always stood in rapt attention whenever anyone recounted some experience with her. For a few minutes, it was like she was alive again to make new memories.

"It was a while ago. I was ten or eleven years old. Your parents were at my house, our dads talking about something or other. I'd just gotten a new book from the school library that I wanted to read, and my brothers were giving me a hard time about it, threatening to chase me down and tear up the book."

Of course they were. Aspen's three older brothers all lived

for hunting and fighting and physical exertion, so Aspen's studious nature was a limitless source for teasing.

"I was trying to hide from them," Aspen says. "But you know it's basically impossible. So we were all running around, and my mom was yelling at us to cut it out because we had company. I finally hid myself in the closet under the stairs and tried to hide my scent under all our coats so I could read my book in peace. And then the door opened and I basically had a heart attack. I was sure it was going to be Ares or Ace, but it was your mom. She smiled and put a finger to her lips and sat down on the floor. She asked me what I was running from. I told her I was hiding from my brothers. She asked why." Aspen leaned back in his chair, a rueful smile on his lips. "I felt really stupid. I didn't want to tell Alpha Lyra herself that I was running around for the sake of some stupid book, but I also couldn't very well lie to her. I can't even remember what the book was now, but I showed it to her. I'm sure I look ashamed and guilty. You know how little pups look." He paused and looked at me, and I was in that closet with them now, with the little boy with wild blonde curls and the beautiful she-wolf with long blonde hair and kind grey eyes. I'd been in that cubby underneath the stairs before, hidden amongst the coats as a small pup. It was dusty and creaky, and it was funny to imagine my full-grown mother sitting on the floor, her knees up to her chest.

"And you know what she did?" Aspen asked me, his eyes still locked on mine. "She asked me all about my book, what I'd read so far. And when I told her, she said it sounded like a very interesting story." He paused again. He looked back at the yard, but his eyes were hazy with memory. "Then she said how she wasn't much of a reader, but that she loved movies. She told me about a couple of her favorites." In the softness of his eyes and face, I saw a genuine love and affection for my mother that reflected my own. Mom was always invariably kind. She had a special way about her, and it was clear that Aspen had felt it even more than most.

"She told me she thought it was very impressive that I could read so well. That I was a smart little pup. She asked me to tell her the end of the story once I had finished it. Of course I said I would." Then his smile faded into something touched with sorrow. "No one had ever treated me like that. No one had looked at my nerdy sape-hobby and told me it was impressive. That it was good. But your mother did, and from then on I always told her about the books I read."

Mom had always liked Aspen. She'd told me so, multiple times. That Aspen was a good kid, that he had a good heart. I had suspected he was one of her favorites amongst the pack, though she never outright said it. While every young wolf boy would trip over themselves to try and impress my father, Aspen always seemed to prioritize Mom, telling her about his books and asking her about her human rom-coms.

"So yeah. I miss her too, Lu," Aspen said. "She wasn't my mom, but I miss her a lot." The raindrops continued to fall, seeping through the cracks in the deck and splashing our faces. "Sometimes, I feel like she was the only person in the whole world who understood me."

CHAPTER 33

CALIFORNIA AND BACK

Aspen is in wolf form when he approaches me, likely so he could better sniff me out. Sunlight peers through the gaps in the trees and dances on his blond coat. He walks on four legs to where I sit and glances at the folder lying next to me on the forest floor. I almost pet him between the ears, but the thought of him flinching away from my touch stays my hand. Aspen shifts into human form and settles cross-legged on the forest floor.

"So. Ani told you, didn't she." His eyes are on the Stanford folder.

The papers rustle as I toss it to him.

"I guess she stole this from my room," Aspen says, opening the folder and sorting the pages. "I didn't even realize it."

I want to scream at him. I want to ask what he was thinking, applying for college, leaving everything behind. I want him to take back those words he said in that essay. I want to hurt him as much as he has hurt me. But I hold my tongue so that he can fill the silence.

Aspen glances at me with the eyes of a guilty pup before

looking back at his folder. "They gave me a scholarship. Stanford, I mean. Because of my background. There are lots of unclaimed funds for werewolf students."

I say nothing.

"It's a school in California. I'm supposed to start in the fall, but I was planning on leaving sooner. Try to start working and setting up my life there in advance."

I say nothing.

"This was the plan, you know?" His hands curl into fists. His body trembles. "I swear Luna, it wasn't personal. I told you it wasn't. I've known for a year—no, longer than that, really—I've known that this is what I wanted to do. To go to college. To make a difference."

I say nothing. I focus on steeling my jaw, keeping my lip from trembling.

Aspen can't seem to meet my eyes, instead focusing on a rock on the ground. "I knew that having a mate would complicate things. I would be dragging her into a lifestyle and world that she wouldn't want. For months, I was terrified I'd run into her, and then what would I do? I'd be stuck. But as time went on, as more and more of my peers turned eighteen, no one turned out to be my mate." He lets out a breath of a laugh. "I thought maybe I was lucky. Maybe I was a Lone Wolf."

Those two sentences clash. "Lone Wolf" and "lucky" do not belong together. There's Kodiak, who's so desperate for a mate that he'd even accept a fake one—and then there's Aspen, praying to the Moon that he'll die alone.

"And then it hit me," Aspen says. "About a month ago, the beginning of May. Everyone had been talking about your birthday and the Blue Moon Hunt for months, but it still hadn't clicked. But then one evening, you walked into school, I was at my locker, and you were talking with Nova. She was saying how your birthday was at the end of the month, she was asking you how you felt about it. And for some reason, that's when it hit me. I realized why I hadn't found a mate yet." He peels his attention from the sticks and stones and looks at me with those soulful blue eyes. "It was you. It was so obvious it was you. There was no one else it could have been."

And just like that, I can't breathe. I'm completely lost in his eyes, like a sailor caught in a whirlpool, and I don't even care that I'm drowning.

His smile is slight. "You're my best friend, Luna."

There's something so significant in that admission, that despite my doubts, despite my theories that he hated me for all my ignorance and shortcomings, I really was his best friend. There's something so sad, that after all that's happened, a best friend is the most I may ever be to him.

"And you're the Alpha Daughter, and the heir of Dakota Ridge. You belong here, and I belong out there." He looks to the side, as if the campus of Stanford University lies before him. In the light of day, it's easy to imagine it. Probably some big red brick building, rows of palm trees, bright sunlight. "A few months ago, I started wondering if there was a way to not be with my mate, if I could cut the ties and venture on my own. I started researching it and found that there was a way to reject your mate, and that a rejected mate could find love again. I had decided that that was what I was going to do to whoever I mated with, even though it might hurt her for a moment." He turns back to me. "And then I realized it was probably you." He scrunches up his mouth in some guilty, pitiful line. "But I really, really, hoped it wouldn't be."

I look down at the forest floor so he cannot see the hurt in my eyes.

"I didn't want to hurt you, Luna. I never have. That's why I came to your room before everyone from the hunt was around.

I didn't want to make you feel worse, with everyone watching, and—"

"Don't lie to me, Aspen." My voice is sharper than Kodiak's canines. "You wanted to spare my feelings?" I look up at him, my eyes ablaze with a purple fire. "They would have ripped you to pieces. You know that. Don't act like you were just trying to save me the humiliation. You were saving your own neck."

Aspen blanches, his ears shifting back. He doesn't speak for a few seconds. "Fine," he acquiesces. "That's fair. I also knew I could never go through with it, not with everyone watching. But I really did want to do it as harmlessly as I could. I really, really didn't want to hurt you, Luna, and I knew that being rejected by your mate would hurt you, but you see why I had to do it, don't you?"

"No," I snap. "I don't."

"I'm leaving, Luna. And I'm not just hopping over to another pack. I'm going to school for at least four years. I'll be living in dorm rooms with humans. It just doesn't make sense for us to be together!"

"It doesn't make sense?!" I jump right up. I can no longer contain the furious energy simmering beneath my skin. "I'm your mate!"

"I know you are." He stands up in turn. "And I know that— I know that it's hard because I am your mate. It's hard for me too, Lu. Harder than I ever imagined. I never knew the mate bond could be this strong." He's clenching his fists against that pervasive mate bond that flows through his veins and screams at him to go to me. A mate bond I haven't felt since the night he rejected me. A mate bond that holds no claim on my emotions.

My voice drops to just above a whisper. "It's not about the mate bond. It's never been about the mate bond." My bottom lip trembles. "Not for me."

And while I no longer feel the bond the way Aspen does, I wonder what traces of it lingers still, if it allows me to read his eyes even better than normal. His eyes do not reveal shock or surprise at my cryptic confession, only increased guilt. He looks down at the ground with pursed lips, and that's when I know. That precious, deepest secret, the one I've held so close to my heart—Aspen knew all along. He knew how I felt about him, or at least he knew my feelings to some extent. He knew I liked him and he just played dumb.

"I was hoping—" he starts. "I was hoping you'd find someone after I rejected you. But Kodiak isn't your real mate, is he?" He's ignoring what I've said. I say nothing. I don't even want to dignify his stupid question with a response.

"I'm so sorry, Luna. I really am. I never meant for all this to happen. The whole situation—moon, it's a mess." He rakes his hand through his hair. "And every part of me is screaming at me to take you in my arms...and it gets so much worse when the Moon's out. And I wish I could have just accepted you as my mate, but it's just impossible. Don't you see it?"

I look at his pained face and realize he's desperate for affirmation. He wants me to tell him that, while difficult, he made the right choice. That it really was impossible. That there was no other way. He wants me to tell him that I understand. And as desperate as he is for that affirmation, my heart is even more desperate to find hope in his words. He didn't reject me because he didn't want me—he rejected me because he respects me too much. He understands my role and my destiny, and he didn't want to take that from me. He only rejected me because he thought he'd be sparing me from sorrow down the road. He only rejected me because he cares about me.

Tears fill my eyes.

"You should have talked to me about it," I say. "You should have explained everything. You didn't even give me that choice." This is what those human rom-coms are all about, isn't it? Just stupid misunderstandings that momentarily break up true love? If only Aspen had explained it all to me, we could have avoided so much heartache because he would have known that I would have walked to California and back to be with him. Just a little miscommunication, that's been the problem.

"I know." He's gripping his folder. "I know I should have."

We stand there, several feet apart, staring into each other's eyes before he rips his gaze from mine.

"I have to go," Aspen says. "I can't—I can't stay here with you. Alone. I just can't."

"What do you mean?"

"We can talk more later, but I just—" Aspen shifts into his wolf form, picks up his folder by the teeth, and runs off. I almost shift in turn, ready to chase after him—to physically pin him down if I must—and determine what our next steps are.

But for some reason, I don't. For some reason, I just watch him run away yet again. Every step he makes to get away from me takes a fraction of my newfound hope with him, and by the time he's completely out of sight, I'm left with almost nothing.

This is all going to be fixed. The last whispers of my desperate hope fling themselves onto my mind.

He didn't know how much you cared.

He just needed to know you would have made it work.

It was just a miscommunication.

He really cares about you.

He loves you.

He wants to be with you.

You both just need to figure out what you want from your future together.

The obstacle is just the college thing. You just have to figure out how to overcome it.

You both just need to figure out what you want from your future together.

He wants to be with you so much that he has to run away to hold himself back.

He is still yours.

And as loud and obtrusive as these thoughts are, I can't shake the feeling in the bottom of my stomach, the thought that underpins all the lighter, happier ones. Aspen should have discussed his plans to leave Dakota Ridge from the very beginning. In fact, if he really was so sure I was going to be his mate, he should have asked me what I thought about this situation before the night of the Blue Moon.

But he didn't do that.

There was no discussion, no weighing of options, and no determining together how our futures should or should not intertwine. He didn't ask for my opinion. He decided all on his own what his future was going to be—and that I wasn't going to be in it.

CHAPTER 34

HEART AND MIND

The noonday sun hangs high in the sky, but Rory is waiting for me in the living room when I get home. She stands up from the sofa as I walk in and rushes towards me.

"You're home late. What happened? Is everything okay?" Her silver eyes are soft, her voice gentle and concerned. Sometimes she looks just like Mom. But Mom is gone. I'll never look into those grey eyes again.

I don't explain that I was roaming the forest for hours, wallowing in all sorts of wretched feelings. I just murmur, "He's leaving." My arm brushes against Rory's as I head towards the kitchen. I'm starving. I haven't had dinner yet.

"What do you mean he's leaving?" she asks, her voice quiet. We don't want Dad to wake up.

I open the pantry, searching for the deer jerky. I hope Dad didn't eat it all. It's both of our favorites.

"What do you mean, he's leaving?" Rory repeats herself. "And who are you referring to? Kodiak or Aspen?"

There's the deer jerky, tucked away on the top shelf. I have to stretch on my tiptoes to grab the container. Dad probably wanted to hide it from me. I take the container to the kitchen counter, unscrewing the lid and gnawing on a strip.

"Who is leaving?" Rory demands.

"Aspen," I say. "He wants to go to college. Way down south in California!" An incredulous laugh escapes me. "He's leaving Dakota Ridge."

Rory's eyes are huge. "He's leaving the pack?" She acts like it's a cardinal sin. Like she didn't do it first. "He's leaving the pack?!"

I take another bite of deer jerky.

"He can't—he's just up and leaving? Like that? Like it's nothing? That's not how it works. That's not who we are."

I laugh again, cold and bitter. "I know, right? I mean, moon, werewolves aren't supposed to leave. We're supposed to stay in our pack. We're supposed to stay together." I look up at the ceiling, shaking my head. "And yet everyone in my life keeps leaving. I don't know why I'm surprised anymore." I swallow the lump that's beginning to form. "I mean, look at this place, this house." I gesture out to the kitchen, with its large granite island and walk-in pantry and eight-burner stove. Overkill for just two people. "Half my own family is gone. First Mom. Then you. Everyone close to me goes away and I'm still here. Alone. Dad is the only one who's stayed."

Rory just stares at me, something dawning on her face. I can't look at her longer; I feel stupid for having said as much as I have. I grab my deer jerky container and start walking out of the kitchen. Dad sure will be mad when he wakes up and finds it empty.

"Luna," Rory's voice stops me just as I'm about to step onto the living room carpet. "You know it's different, don't you? I never would have left Dakota Ridge for something like college. I never would have done that. Not to Dakota Ridge—and especially not to you."

I'm grateful my back is to her, that she can't see my face. "Of course," I mumble. What a stupid thing for her to say, that she wouldn't have abandoned us for college. She hated school—she didn't even finish her senior year.

"Luna, look at me," Rory says.

I grit my teeth. Why did I even allude to this issue? This discussion isn't going to change anything—Rory still has to go back to Grey at some point. I have so many things to worry about, and Rory abandoning us to go live her happily ever after is the least of my worries. It's ancient history now.

"Luna," she repeats.

I slowly turn to her, gripping my deer jerky container. "Yeah, *Aurora*. I know. You never would have gone to college."

"Nor would I have left for any other reason. Grey is my mate—I had to go be with him, and he's the Alpha Heir of his pack."

"And you were the heir of *our* pack." It just slips out, even though it won't help with cutting off this conversation. Maybe I'm too inebriated with sleeplessness to withhold my thoughts and feelings.

"Male heirs take precedence; you know this."

"I know." I purse my lips. I know all this. I know it was only natural for Rory to leave, and I know that I'm not supposed to care as much as I do. If anything, I should be jumping up and down for joy that Grey didn't decide to derail the Moon's plan the way Aspen did.

"You still seem upset," Rory says.

"It doesn't matter."

"Of course it matters."

"No, Rory. It doesn't." I take a couple steps towards the kitchen table and slam the jerky container down. "You have Grey now, and he is your whole entire world, and he's the only thing that matters. You followed tradition. That's what matters.

And it doesn't matter that you were supposed to be the heir. Now *I* have to be the heir, and now all my peers look to me—and I never wanted any of that. And now the boy I love is leaving and I'll never see him again—but it doesn't matter, does it?" When my voice breaks, I look down at the hardwood floor and grab my left arm with my right hand. I want to run away from this conversation, the way Aspen ran away from me, but I'm already this far into it, aren't I? "This is the most I've seen you in years, Rory. It took a Blue Moon and a basically unprecedented, cataclysmic event for me to see you for more than a couple of days. You hardly call. You hate texting. You only visit every few months, and when you do, you're always with Grey. I never get you to myself. Ever. He's the only person that matters anymore. So I found someone else who I thought I mattered to—and now he's leaving too." I tighten my grip on my arm. I think about the first night of the Blue Moon Hunt, when Rory chastised me for my stupid crush on Aspen. Like she had any say in a life she'd opted out of. "But I don't know why that would matter to you, because you have your wonderful life in Northern Skies with your mate, so it doesn't matter what's going on with me and my mess of a life."

Years of pent-up emotion flow down my cheeks, and when I steal a glance at Rory, I'm shocked to find tears in her eyes. Outside of Mom's sickness and subsequent death, I could probably count the number of times I've seen Rory cry on one hand.

"Luna." Her voice is thick with emotion. It sounds so foreign, so unlike her. "Why didn't you ever tell me you felt this way?"

It takes me a few seconds to process the question, to try and find the answer. Why didn't I tell her I felt this way? Rory and I used to be so close. I used to tell her everything. I try to remember the beginning of her marriage with Grey—how helpless I felt, watching her slip away from my life and into his. I guess I felt some mixture of happiness and envy; I was glad that my sister had found her true mate, but jealous that she was so happy when I was still so sad. I was bitter that she could leave those heavy emotions and responsibilities behind while I had to bear them alone. But despite my resentment, I guess I wanted her to be light and happy with her mate, even though it was far off in the mountains of Northern Skies. It didn't seem right to chain her life to a little sister who felt far too much for an alpha, especially when Rory was only doing exactly as she should.

"It's just...it's because this is the way it is, right?" I say. "You get a mate and all your love goes to them. So really, I didn't have a right to be upset about it, you know? To be upset with nature. And I...I want you to be happy. I really do."

Rory walks up to me, takes my hands in her own, and stares at me with all the emphatic intensity of her silver eyes. "Luna, my love is not finite. Loving Grey doesn't mean I love you any less. He may be my mate, but you are and always have been my sister. I love you more than the Moon herself. You and I share memories, joys, and sorrows that he will never know."

I look down at our hands as Rory squeezes them.

"Luna, I am sorry," she says. "I didn't realize you felt this way. I didn't know you felt that I'd abandoned you or that I didn't care about you." I look up, and her eyes are full of sincerity.

I swallow the lump in my throat.

"I guess...I just got so caught up in where I was. I was so busy, and I just assumed you were fine here without me. I didn't think enough." She scoffs at herself. "I never do."

"It's okay," I say. I mean, really, how was Rory supposed to know when I never told her? It's my fault for not communicating. If anyone is to blame, it's me.

"No, it's not," Rory says. She sighs. "It's why the Moon has surrounded me with such thoughtful people throughout my life, you know? Grey...you..." She pauses. "Mom." She lets go of my hands, taking a half step back and watching me with those careful, scanning eyes. "Stars, you remind me so much of her, Luna."

My eyes flare open wider. Did I mishear her? "Me? I remind you of Mom?"

She nods her head.

That's not right, though. It can't be. Mom was wise and kind and perfect and I'm...not. I'm literally nothing like her. I don't even look that similar to her, with Dad's black hair and purple eyes. "But...but you're the one who reminds everyone of Mom," I say. "You're almost her spitting image."

"Yeah, I look like her," Rory admits. "But you *are* like her. You always have been."

I purse my lips and shake my head. I guess the tears have gotten to Rory's head, like some sort of noxious gas. It probably happens when you've gone too long without crying—it's distorting her memories the way tears blur vision.

"No. That's not true," I say. "I'm not like her. She...she wouldn't have gotten into this mess." Never ever. She might even be rolling in her grave at such a comparison.

Rory tilts her head, then gently takes my arm. "Let's sit down, alright?" She guides me to the couch and sits next to me. "Mom was always compassionate, thoughtful, and full of emotion. Traits I see in you. I mean, I think of the way you've taken Nova under your wing."

I feel a stab of guilt at the mention of Nova. "No, you've got it wrong," I say. "I haven't been a good friend to her, not at all. And I've only just realized it, too. I could have been so much better and I wasn't."

"Sure, maybe you could have been better," Rory says. "Maybe there's still room for improvement—I don't really know your relationship with her. But Luna, you understand, don't you? That I *never* would have associated with her like that. I would have been too proud for it. But Mom would have. You know she would have. And so have you."

I don't know if I can agree with Rory on this one, not fully. Mom would have been so much better than me. And yet, I find my heart warming at her words; I feel some easement of the guilt that weighs down my shoulders.

"Sometimes," Rory continues, "you're sitting there quietly, and I just know you're thinking about everything. Watching everything. That's how Mom was, too. A deep thinker, always wondering. Me? Not so much." She wears a lopsided smile. "I'm like Dad, you know? Kind of more straightforward. I see things as they are, but sometimes, I think you see the world as it could be."

As I try to picture how I could be comparable to Mom, I can't help but think that these traits could also describe Aspen. *It was you. It was so obvious it was you. There was no one else it could have been.* Maybe he knew we were more alike than I had ever realized.

"You've always had this softness to you, deep down, that's like her," Rory continues. "It was a big comfort to me, you know? After she died. I was lost without her, but there you were. Like a piece of her still living on the earth. It's what kept me going."

Tears mist my eyes. "You really mean that?"

"Of course I do." Then she smiles ruefully. "Actually, sometimes I think that's why the Moon put me with Grey."

"What are you talking about?"

She chuckles. "Honestly, he reminds me a lot of you at times, too."

I wrinkle my nose. "Alright, seriously? Does everyone remind you of me?"

"No, no. I swear it's just you two!" She leans back into the cushions, looking at me like I'm some sort of treasure. "You both are more quiet, you like to hold back what you feel. You both think a lot more than I do, though that's a pretty low bar. Plus, Grey also gets pretty sulky!"

I grimace, and she laughs.

"I know he's not the most extroverted—that you maybe aren't that close to him. But seriously, I think you two might understand each other more than you think."

I eye her suspiciously. "Maybe."

"I'll take a maybe." She grins, but then her features soften. Her eyes become solemn. "Luna, I know you think you've ruined everything. But you know what? You're one of the four people I love most in the world: Mom, Dad, Grey, and you. You look a lot like one of them, and you're really similar to the other two." She clasps a hand on my shoulder. "Mom had a great heart, and yours is a lot like hers. So I believe in you, Luna. I believe you'll make the right decision for you. And if Mom were here, I think she'd tell you to follow your heart and mind."

Rory's words echo Kodiak's, the advice he gave as we gazed at the canopy of stars. I need to follow my heart and mind, but that advice sounds so much easier in vague words than in practicality. I know what my heart wants, what my heart has always wanted...but is it right? Perhaps the problem with following my heart is that it's not fully mine anymore. Whether he wanted it or not, I gave it to Aspen for unsafe keeping years ago. He's the boy of my dreams. I'm not the girl of his. I'm torn straight down the middle between letting him go and fighting for love like they do in Mom's movies.

"I don't know if I can do it," I whisper.

"Do what?" Rory asks, her voice as quiet as the rustling breeze.

"Set us free." That heart I'm supposed to follow pounds in my chest. I see Aspen's bright smile, his sun-kissed skin, his cheeks with summer freckles. I smell the books and the chess pieces and the ocean breeze. I feel the way my heart stirs when he looks at me with those deep blue eyes. How can I let go of that remaining string that holds us together?

"It's up to you." Rory strokes my hair, tucking it behind my ear. "Your fate is in your hands."

CHAPTER 35

FATE IS LIKE THE OCEAN
A FEW MONTHS AGO

"What if a Midnight River wolf catches us?" Nova asked, her face pale.

"Moon, grow a spine, Nova. Quit acting like some nervous sape," Anika drawled.

A few months ago, my friends and I decided we were going to have a beach day whether Midnight River liked it or not. We had snuck out in the middle of the day and run into their territory in wolf form. We'd found a rocky cliff with enough footing to make our way down to the sandy shore, and we'd all taken our shoes off.

"Don't worry," Raff said, slinging an arm around Nova's neck. "If they catch us, we'll just have to try and kill them. May the best wolves win."

"Oh," she peeped.

Aspen rolled his eyes and smacked Raff's arm off Nova. "He's just messing with you," he said. "Nobody's going to die just because we came to the beach."

"You never know," Raff said, his mouth widening into a sharp smile. "Maybe we'll get lucky." Logan and Anika and I laughed, and even Aspen chuckled at Raff's comedic bloodlust.

"Or maybe," I offered. "We'll go completely undetected, and I won't have to hear a lecture from my dad about 'respecting other packs.'" I used a deep voice to impersonate Dad, and everyone chuckled.

Raff groaned. "Lame."

Anika started pulling off her shirt, revealing a pretty green bikini that matched her eyes. "I'm getting in."

"You're going swimming?" Aspen asked. "The water's going to be freezing." In late February, the water was cold and the beach was windy. I was wearing a long sleeve shirt and a jacket over jeans I'd rolled up to walk along the beach. I thought we were only going barefoot.

"Of course," she grinned. "Wanna join, Aspen?"

His eyes scanned her fit physique in a way that made my stomach curl. "Tempting," he said. "But I'm going to have to pass on your offer." He shoved his hands in the pockets of his brown corduroy jacket and opened the jacket up, showing it off as the reason he wouldn't be taking a swim.

"Hmm." She narrowed her eyes and took a step closer, leaning in with a grin. "Your loss." She turned on her heel and darted towards the ocean. She squealed when she crashed into the water and then howled. Logan and Raff already had their clothes off, and Logan was running towards her in nothing but his boxers. Raff ran to Nova, his rusty red hair flying behind him, and picked her up and threw her over his shoulders like she was a sack of potatoes.

"RAFF!" she screamed. He cackled as he threw himself and her into the ocean.

"They're nuts," Aspen said, grinning. "The whole lot of them."

I was laughing so hard I was hunched over, especially as

Nova came out of the water, sputtering and spitting out salt water. "Raff!" she yelled in uncharacteristic anger.

"Nova, I'm sooooorry." Raff said, though no one really believed him. He was wading towards her with wide open arms, and Nova whacked one of his arms away.

"I hope Nova's alright," Aspen said. I could tell he was trying not to laugh.

"She's fine," I assured him. "Besides, with Raff around, you have to expect some casualties."

Aspen shook his head, laughing. "He's rabid."

Anika beckoned us with big, sweeping strokes of her arms. "Come join us! The water's nice!"

I highly doubted that.

As fun as it was watching my friends, very few things sounded less appealing than plunging into the saltwater ocean in February. I'd wanted to enjoy the shore, watch the waves, maybe hunt a little and start a fire on the sand.

"Am I a bad alpha if I don't go in?" I asked Aspen, quiet enough so no one else would hear me over the waves. It meant to come out as a joke, but my tone was flatter than I'd hoped.

"No," he said. "Am I a bad beta if I don't go in?"

I smiled. "Only if I had commanded you to do so."

There was a twinkle in his eyes. "Good thing you never beat me at chess."

"Good thing I don't want you to throw yourself in the ocean."

"How benevolent," Aspen said.

"Get in here, you two!" Logan called, joining Anika in waving us to them. Raff was distracted chasing Nova around and splashing her. "Are you not tough enough?"

I bristled. Now I had to go in to prove I wasn't some wuss. Why hadn't I brought my swimsuit? It was one thing jumping in naked in wolf form, but it felt uncomfortable in my underwear in human form. Should I go in wearing all my clothes like Nova had?

"Duty calls," I sighed. Besides, it was just skin. It didn't really matter. I started to unzip my jeans.

"You don't have to get in the ocean if you don't want to," Aspen said softly. "Just ignore them."

"I can't," I whispered. These weren't just my friends. They were my people, the future betas under me in the pack. Maintaining their respect was of the utmost importance. I could feel Aspen reading me, detecting some code in my eyes. Somehow, I knew he understood the implications of it all.

"Sure you can," he said. He winked at me and grabbed my hand, pulling me along the sand in a sprint. A blush crept up my cheeks, one hand in his and the other keeping my unzipped pants from falling down. "Sorry!" Aspen yelled, sounding as remorseful as Raff had been. "But I'm stealing her!"

Logan and Ani called for him to come back, starting to make their way out of the water, but Aspen kept running and when he started to laugh I joined in. This was, without a doubt, the best possible outcome for this beach trip. In a moment, it didn't matter if they still thought I was weak, or if I was abandoning my people. What mattered was Aspen's warm hand in mine and the sound of my heartbeat pounding in my ears.

The beach was backed by cliffs that created walls and alcoves that hid us from plain sight. When we stopped running, Aspen took a couple of seconds to let go of my hand, leaving it warm and tingly. I zipped up my pants and he fell back onto the sand, a joyful laughter bubbling over the sound of the crashing waves. His blond, windswept curls blended in with the sand.

"Problem solved," he said. "We're safe from them and the ocean."

I plopped down next to him, digging my bare feet in the sand. "Until they chase us down."

"Hmm. Maybe. We'll just have to run again if they come."

I chuckled. "I'll never hear the end of it if I keep running from them. 'Alpha Heir, running from conflict.'"

"You should just punch Logan in the face then." Aspen sat up and looked at me with a goofy grin. "That might shut him up. Or maybe he'd like it. Honored to be punched by her royal highness, our illustrious morning star, Alpha Heir Luna." He was leaning in closer as he teased me, a wicked smile on his lips.

"Oh moon," I rolled my eyes and whacked his arm.

"You know he has a crush on you."

"He does not."

"Does too. He's all puppy eyes around you. He's probably livid I ran off with you, holding your hand and everything."

Little butterflies flit in my stomach as he mentioned holding my hand, the action still a kiss of warmth in my palm. "Even if you're right, he's probably more smitten with *what* I am rather than *who* I am."

I expected Aspen to laugh, to throw another joke or quip my way, but instead his face stilled and he looked at me with those eyes, eyes that made me feel more bare and naked than if I'd taken off all my clothes. I broke eye contact with him and watched the waves crash on the shore, wash over the sand, and retreat back to the ocean. Over and over and over again. A wave came so close to us that I could have leaned forward and touched the foam.

Then, Aspen spoke. "I know who you are."

I looked at him, and his eyes and face held such sincerity that if I opened my mouth, I was certain my feelings would flow out unbidden onto the sand.

"I see you, Lu. And I'm here for you."

I turned my cheek, but I could feel his piercing gaze on my skin. To have him looking at me like that was exciting and scary all at once. It was the conundrum of vulnerability—beautiful to share yourself with another, terrifying to let someone in to see what a mess you truly were.

Several seconds passed before I replied. "I never thought I'd be the heir." The ocean waves danced ever closer before pulling away. "And I never wanted to be."

Aspen didn't say anything, and I knew he was waiting for me to continue.

"I love being alpha-blooded," I admitted. "I know I can see and hear further and better than most can. I know I get to enjoy privileges within the pack that I otherwise wouldn't have. I've always loved it." I furrowed my brow. "But being the heir? I mean, that was for Rory. It always was. I mean, you know how she was. She was perfect. Breathtaking, even. It was her destiny, not mine. At least, that's what I thought. I guess fate had other plans."

A few gulls flew overhead, barking their song in the pause that followed.

"Do you think fate is so fixed?" Aspen asked. "That we all have some predetermined path that we're forced to follow?"

I glanced at the sky instinctually, though only the sun stood above us. Such conversations felt easier in its light, away from the watching eye of the Moon. "I don't know. I think so," I said. The latest wave was spilling towards us, touching our toes.

"We should move back," Aspen said. "The tide is coming in." We shifted several feet back, close to the black rock cliff behind us. When we'd settled into the sand once more, he spoke. "I find it hard to believe that fate is set in stone. Sure, there might be an obvious path, but it doesn't mean you can't make your own way."

"I don't believe in an all-consuming fate," I said. "I don't believe that what I choose to eat for breakfast or wear to school is predetermined. And I'm not even sure that you can't derail your destiny. But there *are* fixed, predestined points of fate. We cannot change what we are born as—an alpha or a beta or an omega child. We cannot change who our mate is. And we all have a role we need to play in our packs, even if we don't always know what that role is at first." I squint at the horizon. "We thought Rory's role was to one day lead Dakota Ridge with her mate, and now we know that it was always supposed to be me and mine. She was always supposed to be with Grey in Northern Skies." No matter how much I hated it. "It's as the Moon designed. She is the author of our destiny, our fate."

The tide was creeping closer, once again promising to kiss our skin. Aspen opened his mouth and drew a breath before closing it, his hesitation as clear as his eyes were blue.

"What are you thinking?" I prompted.

He glanced at me, analyzing if he should say what was on his mind. I kept my face calm and neutral, hiding my desperate desire for him to trust me, to open up to me. He spoke. "I think we may give the Moon too much credit when it comes to fate. Has it ever talked to you, given you a step-by-step guide of what to do?" I looked at him with wide eyes. I didn't tell him that that wasn't how it worked, that what he was saying was disrespectful, or that I didn't want to hear any more of this. Because I *did* want to hear more, to my own shame. I wanted to hear more because I wanted to hear him.

"I think we're the ones who hold ourselves back," he said, "who refuse to look past what has always been done, who assume we cannot change who we are. We make our own fate and call it providence."

And though his words danced on the line of disrespect, I wondered if he wasn't right. Maybe we dug our own graves and blamed the Moon for it. And yet, as werewolves, we weren't like the humans Aspen spent so much time with. Our soul-mates were proof of a fate beyond our control. "I think you might be right. At least partway. Some people might use the Moon as an excuse when she has no part in some of the details of our lives." I looked back out at the ocean. "But I still believe in a larger destiny. I believe that..." A big wave was rolling towards us, faster and more powerful than its predecessors. "That's a big wave coming in!"

"We gotta move!" Aspen offered me a hand as we scrambled to our feet. The wave was rushing towards us with a surprising ferocity, and we ran as far as we could before we were met with the cliff wall.

"Aspen..."

"We're screwed," he said. With nowhere to run, the merciless tide rushed in and crashed against us. We shrieked as the cold water hit our legs, soaking our pants and leaving us with cold denim before retreating to the ocean. We stood there in stunned silence for a moment before we looked at each other and started to laugh.

"We're so wet!" Laughter rippled through my voice.

"Look at us!" Aspen said, holding his arms to show off his pants. He was smiling and shaking his head. "This is terrible."

"Anika and Logan got their way after all."

"Somehow they always do, those freaking mutts!" he cried, his tone jovial.

I laughed, and then an idea struck me. There it was before me, the answer clearer than the ocean water. "I've got it!"

"Got what?"

"Fate is like the ocean."

Aspen was trying to roll up his sopping wet jeans with little success. "Big and cold and wet?"

I laughed again. "It's like the waves. The tides. We can try to stop them, try to run away, but the waves are always going to come. We do not control the tides." My smile widened. "The Moon does." I looked down at my clothes, just as dripping and soaked as Aspen's were. The ocean breeze was whipping his curls and twirling my hair and sending shivers down our spines. "The waves are always going to come, and there's nothing we can do to stop it. We can't fight the tide any more than we can fight fate." I was looking at him as I took a step backwards into the ocean that had claimed us soaking wet victims. "We're going to get wet either way, so we might as well dive in." And in a moment of girlish delight, I took Aspen's hand and dragged him towards the ocean.

"Luunaaa," he whined, but there was a lightness to it. Just as I let go of his hand, I tripped and fell into the water, crashing against the ground and sputtering against the salt water in my eyes and ears.

"Ick," I said, trying to spit out the salty taste in my mouth.

Aspen burst out laughing. "I can't believe you biffed it!" he said, reaching down to offer me his hands. I took them, and in another girlish, impulsive moment, I pulled him down so that he crashed beside me.

"Luna!" he cried, pushing my arm lightly. "And here I was trying to be a gentleman."

I grinned. "But you know I'm hardly a lady."

"I think you're more of a lady than you give yourself credit for," he said. He nestled beside me in the sand and pressed his arm against mine, the water rushing up against us up to our chests before pulling back. It was cold, but watching the ocean was mesmerizing. It seemed to wash a hypnotic calm over me.

"Whether I knew it or not, whether I *wanted* it or not, I was always destined to be the Alpha Heir," I said. "All that's left to do is accept my destiny. I might as well dive deep, right? Instead of dipping my toes in the water."

I glanced over at him. Aspen's eyes were trained on the

horizon, on that line that seemed so impossibly far away. "I suppose so," he said. I could see his mind churning, like gears working to produce something to say. "You know, you've got a poetic mind, Luna." Anyone else referring to me as a poet would have meant it as an insult, but with Aspen, I knew it was a compliment—one that warmed me from the inside out and fought against the cold water. "I've never thought of it that way before, fate being like the ocean." Aspen released the tiniest of sighs. There was something almost sad in his eyes. "Both werewolves and waves controlled by some orb in the sky we cannot touch."

Referring to the Moon as "some orb" bordered on blasphemous, like many of his remarks in this conversation had, but I let the comment slide. In that moment, it felt more important to listen to the breathing, heart-beating boy next to me than to jump to the defense of that orb. He looked at the horizon like he was searching for something, the intensity in his gaze arresting mine. "We cannot control the tides," Aspen said. When he turned to me, the look in his face softened, and he stared at me with those ocean blue eyes. "But Lu, we can always leave the beach."

CHAPTER 36
THE END OF US

Queenie's yellowed page lurks in the corner of my nightstand, and I pull it out to read in the light of the afternoon sun. I should be sleeping—it's 4:00, but I find that sleep evades me. My mind is far too active to rest. I tried shifting into wolf form to still my thoughts, but the gnawing anxiety kept me wide awake.

My eyes move over the scrawl of words as my heart hammers against my chest. It's a dangerous piece of paper with dangerous words that can undo everything we are, and yet I haven't thrown it away. I've tried, and when I couldn't bring myself to burn it or throw it in the trash can, I hid it away in my nightstand. But this page still calls out to me: The End of Us, spelled out in perfect cursive.

Aspen is all I can think about—every moment we have shared, and every moment we should have shared. I look through the sliding glass door at the balcony, at the hard wooden planks I fell to when he uttered those cursed words. I shove Queenie's note in the pocket of my shorts and step outside. The sun is warm on my skin, and I'm grateful that it's the sun's light on me instead of the Moon. It was under her light and her care that so much heartache came to pass. I harbor unfair feelings towards her, that she betrayed me, and I don't want the Moon to see my traitorous heart.

I slump over with my forearms on the railing and look out to the woods, where even the trees remind me of him. Their rustling leaves echo the words he spoke to me in the forest. *It was you. There was no one else it could have been.* Before my birthday, I'd been terrified my mate wouldn't be Aspen, but he'd *known* it was going to be us. Maybe Kodiak is right, maybe there is a pool of werewolves who could be our mates—but maybe there really is just one. Maybe it's only Aspen for me. I mean, as he said, it was obvious, wasn't it? Of course it was going to be us. That's just how fate works. Then again, everyone thought it was going to be Kodiak and Aurora. "It's obvious," they said. Look at all of us now.

Alright. Enough pacing around the room and the balcony.

I put on a faded blue t-shirt over jean shorts and let my hair fall loose before climbing down the balcony and heading into the woods. I imagine the North Star in the sky, providing whispered clues of where my feet should go. I just keep walking, hoping I'll find some answer on my way. The sunlight casts golden drips on the forest, and each little ray seems to illuminate the path I should take. I brush past branches and step onto twigs and plow through clearings. Step after step, thought after thought, memory after memory. I can almost feel the wisdom of the trees seeping into me as I step over their roots. I walk until I smell the whiff of salty sea air and hear the caw of barking seagulls. I must be in Midnight River now, close to the ocean. When I make it out of the woods, I see the sun sitting low above the ocean, a glittering orange jewel that makes the water sparkle. The sky is a breathtaking painting of pink and blue and apricot, the same strokes of color on the evening of the Blue

Moon Hunt. I turn. Behind me, the edge of the waning Moon is smudged, but still undeniably there, looking over me once more. I apologize for blaming her for the current outcome of my fate. I turn back towards the ocean and peer over the cliff, watching and listening to the roar of waves as the tide pushes against the sand. In and out, in and out.

Once, I had said that fate is like the ocean—uncontrollable, a powerful entity of its own, only to be tempered by the Moon. I don't know that I believe that anymore.

Just as the sun kisses the horizon, I sense him coming in wolf form. I didn't expect him to find me here. I should be absolutely exhausted after a sleepless night, but I find myself wide awake.

Aspen's wolf form emerges from the woods, and once he lays eyes on me, he stops and stares for several seconds before shifting into human form. He's wearing a faded blue t-shirt, same as my own. It's from a school trip we took a couple of years back.

"Hi Aspen." My voice is half a whisper. My hair blows gently in the wind, curling strands that reach out towards him. Aspen and I have always loved the ocean, always felt its rhythmic call. I'm not surprised that we both ended up here, right by the cliff we so often climbed to get down to the water.

Aspen's eyes are soft, almost defeated. His voice is even softer. "Hi, Luna."

I turn back to the water, the sight of him spurring an ache in my heart. I take a seat at the edge of the cliff, my legs dangling over the rocks. Aspen sits next to me, his arm so close to mine that his sleeve brushes my own. I breathe in his scent, letting it fill my lungs and my heart and my soul. "I didn't expect you to come here," I say.

"I couldn't sleep," he says. I glance over his messy wind-tossed hair and the dark circles under his eyes. "I hardly sleep anymore." When he sighs, his body deflates. "All I can ever think about is you. I tried to distract myself with Anika, but it didn't work." He turns to me with wide, wild eyes. "You drive me mad, Lu. It's no use. I can't fight this desire anymore." And then, he reaches for my face with an unsteady hand, and as soon as his palm touches my cheek, I feel a spark zing through my body. There it is, a hint of that mate bond feeling that I felt the night of the Blue Moon—a feeling that seems so long ago now.

Aspen exhales in relief the moment he touches me, like some sharp pain has been nullified. "Oh, moon," he whispers. And then he pulls me to him and wraps his arms around me. He's running his hands along my back, he's pressing his chest against mine, he's burying his nose into the crook of my neck and breathing in deeply, like my scent is a drug he can't get enough of.

All this time, I've wondered if the Moon wanted to curse me for my incompetence, to gift me a mate who would reject me, but it's clear she's been doing all in her power to bring us together. She has not punished me, but Aspen. She's been cursing him with that unbearable agony of desire.

And for a few blissful moments, I let him hold me. I enjoy every butterfly and every zing. I hold onto him the way a drowning man clings to his last moments of life. Aspen pulls back just enough to look at me. He places both hands on my cheeks, looking at me with heated and shallow blue eyes the way I've always wanted him to. But for a moment, the carnality in his gaze slips away, and he's the Aspen I've known once more. Deep eyes, blue like the ocean. Something genuine, something sad. There's some hopeless resignation in his face.

"You know I love you, don't you?"

As tears surface to my eyes, so do memories surface to my mind. The pretty daisy he picked for me as a young pup, the way he patiently explained how to play a board game, the secret handshake we made at age twelve, the hours he spent helping me with my homework, the card he gave me at Mom's funeral, the evening he surprised me with a milkshake, the journal he gave me so I could write my thoughts down, the texts to ask how I was doing, the way he always looked at me to make sure I was alright, the time he lied on my behalf, the night he explained all the constellations, and every moment when he held me in his arms as I cried. I know that Aspen loves me. His words are true, and that's what makes it all the more heart-breaking.

"I know," I say. "And I love you, Aspen." My voice breaks. "More than you'll ever know."

Aspen has always loved me, just not how I've loved him.

I take his hands from my face and press my lips to his fore-head, tears streaming down my cheeks. Then, holding his hands in my own, I give them a squeeze and look straight into his eyes. The sun is setting on my left. The moon is watching over us on my right.

"Aspen," I say. "I, Luna, under the light of the Moon..." I pause, the words catching in my throat. "I, Luna," I repeat, my voice skewing several pitches too high. "Under the light of the Moon, accept your rejection, and sever our remaining connec-tion. Aspen, I shall no longer be your mate."

CHAPTER 37

ONCE IN A BLUE MOON

Aspen crumples like a piece of paper, caving in on himself and letting out a cry of pain that could be heard for miles. I pull him back, keeping him away from the edge of the cliff, and wrap my arms around him as best I can, tears flowing down my cheeks.

"It hurts so much!" His words are a desperate gasp for air.

"I know," I say, keeping my voice as steady as I can. "I know."

"Luna." The veins on his neck are popped, his body is fraught with tension. "Moon, Luna. Did you have to go through this?" His fisted knuckles are white and his teeth are clenched.

"Yes," I say.

As for me, the moment I accepted his rejection, I did not feel that overwhelming surge of pain. Instead, some quiet unease has settled in my stomach. It's that empty feeling, like something is missing, coupled with the uncertainty of ever getting it back again. I feel hollowed out, and I don't know how much of that is attributed to the mate bond and how much of that is just myself.

"I'm so sorry!" Aspen sobs. "I never should have done this to you. Oh I'm so sorry! I never should have rejected you!"

We stay there, on the edge of that cliff, until the sun has slipped past the horizon and the Moon is shining bright in the sky. I wonder what she thinks of this, if she thinks I made the right decision. I wonder what Mom thinks, watching over me now. Aspen finally succumbs to the exhaustion of prolonged pain, and when he's knocked out fast asleep, I take a few moments to drink him in. His head rests on my lap, his face almost peaceful. I run my hand through his hair and kiss his forehead for the last time. Then I shift into wolf form, get his limp human form onto my back, and drop him off outside his house.

By the time I get home, Rory and Dad are awake, but I tell them I need to lie down and get some rest. Rory comes into my room as I'm crawling under the covers.

"Where were you?" she asks, stepping into the room.

I close my eyes. "With Aspen," I say. "It's—" I pause. Suddenly, three little words feel so insurmountable. Rory just waits for me. "It's over now," I whisper. "And I'd like to be alone."

Rory hovers for a moment. "Okay. Please, let me know if you need anything. I'll be here."

And as soon as she shuts the door, I give myself away to tears. When my cheeks are slick and shiny, there's another little knock on the door. I stiffen. It's Dad. He steps into the room and looks at me with all the tenderness of a devoted father. Then he comes up to my bed and pulls me into one of his hugs, so big and strong and loving that my sorrow starts to float away with my tears. He does not ask me any questions, and I wonder how much he knows, how much he's secretly overheard. Maybe he knows it all. He ruffles my hair with a big, scarred hand, and tells me, "I love you, Lulu."

With a stuffy voice, I tell him I love him too. And somehow, I feel that Mom is with us in this room, offering an unseen hug around both of us.

Dad leaves, and Aspen plagues my dreams. After several hours of fitful sleep, I wake up in the middle of the night and hear Rory mulling around downstairs. Dad has probably gone out for pack business. I click open my phone to see a text from Kodiak.

Kodiak: *Hey Luna. Hope you're doing alright.*

And there it is. Amidst my gloom, amidst that horrifying reality that I've just rejected my one and only mate, there's a glimmer of hope. I once told the Moon that if Aspen could just be my mate, I'd never ask for anything again. I wonder if she's willing to answer just one more prayer.

I call Kodiak's number, surprised at the way my heart pounds faster and faster with each ring.

"Hello?" I hear his voice through his end of the speaker.

"Hi," I say.

"Hey, how are you?"

I shrug, though he can't see it. "I don't know. I'm okay." Though it doesn't feel like the truth. "I was wondering...I'd like to see you today. If you could come over."

"Yeah, of course. I have to finish up a couple of things, but I'll be there in an hour or two, is that alright?"

"Sounds great."

"Sweet. Well I'll see you in a couple of hours then."

"Okay."

"Talk to you—"

"Kodiak?"

"Yes?"

I pause. I don't even know what to say.

I rejected Aspen.

I'm a mess.

When I saw your text, it made me feel like life might be okay.

I wait a couple of seconds.

"I hope it's you," I murmur.

"What did you say?" he asks.

I purse my lips. I don't want to get his hopes up for something that might not even be possible.

"I said 'I'll see you soon.'" I hang up the phone, my heart pounding in my chest.

The smell of frying bacon encourages me to get out of bed and steal some food from Rory. But by the time I make it down to the kitchen, the whole place smells burnt, smoke is coming out of the pan, and Rory is unleashing a barrage of curse words at the food.

"It burned!" she barks, shoving the pan in my direction as proof.

"I can smell that," I say.

"Moon, I'm so hungry!" She slams the pan down onto the stovetop. She always gets angry when she's hungry.

"Let's go to Bruno's," I say, a small smile on my face. "He actually knows how to cook."

Her face softens. "Sorry, I'm over here ranting about bacon. Stars, how are you, Lulu?"

"I'm okay. I think," I say. "I don't know."

Rory comes up to me and wraps me in a hug, and I sigh as I lean into her. "Better that you're here," I say.

"I'll always be here for you. I'm just a phone call away, you understand?"

"Mmhmm," I say, nodding.

Rory takes a step back, smiling sadly at me.

"Let's get food at Bruno's," I repeat. "Maybe Dad can meet us there for an early dinner."

"You sure you want to go out?" Rory asks.

"Oh, I'm sure. I'm starving."

She laughs. "A wolf after my own heart."

But there's a knock at my door, and it only takes me a moment to sniff out who it is. My heart drops and Rory's face turns dark and cold.

"Alright, can I kill him now?" she asks.

"No," I say. "You can't kill Aspen."

"Are you sure?"

I chuckle. "Would you mind getting the food to-go? He probably wants to talk with me, and I'd rather be alone for that."

She eyes me warily, but agrees. "Okay. But if he does anything funny, I will kill him."

"I know you will."

Rory grabs her wallet and opens the front door. I'm in the kitchen so I can't see them, but I can imagine the look on her face.

"Aspen." Her voice is frostier than a winter's morning. "She's in the kitchen."

"Oh, thanks."

I hear his footsteps as he walks in, the sound of rolling wheels, and the giant *thud* of Rory slamming the door behind her as she leaves for food.

Aspen takes tentative steps into the kitchen. He's wearing a backpack and dragging a large suitcase across the wooden floors. It only takes a couple of seconds to piece it together.

"You're leaving," I say.

He smiles sadly. "I figure...soon Anika is going to tell everyone about Stanford and everyone's going to try and stop me. It's better that I leave now. Make some actual money for the summer before I start school."

"I see."

A silence settles between us.

"But I couldn't leave without saying goodbye," he says. "Without seeing you before I go."

My smile is slight. I wonder if he can see how sad it is. "We've been through a lot."

Aspen leans on the handle of his suitcase. "More than anyone will really know." And he's right. Sure, Kodiak and Rory might know that I was rejected, they might know that I liked Aspen well before he was my mate, but they'll never really know just what we were and all that we felt. This relationship is ours and ours alone, an experience only the two of us will ever know. Then again, I don't think I'll ever know just how Aspen felt. And he'll never know how I felt everything.

I fight the emotion rising in my throat. "It's hard to believe that you're leaving." And yet, it's hard to believe I once thought it would be us in the end. A hope so blinding I really believed true love could conquer all.

"It's not goodbye forever." He tightens his grip on his suitcase handle. "I'll be back."

"That's good," I say. But we'll never be back to the way we were. Our golden childhood together is over, and the soulmate I thought I would have forever had the permanence of footprints in the sand.

Aspen shrugs off his backpack, lets go of his suitcase, and walks up to me, pulling me in a strong, warm embrace. As I hold onto him, I am grateful he cannot see the way my lip quivers and the way my eyes water. Aspen was never truly mine, and even the Moon couldn't make him really love me, but once more, I see the future I've imagined so often flash before my eyes. Mornings curled up next to each other, children with curly hair and vivid eyes, pack meetings led with his wisdom and kindness, summer nights showing our children the fireflies, and nightly story time by the fireplace with dad and his books. I watch it all slip away as tears slip down my cheeks.

I do not cry for what Aspen and I were, but for all we could have been.

He pulls back and stares at me with those ocean blue eyes, brightened by his own tears. "I'll miss you, Lu."

"I'll miss you too."

Then Aspen puts on his backpack and starts rolling his suitcase. I follow him to the front door, as though he's pulling my heart toward him by a string. He puts his hand on the doorhandle and turns back to give me one final, long gaze.

"Goodbye, Luna." His voice is so quiet.

I draw in a deep, shaky breath. "Goodbye, Aspen."

And then he leaves, and as he shuts the front door, it's as though another door is closing on a huge part of my life. Like that big oak door, our end feels hard and cold and lifeless, a tragic finale to all I hoped we could be. My heart wavers. Have I made a mistake? I could have restored the mate bond. He was desperate for me, wasn't he? Everything in his body telling him that I should be his? Maybe it doesn't matter that he didn't really love me. With the mate bond, it could have been enough. *I* could have been enough. Now, I may never feel that way again.

I sit on the floor and lean my back against the wall, looking up at the chandelier dangling over me. Light is beginning to shine through the windows, marking the dawn of the sun's new day.

A knock at the door sends my heart into a furious drum, pounding against my chest. It's Kodiak. This is it. It's the first time I'll see Kodiak after turning eighteen, without a mate bond tying me to another.

"It's me," I hear him say through the door.

I rise to my feet and take slow steps toward the door, watching my feet so that I don't catch his eyes through the window. The metal door handle is cool to the touch, and I take a deep breath. I don't know what will happen when I look into Kodiak's eyes—if everything will change or nothing. It's hard to believe something so good could happen amidst my sorrow and disappointment. It seems so obvious that I won't get that lucky. It's clear that I'm doomed to a life without true love. It's foolish to hope for some great fortune when I was so mistaken in my blinding belief before. *But then again,* I think, turning the door handle. *Maybe I'm wrong.*

Maybe it's okay to allow myself to hope once more, to embrace the possibility of a new love, to believe that, in the end, everything will work out as it was always meant to be. Perhaps I may petition the Moon and the stars to grant me one more chance, one more golden gift. I open the door, and when I lift my eyes, they are no longer brimming with tears, but with hope.

After all, even miracles happen once in a Blue Moon.

THANK YOU

Thank you so much for reading *Blue Moon*. By reading it, you've made the story book so much bigger than the little story that's been swimming around in my head for years.

If you enjoyed the book, I would really appreciate your review on Amazon or Goodreads. Even a sentence or two can help other readers find the story.

You can find more from me at kaylalafroth.com.

ACKNOWLEDGMENTS

✦ ☾ ✦

It's finally complete. My first, official novel. There were doubters that the day would come...

It was me. I was the doubter.

But my mother was not one. She has often expressed her love for my writing, and she has continually encouraged me to pursue my dream of publishing a book. Her strong, infectious faith gave me the courage to self-publish *Blue Moon*, despite my abject fear of failure. Both she and my father have been my champions throughout my various creative endeavors, and when I think about the parents I've been blessed with, I feel like the luckiest girl in the world. Thank you, Mom and Dad.

I'd like to thank my editor, Jessica King, for her edits and her encouragement. It was very reassuring to have someone as smart and insightful as Jessica—and someone who wasn't related to me—believe in my project. Her help with both the editing and publishing fronts was invaluable. I'd also like to thank Destinee Nelson for her work on my cover. I love it. I was very picky and a touch neurotic, but she was kind, patient, and detail-oriented. She handled both me and the cover beautifully.

To Sloan, Olivia, and Emily—you three are such true

friends. Thank you for being the first beta readers, for reading the book when no one else would. Your time meant the world to me.

I'd like to thank a couple of my BYU professors: Spencer Hyde, for your incredible creative writing classes and for your help with the first few chapters, and Quint Randle, for believing in me and my potential when I felt like a failure.

Thank you to the Ink Swingers—the best writing group I could have asked for. And thank you to all my Wattpad fans, who followed me in my writing infancy through the rough drafts of four romance novels. Your excitement and support have given me a lot of confidence to continue my author journey.

And while I am deeply grateful to all those aforementioned, I'd be remiss if I didn't acknowledge the most important contributors of all. Without you, there would be no *Blue Moon*.

So thank you—to all the boys who broke my heart.

–Kayla

About the Author

Kayla LaFroth is a middle school teacher with precisely two claims to fame: her Wattpad series and her LEGO YouTube channel. While writing Ninjago fan fiction and making LEGO videos didn't exactly make her popular as a teenager, they did reignite her love for storytelling, leading her to post episodic updates of a four-book romance series on Wattpad, *Maid For You*.

Outside of writing, Kayla enjoys reading, watching TV and movies, going for walks, cosplay, travel, and talking about dating. Seriously. She'll ask just about anyone for their opinions on relationships.

Kayla graduated from Brigham Young University with a Bachelor's degree in Communications and a minor in Creative Writing, and now lives in her home state of Virginia. *Blue Moon* is her debut novel.

www.ingramcontent.com/pod-product-compliance
Lightning Source LLC
Chambersburg PA
CBHW051303130726
47987CB00004B/1645